D0091362

KISS NUMBER 8

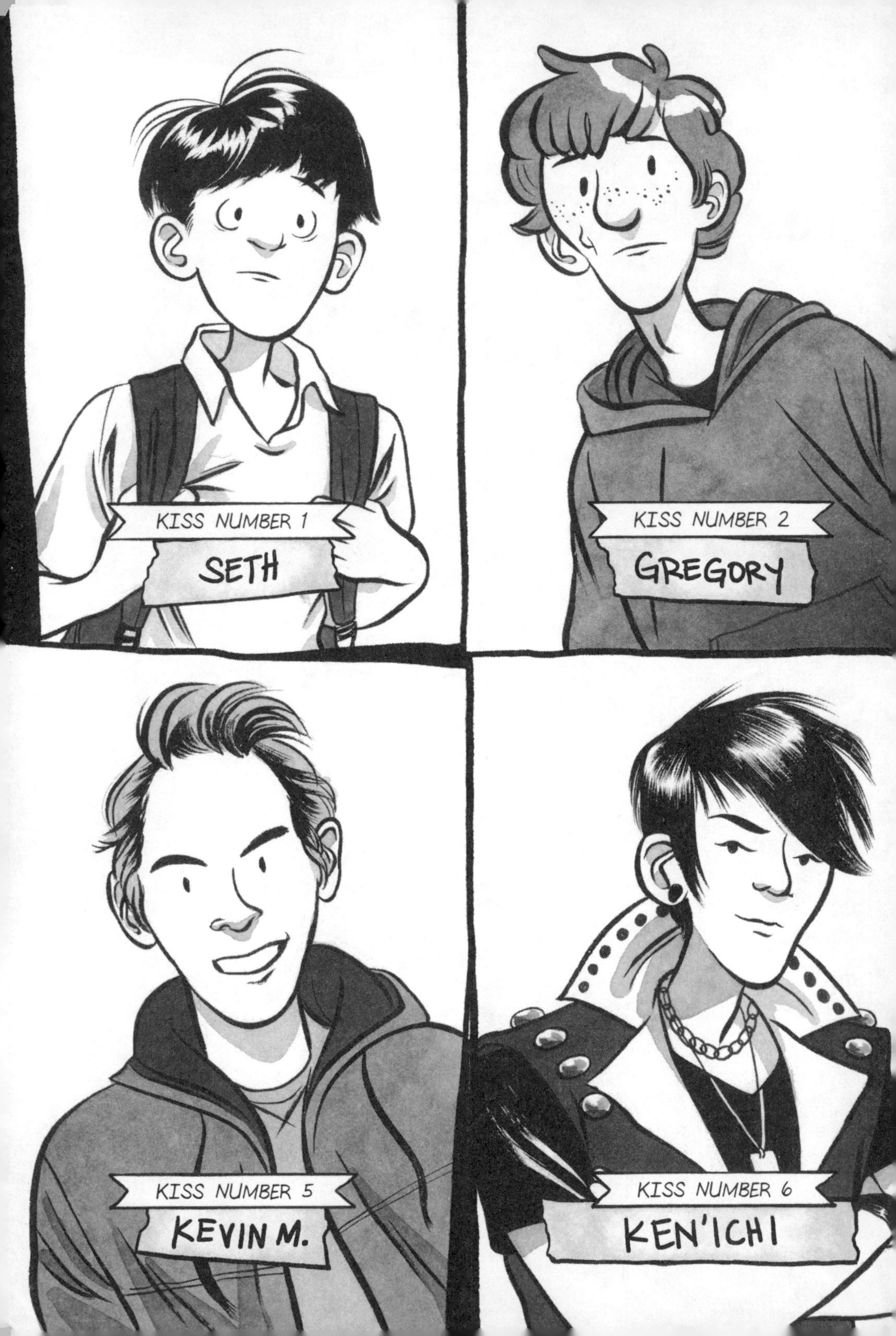
KISS NUMBER 1
SETH
KISS NUMBER 2
GREGORY
KISS NUMBER 5
KEVIN M.
KISS NUMBER 6
KEN'ICHI

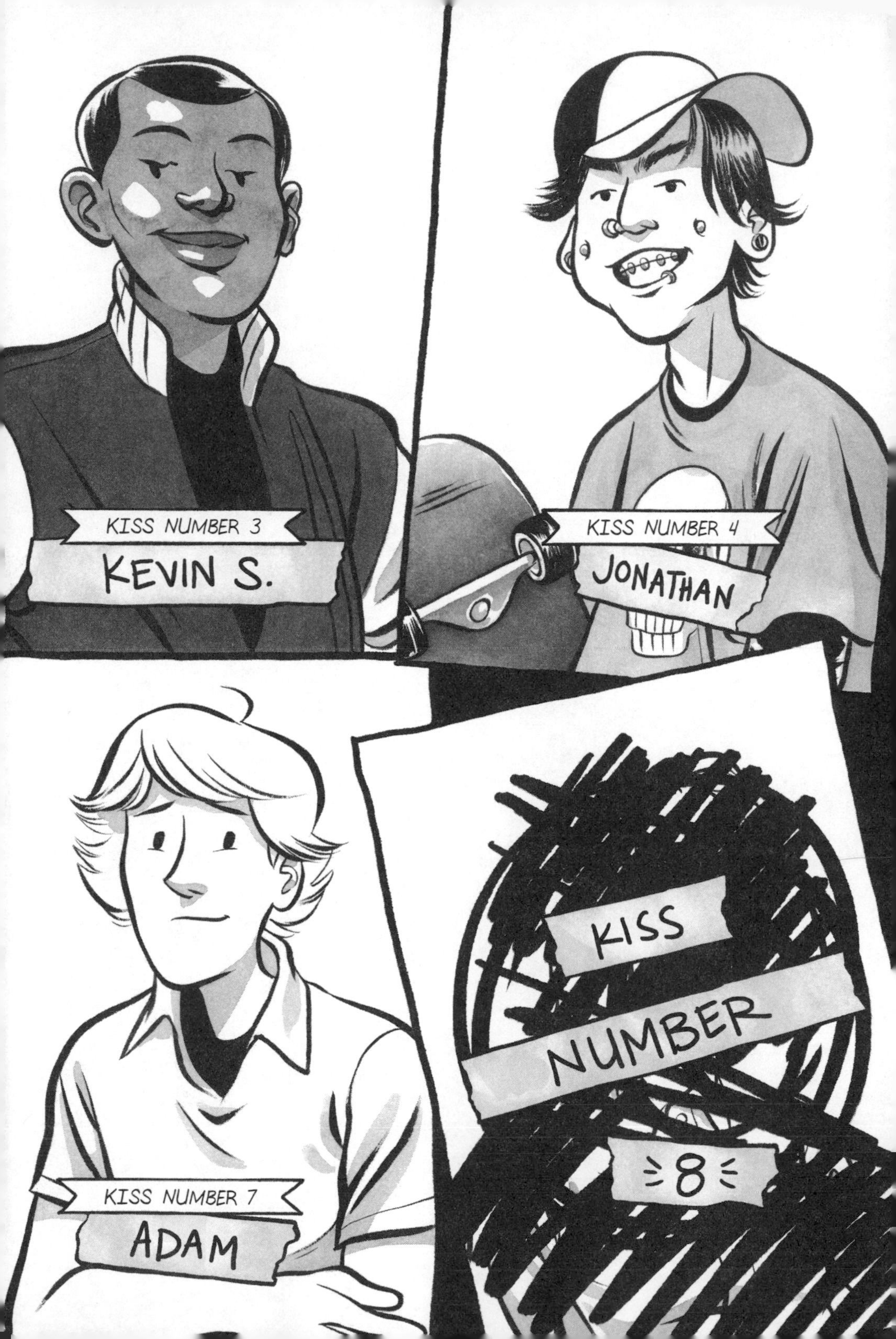
KISS NUMBER 3
KEVIN S.
KISS NUMBER 4
JONATHAN
KISS NUMBER 7
ADAM
KISS
NUMBER
8

KISS NUMBER 8

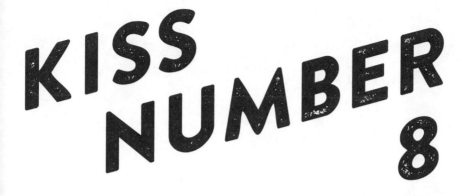

WRITTEN BY
COLLEEN AF VENABLE

ARTWORK BY
ELLEN T. CRENSHAW

:01
First Second
NEW YORK

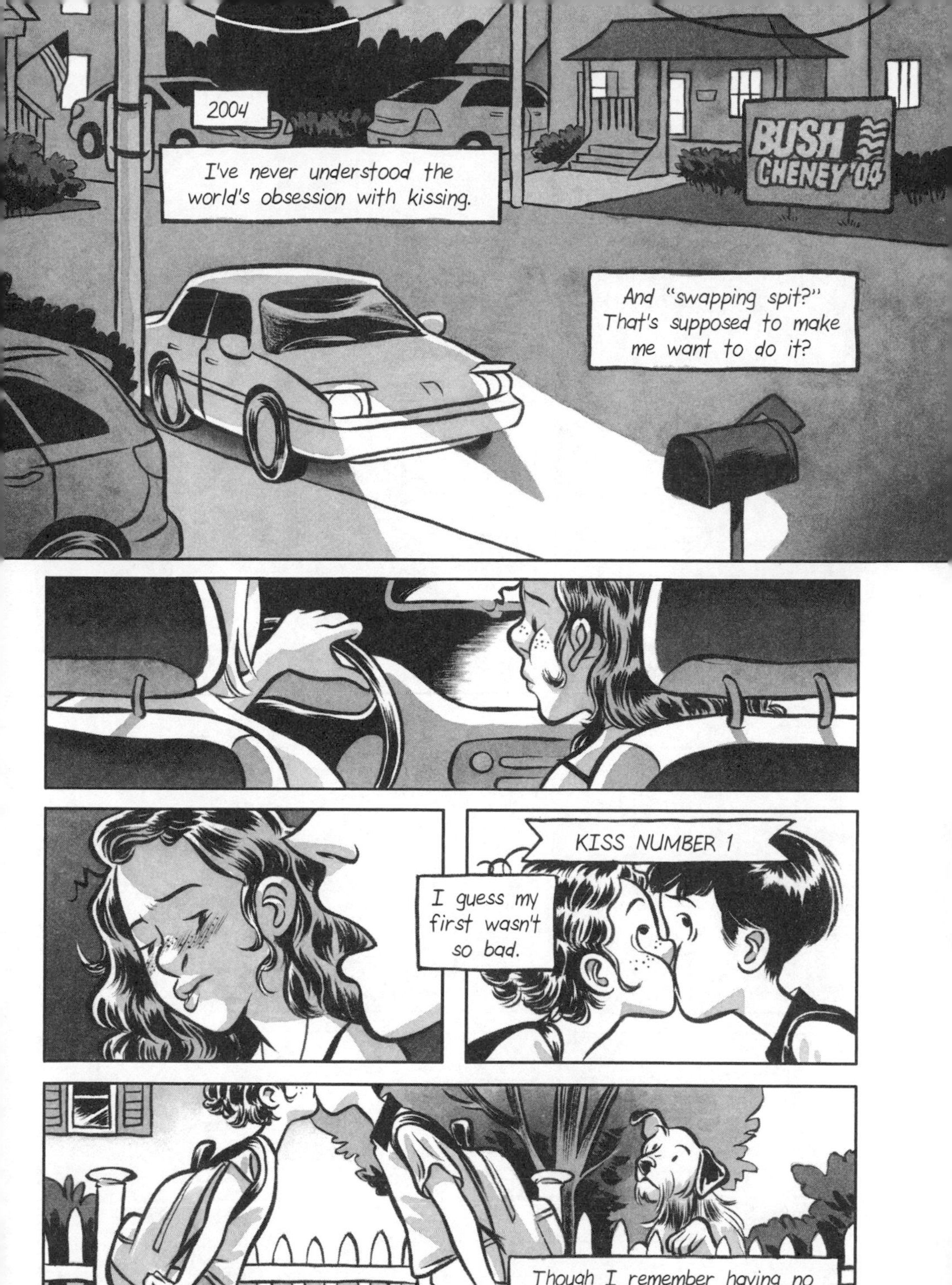
2004
I've never understood the world's obsession with kissing.
BUSH CHENEY '04
And "swapping spit?" That's supposed to make me want to do it?
KISS NUMBER 1
I guess my first wasn't so bad.
Though I remember having no idea what to do with my arms.

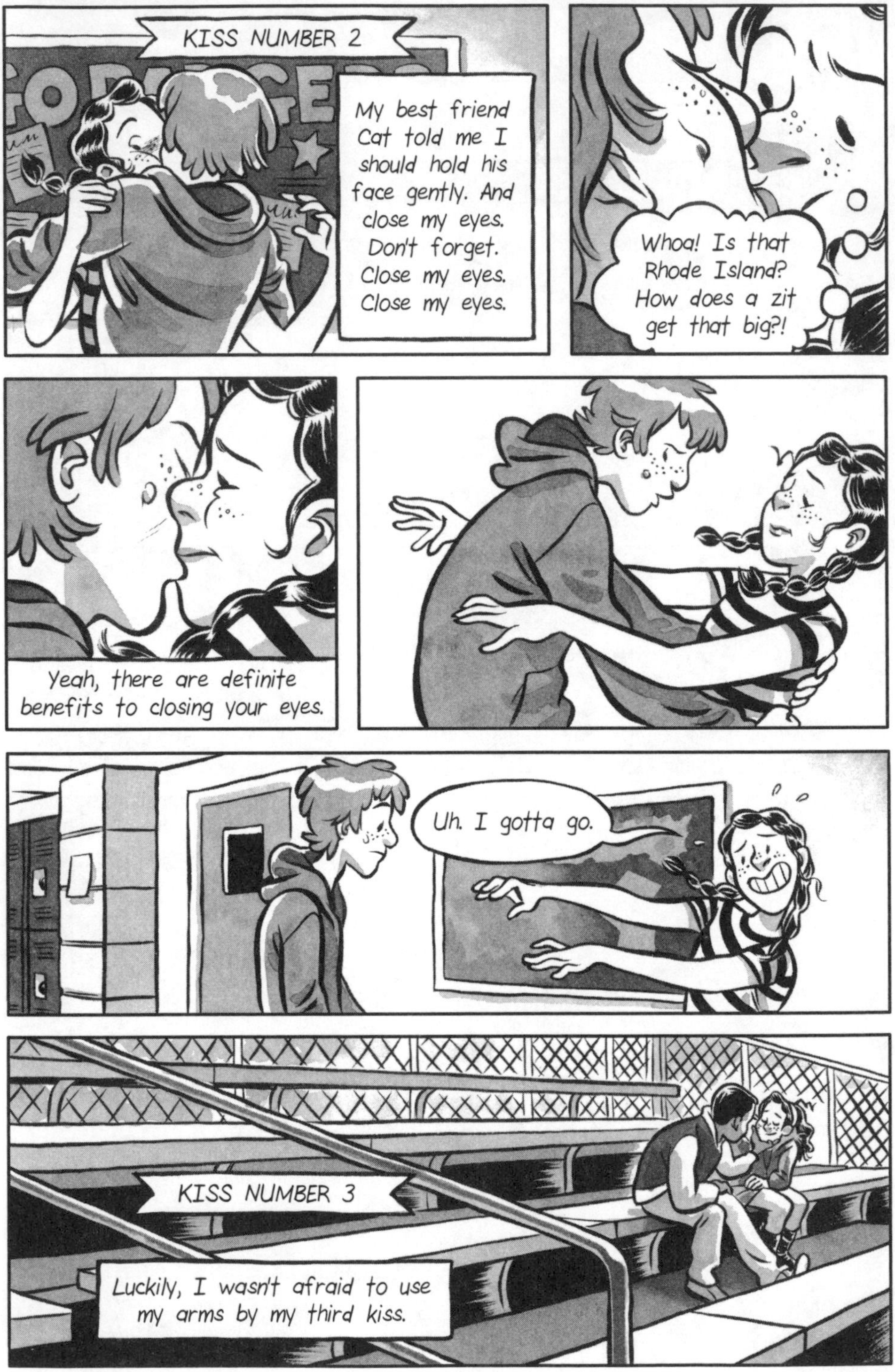
KISS NUMBER 2
My best friend Cat told me I should hold his face gently. And close my eyes. Don't forget. Close my eyes. Close my eyes.
Whoa! Is that Rhode Island? How does a zit get that big?!
Yeah, there are definite benefits to closing your eyes.
Uh. I gotta go.
KISS NUMBER 3
Luckily, I wasn't afraid to use my arms by my third kiss.

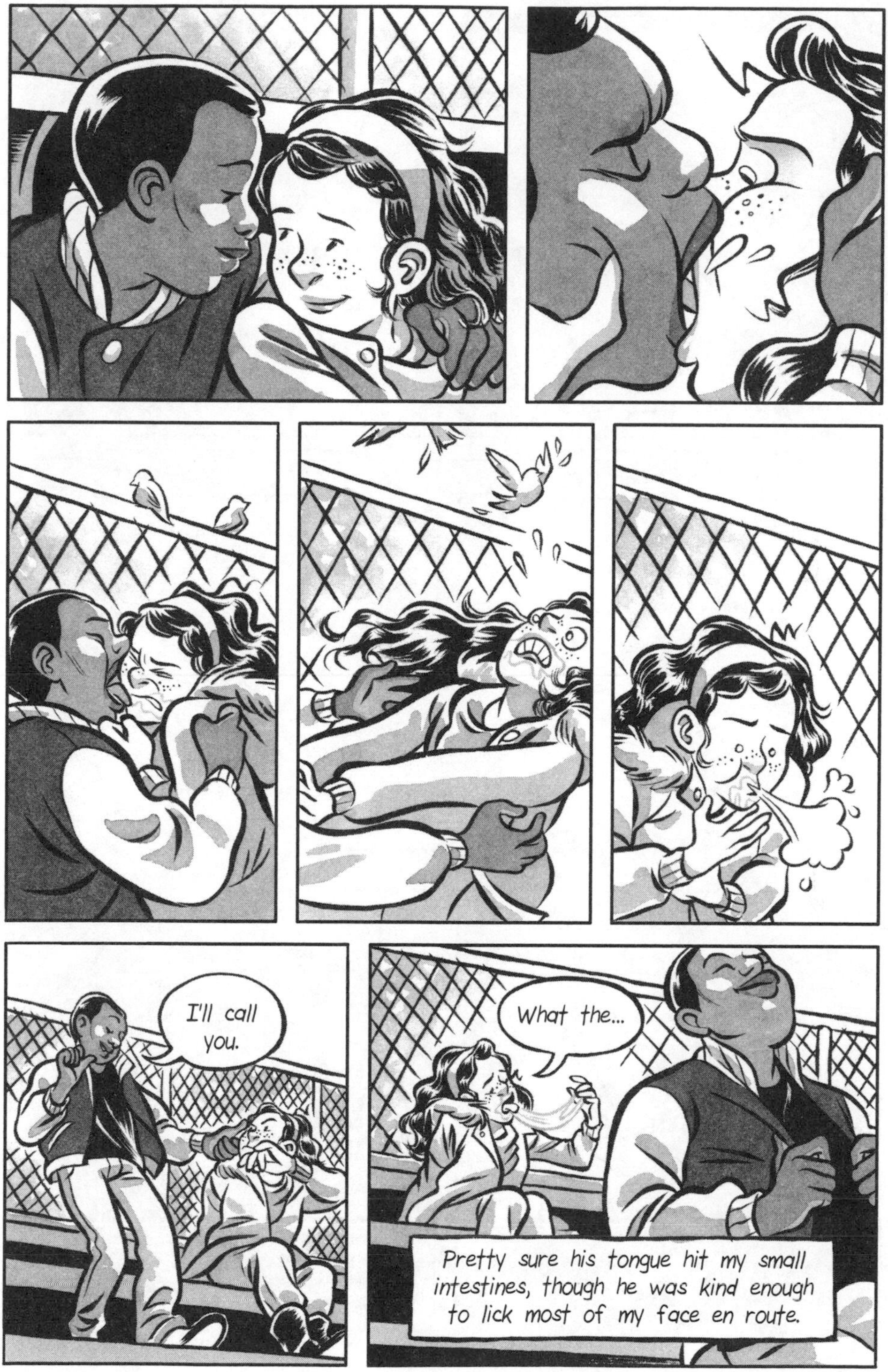
I'll call you.
What the...
Pretty sure his tongue hit my small intestines, though he was kind enough to lick most of my face en route.

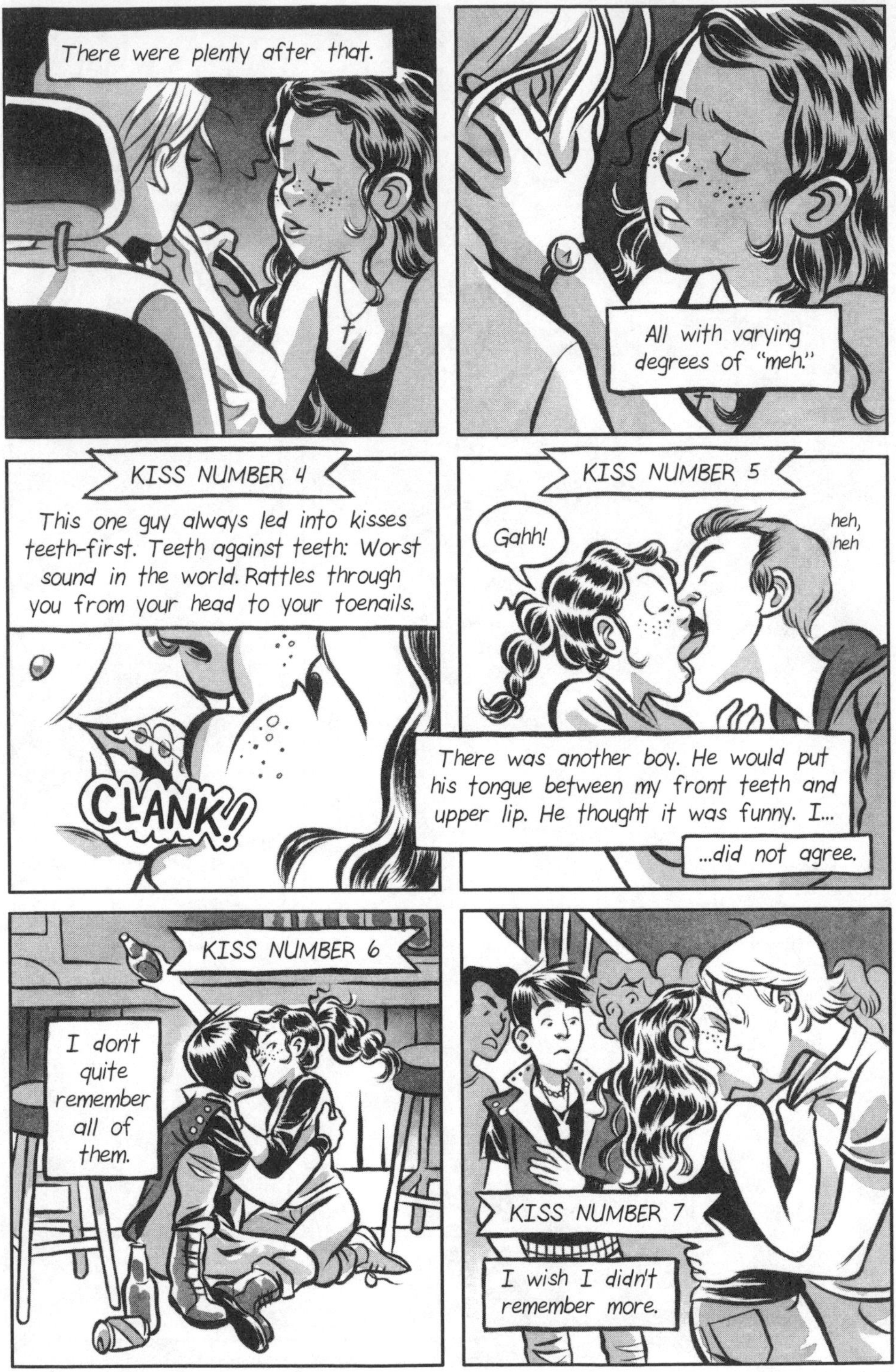

There were plenty after that.
All with varying degrees of "meh."
KISS NUMBER 4
This one guy always led into kisses teeth-first. Teeth against teeth: Worst sound in the world. Rattles through you from your head to your toenails.
CLANK!
KISS NUMBER 5
Gahh!
heh, heh
There was another boy. He would put his tongue between my front teeth and upper lip. He thought it was funny. I...
...did not agree.
KISS NUMBER 6
I don't quite remember all of them.
KISS NUMBER 7
I wish I didn't remember more.

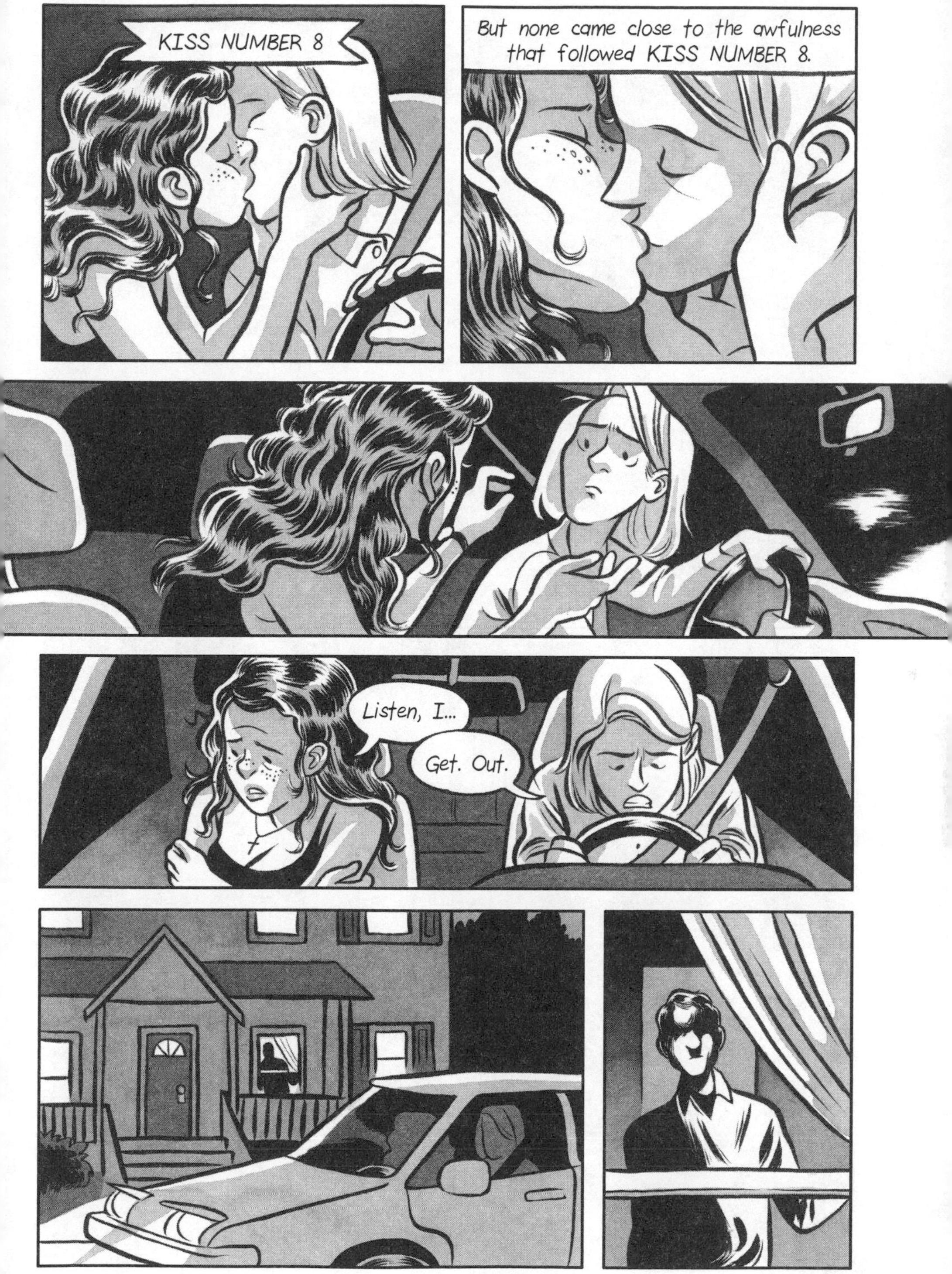
KISS NUMBER 8
But none came close to the awfulness that followed KISS NUMBER 8.
Listen, I...
Get. Out.

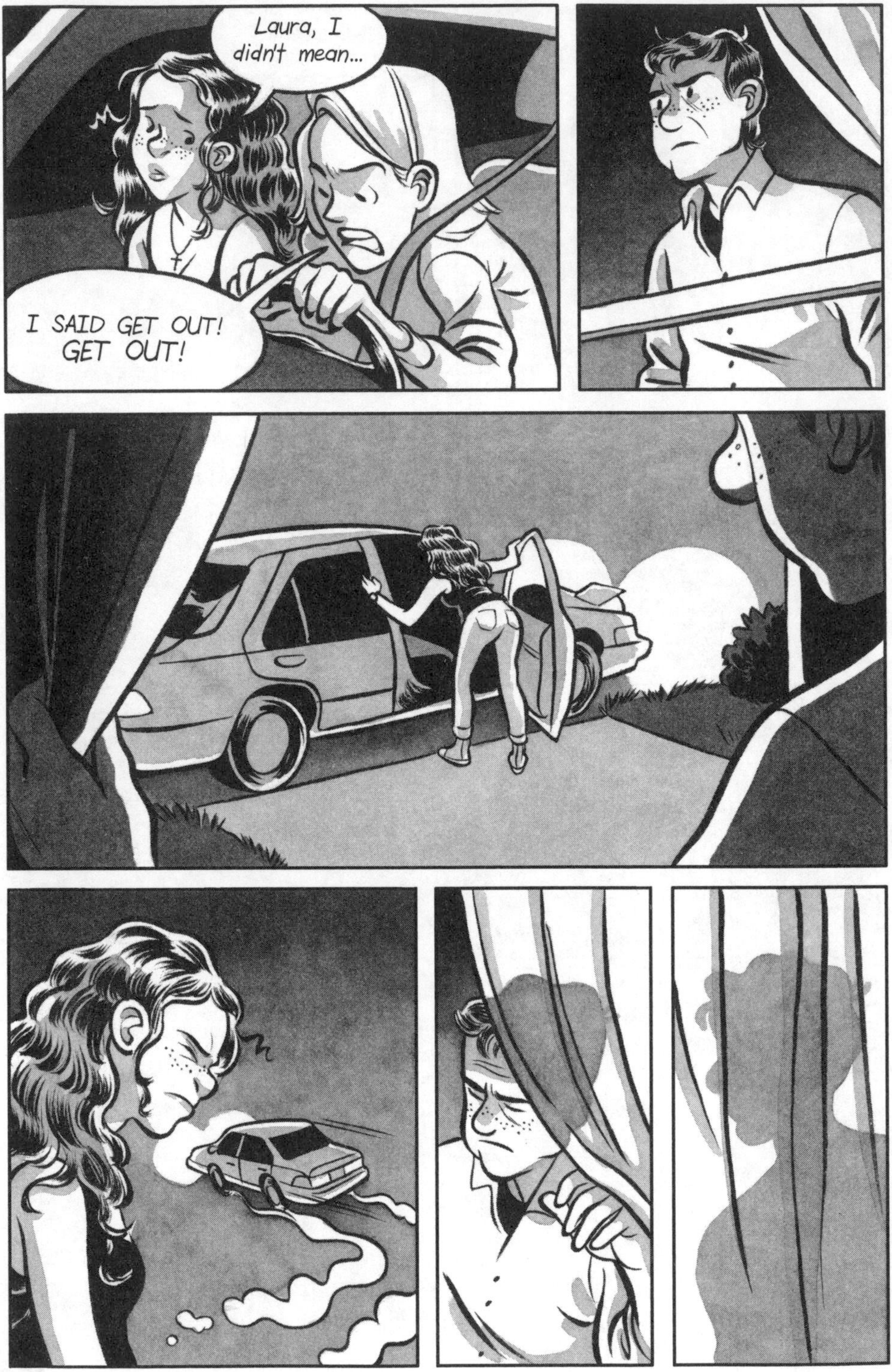
Laura, I didn't mean...
I SAID GET OUT! GET OUT!

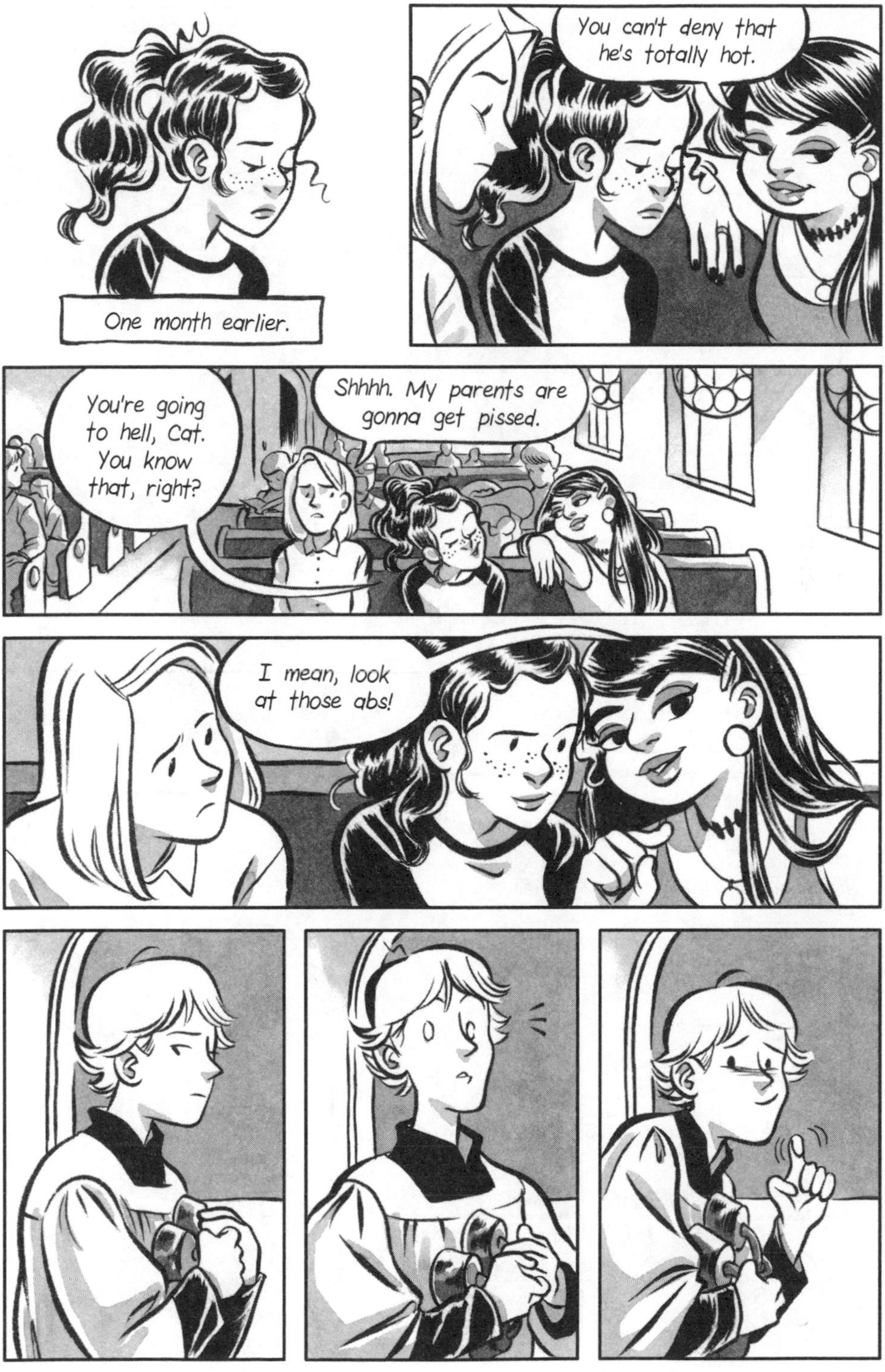

One month earlier.
You can't deny that he's totally hot.
You're going to hell, Cat. You know that, right?
Shhhh. My parents are gonna get pissed.
I mean, look at those abs!

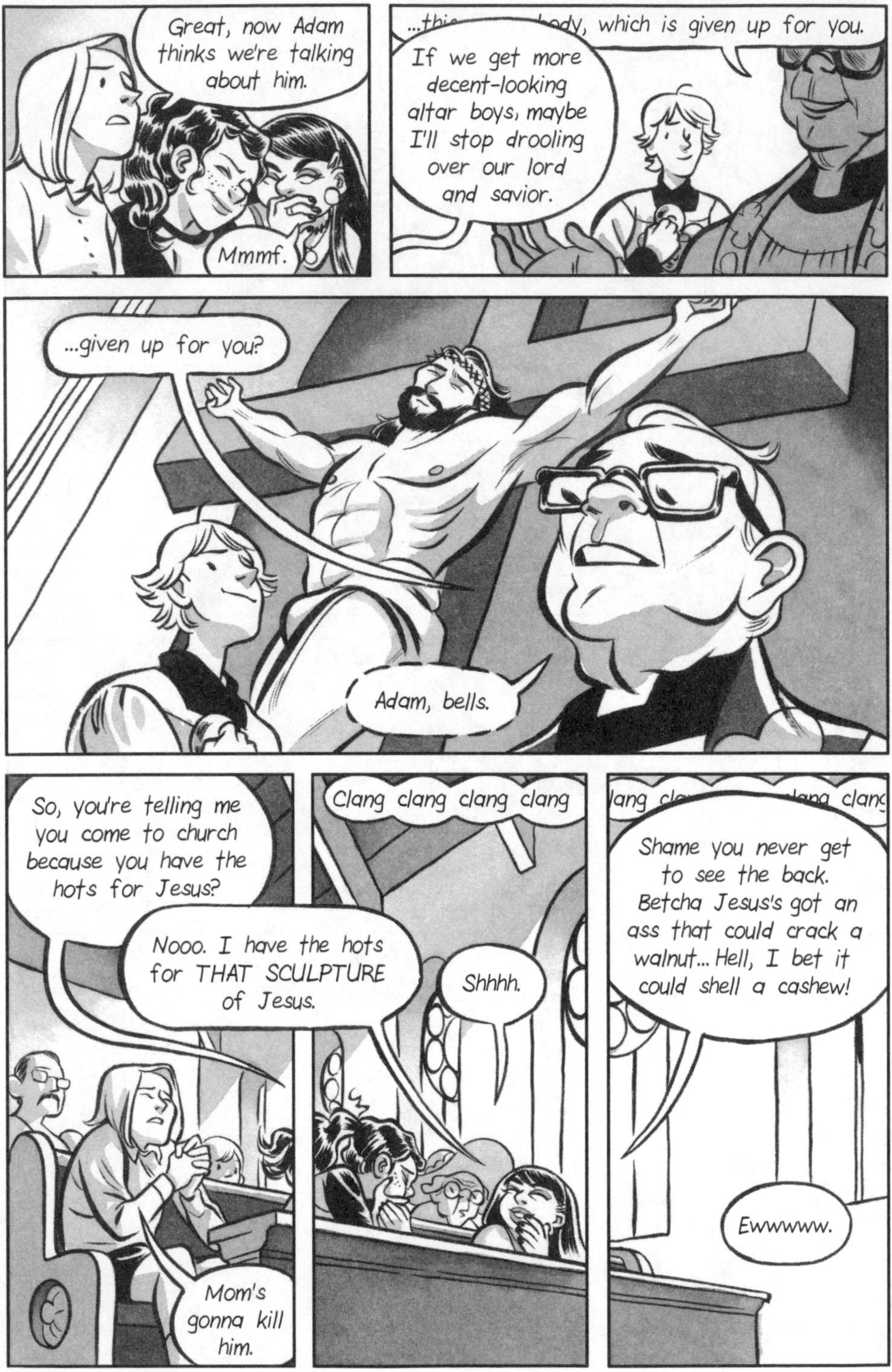
Great, now Adam thinks we're talking about him.
Mmmf.
...thi body, which is given up for you.
If we get more decent-looking altar boys, maybe I'll stop drooling over our lord and savior.
...given up for you?
Adam, bells.
So, you're telling me you come to church because you have the hots for Jesus?
Nooo. I have the hots for THAT SCULPTURE of Jesus.
Mom's gonna kill him.
Clang clang clang clang
Shhhh.
Shame you never get to see the back. Betcha Jesus's got an ass that could crack a walnut... Hell, I bet it could shell a cashew!
Ewwwww.

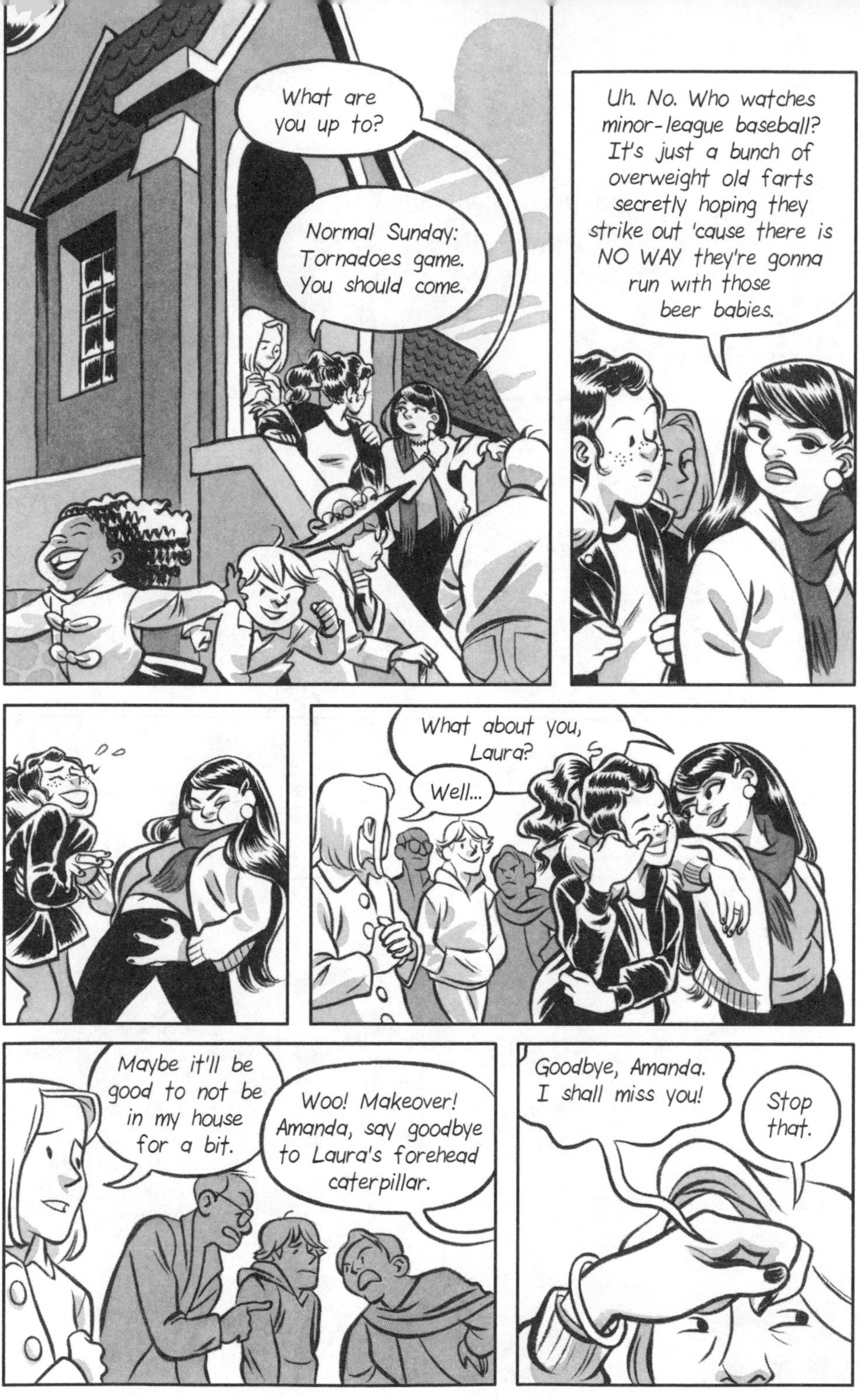
What are you up to?
Normal Sunday: Tornadoes game. You should come.
Uh. No. Who watches minor-league baseball? It's just a bunch of overweight old farts secretly hoping they strike out 'cause there is NO WAY they're gonna run with those beer babies.
What about you, Laura?
Well...
Maybe it'll be good to not be in my house for a bit.
Woo! Makeover! Amanda, say goodbye to Laura's forehead caterpillar.
Goodbye, Amanda. I shall miss you!
Stop that.

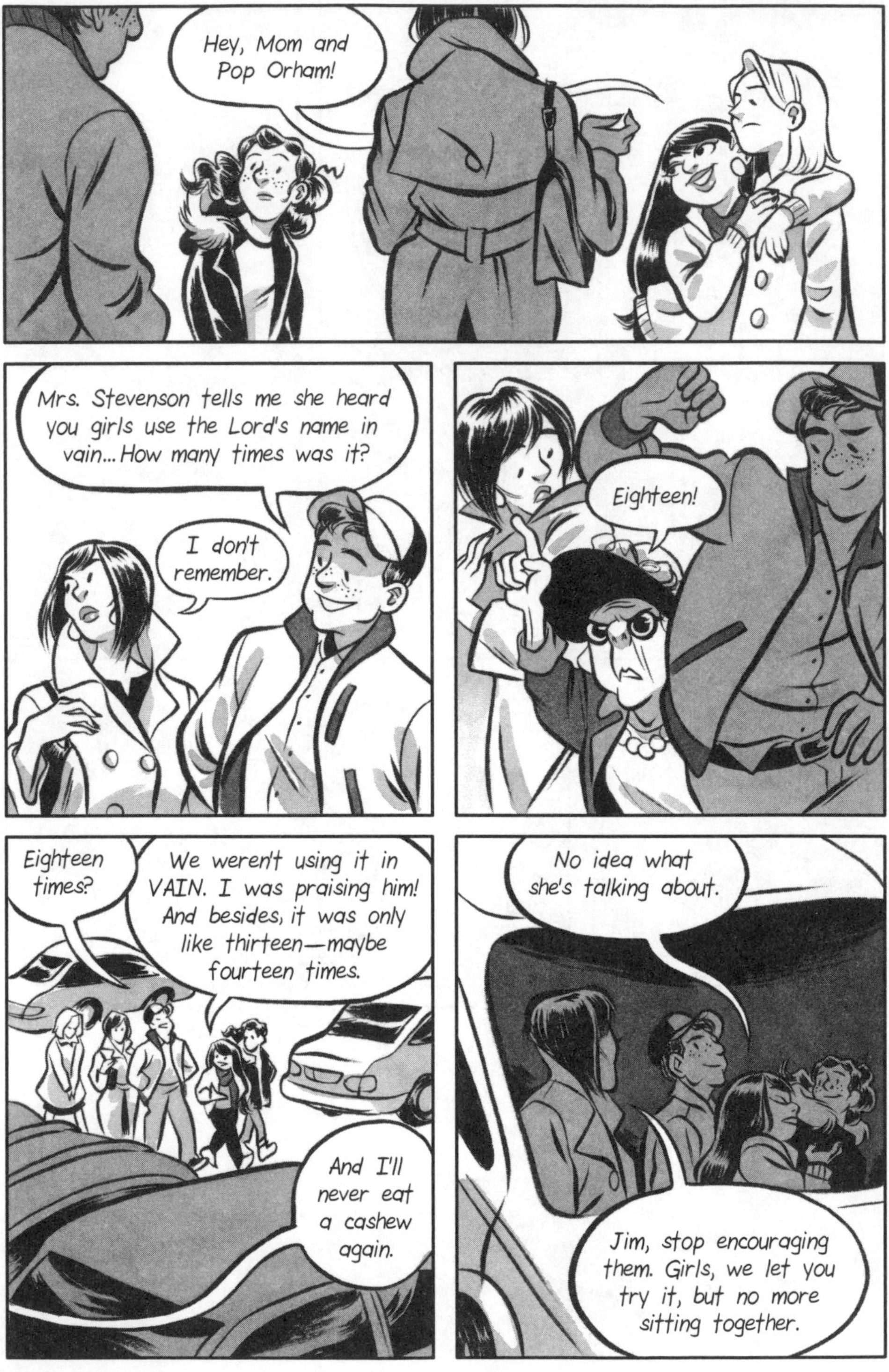

Hey, Mom and Pop Orham!
Mrs. Stevenson tells me she heard you girls use the Lord's name in vain... How many times was it?
I don't remember.
Eighteen!
Eighteen times?
We weren't using it in VAIN. I was praising him! And besides, it was only like thirteen—maybe fourteen times.
And I'll never eat a cashew again.
No idea what she's talking about.
Jim, stop encouraging them. Girls, we let you try it, but no more sitting together.

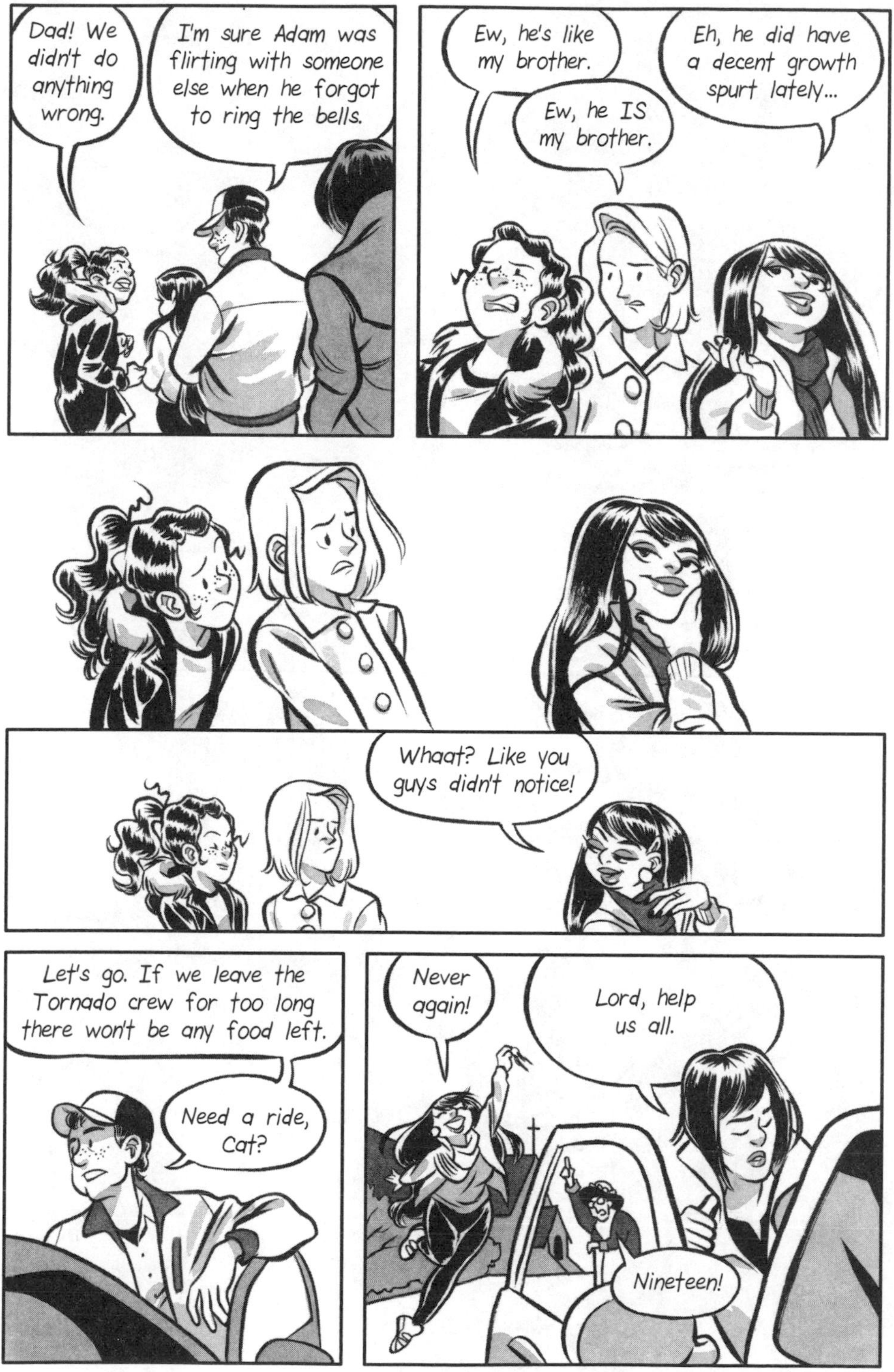
Dad! We didn't do anything wrong.
I'm sure Adam was flirting with someone else when he forgot to ring the bells.
Ew, he's like my brother.
Ew, he IS my brother.
Eh, he did have a decent growth spurt lately...
Whaat? Like you guys didn't notice!
Let's go. If we leave the Tornado crew for too long there won't be any food left.
Need a ride, Cat?
Never again!
Lord, help us all.
Nineteen!

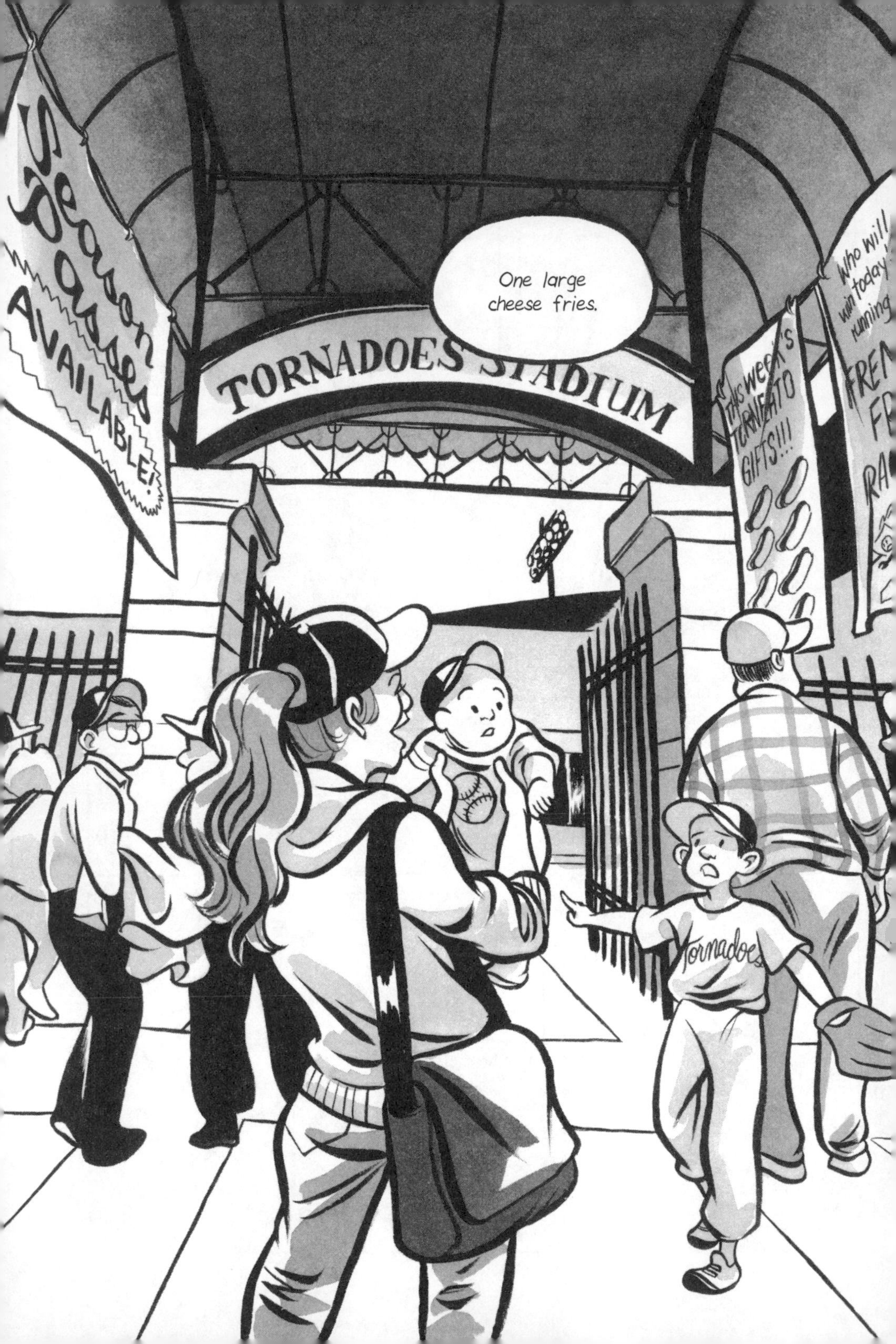
Season Passes AVAILABLE!
TORNADOES STADIUM
One large cheese fries.
THIS WEEK'S
GIFTS!!!
Tornadoes

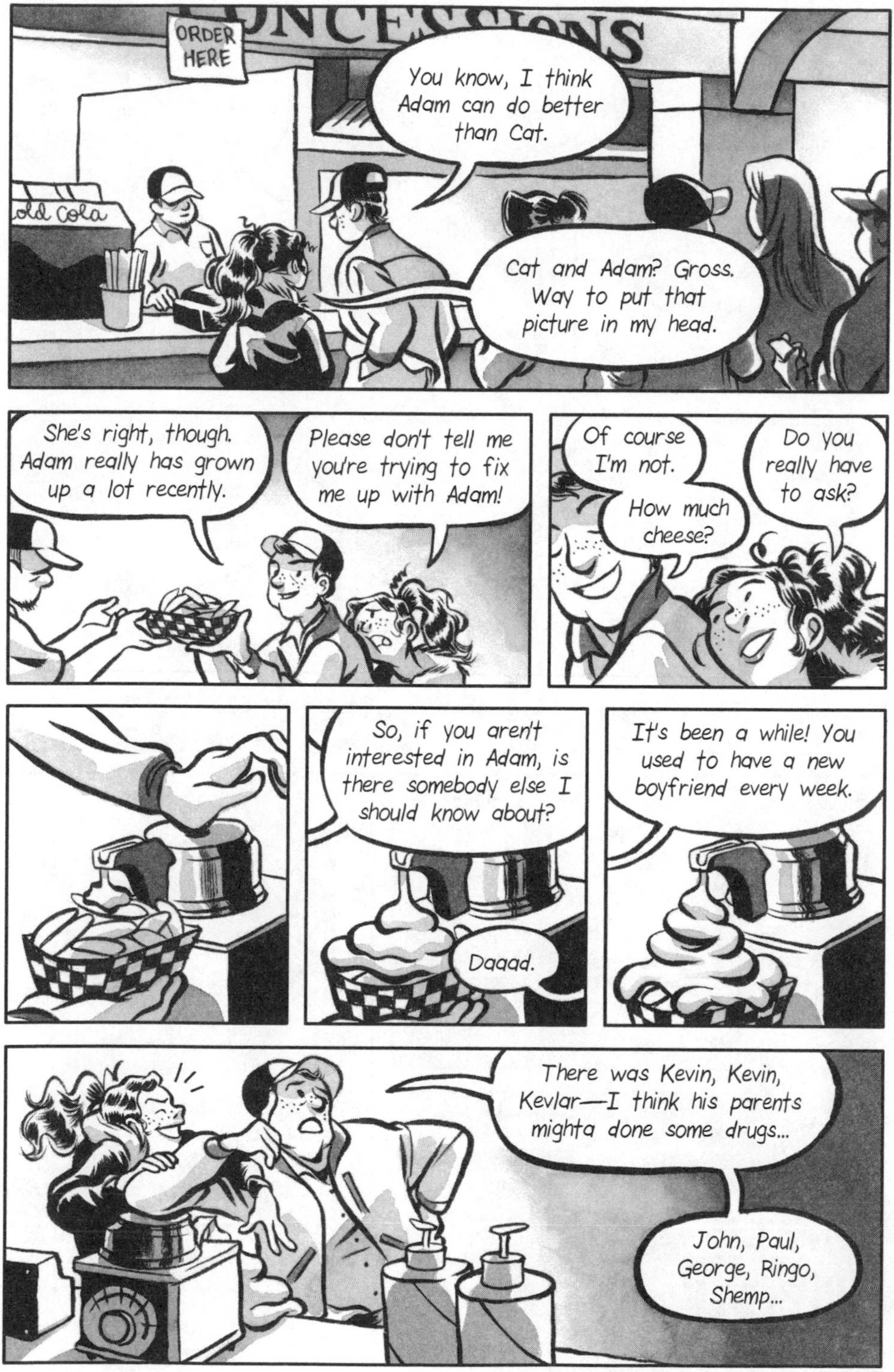
ORDER HERE
CONCESSIONS
Cold Cola
You know, I think Adam can do better than Cat.
Cat and Adam? Gross. Way to put that picture in my head.
She's right, though. Adam really has grown up a lot recently.
Please don't tell me you're trying to fix me up with Adam!
Of course I'm not.
How much cheese?
Do you really have to ask?
So, if you aren't interested in Adam, is there somebody else I should know about?
Daaad.
It's been a while! You used to have a new boyfriend every week.
There was Kevin, Kevin, Kevlar—I think his parents mighta done some drugs...
John, Paul, George, Ringo, Shemp...

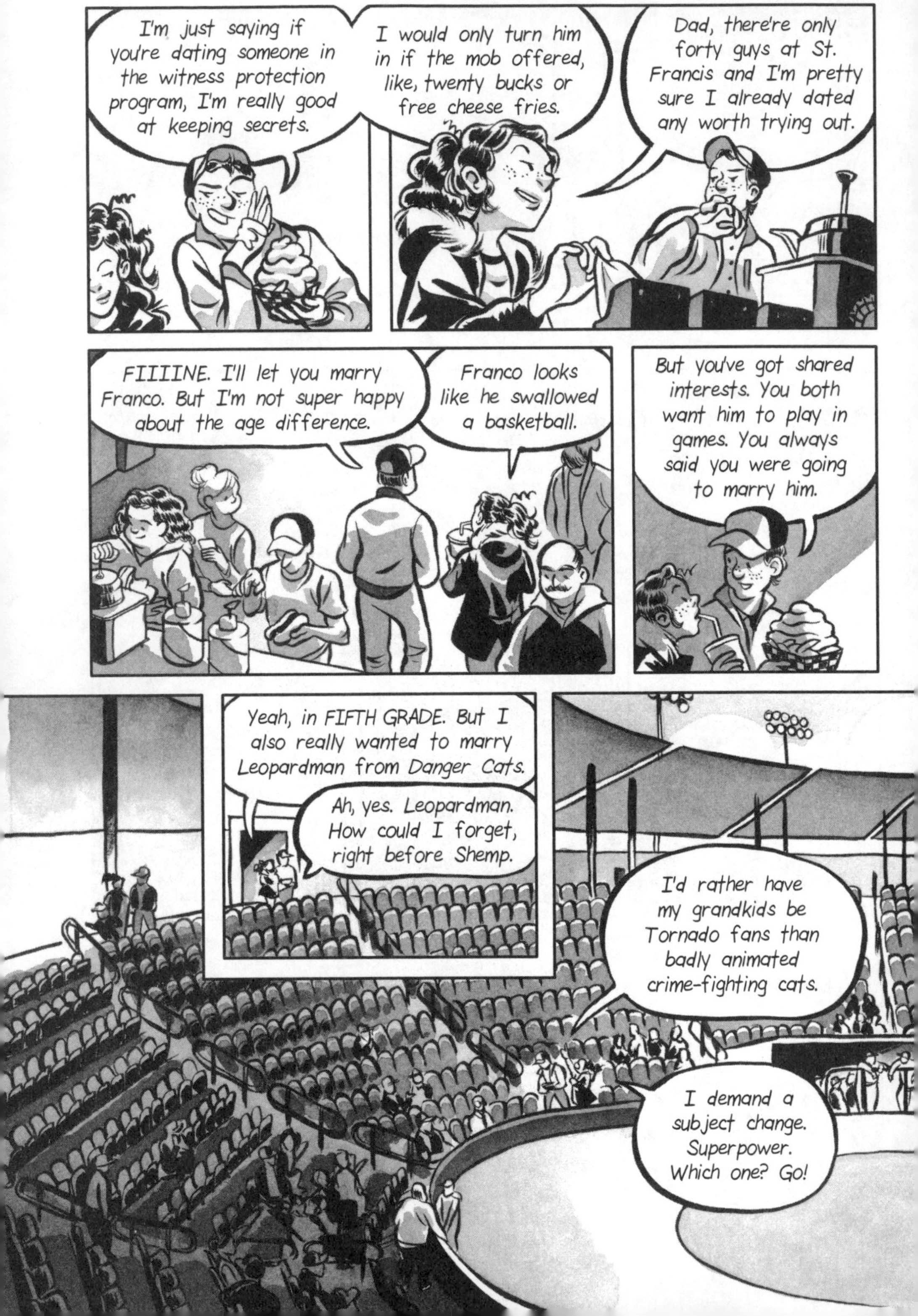
I'm just saying if you're dating someone in the witness protection program, I'm really good at keeping secrets.
I would only turn him in if the mob offered, like, twenty bucks or free cheese fries.
Dad, there're only forty guys at St. Francis and I'm pretty sure I already dated any worth trying out.
FIIIINE. I'll let you marry Franco. But I'm not super happy about the age difference.
Franco looks like he swallowed a basketball.
But you've got shared interests. You both want him to play in games. You always said you were going to marry him.
Yeah, in FIFTH GRADE. But I also really wanted to marry Leopardman from Danger Cats.
Ah, yes. Leopardman. How could I forget, right before Shemp.
I'd rather have my grandkids be Tornado fans than badly animated crime-fighting cats.
I demand a subject change. Superpower. Which one? Go!

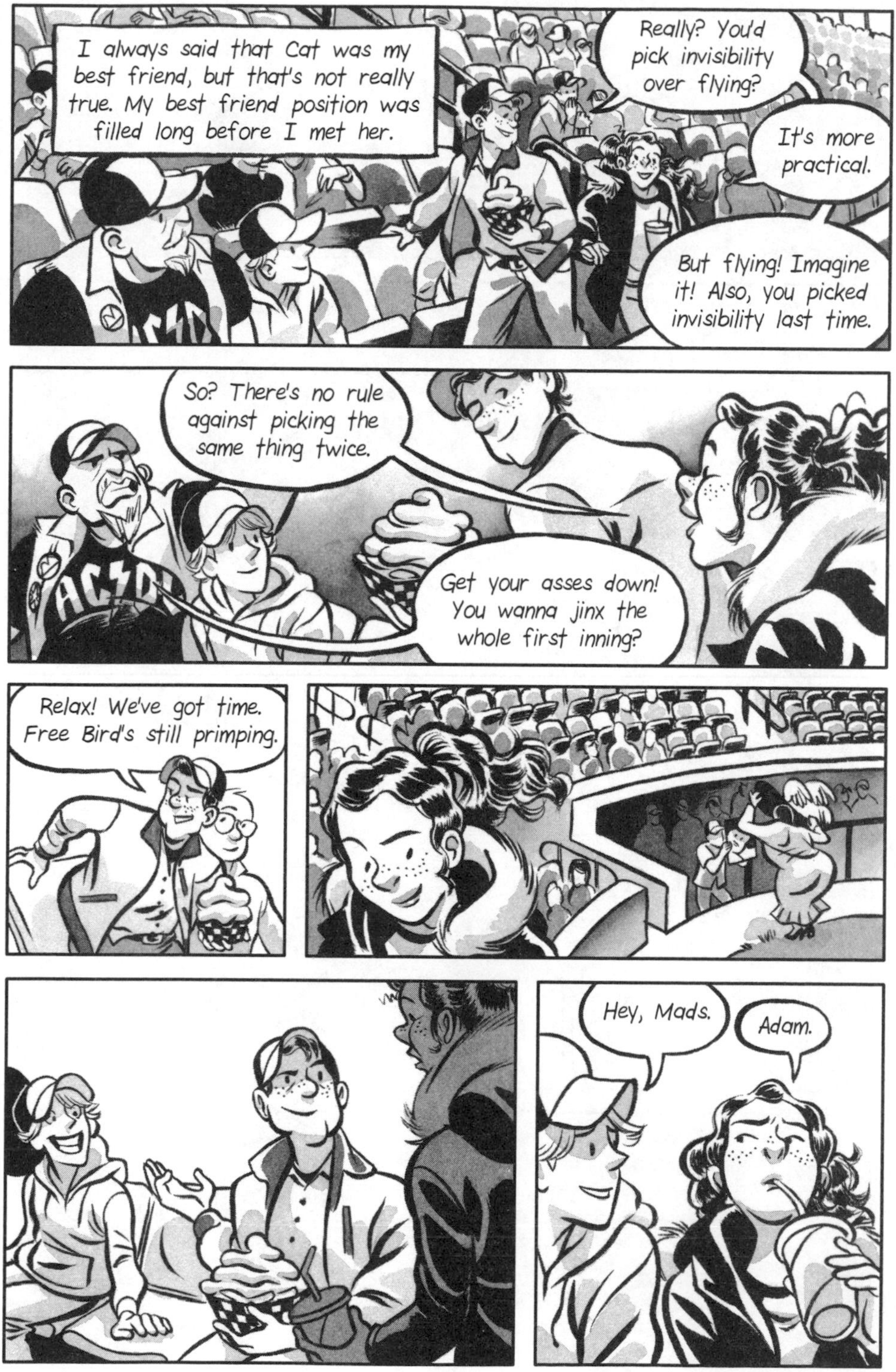
I always said that Cat was my best friend, but that's not really true. My best friend position was filled long before I met her.
Really? You'd pick invisibility over flying?
It's more practical.
But flying! Imagine it! Also, you picked invisibility last time.
So? There's no rule against picking the same thing twice.
Get your asses down! You wanna jinx the whole first inning?
Relax! We've got time. Free Bird's still primping.
Hey, Mads.
Adam.

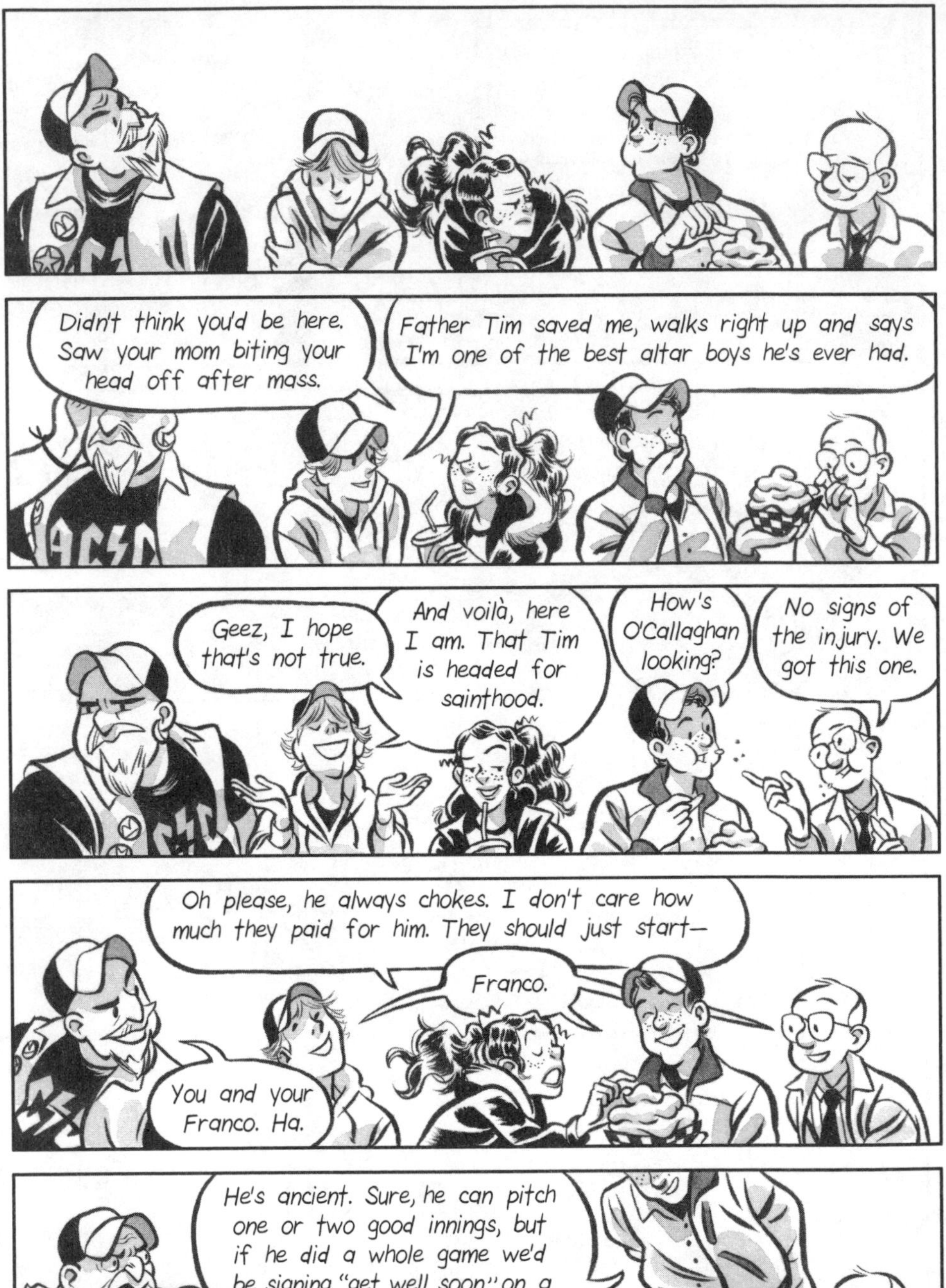
Didn't think you'd be here. Saw your mom biting your head off after mass.
Father Tim saved me, walks right up and says I'm one of the best altar boys he's ever had.
Geez, I hope that's not true.
And voilà, here I am. That Tim is headed for sainthood.
How's O'Callaghan looking?
No signs of the injury. We got this one.
Oh please, he always chokes. I don't care how much they paid for him. They should just start—
Franco.
You and your Franco. Ha.
He's ancient. Sure, he can pitch one or two good innings, but if he did a whole game we'd be signing "get well soon" on a
What are you doing?! Sit down!

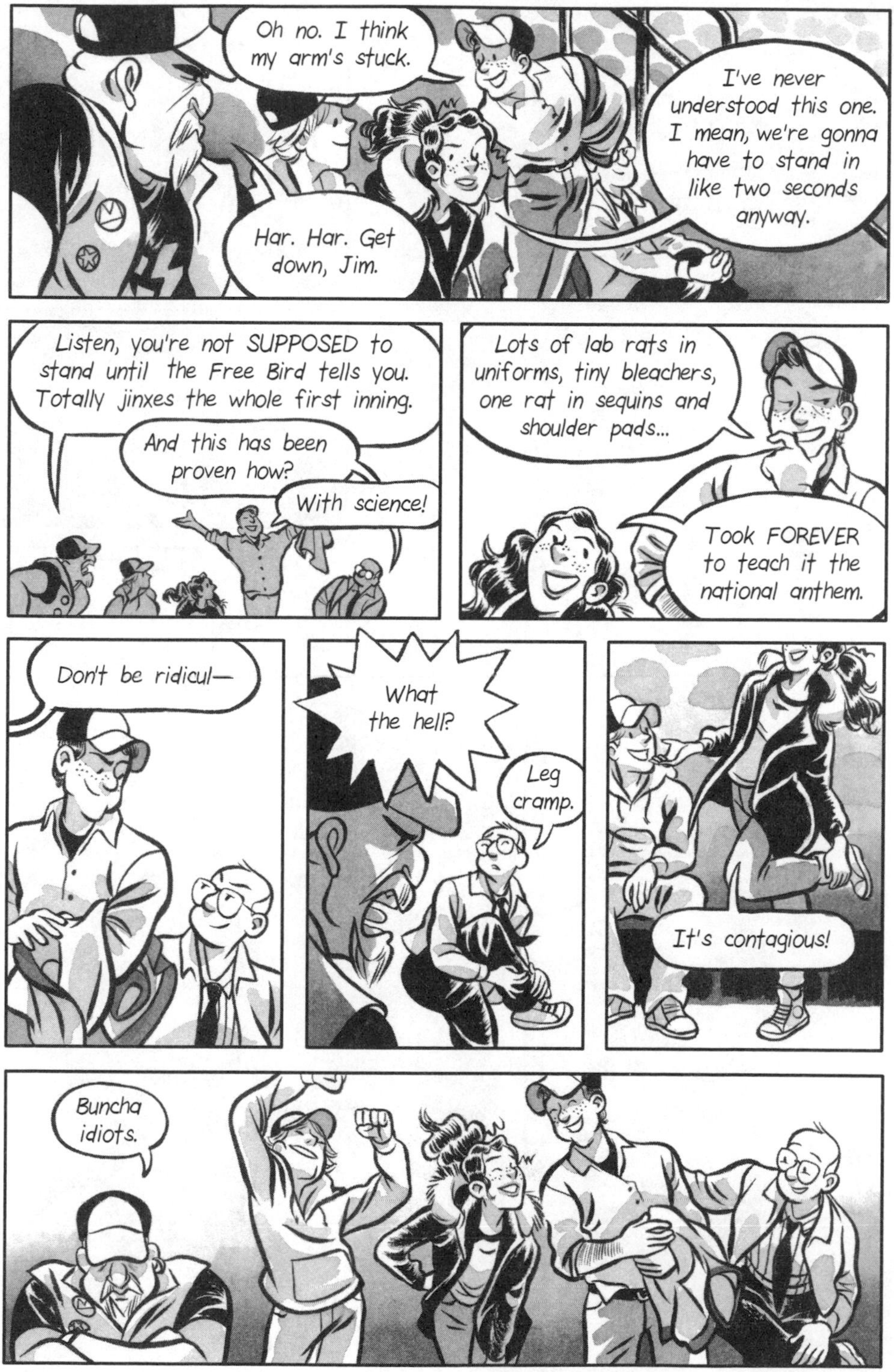
Oh no. I think my arm's stuck.
I've never understood this one. I mean, we're gonna have to stand in like two seconds anyway.
Har. Har. Get down, Jim.
Listen, you're not SUPPOSED to stand until the Free Bird tells you. Totally jinxes the whole first inning.
And this has been proven how?
With science!
Lots of lab rats in uniforms, tiny bleachers, one rat in sequins and shoulder pads...
Took FOREVER to teach it the national anthem.
Don't be ridicul—
What the hell?
Leg cramp.
It's contagious!
Buncha idiots.

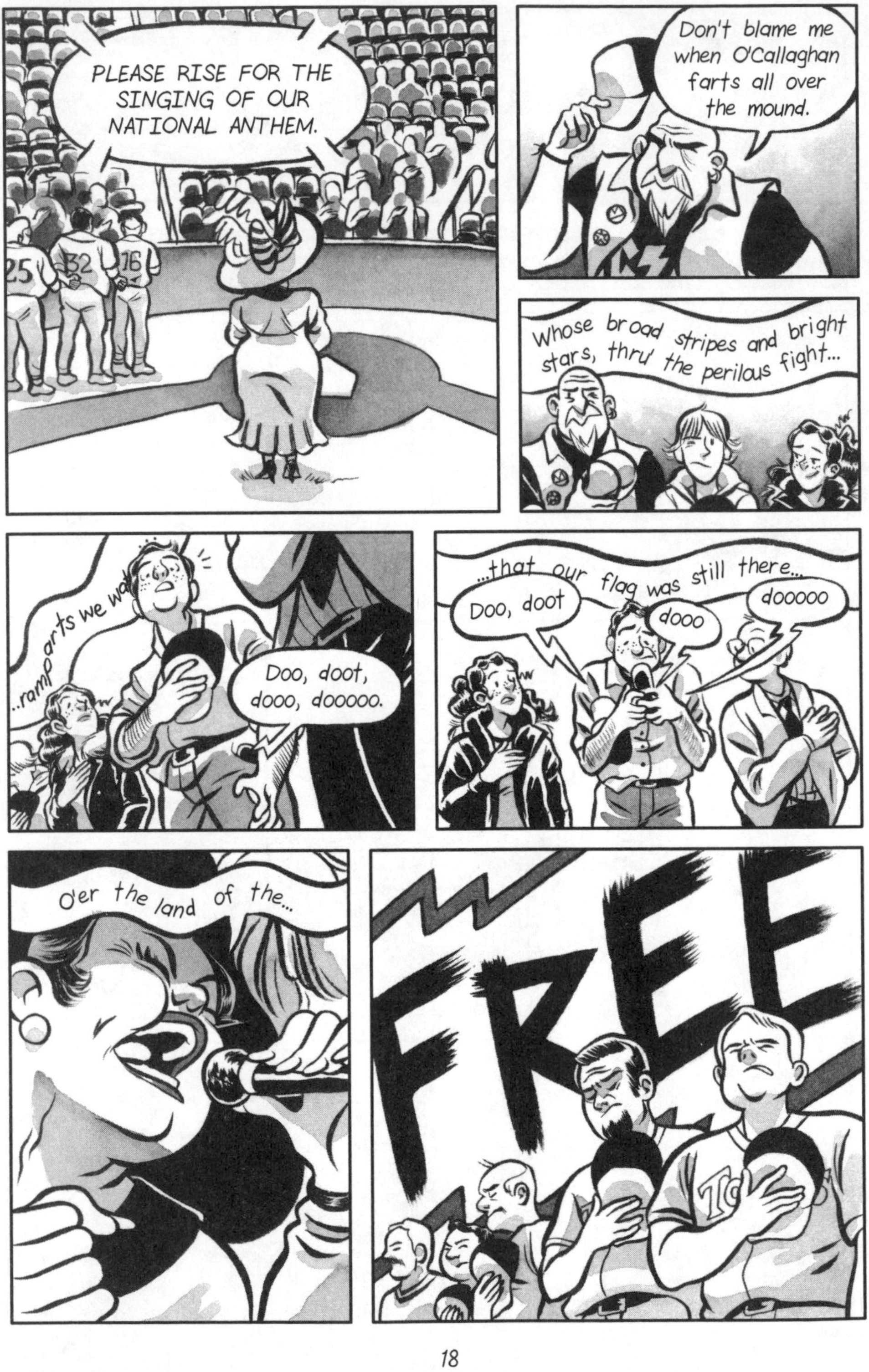
PLEASE RISE FOR THE SINGING OF OUR NATIONAL ANTHEM.
Don't blame me when O'Callaghan farts all over the mound.
Whose broad stripes and bright stars, thru' the perilous fight...
...ramparts we wa
Doo, doot, dooo, dooooo.
...that our flag was still there...
Doo, doot
dooo
dooooo
O'er the land of the...
FREE

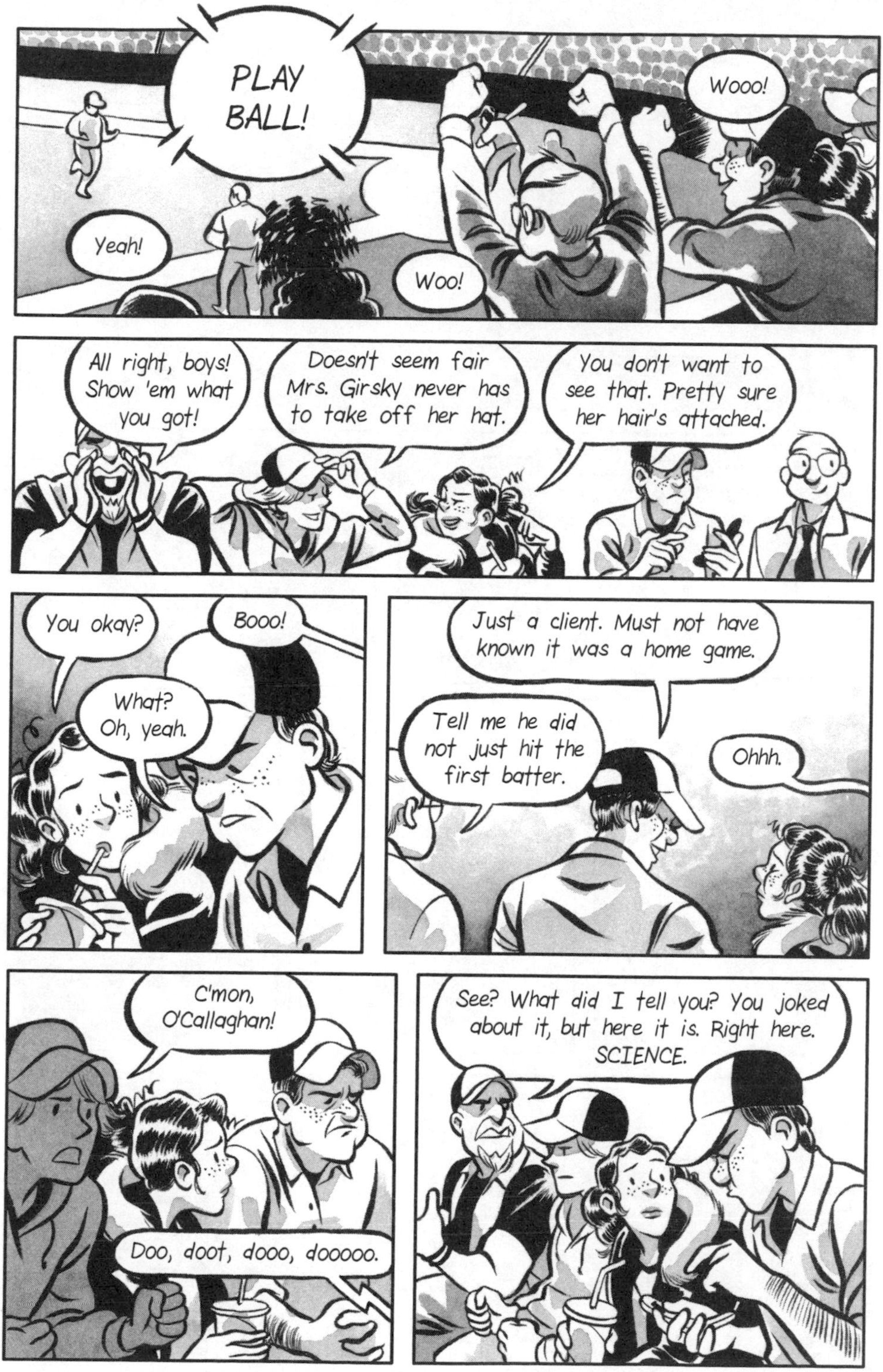
PLAY BALL!
Wooo!
Yeah!
Woo!
All right, boys! Show 'em what you got!
Doesn't seem fair Mrs. Girsky never has to take off her hat.
You don't want to see that. Pretty sure her hair's attached.
You okay?
Booo!
What? Oh, yeah.
Just a client. Must not have known it was a home game.
Tell me he did not just hit the first batter.
Ohhh.
C'mon, O'Callaghan!
Doo, doot, dooo, doooooo.
See? What did I tell you? You joked about it, but here it is. Right here. SCIENCE.

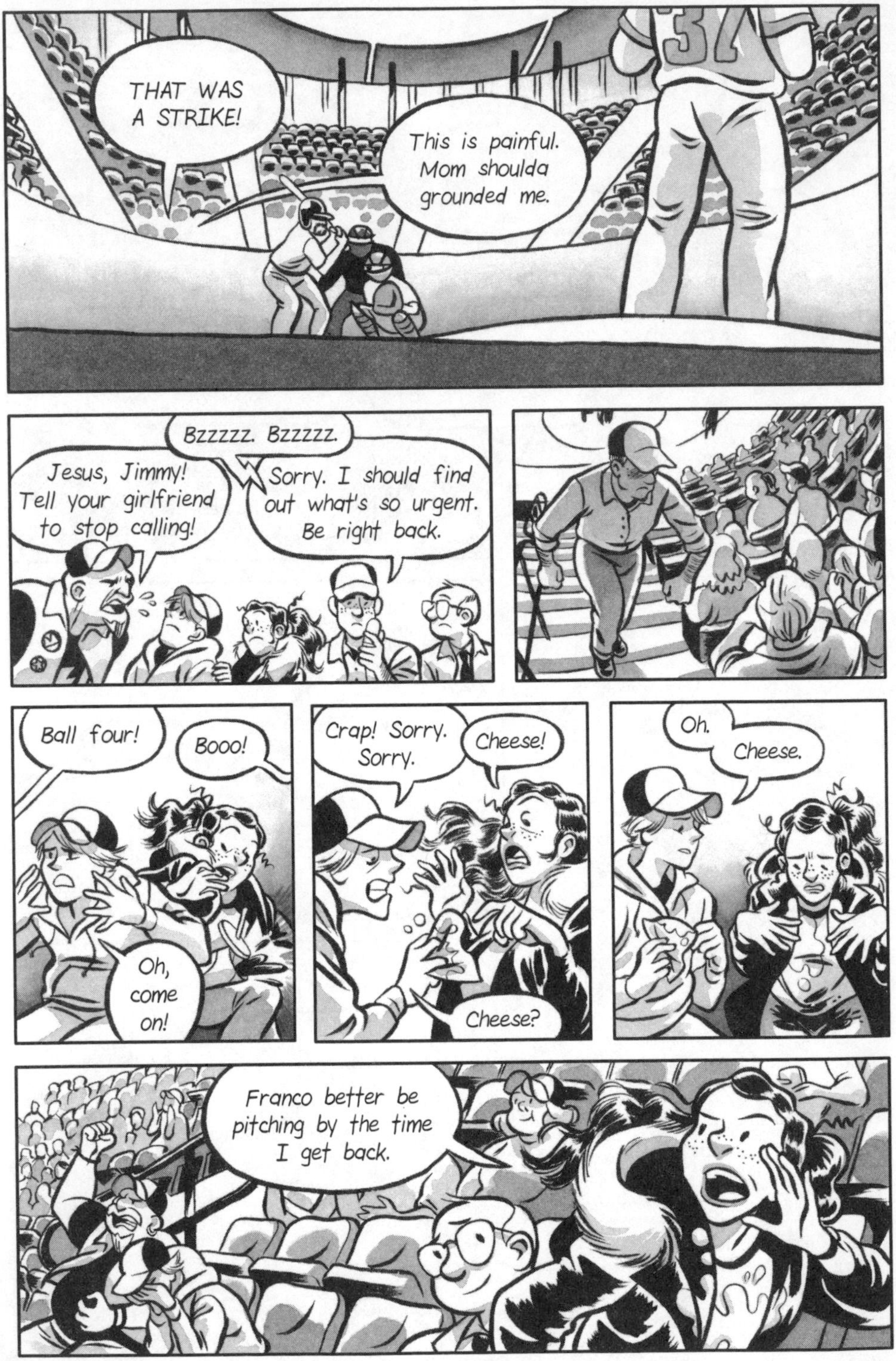
THAT WAS A STRIKE!
This is painful. Mom shoulda grounded me.
Bzzzzz. Bzzzzz.
Jesus, Jimmy! Tell your girlfriend to stop calling!
Sorry. I should find out what's so urgent. Be right back.
Ball four!
Booo!
Oh, come on!
Crap! Sorry. Sorry.
Cheese!
Cheese?
Oh.
Cheese.
Franco better be pitching by the time I get back.

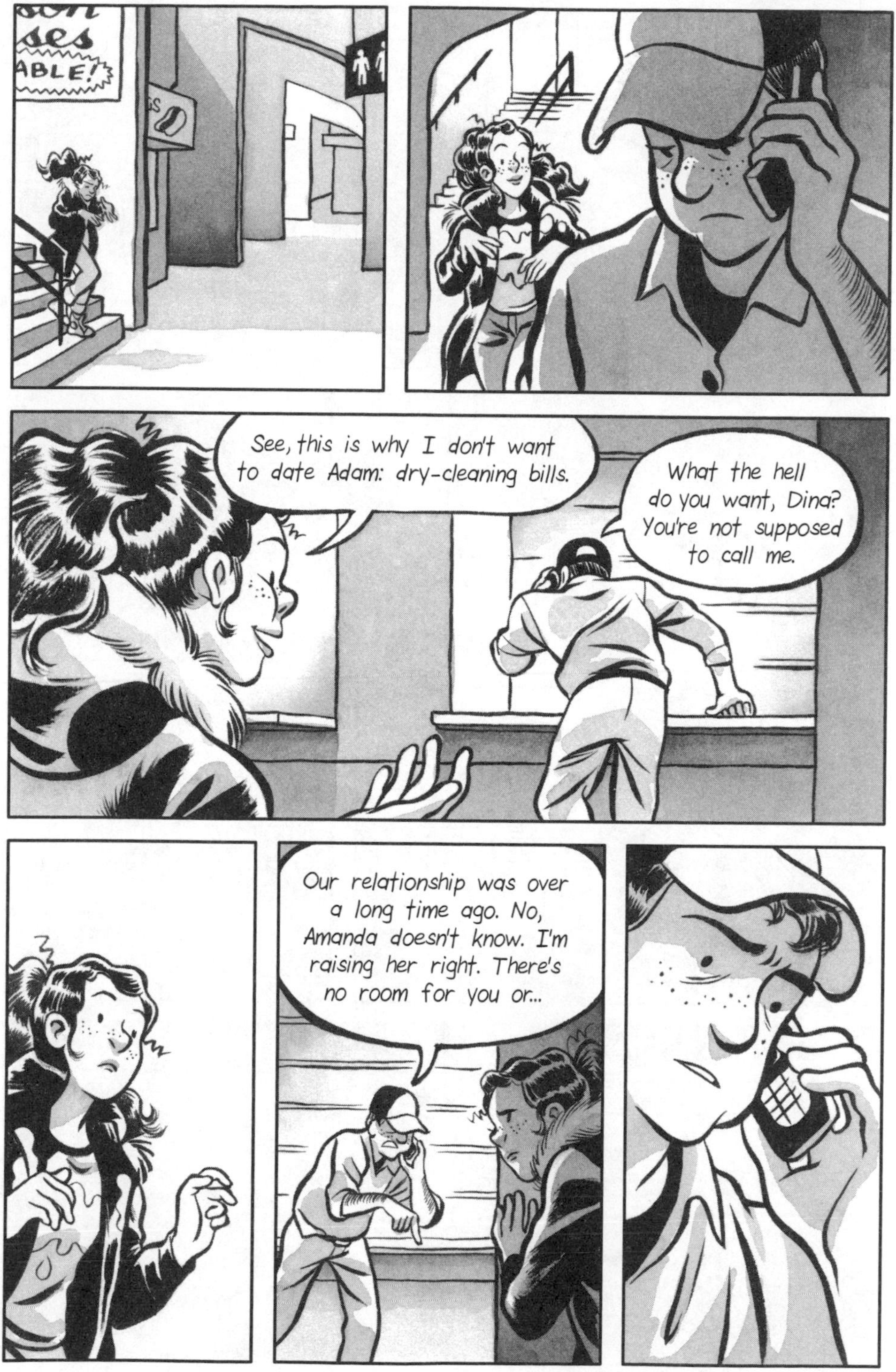
See, this is why I don't want to date Adam: dry-cleaning bills.
What the hell do you want, Dina? You're not supposed to call me.
Our relationship was over a long time ago. No, Amanda doesn't know. I'm raising her right. There's no room for you or...

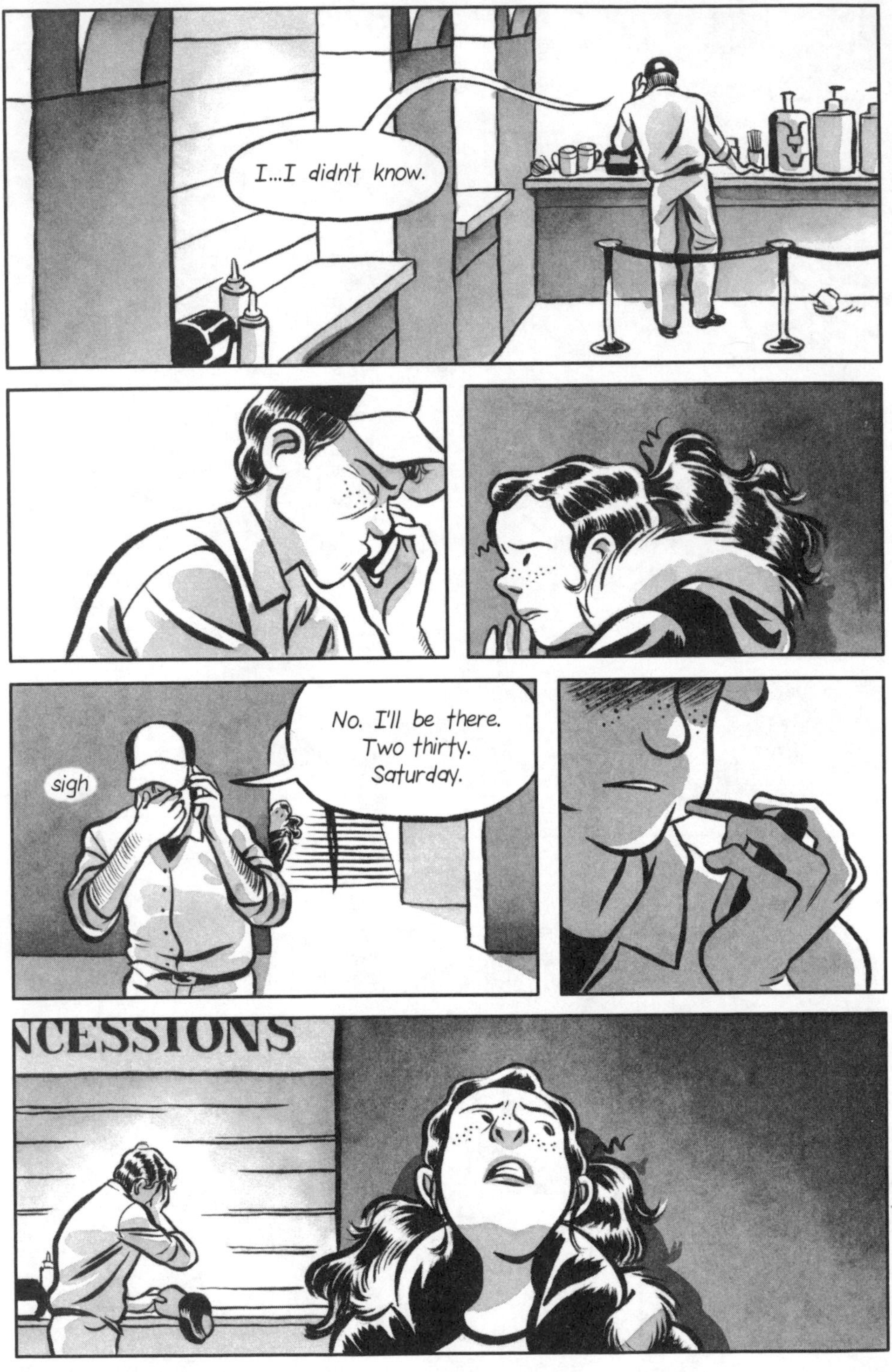
I...I didn't know.
sigh
No. I'll be there. Two thirty. Saturday.
NCESSIONS

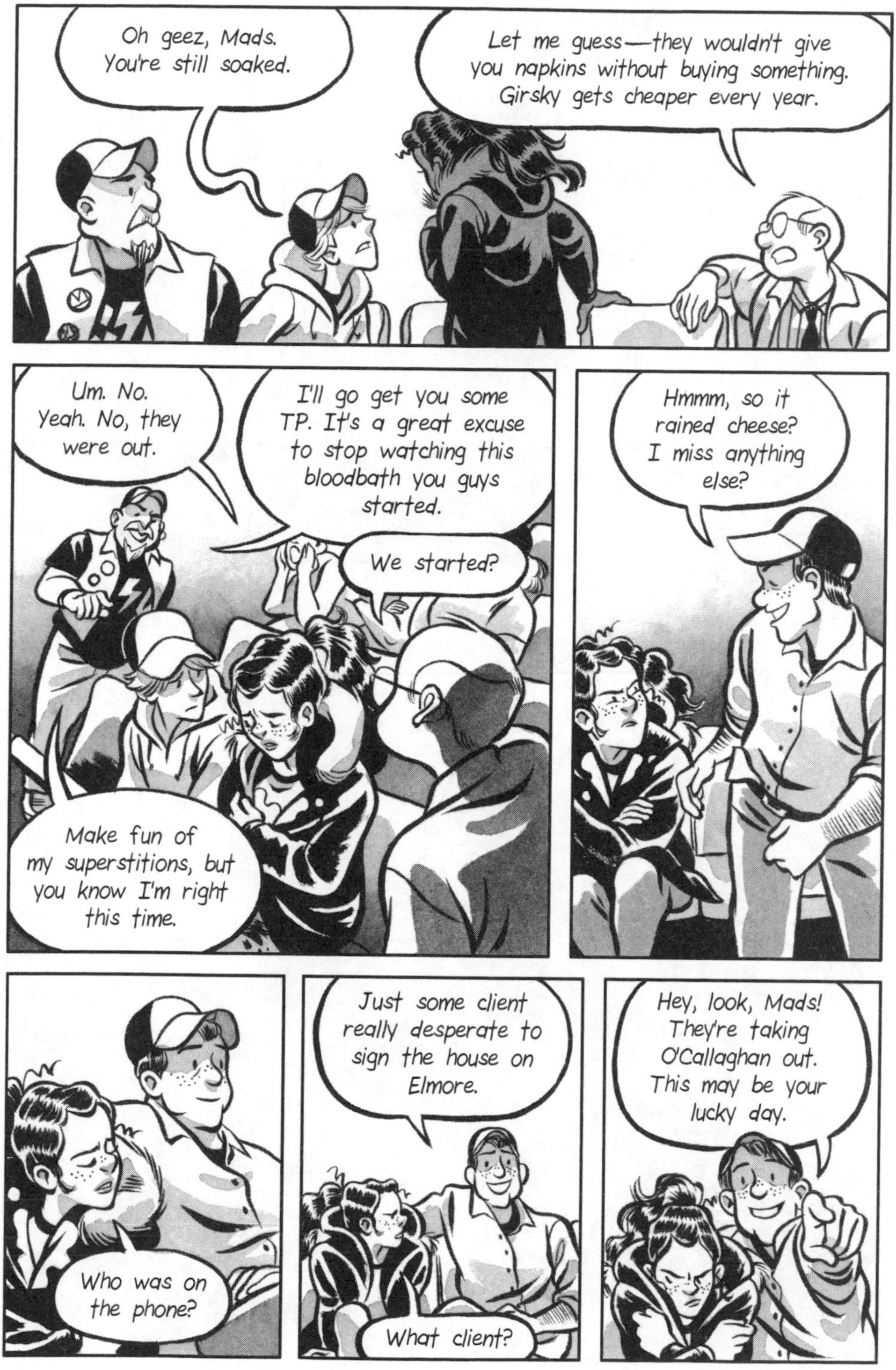

Oh geez, Mads. You're still soaked.
Let me guess—they wouldn't give you napkins without buying something. Girsky gets cheaper every year.
Um. No. Yeah. No, they were out.
I'll go get you some TP. It's a great excuse to stop watching this bloodbath you guys started.
We started?
Make fun of my superstitions, but you know I'm right this time.
Hmmm, so it rained cheese? I miss anything else?
Who was on the phone?
Just some client really desperate to sign the house on Elmore.
What client?
Hey, look, Mads! They're taking O'Callaghan out. This may be your lucky day.

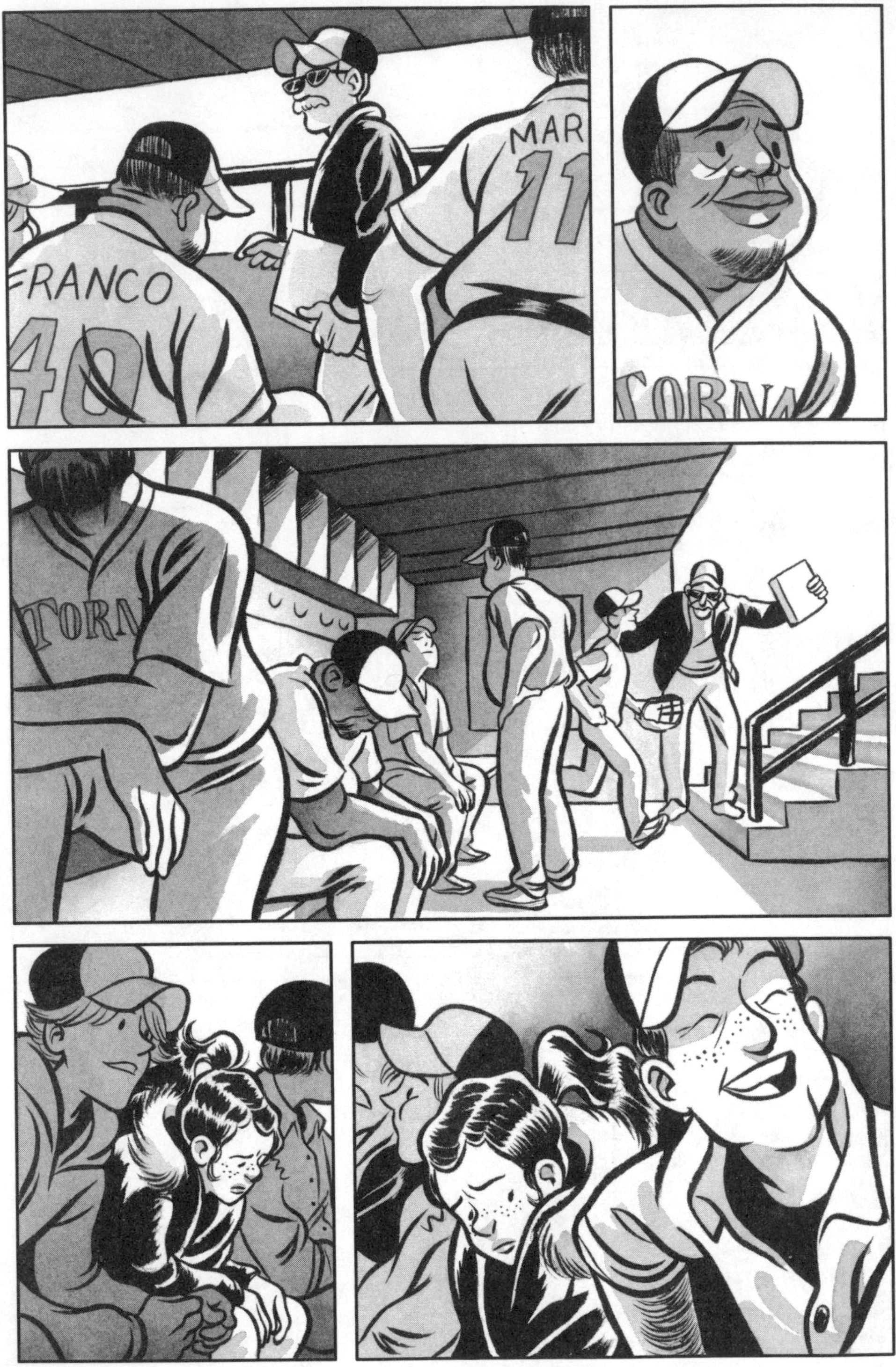
MAR
11
FRANCO
40
TORN

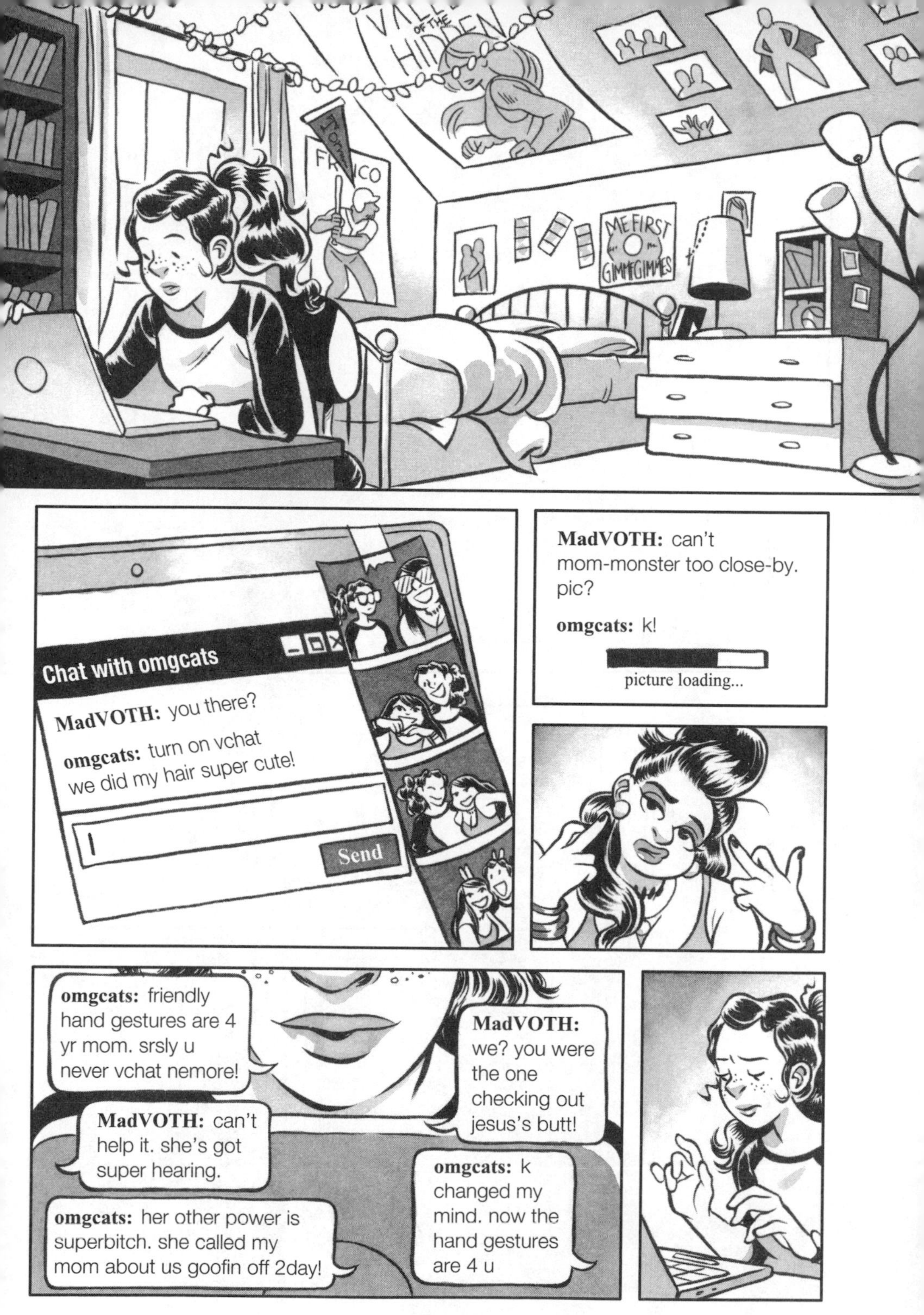
ME FIRST
GIMMEGIMMES
Chat with omgcats
MadVOTH: you there?
omgcats: turn on vchat
we did my hair super cute!
Send
MadVOTH: can't
mom-monster too close-by.
pic?
omgcats: k!
picture loading...
omgcats: friendly hand gestures are 4 yr mom. srsly u never vchat nemore!
MadVOTH: can't help it. she's got super hearing.
omgcats: her other power is superbitch. she called my mom about us goofin off 2day!
MadVOTH: we? you were the one checking out jesus's butt!
omgcats: k changed my mind. now the hand gestures are 4 u

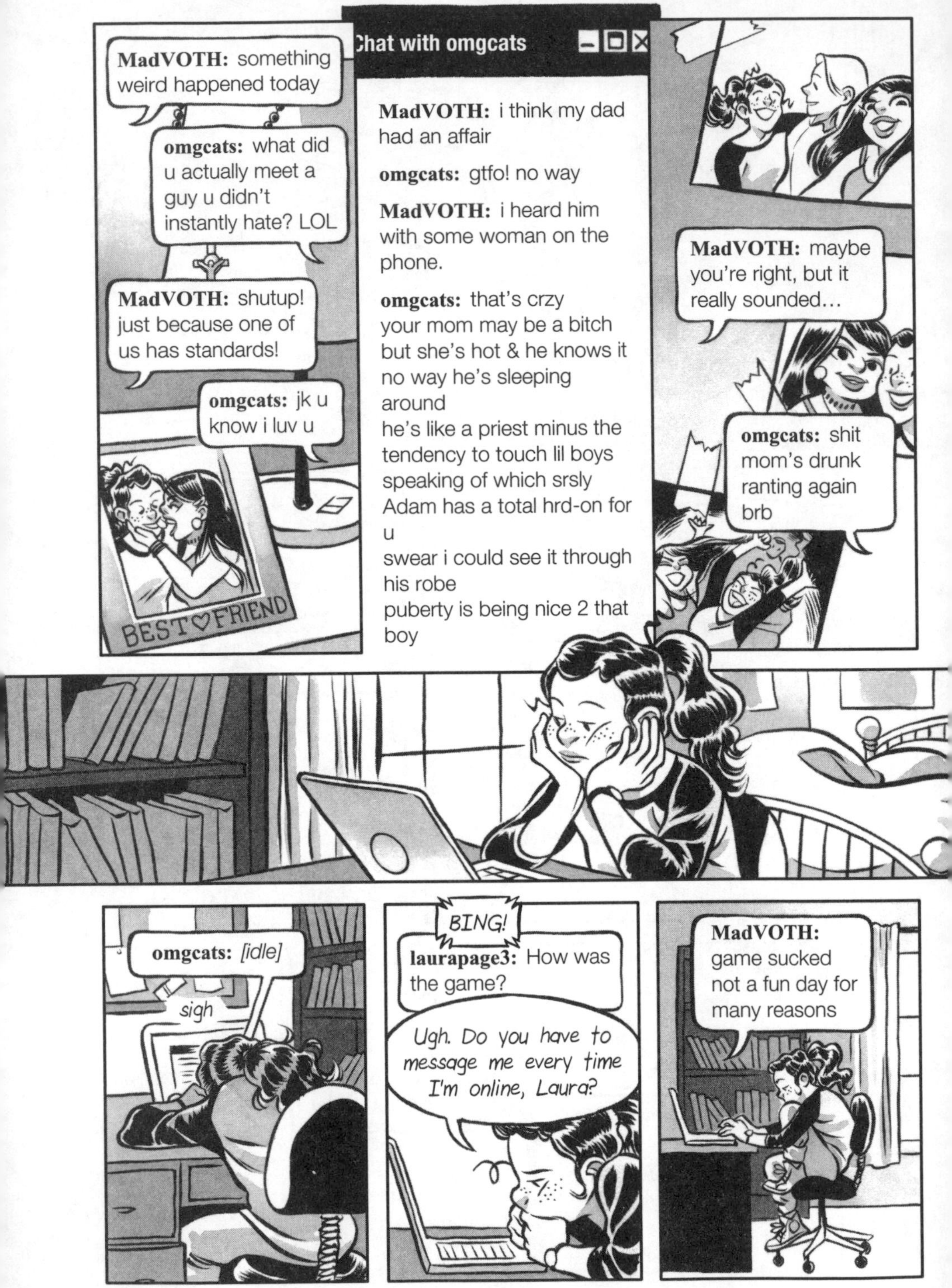
Chat with omgcats
MadVOTH: something weird happened today
omgcats: what did u actually meet a guy u didn't instantly hate? LOL
MadVOTH: shutup! just because one of us has standards!
omgcats: jk u know i luv u
BEST♡FRIEND
MadVOTH: i think my dad had an affair
omgcats: gtfo! no way
MadVOTH: i heard him with some woman on the phone.
omgcats: that's crzy
your mom may be a bitch
but she's hot & he knows it
no way he's sleeping around
he's like a priest minus the tendency to touch lil boys
speaking of which srsly
Adam has a total hrd-on for u
swear i could see it through his robe
puberty is being nice 2 that boy
MadVOTH: maybe you're right, but it really sounded…
omgcats: shit mom's drunk ranting again brb
omgcats: [idle]
sigh
BING!
laurapage3: How was the game?
Ugh. Do you have to message me every time I'm online, Laura?
MadVOTH: game sucked not a fun day for many reasons

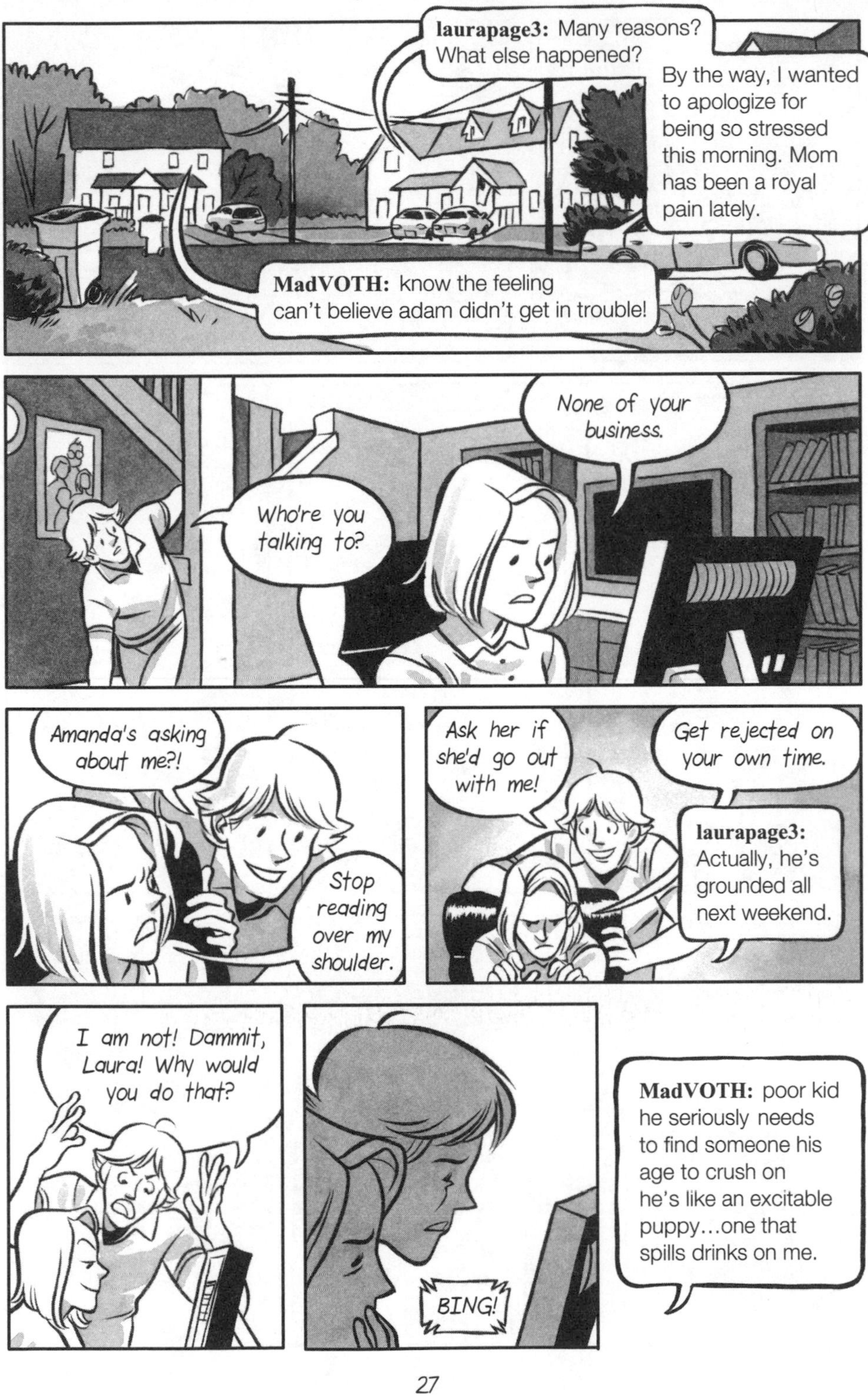
laurapage3: Many reasons? What else happened?
By the way, I wanted to apologize for being so stressed this morning. Mom has been a royal pain lately.
MadVOTH: know the feeling can't believe adam didn't get in trouble!
Who're you talking to?
None of your business.
Amanda's asking about me?!
Stop reading over my shoulder.
Ask her if she'd go out with me!
Get rejected on your own time.
laurapage3: Actually, he's grounded all next weekend.
I am not! Dammit, Laura! Why would you do that?
BING!
MadVOTH: poor kid he seriously needs to find someone his age to crush on he's like an excitable puppy…one that spills drinks on me.

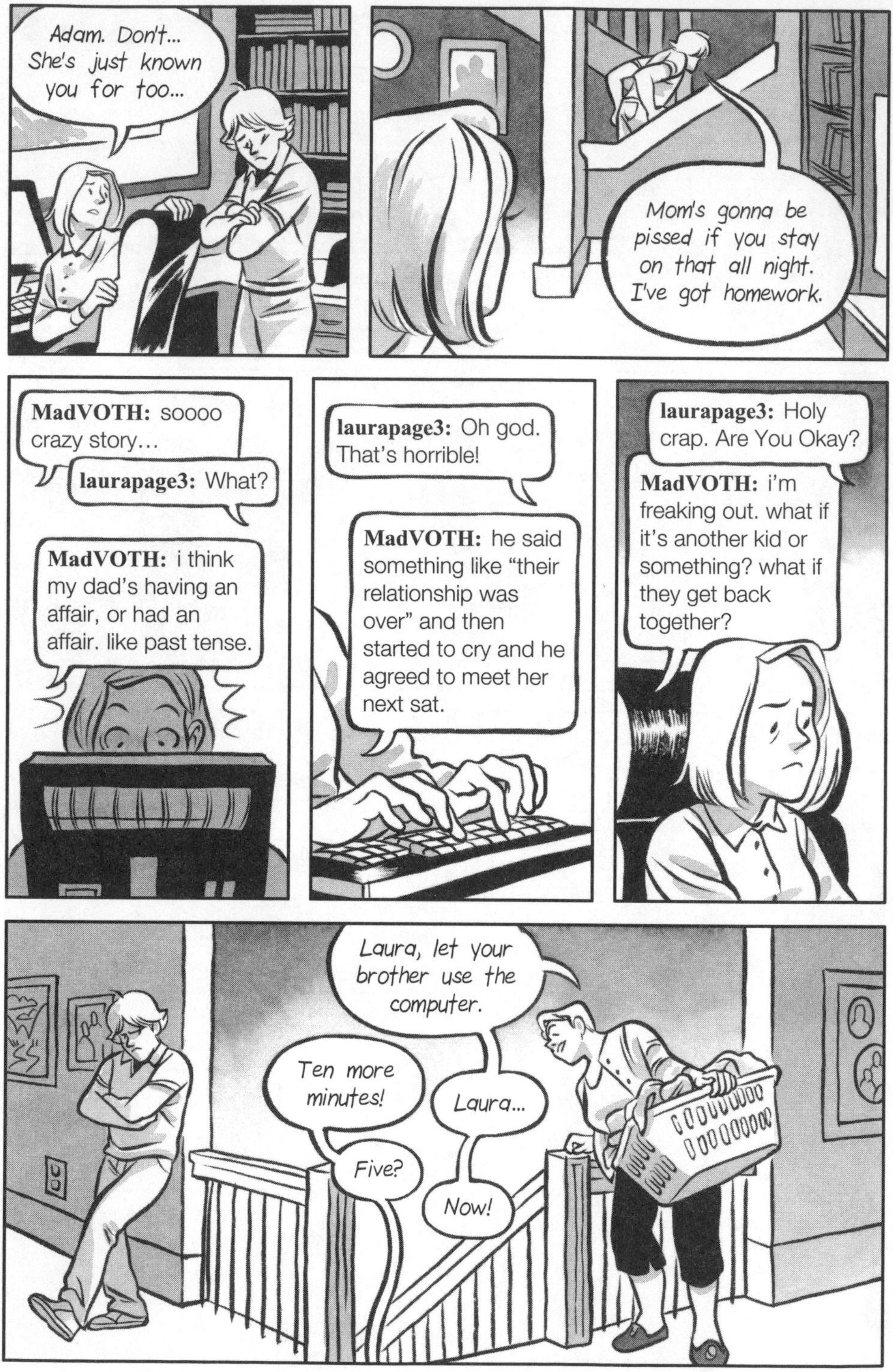
Adam. Don't... She's just known you for too...
Mom's gonna be pissed if you stay on that all night. I've got homework.
MadVOTH: soooo crazy story…
laurapage3: What?
MadVOTH: i think my dad's having an affair, or had an affair. like past tense.
laurapage3: Oh god. That's horrible!
MadVOTH: he said something like "their relationship was over" and then started to cry and he agreed to meet her next sat.
laurapage3: Holy crap. Are You Okay?
MadVOTH: i'm freaking out. what if it's another kid or something? what if they get back together?
Laura, let your brother use the computer.
Ten more minutes!
Laura...
Five?
Now!

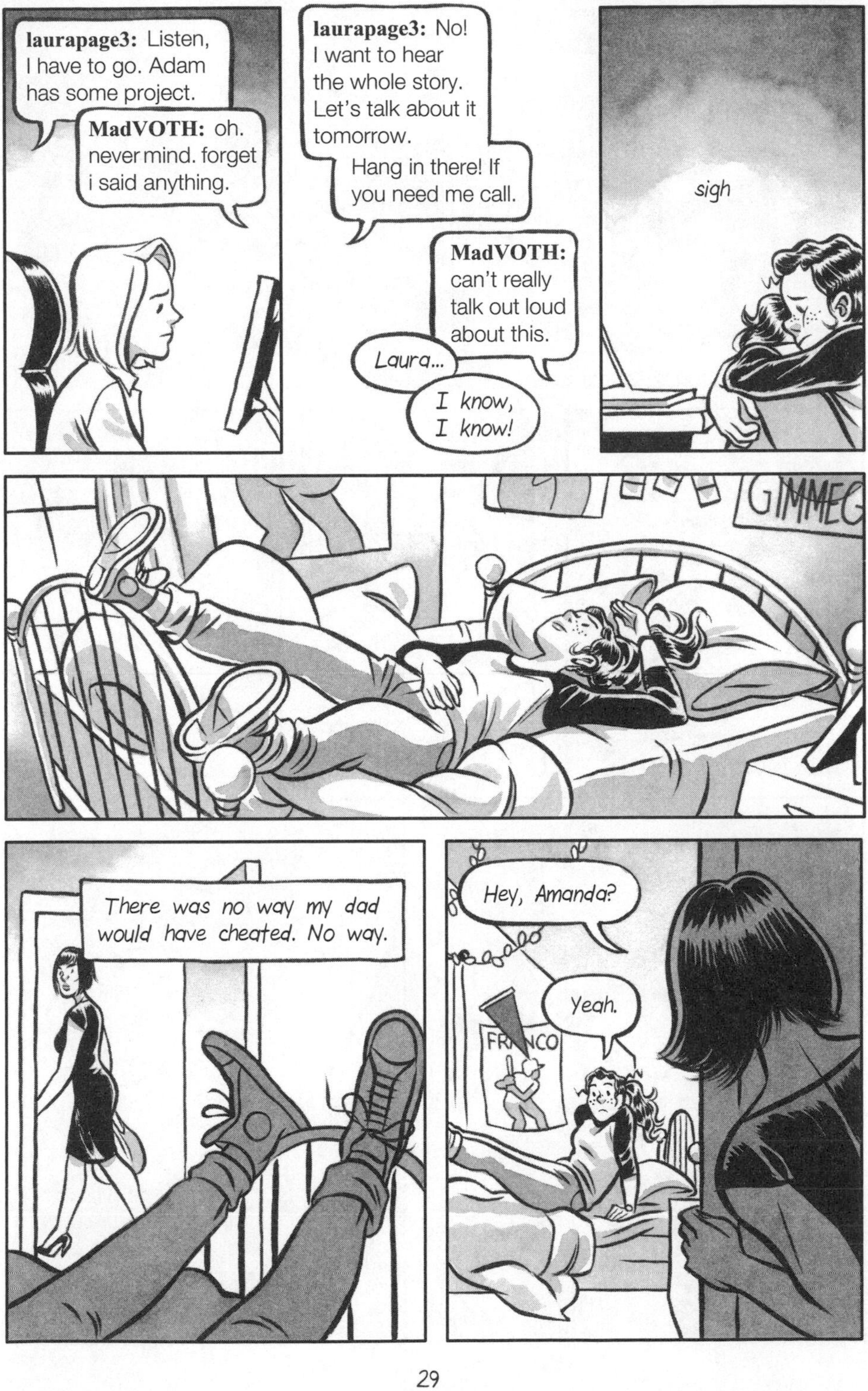
laurapage3: Listen, I have to go. Adam has some project.
MadVOTH: oh. never mind. forget i said anything.
laurapage3: No! I want to hear the whole story. Let's talk about it tomorrow.
Hang in there! If you need me call.
MadVOTH: can't really talk out loud about this.
Laura...
I know, I know!
sigh
GIMMEG
There was no way my dad would have cheated. No way.
Hey, Amanda?
Yeah.
FRANCO

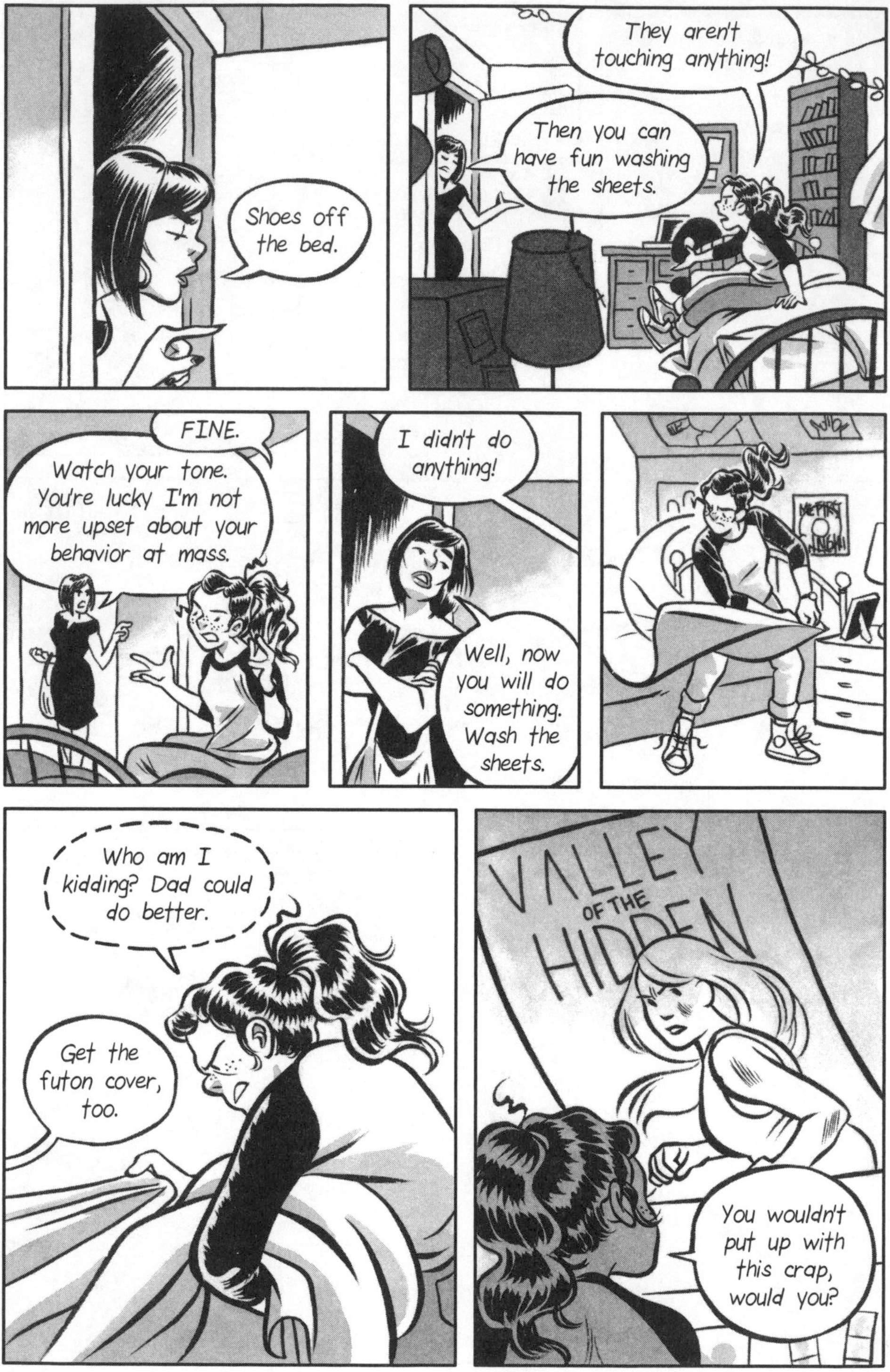
Shoes off the bed.
They aren't touching anything!
Then you can have fun washing the sheets.
FINE.
Watch your tone. You're lucky I'm not more upset about your behavior at mass.
I didn't do anything!
Well, now you will do something. Wash the sheets.
Who am I kidding? Dad could do better.
Get the futon cover, too.
VALLEY OF THE HIDDEN
You wouldn't put up with this crap, would you?

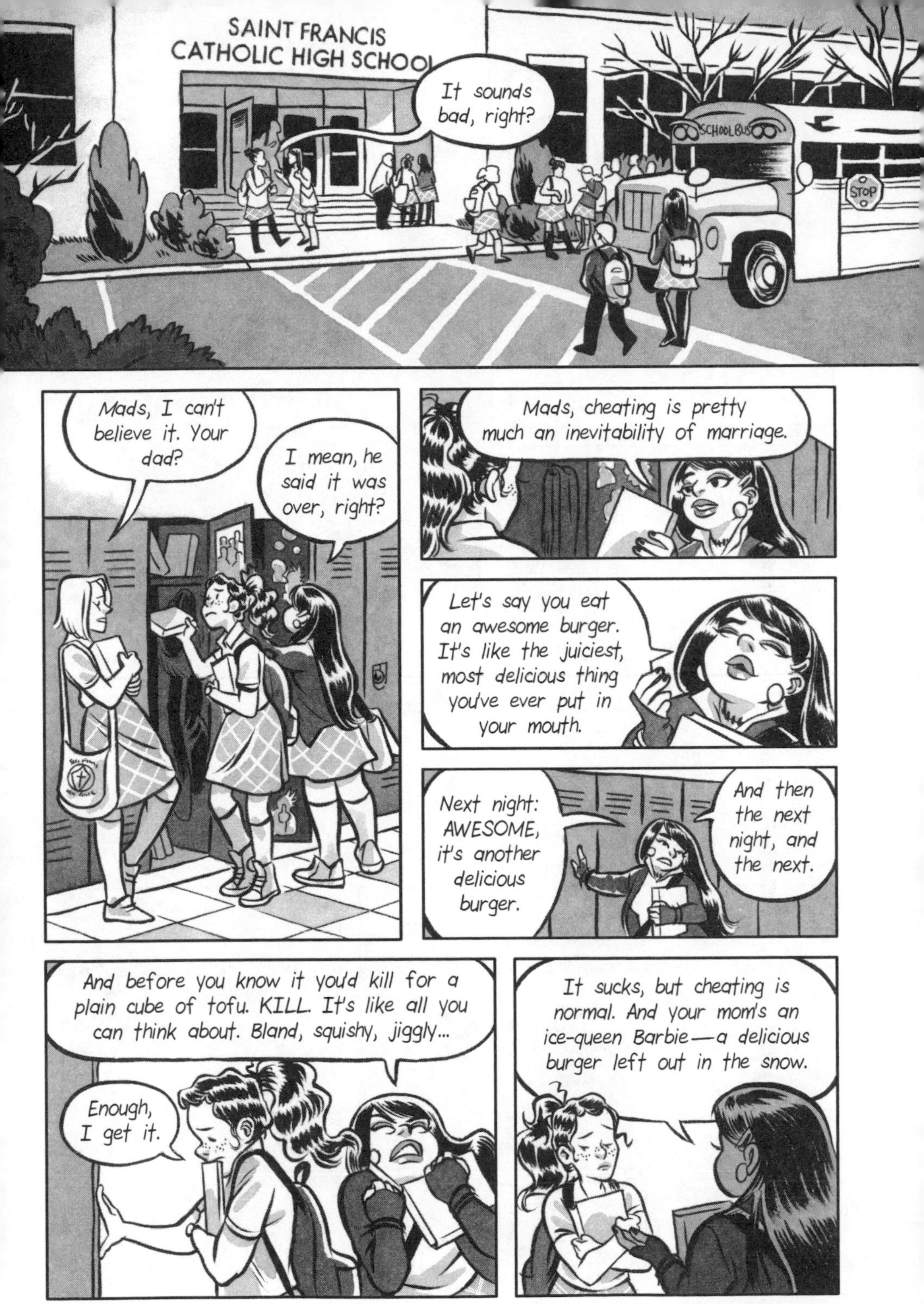
SAINT FRANCIS CATHOLIC HIGH SCHOOL
It sounds bad, right?
SCHOOL BUS
STOP
Mads, I can't believe it. Your dad?
I mean, he said it was over, right?
Mads, cheating is pretty much an inevitability of marriage.
Let's say you eat an awesome burger. It's like the juiciest, most delicious thing you've ever put in your mouth.
Next night: AWESOME, it's another delicious burger.
And then the next night, and the next.
And before you know it you'd kill for a plain cube of tofu. KILL. It's like all you can think about. Bland, squishy, jiggly...
Enough, I get it.
It sucks, but cheating is normal. And your mom's an ice-queen Barbie—a delicious burger left out in the snow.

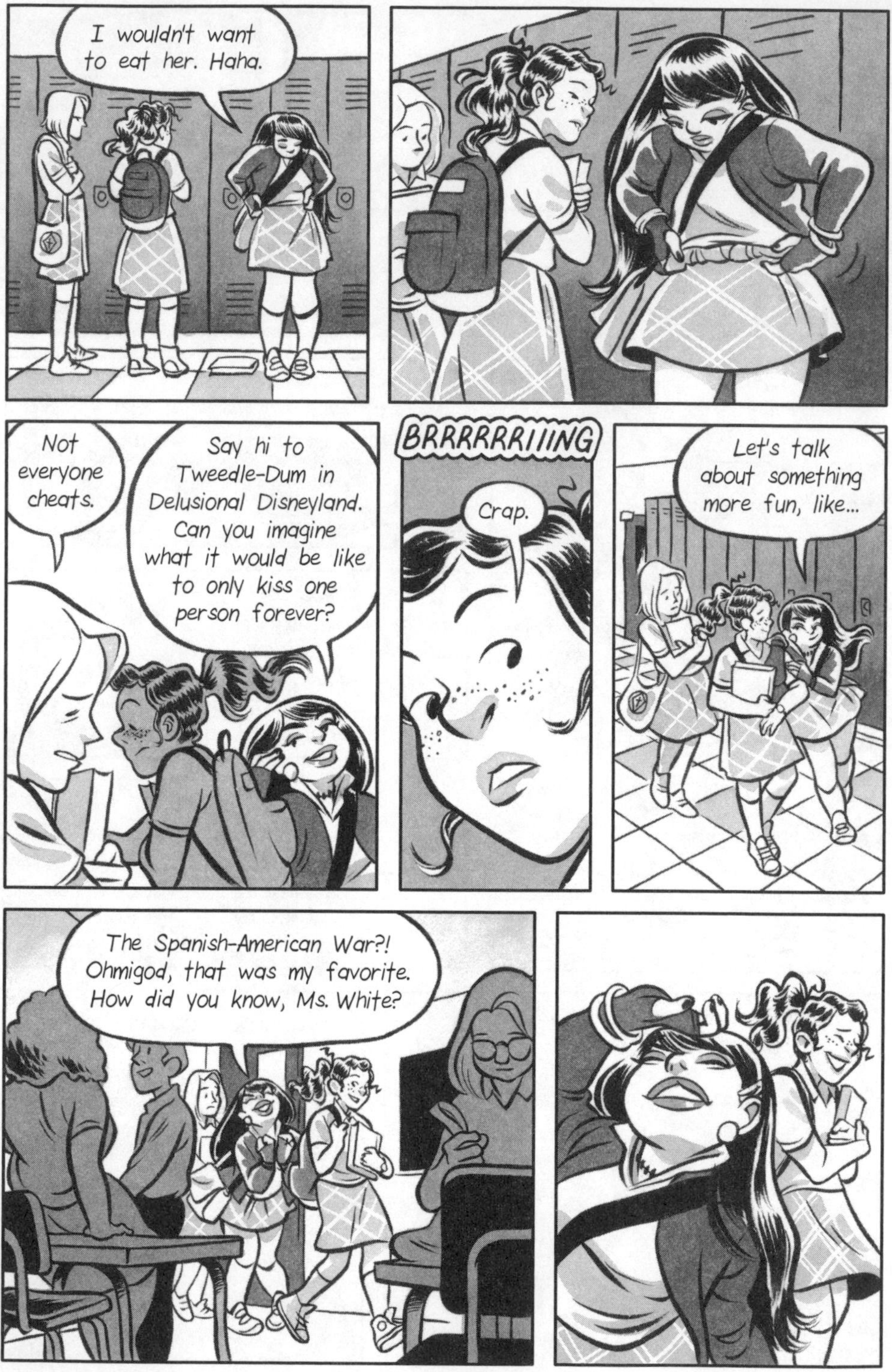
I wouldn't want to eat her. Haha.
Not everyone cheats.
Say hi to Tweedle-Dum in Delusional Disneyland. Can you imagine what it would be like to only kiss one person forever?
BRRRRRRIIING
Crap.
Let's talk about something more fun, like...
The Spanish-American War?! Ohmigod, that was my favorite. How did you know, Ms. White?

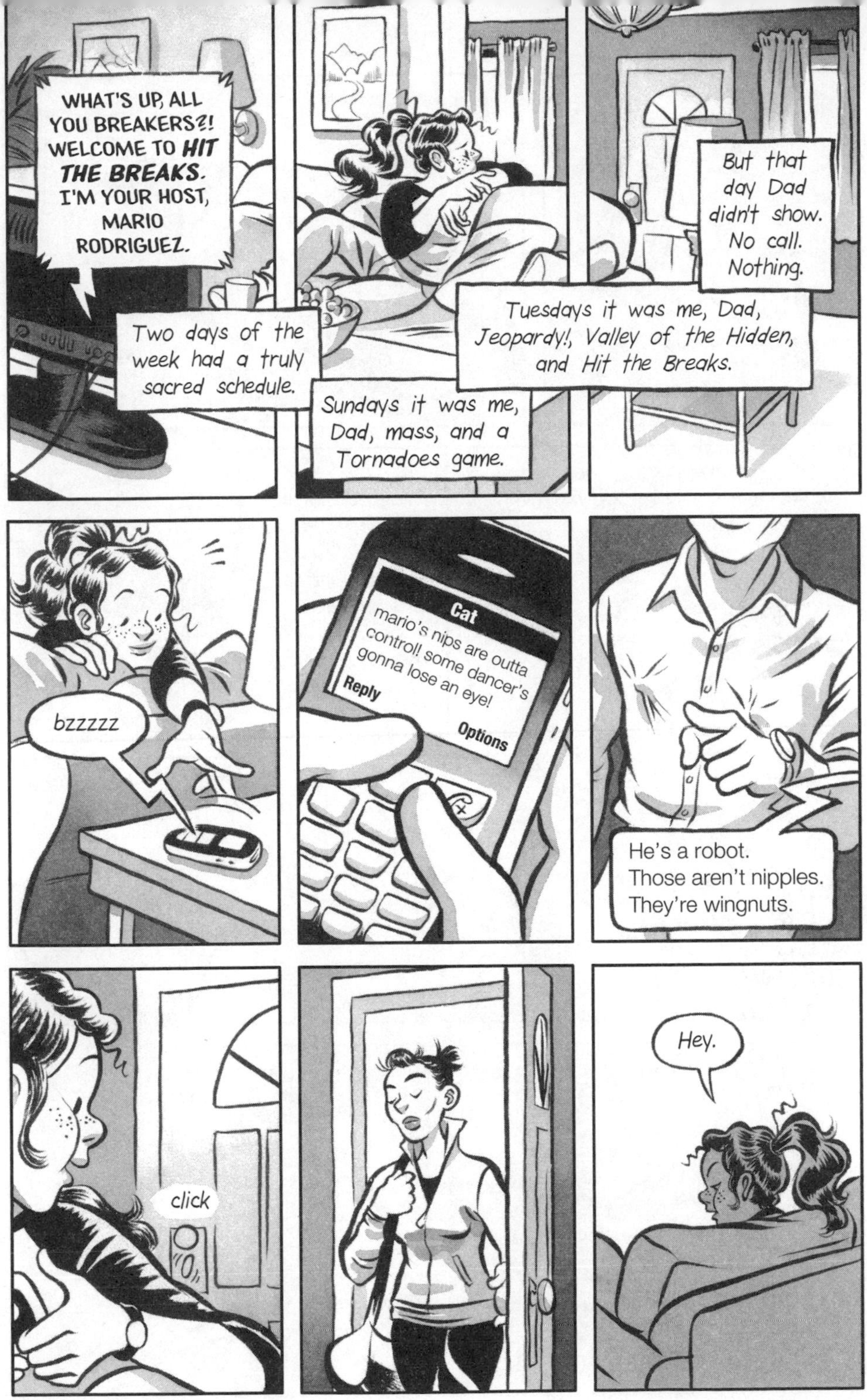
WHAT'S UP, ALL YOU BREAKERS?! WELCOME TO HIT THE BREAKS. I'M YOUR HOST, MARIO RODRIGUEZ.
Two days of the week had a truly sacred schedule.
Sundays it was me, Dad, mass, and a Tornadoes game.
Tuesdays it was me, Dad, Jeopardy!, Valley of the Hidden, and Hit the Breaks.
But that day Dad didn't show. No call. Nothing.
bzzzzz
Cat
mario's nips are outta control! some dancer's gonna lose an eye!
Reply
Options
He's a robot. Those aren't nipples. They're wingnuts.
click
Hey.

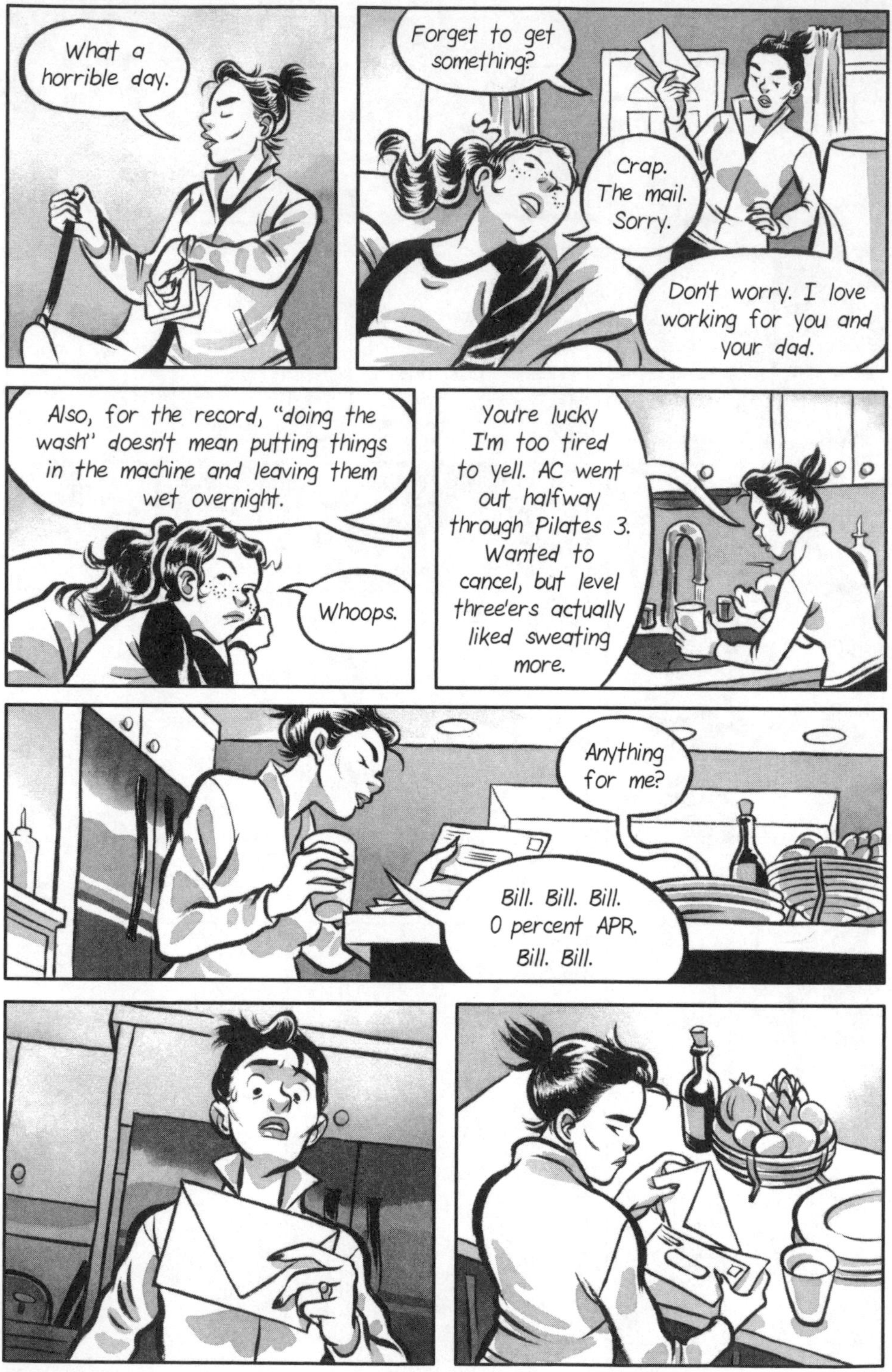
What a horrible day.
Forget to get something?
Crap. The mail. Sorry.
Don't worry. I love working for you and your dad.
Also, for the record, "doing the wash" doesn't mean putting things in the machine and leaving them wet overnight.
Whoops.
You're lucky I'm too tired to yell. AC went out halfway through Pilates 3. Wanted to cancel, but level three'ers actually liked sweating more.
Anything for me?
Bill. Bill. Bill. 0 percent APR. Bill. Bill.

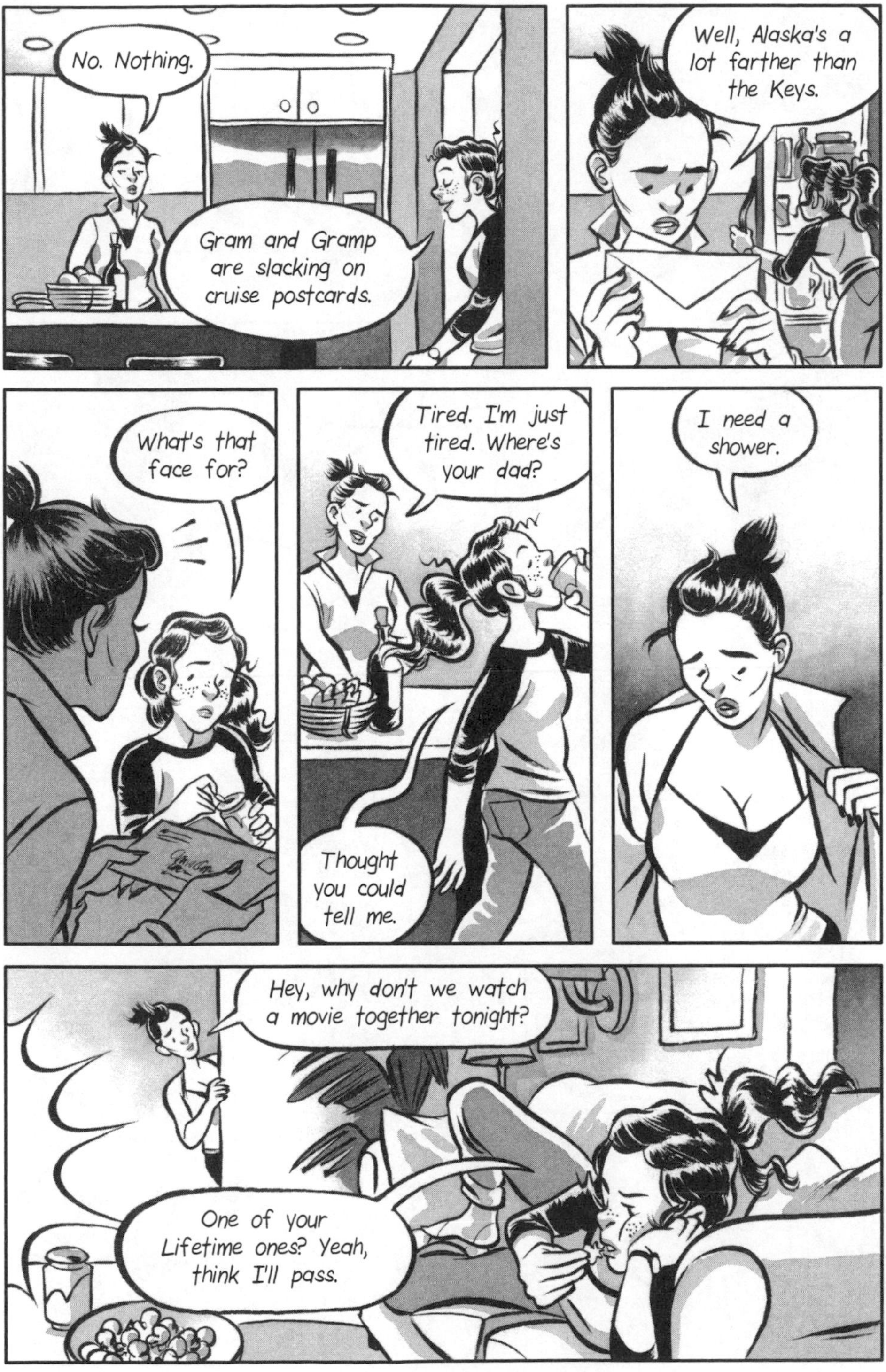
No. Nothing.
Gram and Gramp are slacking on cruise postcards.
Well, Alaska's a lot farther than the Keys.
What's that face for?
Tired. I'm just tired. Where's your dad?
Thought you could tell me.
I need a shower.
Hey, why don't we watch a movie together tonight?
One of your Lifetime ones? Yeah, think I'll pass.

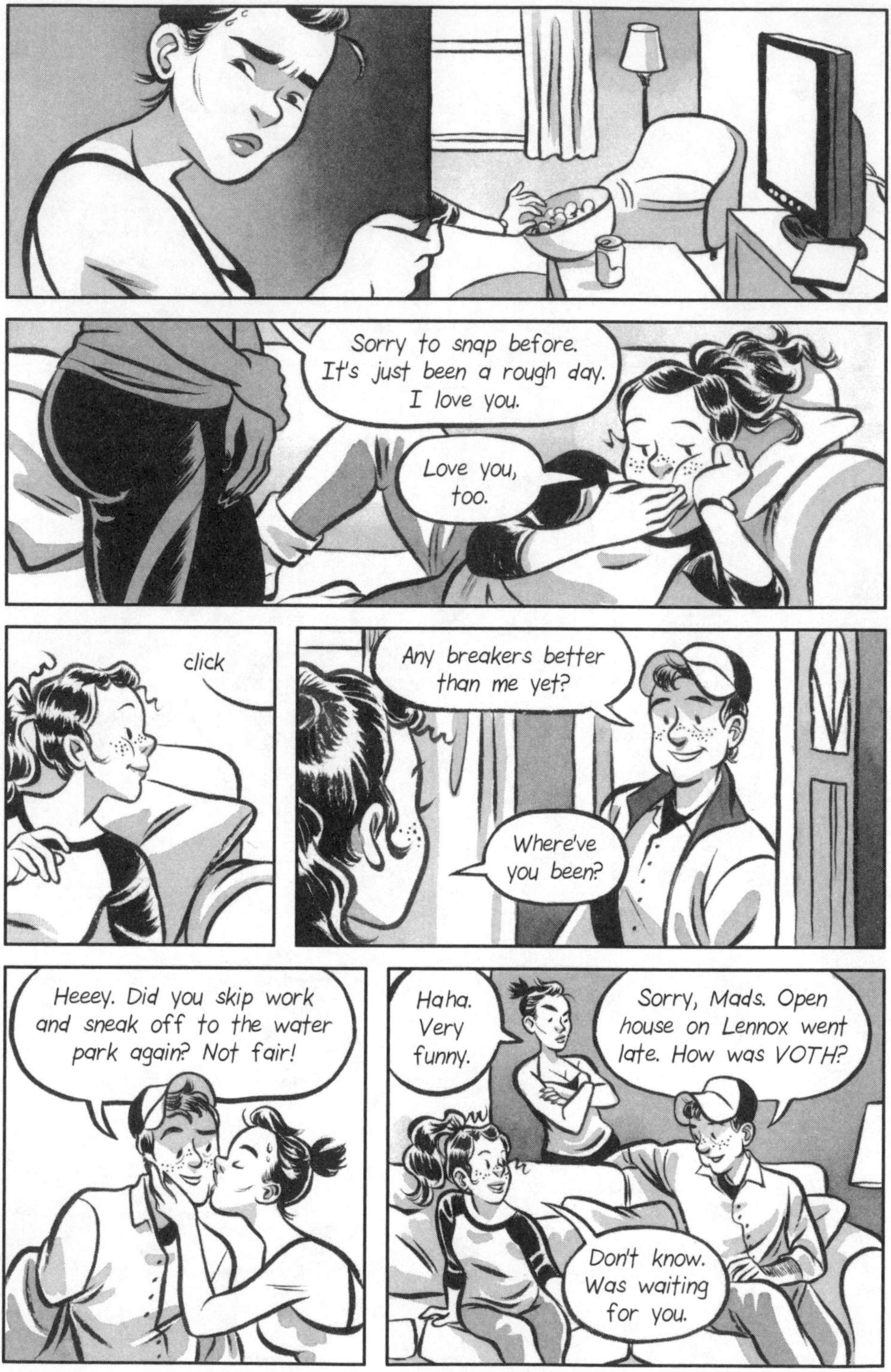
Sorry to snap before. It's just been a rough day. I love you.
Love you, too.
click
Any breakers better than me yet?
Where've you been?
Heeey. Did you skip work and sneak off to the water park again? Not fair!
Haha. Very funny.
Sorry, Mads. Open house on Lennox went late. How was VOTH?
Don't know. Was waiting for you.

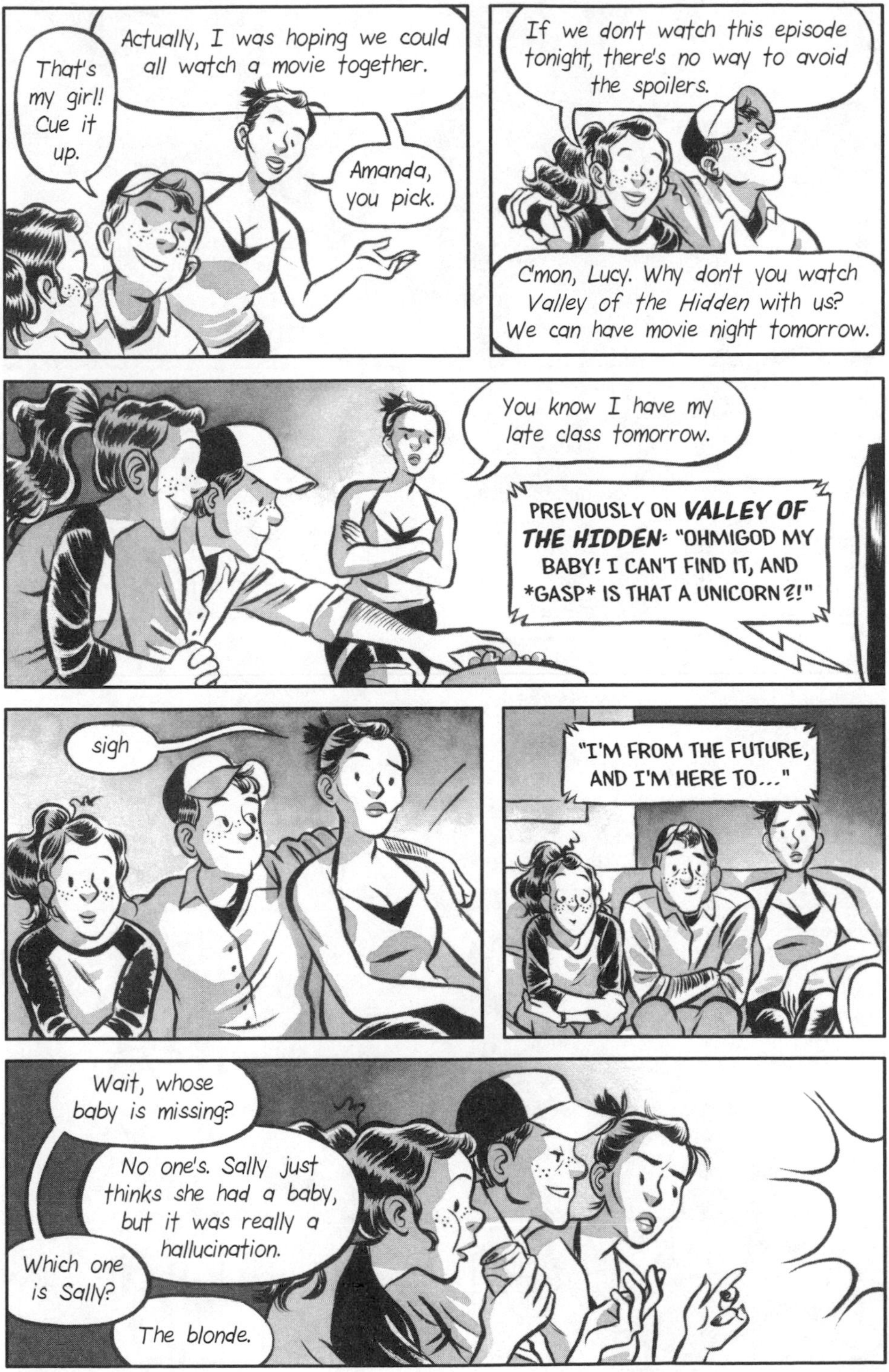
Actually, I was hoping we could all watch a movie together.
That's my girl! Cue it up.
Amanda, you pick.
If we don't watch this episode tonight, there's no way to avoid the spoilers.
C'mon, Lucy. Why don't you watch Valley of the Hidden with us? We can have movie night tomorrow.
You know I have my late class tomorrow.
PREVIOUSLY ON VALLEY OF THE HIDDEN: "OHMIGOD MY BABY! I CAN'T FIND IT, AND *GASP* IS THAT A UNICORN?!"
sigh
"I'M FROM THE FUTURE, AND I'M HERE TO..."
Wait, whose baby is missing?
No one's. Sally just thinks she had a baby, but it was really a hallucination.
Which one is Sally?
The blonde.

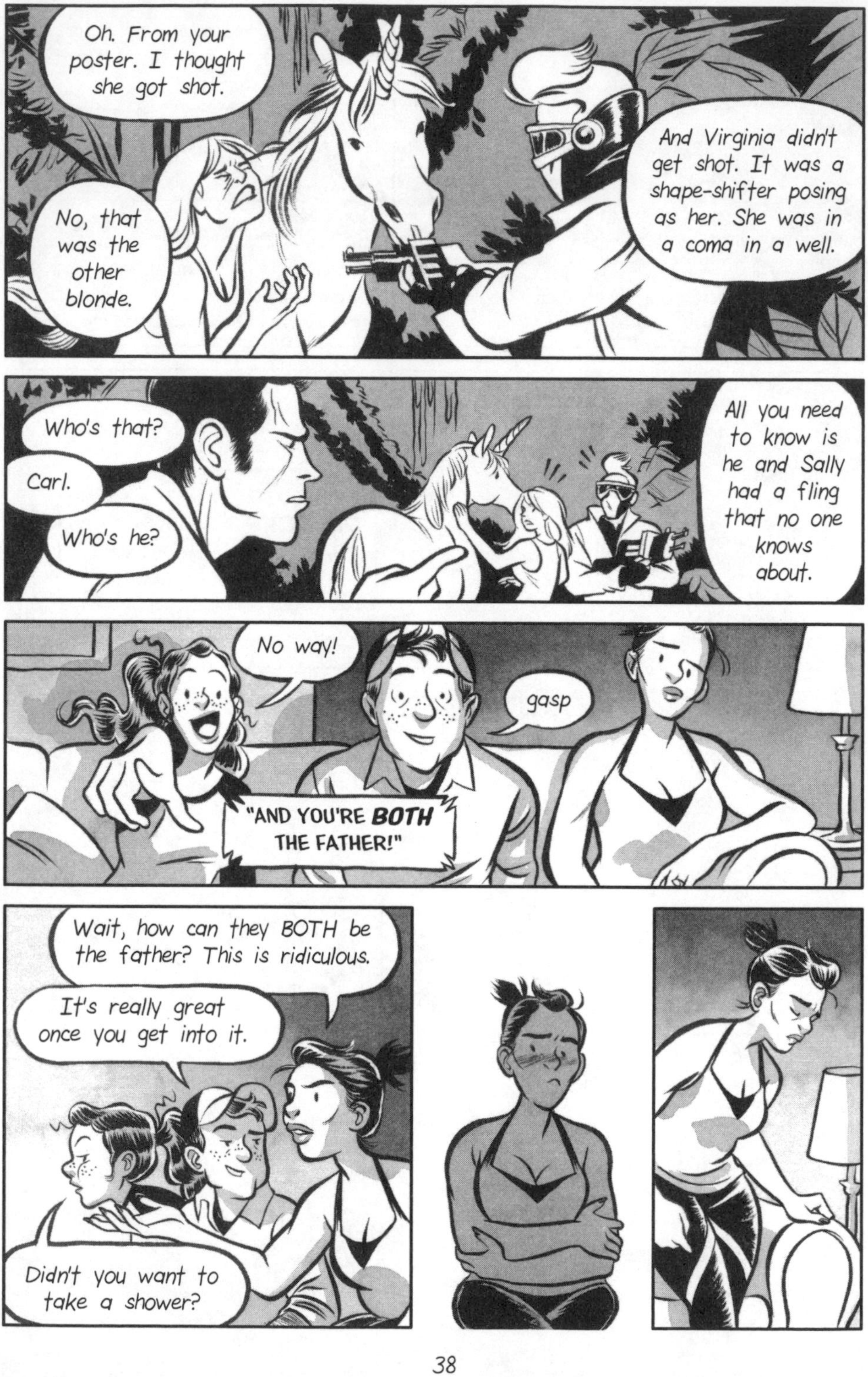

Oh. From your poster. I thought she got shot.
No, that was the other blonde.
And Virginia didn't get shot. It was a shape-shifter posing as her. She was in a coma in a well.
Who's that?
Carl.
Who's he?
All you need to know is he and Sally had a fling that no one knows about.
No way!
gasp
"AND YOU'RE **BOTH** THE FATHER!"
Wait, how can they BOTH be the father? This is ridiculous.
It's really great once you get into it.
Didn't you want to take a shower?

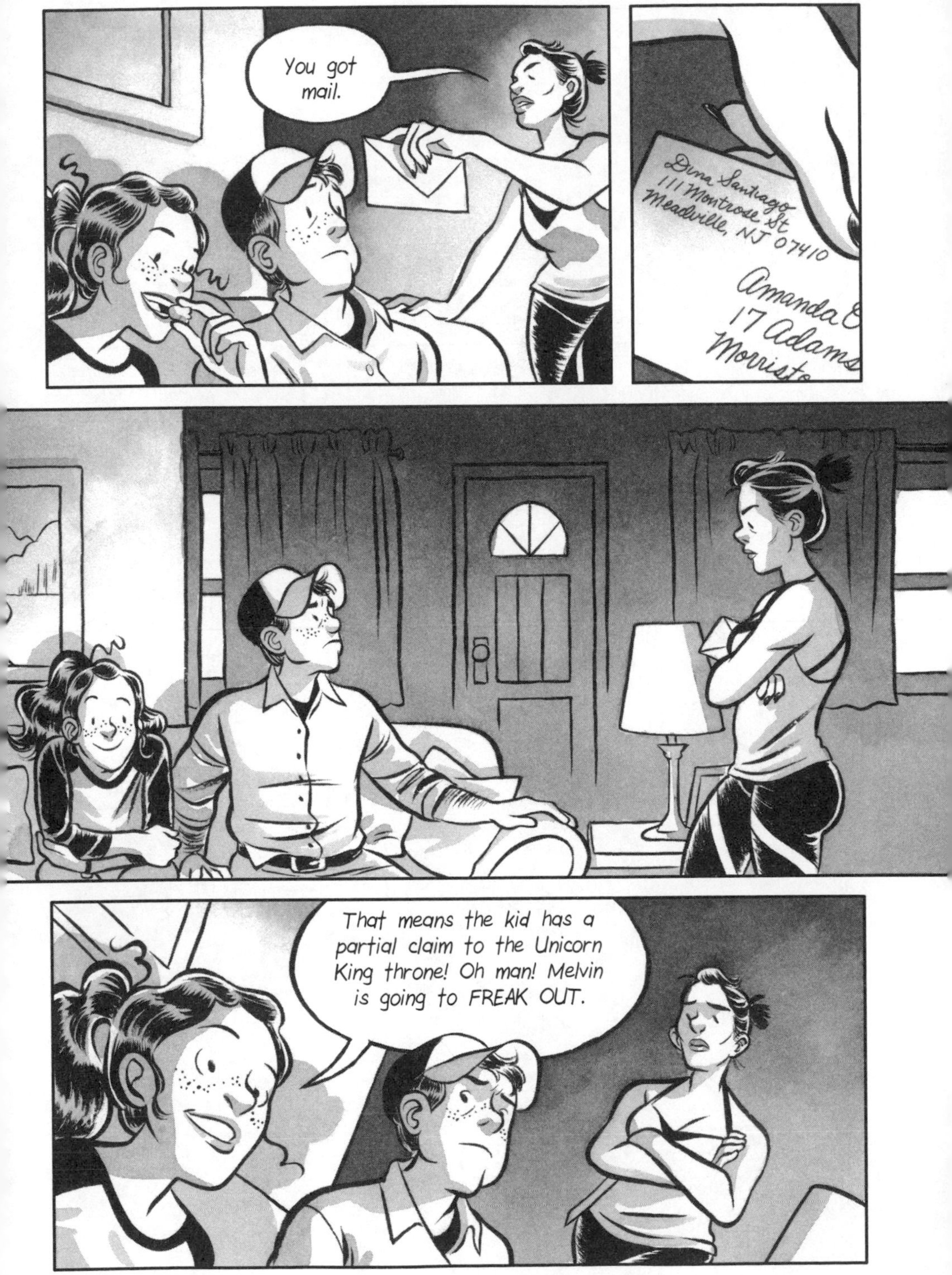
You got mail.
Dina Santiago
111 Montrose St
Meadville, NJ 07410
Amanda
17 Adams
That means the kid has a partial claim to the Unicorn King throne! Oh man! Melvin is going to FREAK OUT.

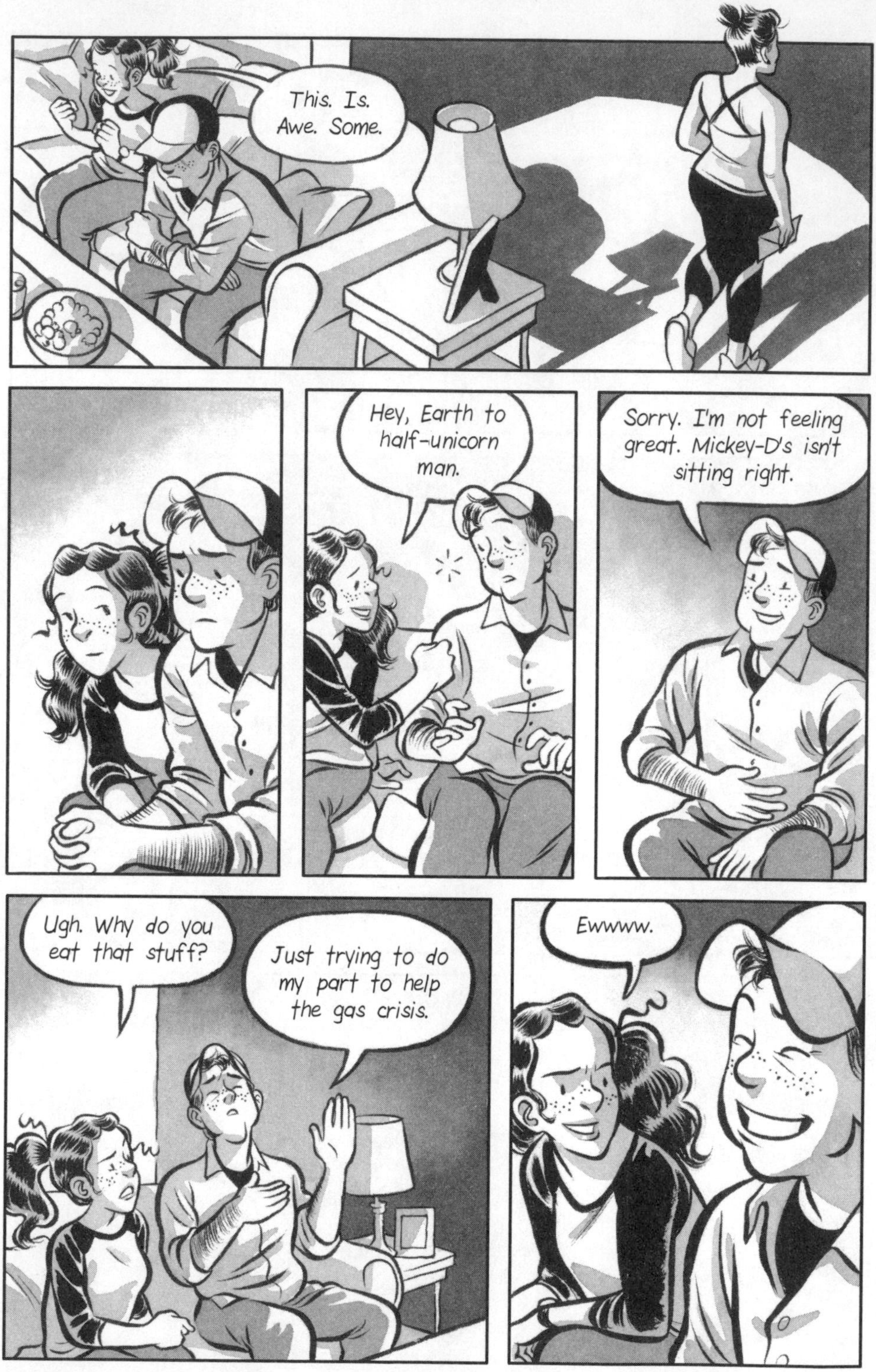
This. Is. Awe. Some.
Hey, Earth to half-unicorn man.
Sorry. I'm not feeling great. Mickey-D's isn't sitting right.
Ugh. Why do you eat that stuff?
Just trying to do my part to help the gas crisis.
Ewwww.

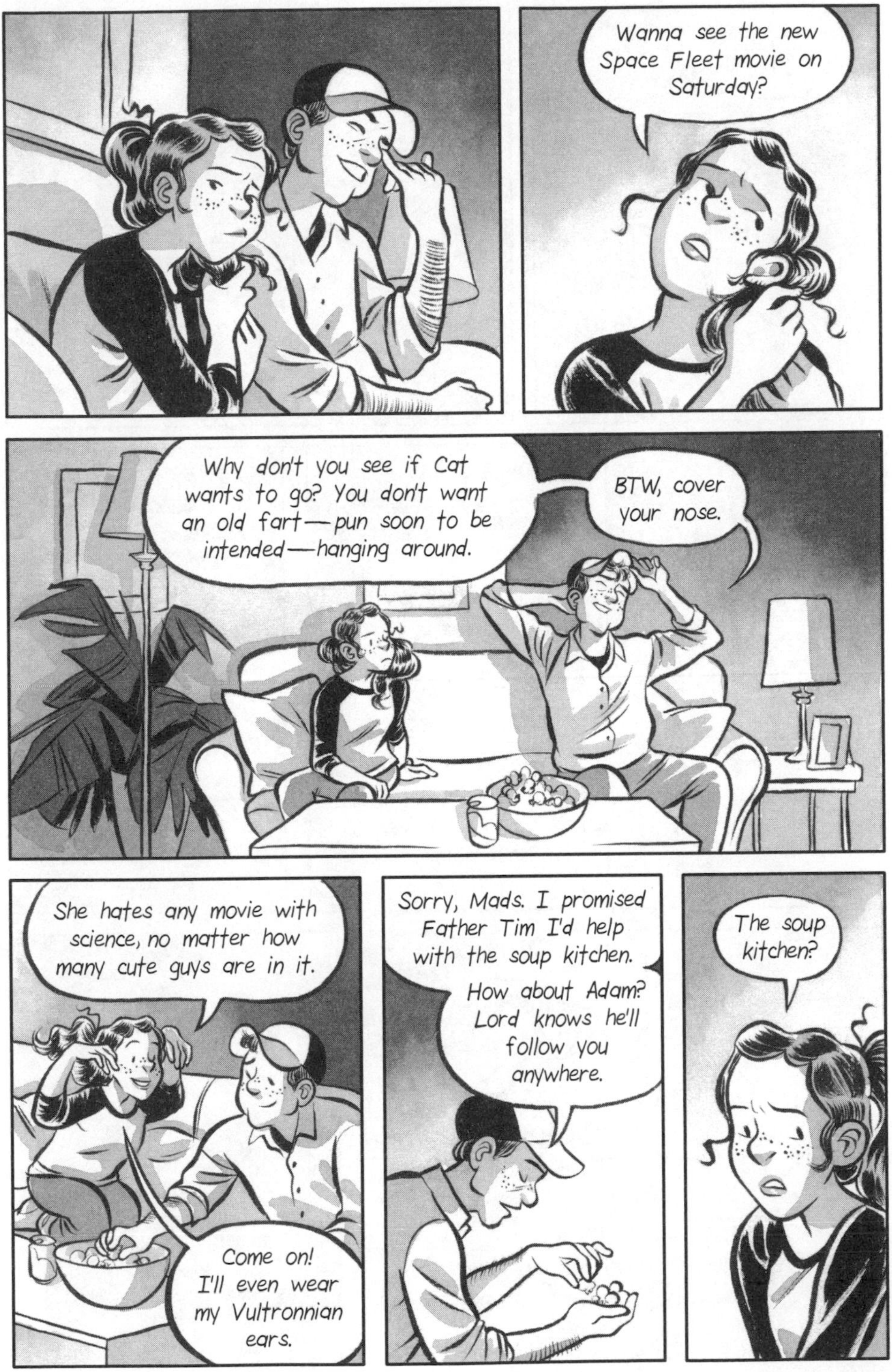
Wanna see the new Space Fleet movie on Saturday?
Why don't you see if Cat wants to go? You don't want an old fart—pun soon to be intended—hanging around.
BTW, cover your nose.
She hates any movie with science, no matter how many cute guys are in it.
Come on! I'll even wear my Vultronnian ears.
Sorry, Mads. I promised Father Tim I'd help with the soup kitchen.
How about Adam? Lord knows he'll follow you anywhere.
The soup kitchen?

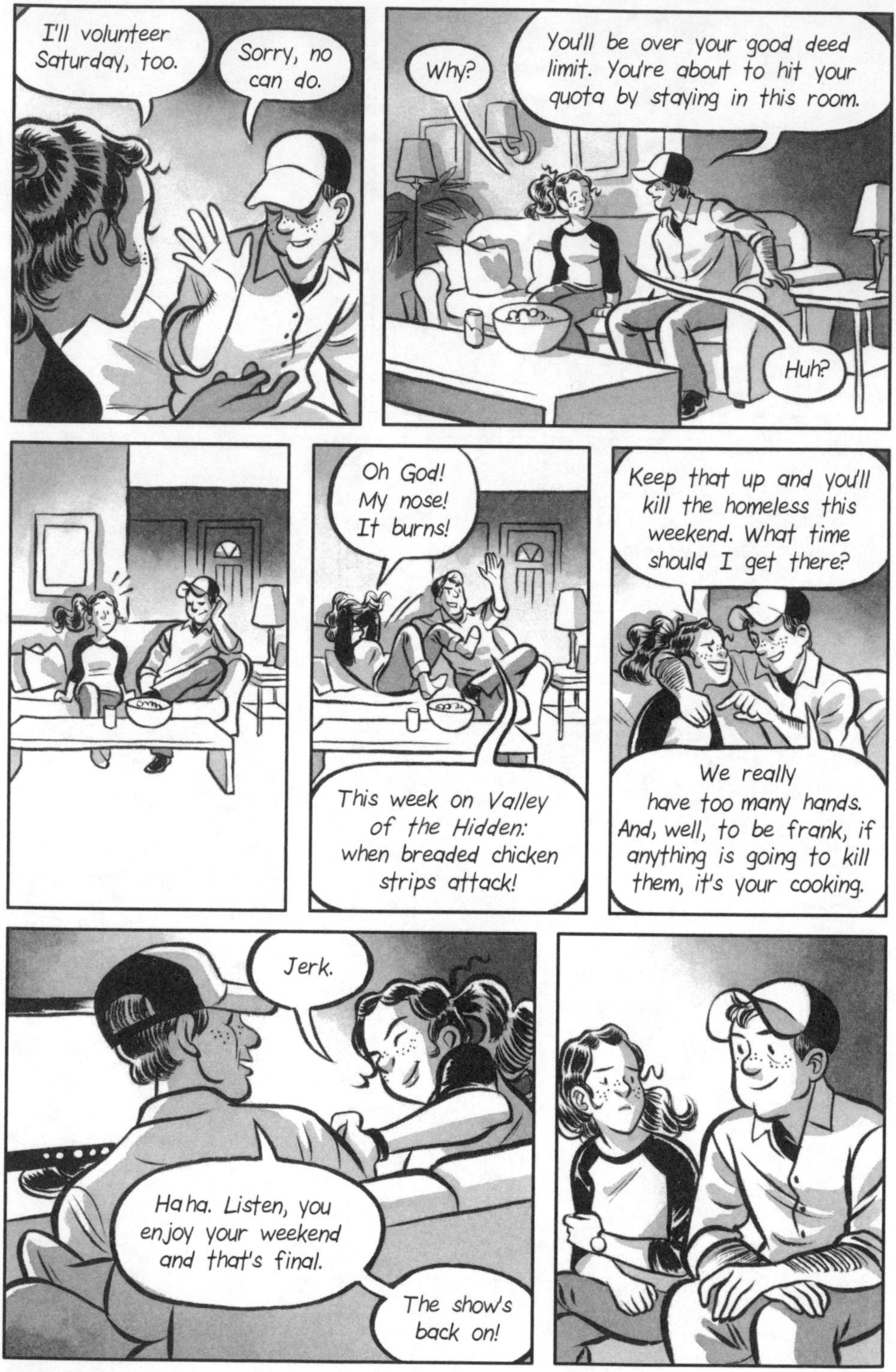
I'll volunteer Saturday, too.
Sorry, no can do.
Why?
You'll be over your good deed limit. You're about to hit your quota by staying in this room.
Huh?
Oh God! My nose! It burns!
This week on Valley of the Hidden: when breaded chicken strips attack!
Keep that up and you'll kill the homeless this weekend. What time should I get there?
We really have too many hands. And, well, to be frank, if anything is going to kill them, it's your cooking.
Jerk.
Ha ha. Listen, you enjoy your weekend and that's final.
The show's back on!

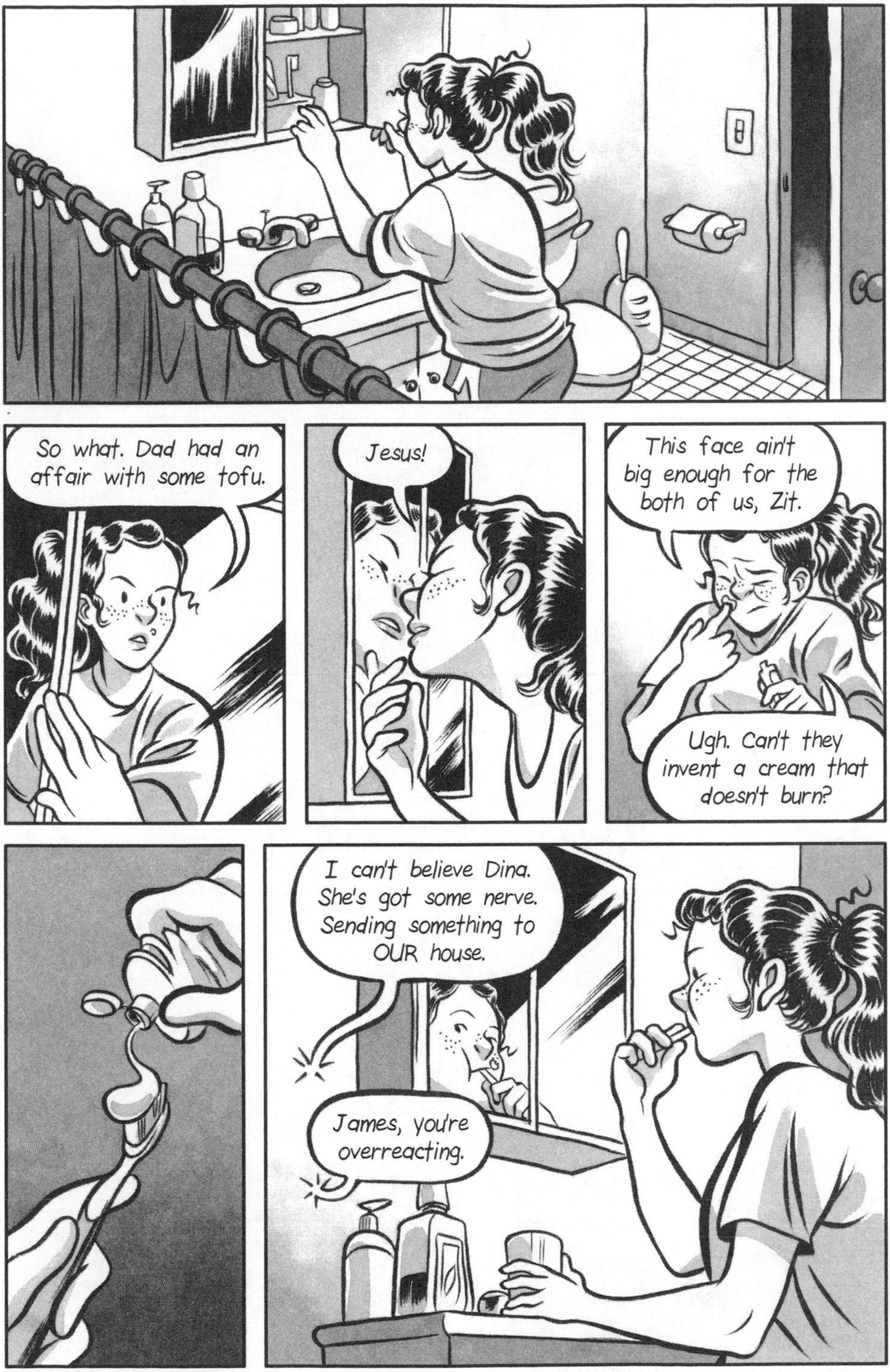
So what. Dad had an affair with some tofu.
Jesus!
This face ain't big enough for the both of us, Zit.
Ugh. Can't they invent a cream that doesn't burn?
I can't believe Dina. She's got some nerve. Sending something to OUR house.
James, you're overreacting.

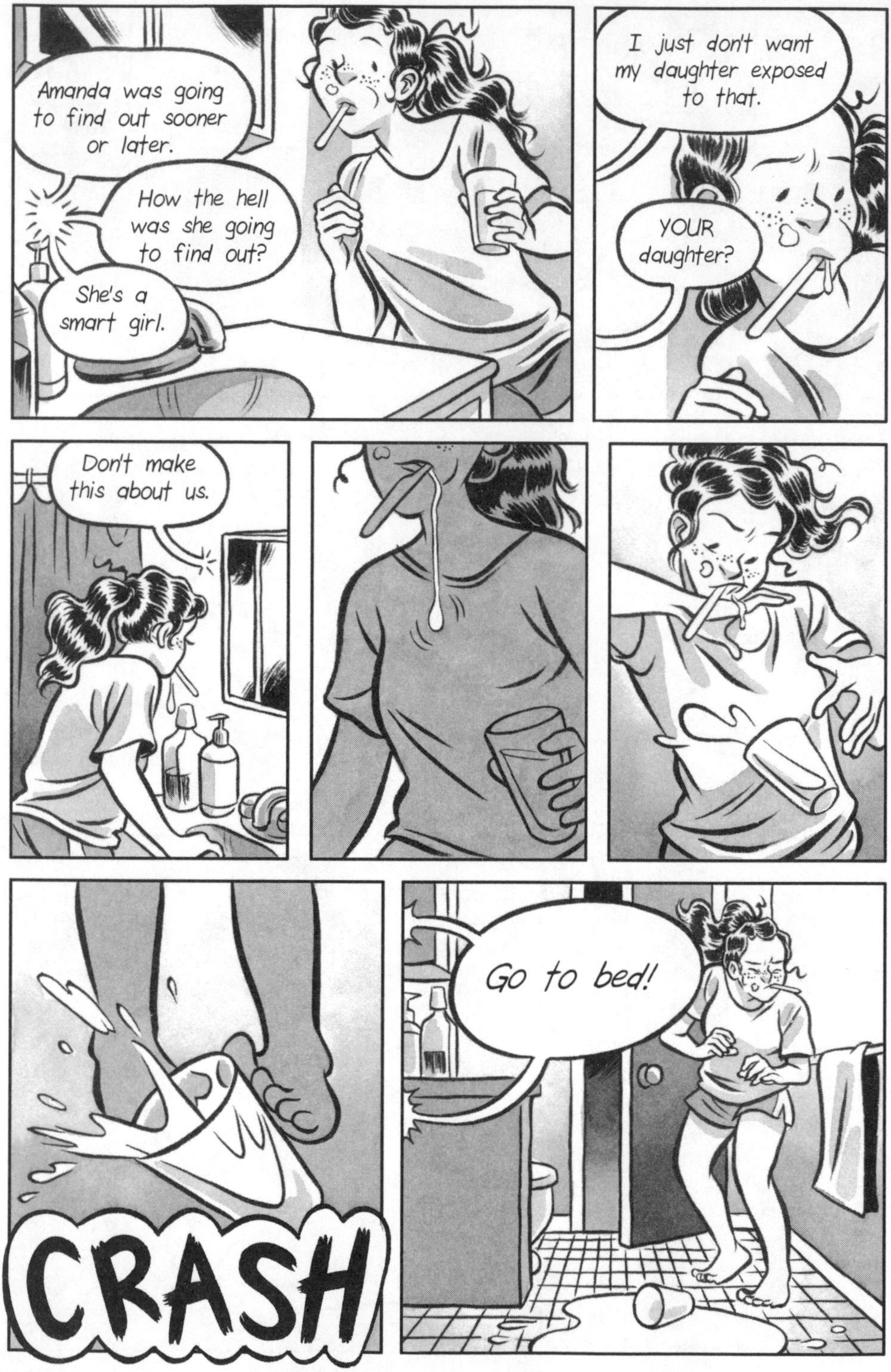
Amanda was going to find out sooner or later.
How the hell was she going to find out?
She's a smart girl.
I just don't want my daughter exposed to that.
YOUR daughter?
Don't make this about us.
CRASH
Go to bed!

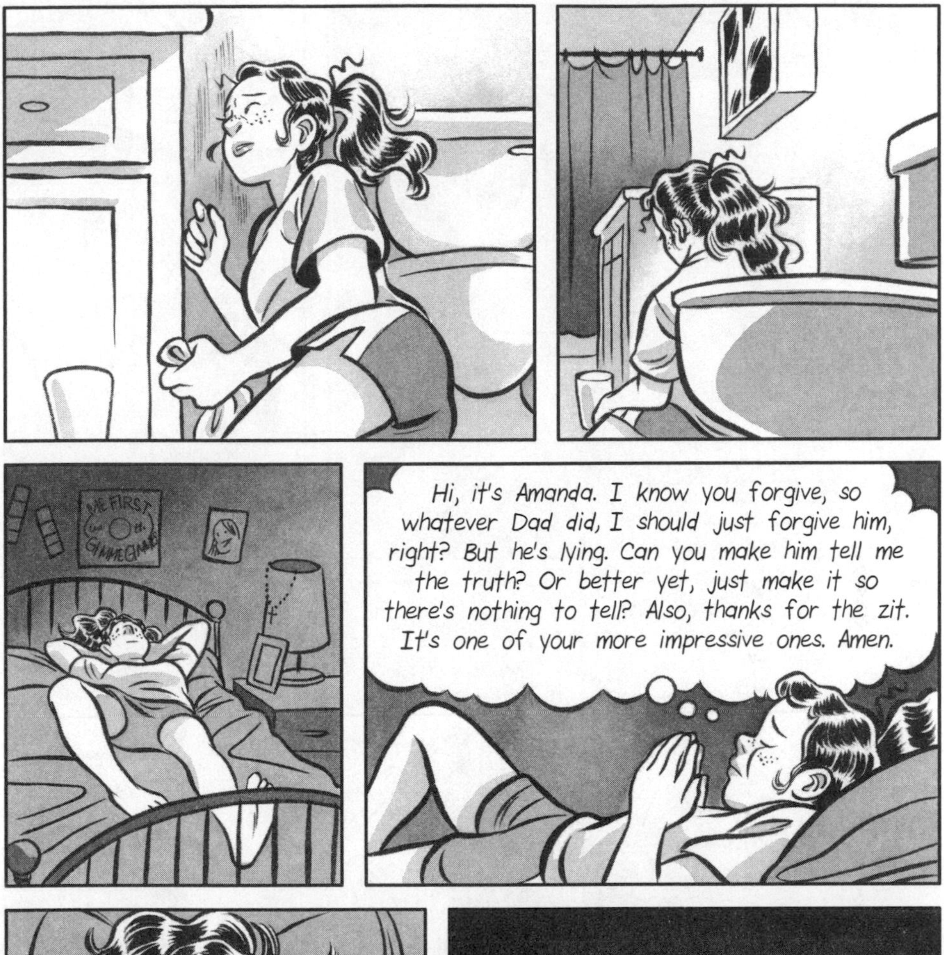
ME FIRST GIMME GIMMES
Hi, it's Amanda. I know you forgive, so whatever Dad did, I should just forgive him, right? But he's lying. Can you make him tell me the truth? Or better yet, just make it so there's nothing to tell? Also, thanks for the zit. It's one of your more impressive ones. Amen.
THUD

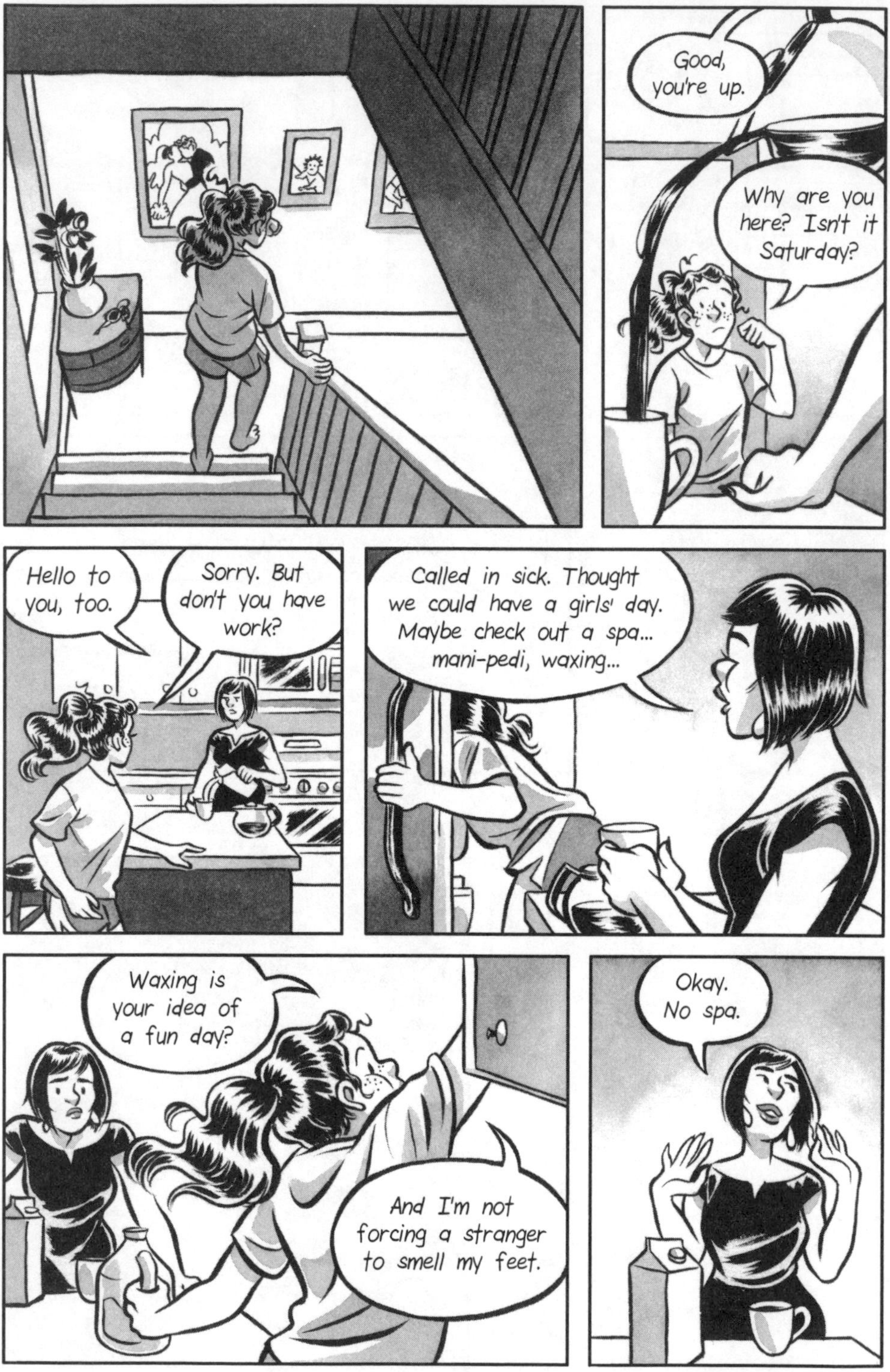
Good, you're up.
Why are you here? Isn't it Saturday?
Hello to you, too.
Sorry. But don't you have work?
Called in sick. Thought we could have a girls' day. Maybe check out a spa... mani-pedi, waxing...
Waxing is your idea of a fun day?
And I'm not forcing a stranger to smell my feet.
Okay. No spa.

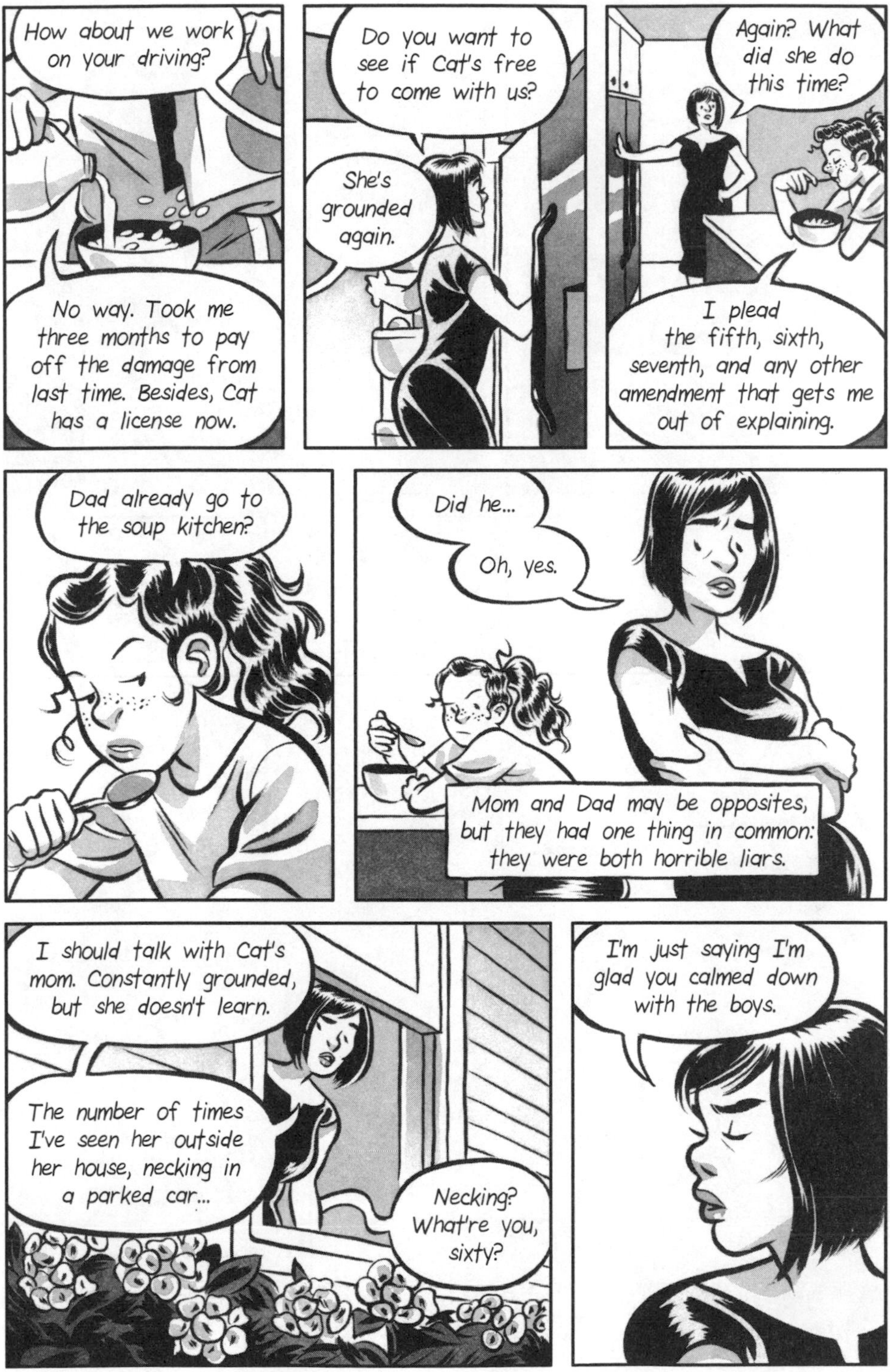
How about we work on your driving?
No way. Took me three months to pay off the damage from last time. Besides, Cat has a license now.
Do you want to see if Cat's free to come with us?
She's grounded again.
Again? What did she do this time?
I plead the fifth, sixth, seventh, and any other amendment that gets me out of explaining.
Dad already go to the soup kitchen?
Did he...
Oh, yes.
Mom and Dad may be opposites, but they had one thing in common: they were both horrible liars.
I should talk with Cat's mom. Constantly grounded, but she doesn't learn.
The number of times I've seen her outside her house, necking in a parked car...
Necking? What're you, sixty?
I'm just saying I'm glad you calmed down with the boys.

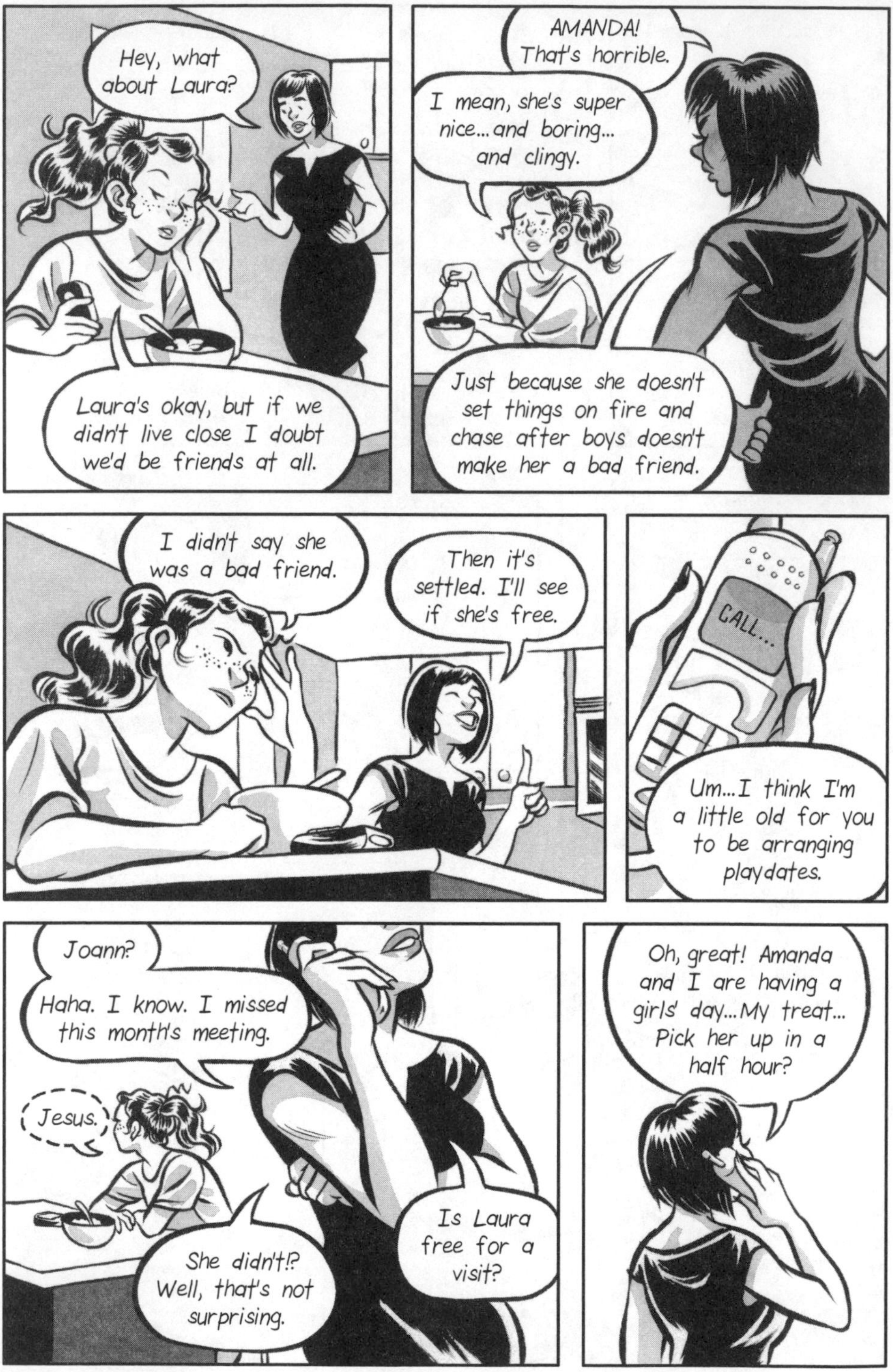
Hey, what about Laura?
Laura's okay, but if we didn't live close I doubt we'd be friends at all.
AMANDA! That's horrible.
I mean, she's super nice... and boring... and clingy.
Just because she doesn't set things on fire and chase after boys doesn't make her a bad friend.
I didn't say she was a bad friend.
Then it's settled. I'll see if she's free.
CALL...
Um...I think I'm a little old for you to be arranging playdates.
Joann?
Haha. I know. I missed this month's meeting.
Jesus.
She didn't!? Well, that's not surprising.
Is Laura free for a visit?
Oh, great! Amanda and I are having a girls' day...My treat... Pick her up in a half hour?

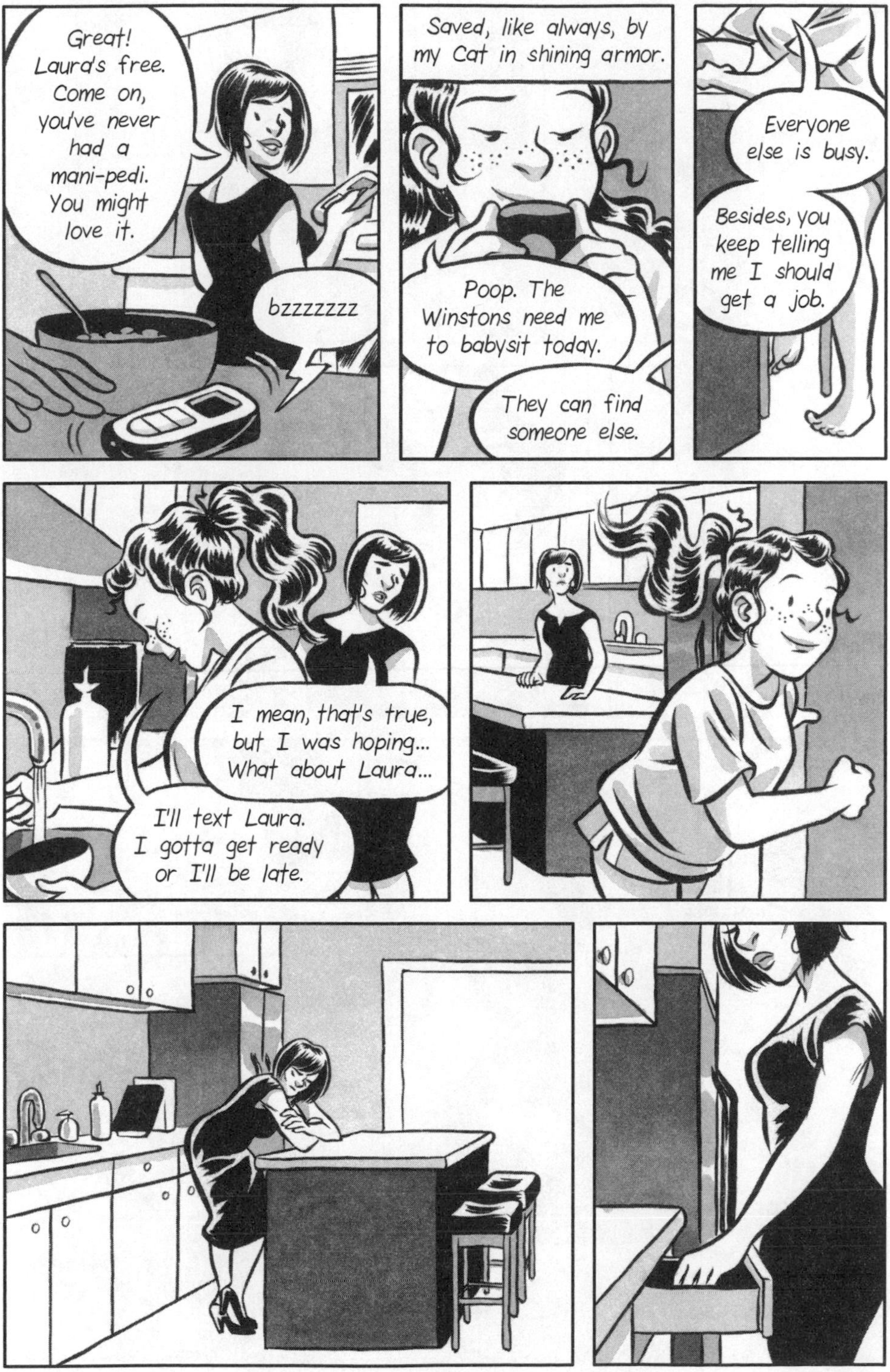

Great! Laura's free. Come on, you've never had a mani-pedi. You might love it.
bzzzzzzz
Saved, like always, by my Cat in shining armor.
Poop. The Winstons need me to babysit today.
They can find someone else.
Everyone else is busy.
Besides, you keep telling me I should get a job.
I mean, that's true, but I was hoping... What about Laura...
I'll text Laura. I gotta get ready or I'll be late.

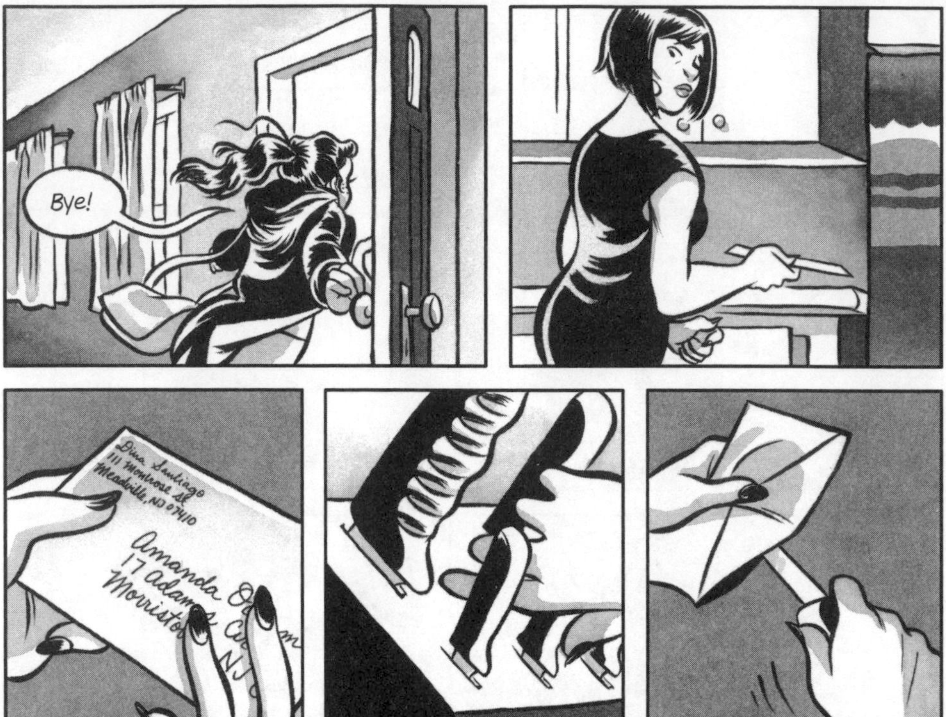

Bye!
Dina Santiago
111 Montrose St
Meadville, NJ 07410
CINEMA
THE APARTMENT
CINEMA
THE APARTMENT

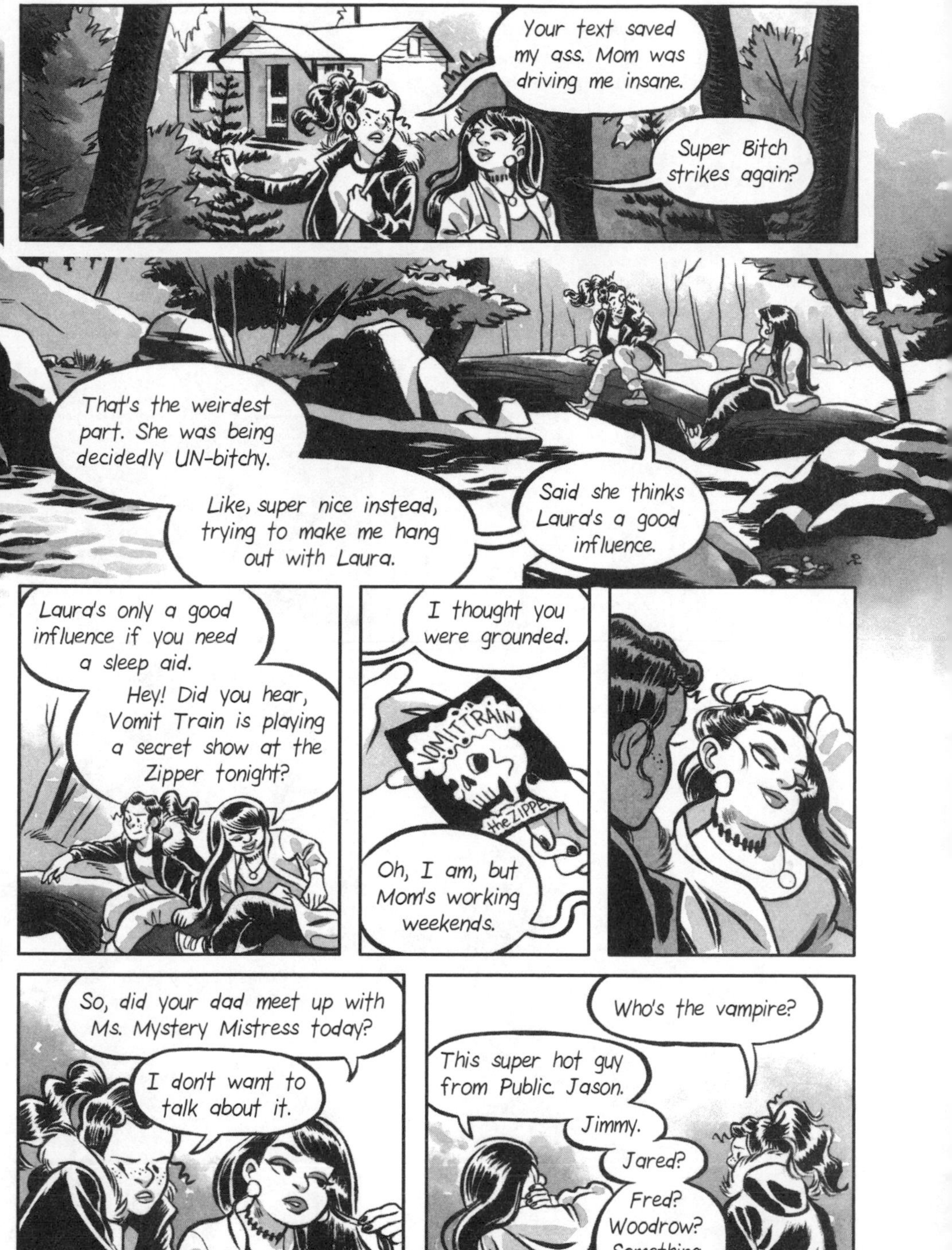
Your text saved my ass. Mom was driving me insane.
Super Bitch strikes again?
That's the weirdest part. She was being decidedly UN-bitchy.
Like, super nice instead, trying to make me hang out with Laura.
Said she thinks Laura's a good influence.
Laura's only a good influence if you need a sleep aid.
Hey! Did you hear, Vomit Train is playing a secret show at the Zipper tonight?
I thought you were grounded.
VOMIT TRAIN
Oh, I am, but Mom's working weekends.
So, did your dad meet up with Ms. Mystery Mistress today?
I don't want to talk about it.
Who's the vampire?
This super hot guy from Public. Jason.
Jimmy.
Jared?
Fred? Woodrow? Something like that.

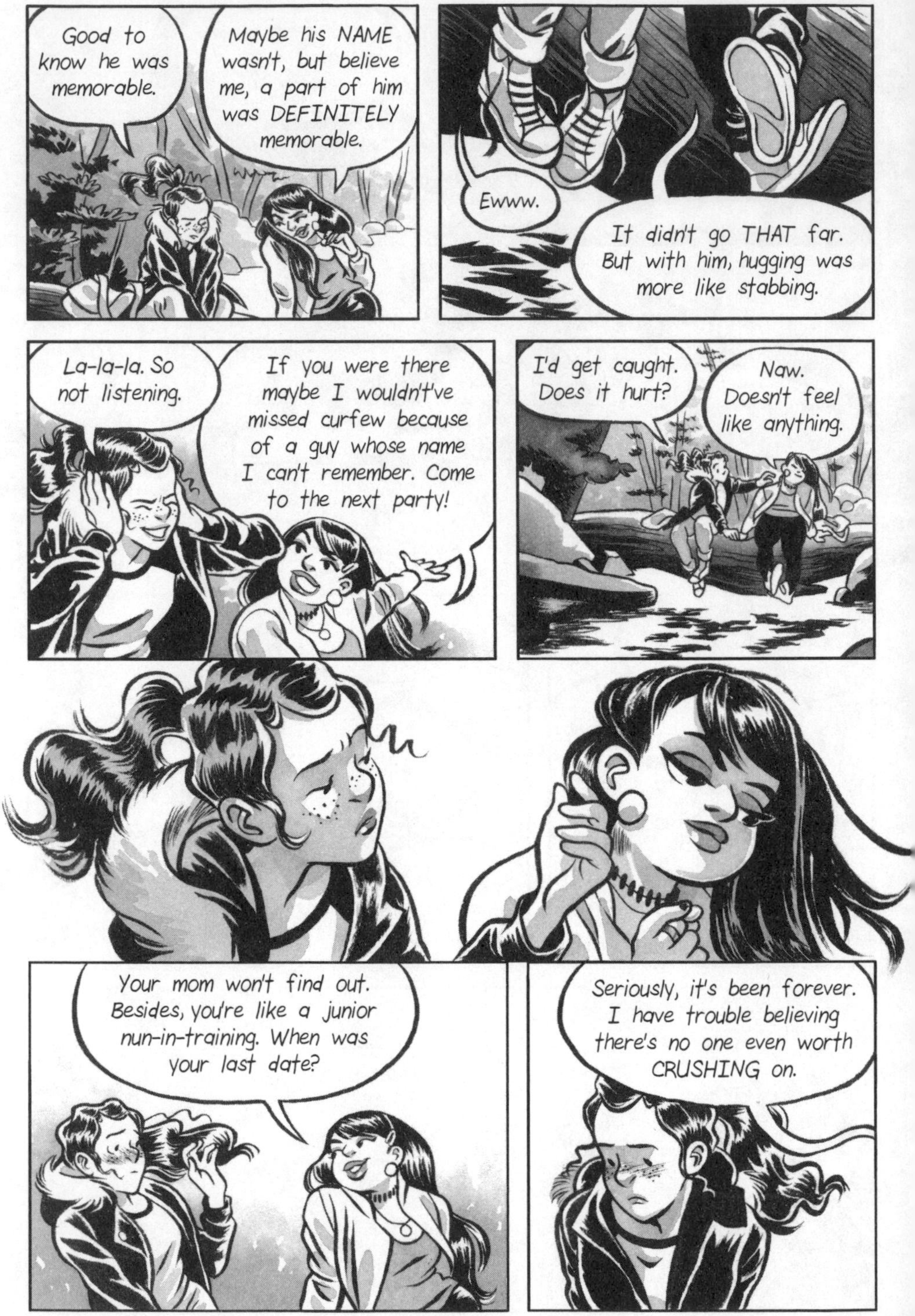
Good to know he was memorable.
Maybe his NAME wasn't, but believe me, a part of him was DEFINITELY memorable.
Ewww.
It didn't go THAT far. But with him, hugging was more like stabbing.
La-la-la. So not listening.
If you were there maybe I wouldn't've missed curfew because of a guy whose name I can't remember. Come to the next party!
I'd get caught. Does it hurt?
Naw. Doesn't feel like anything.
Your mom won't find out. Besides, you're like a junior nun-in-training. When was your last date?
Seriously, it's been forever. I have trouble believing there's no one even worth CRUSHING on.

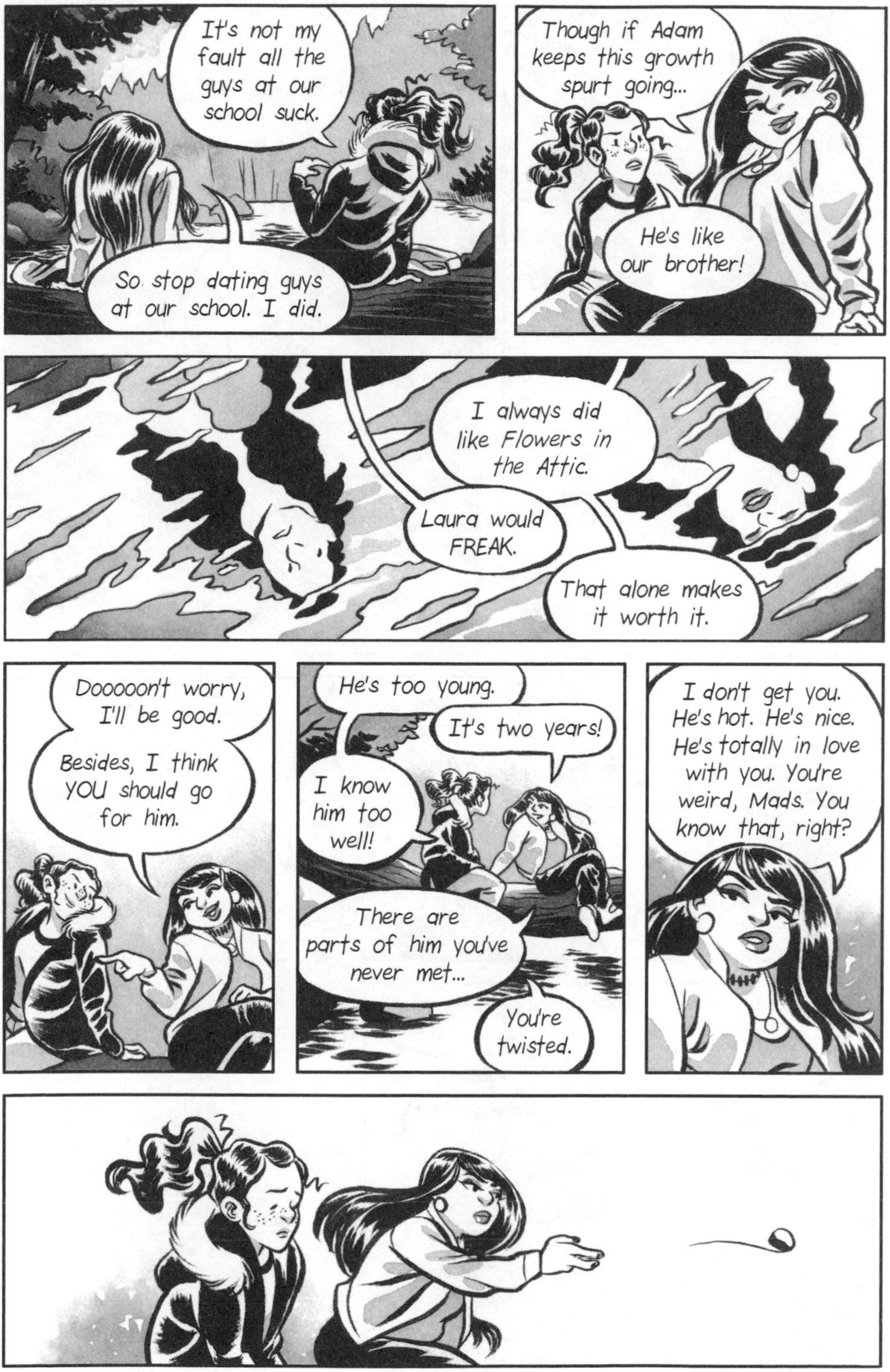
It's not my fault all the guys at our school suck.
So stop dating guys at our school. I did.
Though if Adam keeps this growth spurt going...
He's like our brother!
I always did like Flowers in the Attic.
Laura would FREAK.
That alone makes it worth it.
Doooooon't worry, I'll be good.
Besides, I think YOU should go for him.
He's too young.
It's two years!
I know him too well!
There are parts of him you've never met...
You're twisted.
I don't get you. He's hot. He's nice. He's totally in love with you. You're weird, Mads. You know that, right?

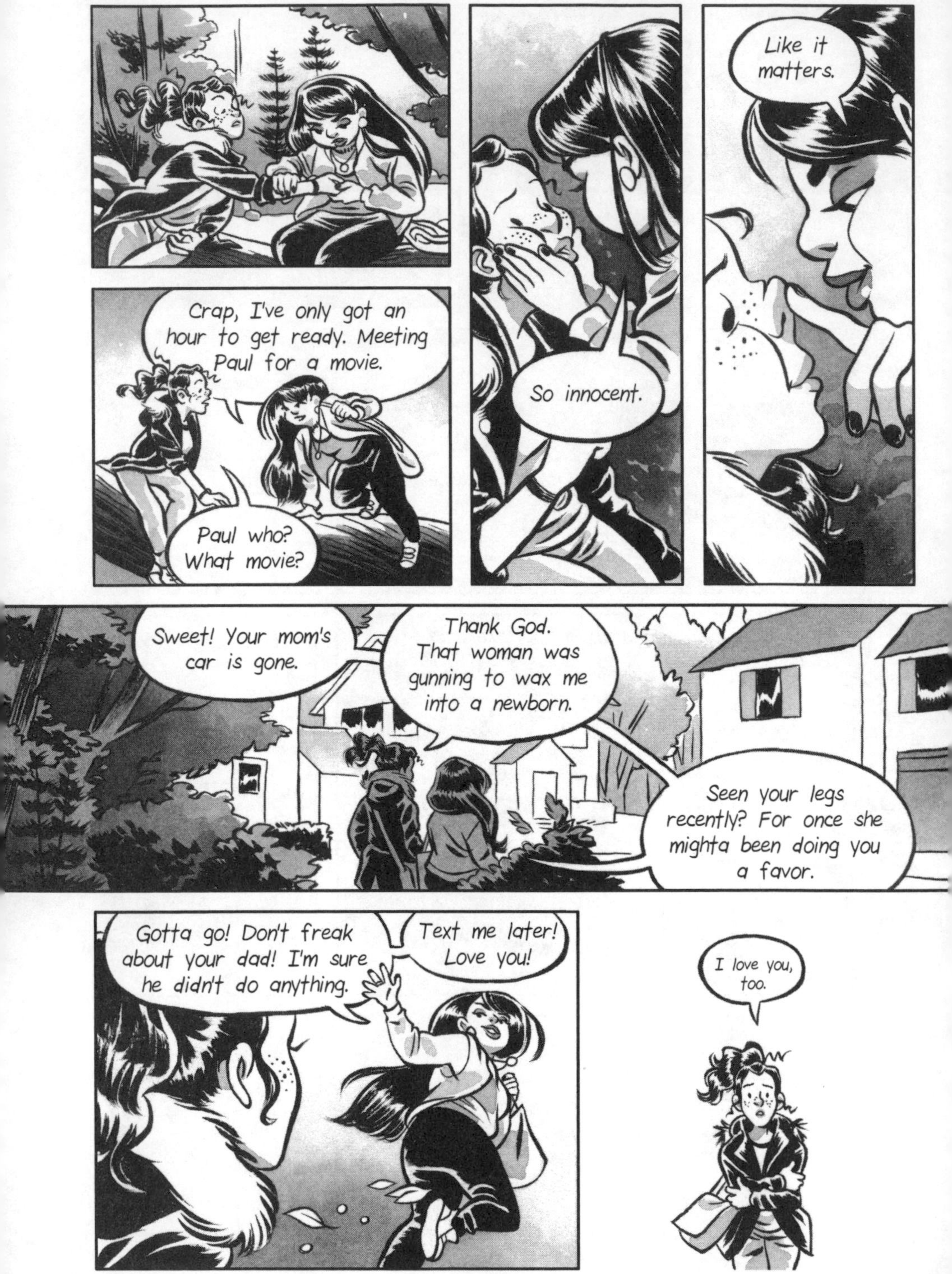
Like it matters.
Crap, I've only got an hour to get ready. Meeting Paul for a movie.
Paul who? What movie?
So innocent.
Sweet! Your mom's car is gone.
Thank God. That woman was gunning to wax me into a newborn.
Seen your legs recently? For once she mighta been doing you a favor.
Gotta go! Don't freak about your dad! I'm sure he didn't do anything.
Text me later! Love you!
I love you, too.

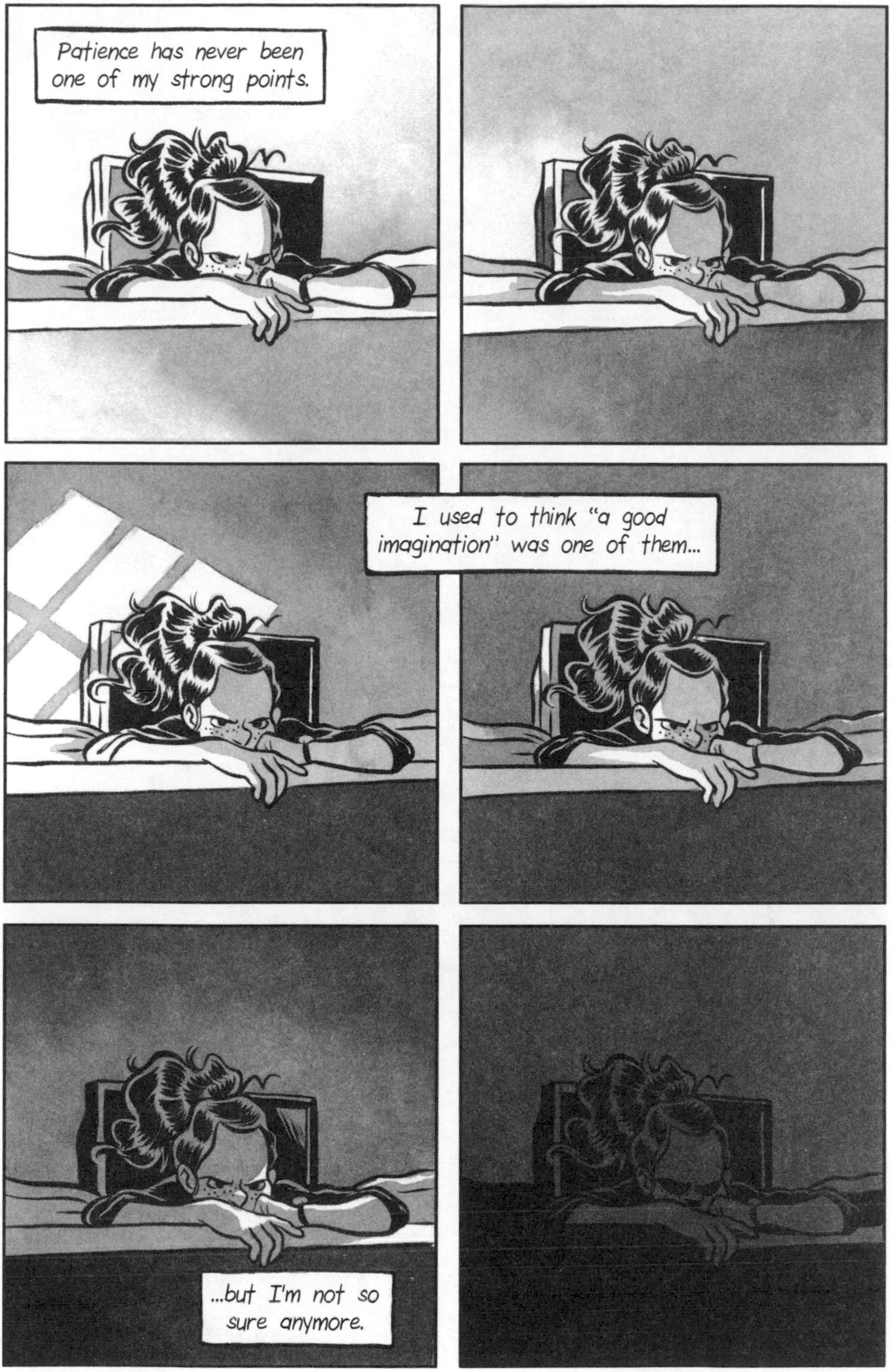
Patience has never been one of my strong points.
I used to think "a good imagination" was one of them...
...but I'm not so sure anymore.

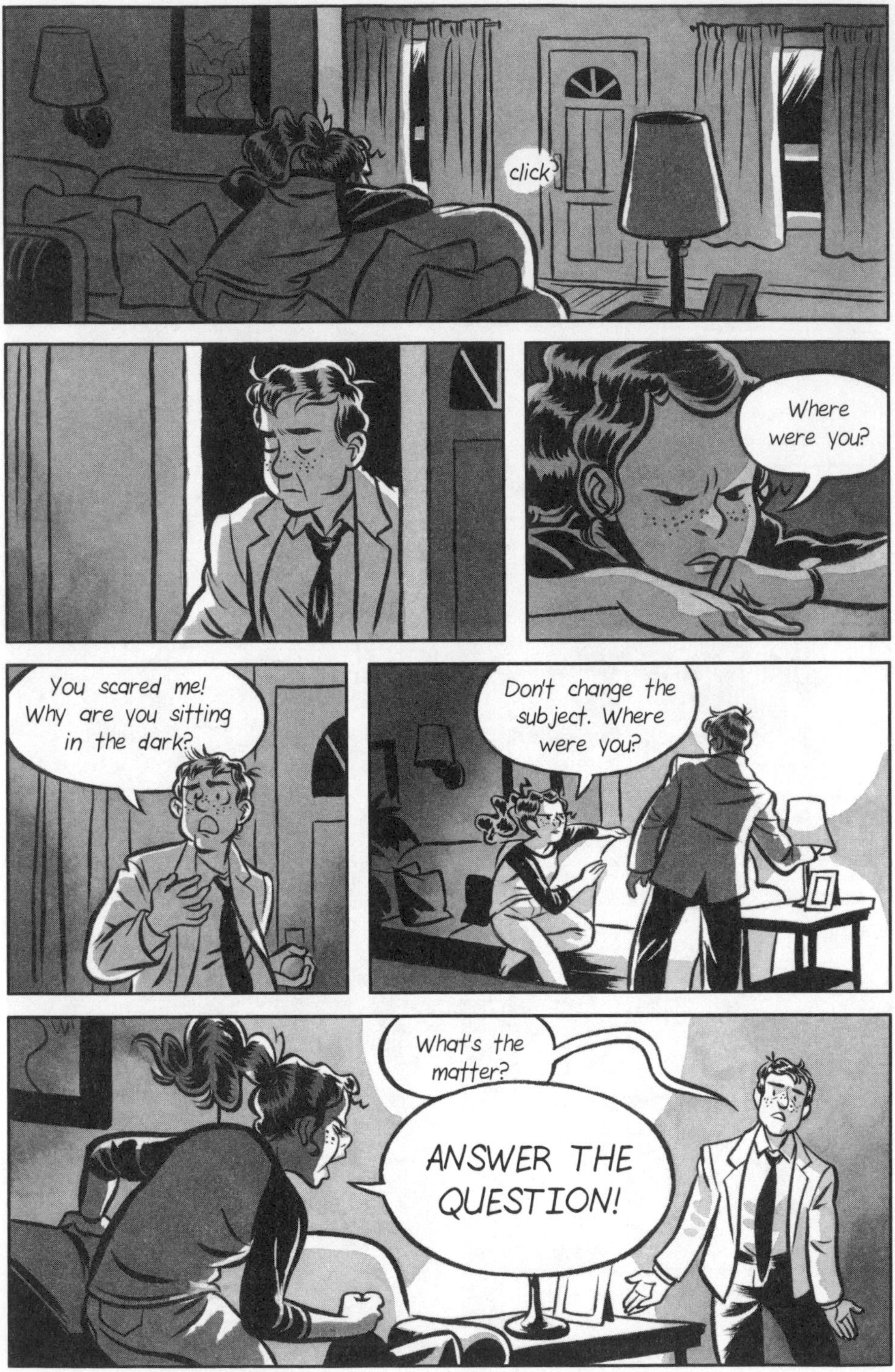
click
Where were you?
You scared me! Why are you sitting in the dark?
Don't change the subject. Where were you?
What's the matter?
ANSWER THE QUESTION!

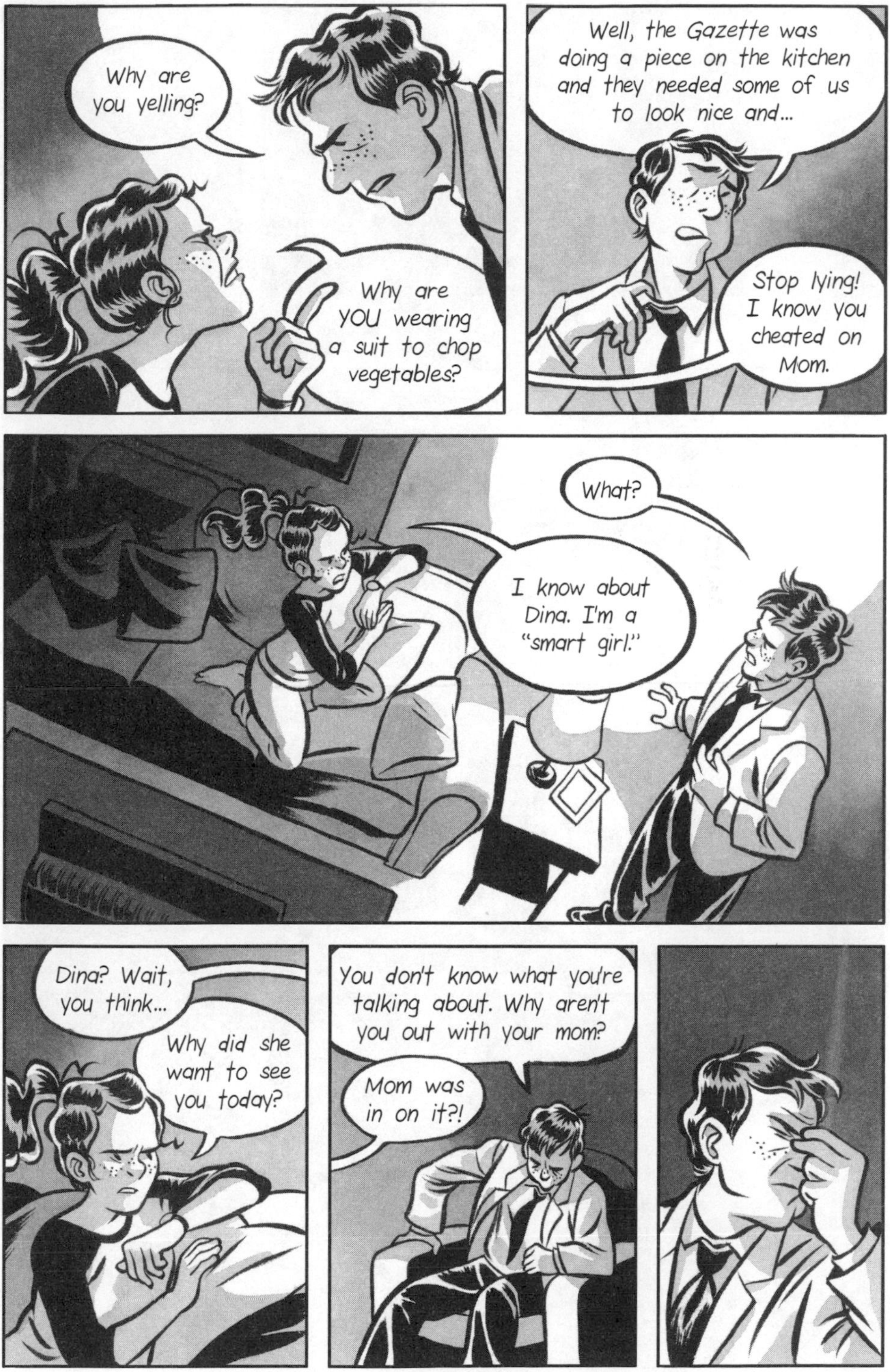

Why are you yelling?
Why are YOU wearing a suit to chop vegetables?
Well, the Gazette was doing a piece on the kitchen and they needed some of us to look nice and...
Stop lying! I know you cheated on Mom.
What?
I know about Dina. I'm a "smart girl."
Dina? Wait, you think...
Why did she want to see you today?
You don't know what you're talking about. Why aren't you out with your mom?
Mom was in on it?!

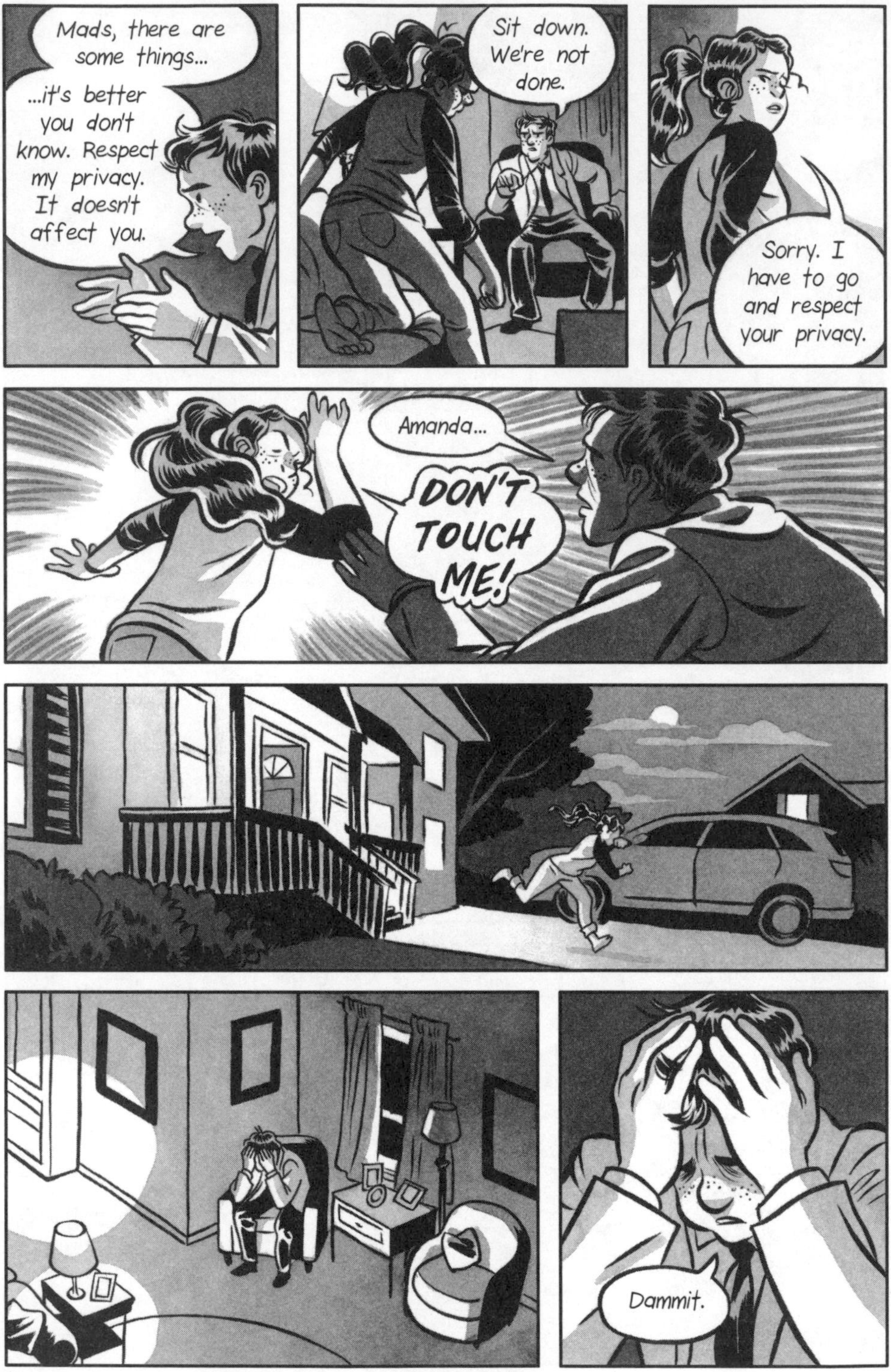
Mads, there are some things...
...it's better you don't know. Respect my privacy. It doesn't affect you.
Sit down. We're not done.
Sorry. I have to go and respect your privacy.
Amanda...
DON'T TOUCH ME!
Dammit.

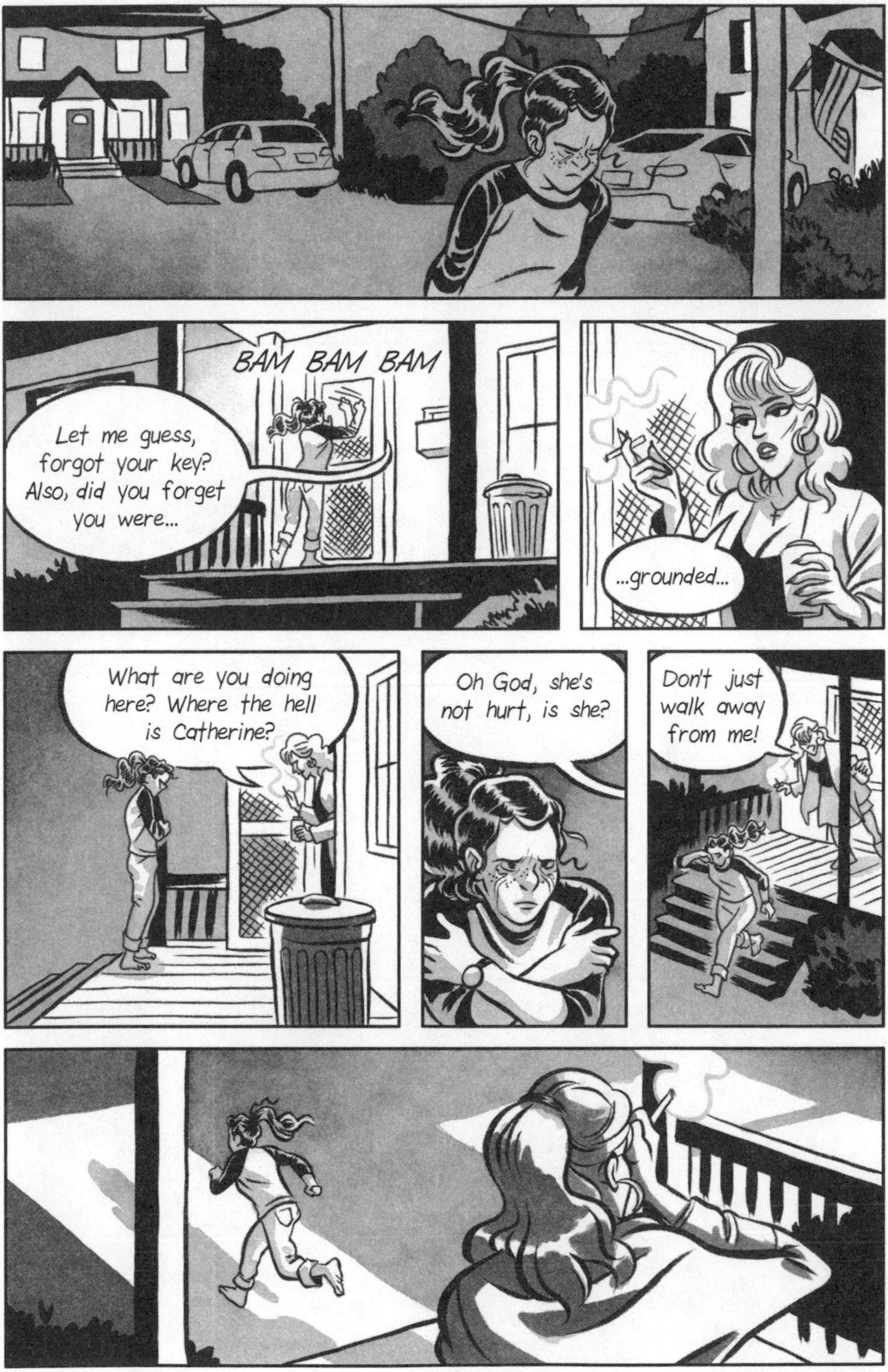
BAM BAM BAM
Let me guess, forgot your key? Also, did you forget you were...
...grounded...
What are you doing here? Where the hell is Catherine?
Oh God, she's not hurt, is she?
Don't just walk away from me!

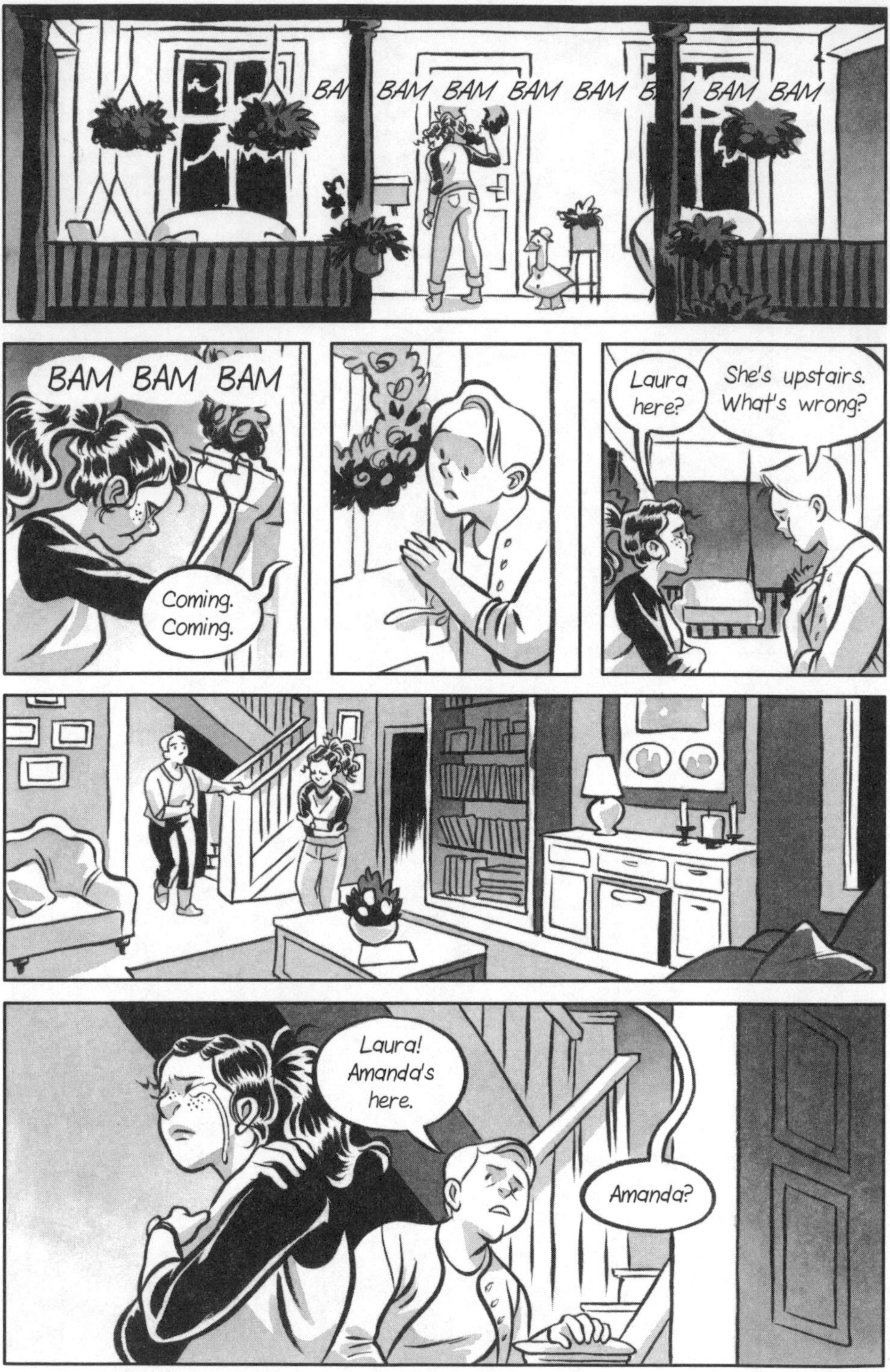
BAM BAM BAM BAM BAM BAM BAM BAM
BAM BAM BAM
Coming. Coming.
Laura here?
She's upstairs. What's wrong?
Laura! Amanda's here.
Amanda?

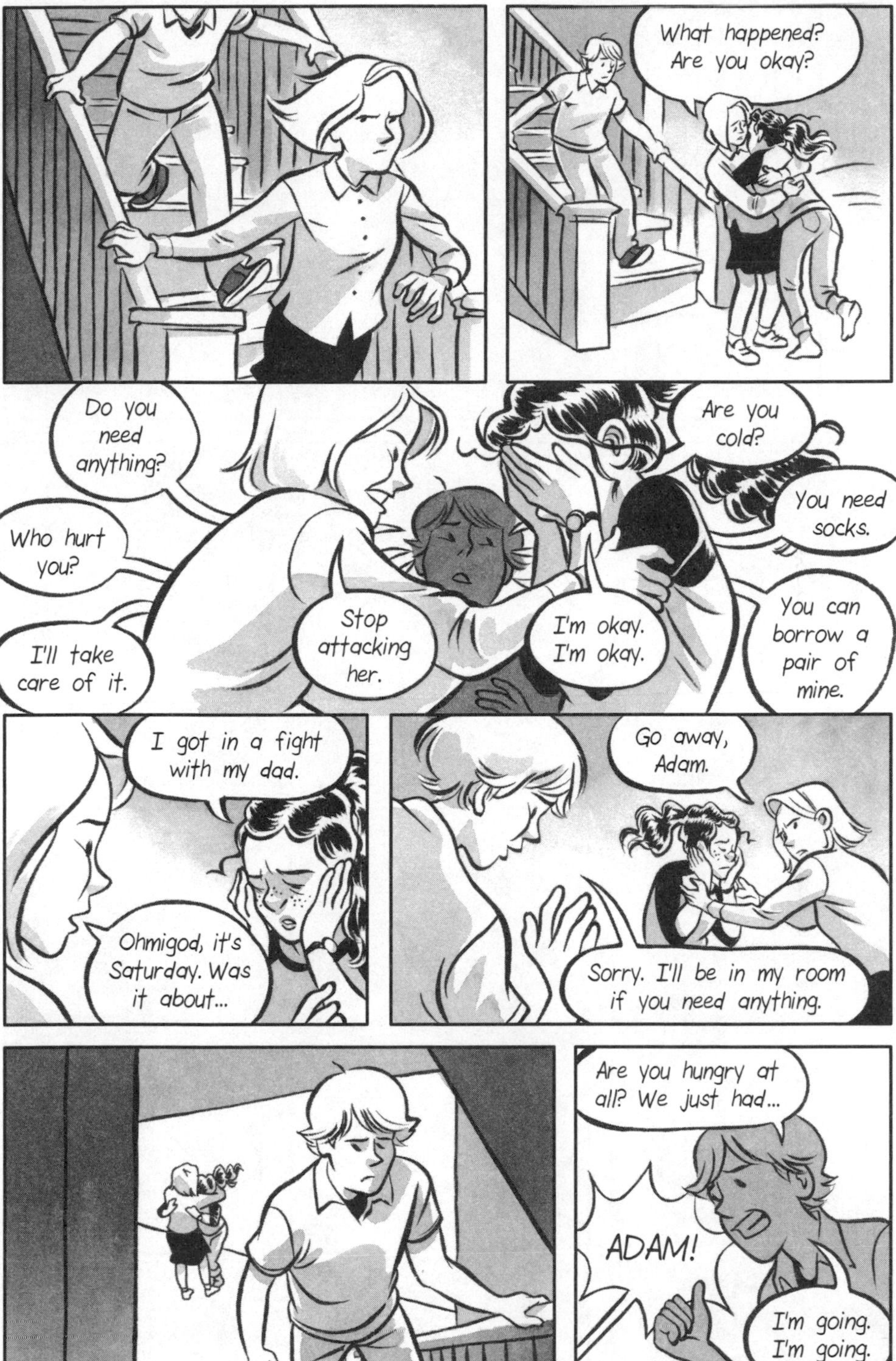
What happened? Are you okay?
Do you need anything?
Who hurt you?
I'll take care of it.
Stop attacking her.
I'm okay. I'm okay.
Are you cold?
You need socks.
You can borrow a pair of mine.
I got in a fight with my dad.
Ohmigod, it's Saturday. Was it about...
Go away, Adam.
Sorry. I'll be in my room if you need anything.
Are you hungry at all? We just had...
ADAM!
I'm going. I'm going.

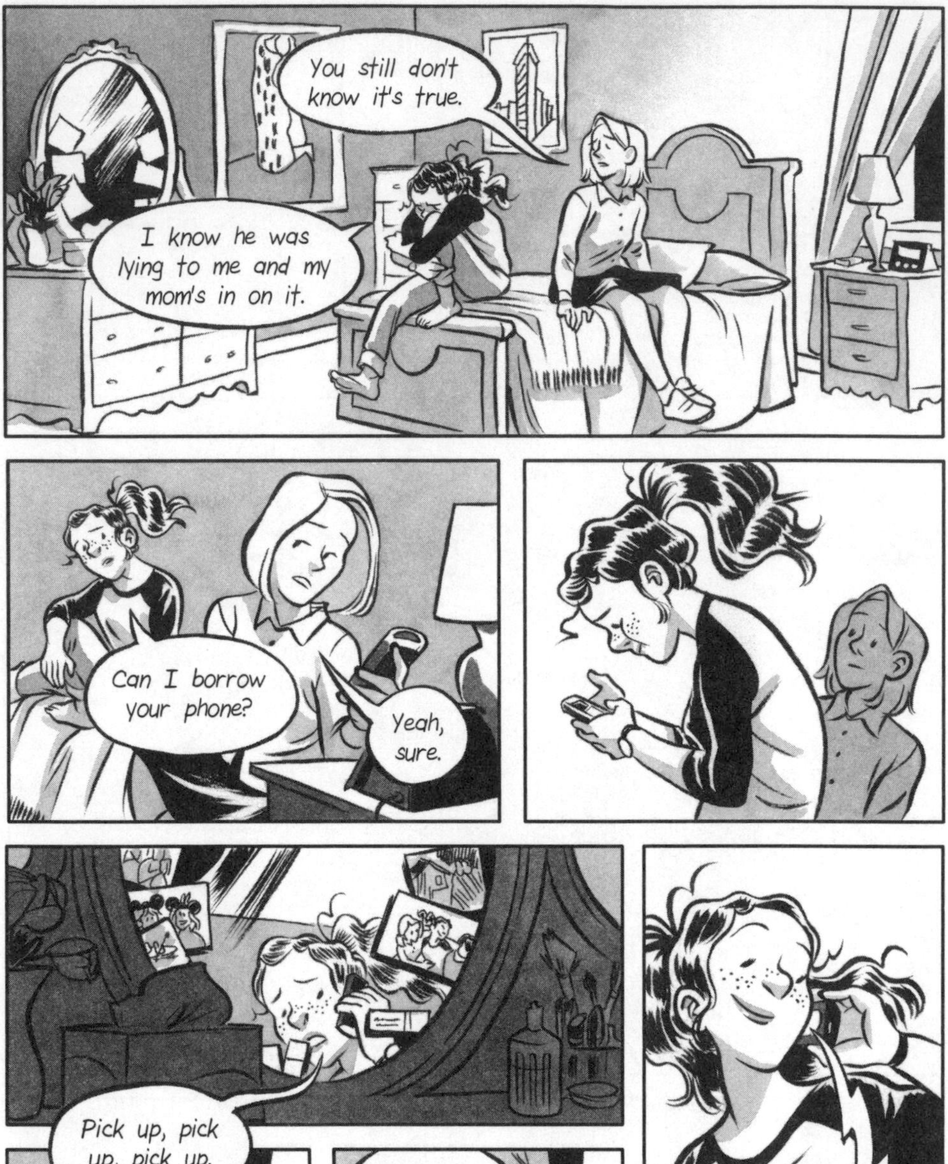
You still don't know it's true.
I know he was lying to me and my mom's in on it.
Can I borrow your phone?
Yeah, sure.
Pick up, pick up, pick up.
Who're you calling?
I'm busy, Laura. What do you want?

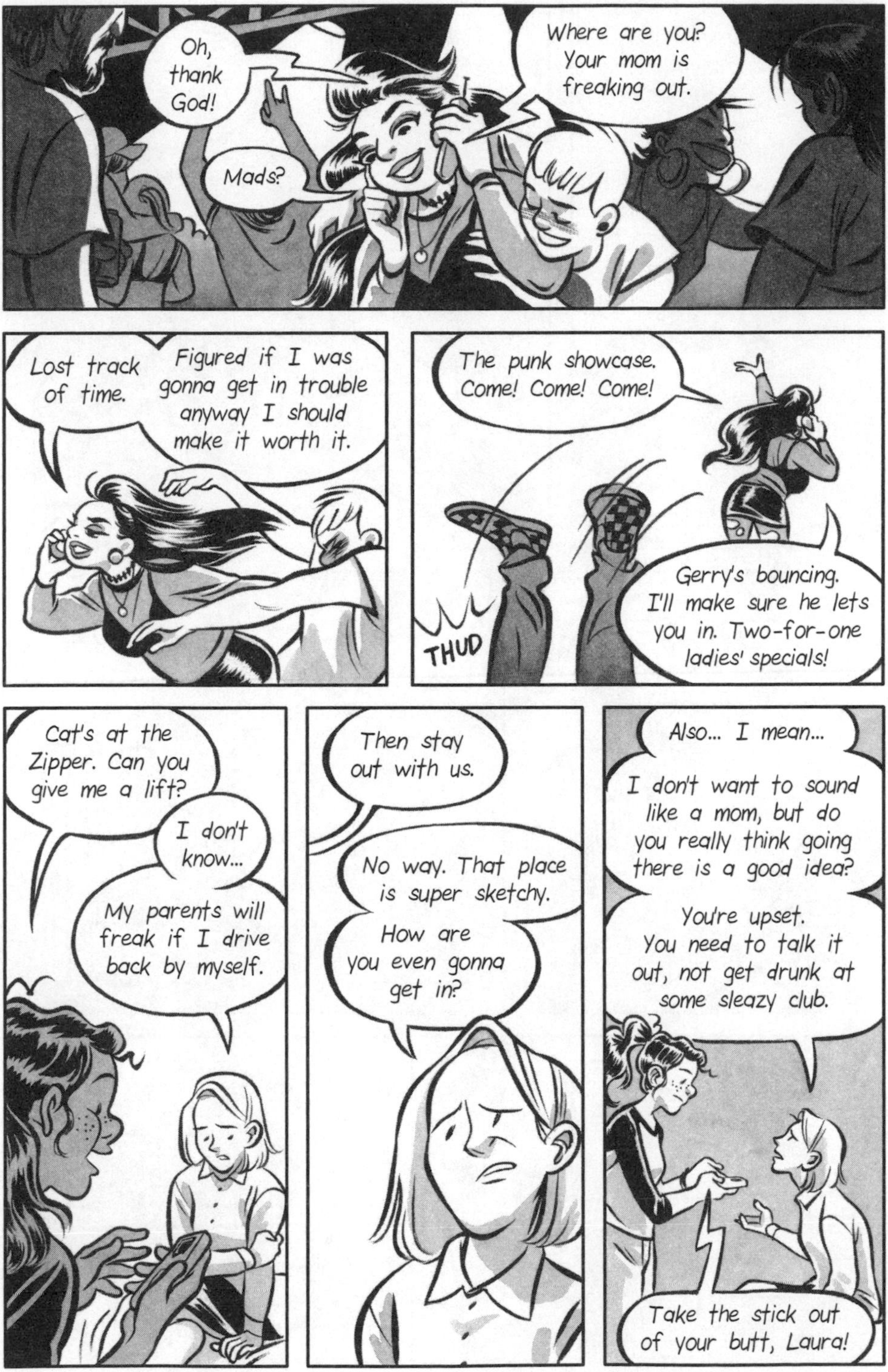
Oh, thank God!
Mads?
Where are you? Your mom is freaking out.
Lost track of time.
Figured if I was gonna get in trouble anyway I should make it worth it.
The punk showcase. Come! Come! Come!
THUD
Gerry's bouncing. I'll make sure he lets you in. Two-for-one ladies' specials!
Cat's at the Zipper. Can you give me a lift?
I don't know...
My parents will freak if I drive back by myself.
Then stay out with us.
No way. That place is super sketchy.
How are you even gonna get in?
Also... I mean...
I don't want to sound like a mom, but do you really think going there is a good idea?
You're upset. You need to talk it out, not get drunk at some sleazy club.
Take the stick out of your butt, Laura!

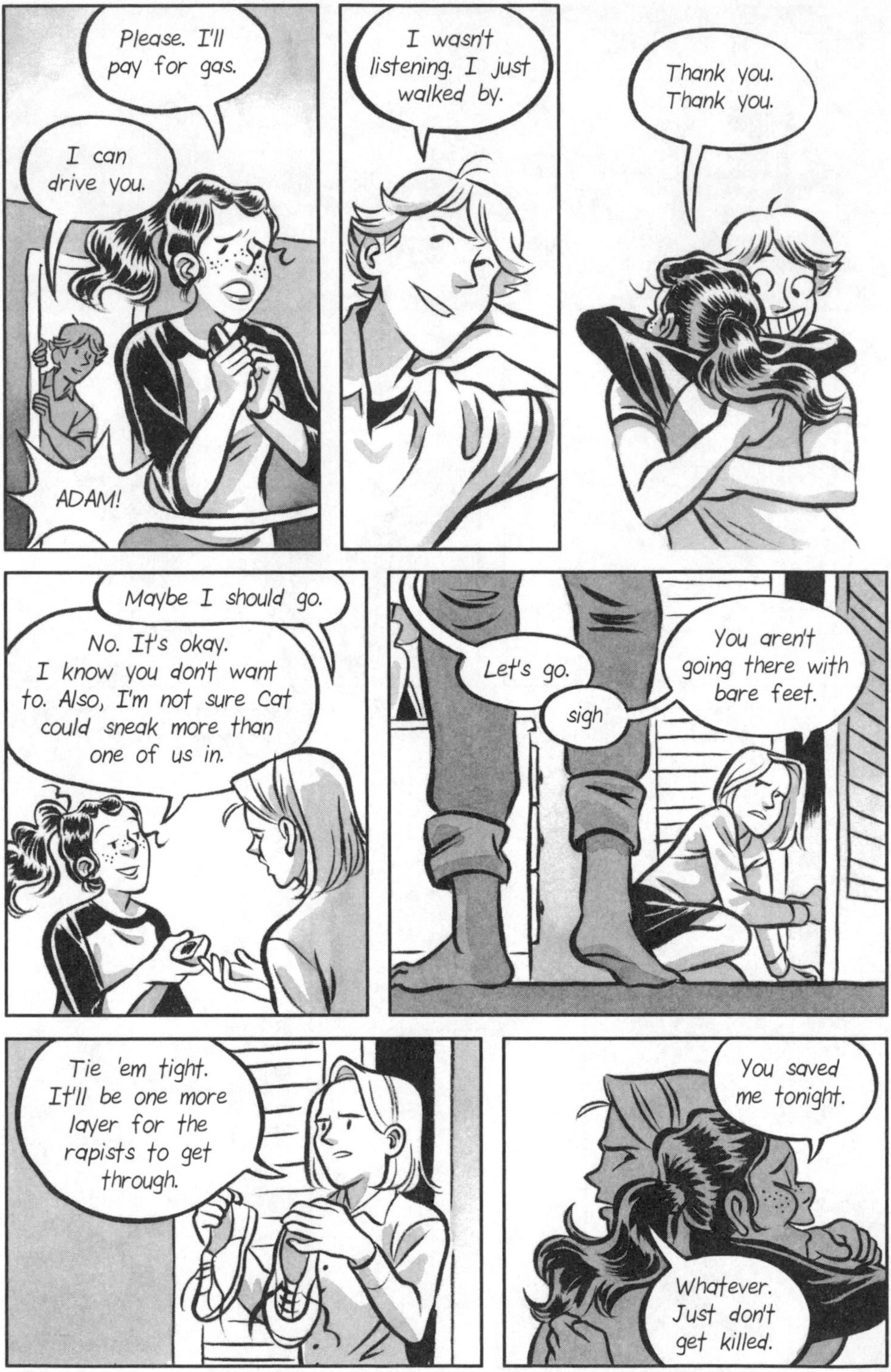
Please. I'll pay for gas.
I can drive you.
ADAM!
I wasn't listening. I just walked by.
Thank you. Thank you.
Maybe I should go.
No. It's okay. I know you don't want to. Also, I'm not sure Cat could sneak more than one of us in.
Let's go.
sigh
You aren't going there with bare feet.
Tie 'em tight. It'll be one more layer for the rapists to get through.
You saved me tonight.
Whatever. Just don't get killed.

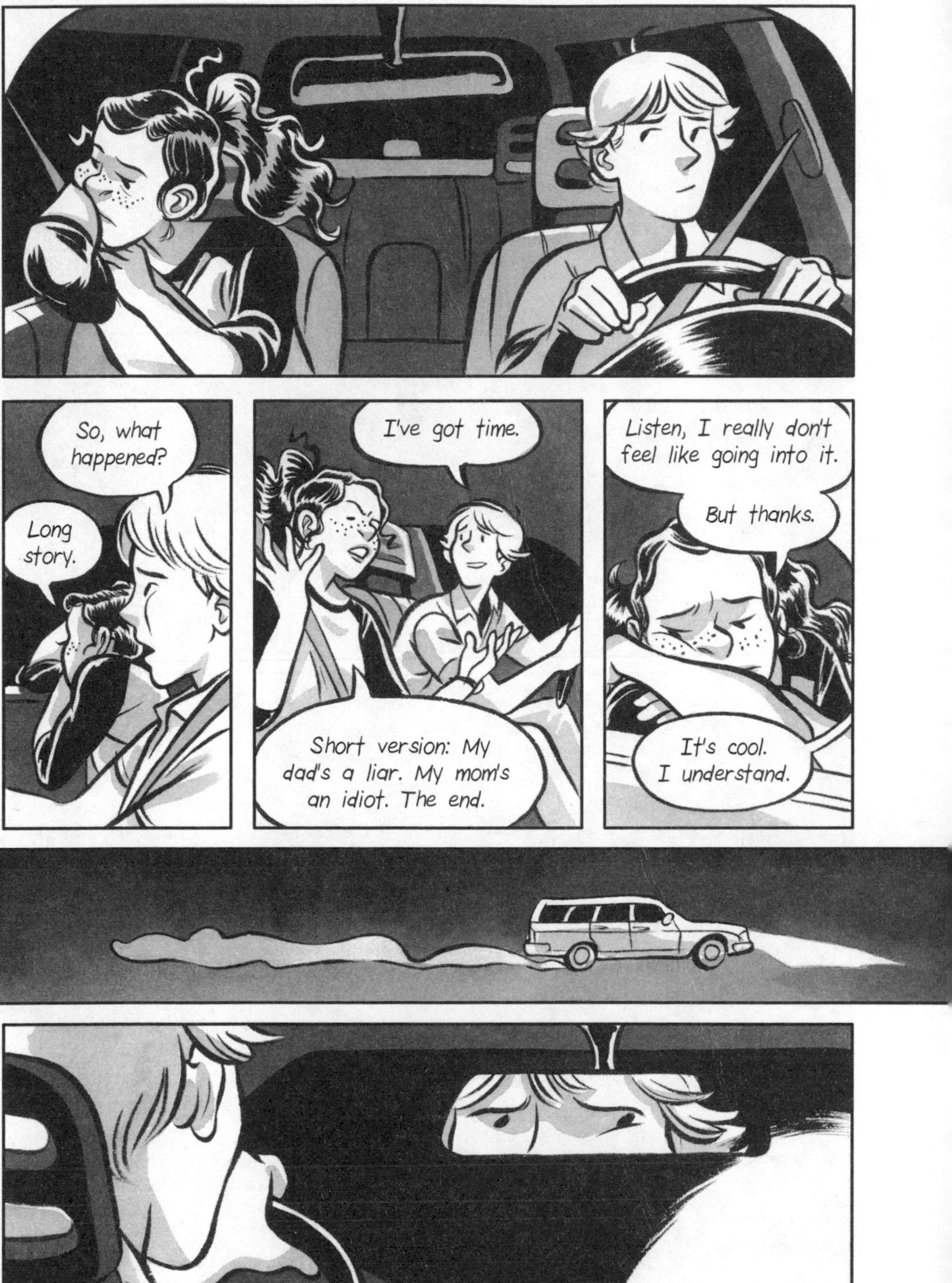
So, what happened?
Long story.
I've got time.
Short version: My dad's a liar. My mom's an idiot. The end.
Listen, I really don't feel like going into it.
But thanks.
It's cool. I understand.

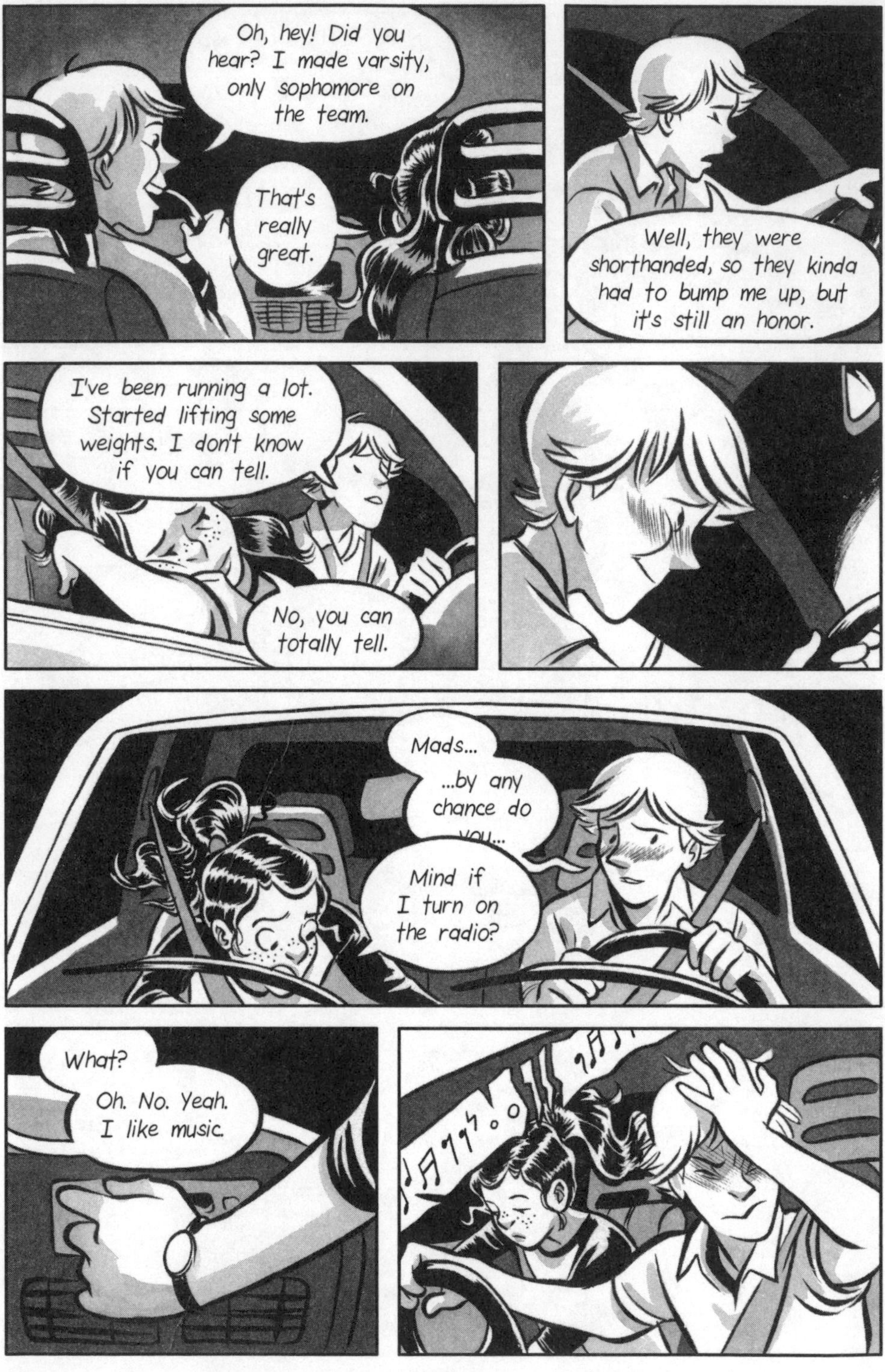

Oh, hey! Did you hear? I made varsity, only sophomore on the team.
That's really great.
Well, they were shorthanded, so they kinda had to bump me up, but it's still an honor.
I've been running a lot. Started lifting some weights. I don't know if you can tell.
No, you can totally tell.
Mads...
...by any chance do you...
Mind if I turn on the radio?
What?
Oh. No. Yeah. I like music.

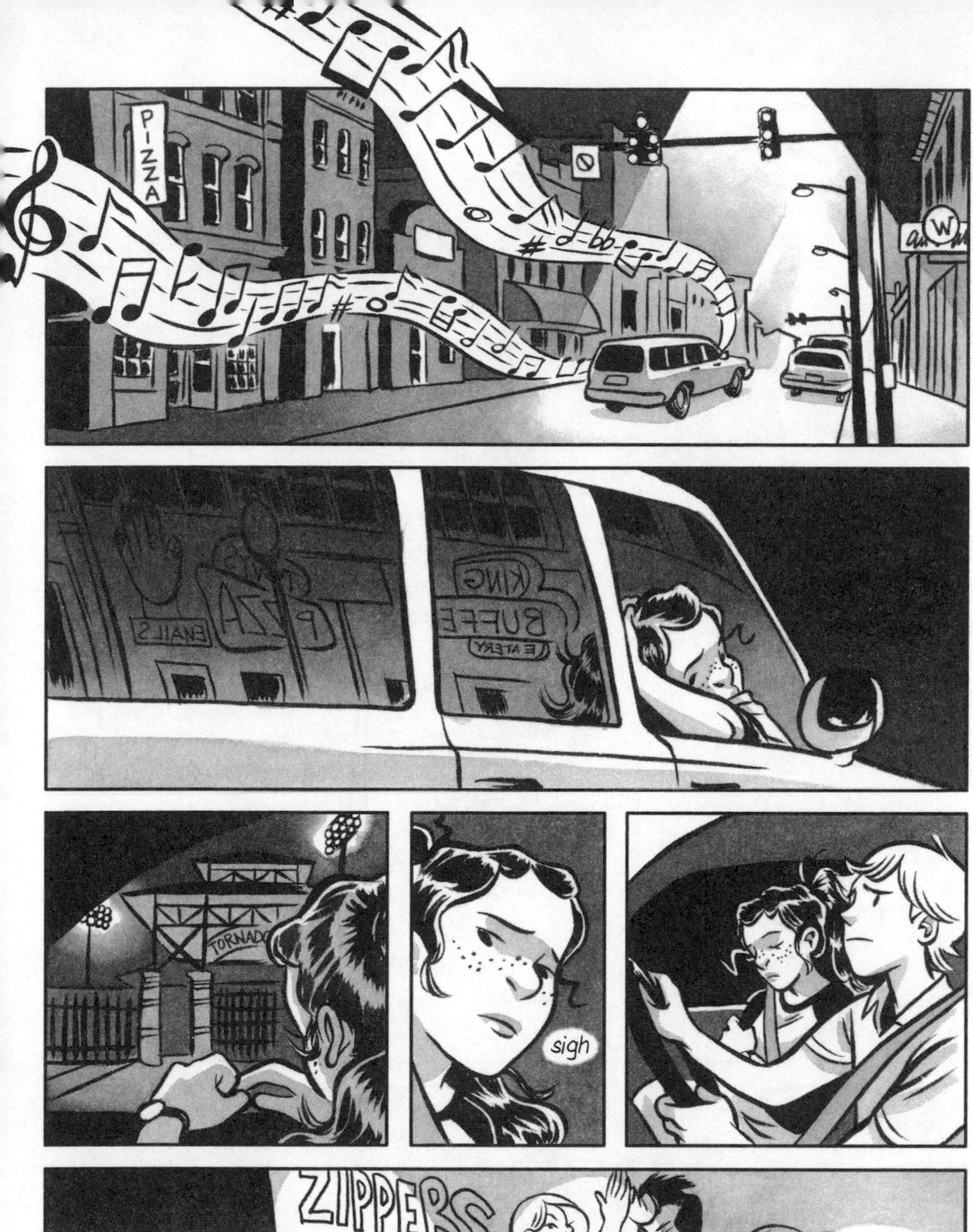
PIZZA
sigh
ZIPPERS
For a night you may never remember!
Live music every night!
Saturday is Ladies Night!

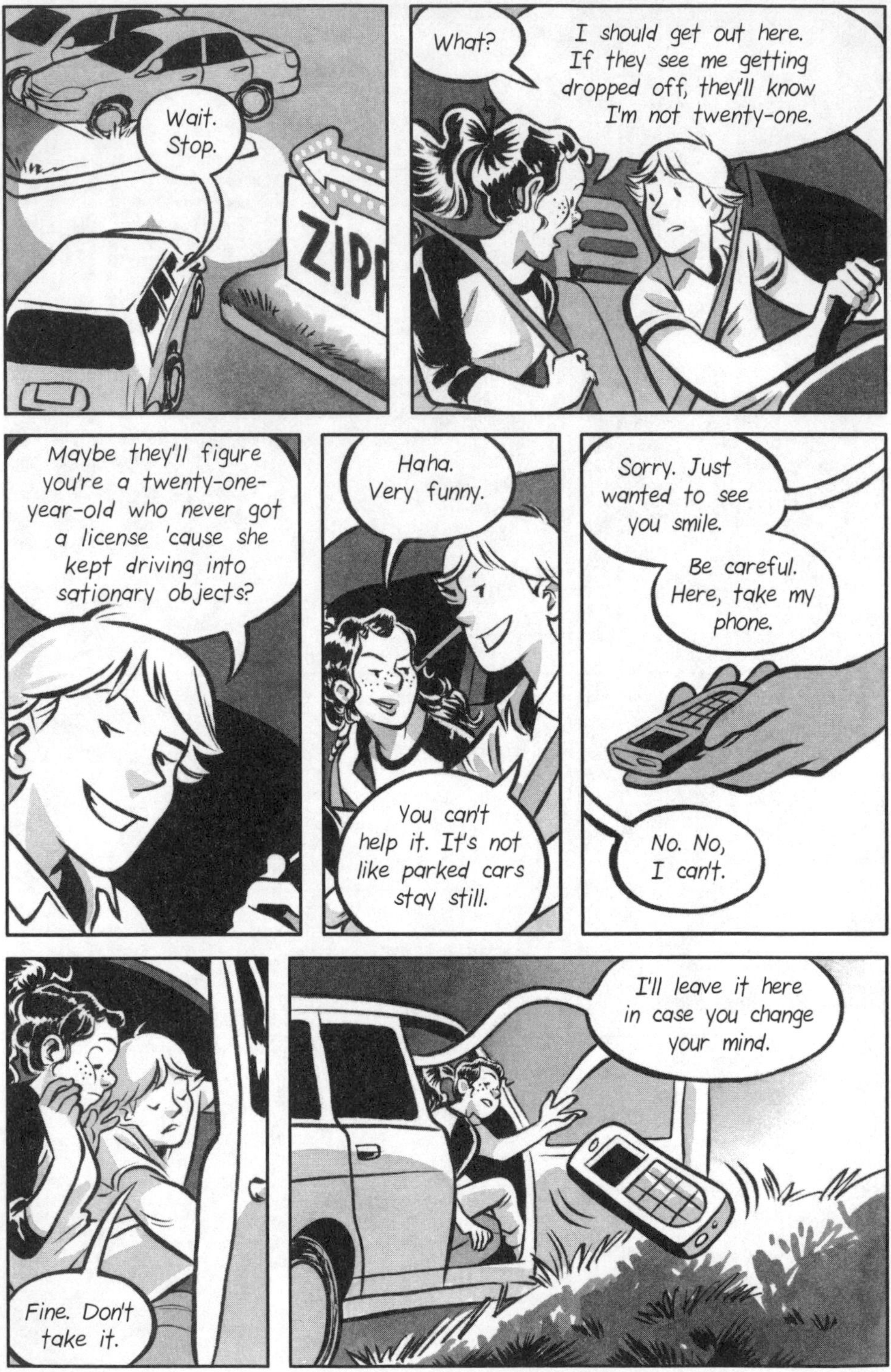
Wait. Stop.
ZIPP
What?
I should get out here. If they see me getting dropped off, they'll know I'm not twenty-one.
Maybe they'll figure you're a twenty-one-year-old who never got a license 'cause she kept driving into sationary objects?
Haha. Very funny.
You can't help it. It's not like parked cars stay still.
Sorry. Just wanted to see you smile.
Be careful. Here, take my phone.
No. No, I can't.
Fine. Don't take it.
I'll leave it here in case you change your mind.

VRRROOOOM

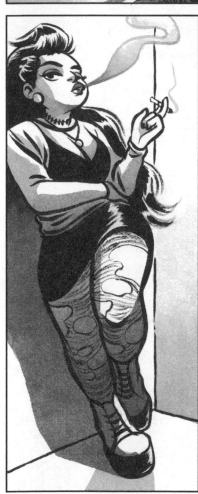

There you are! Gerry, Mads. Mads, Gerry.

Hi.

grunt

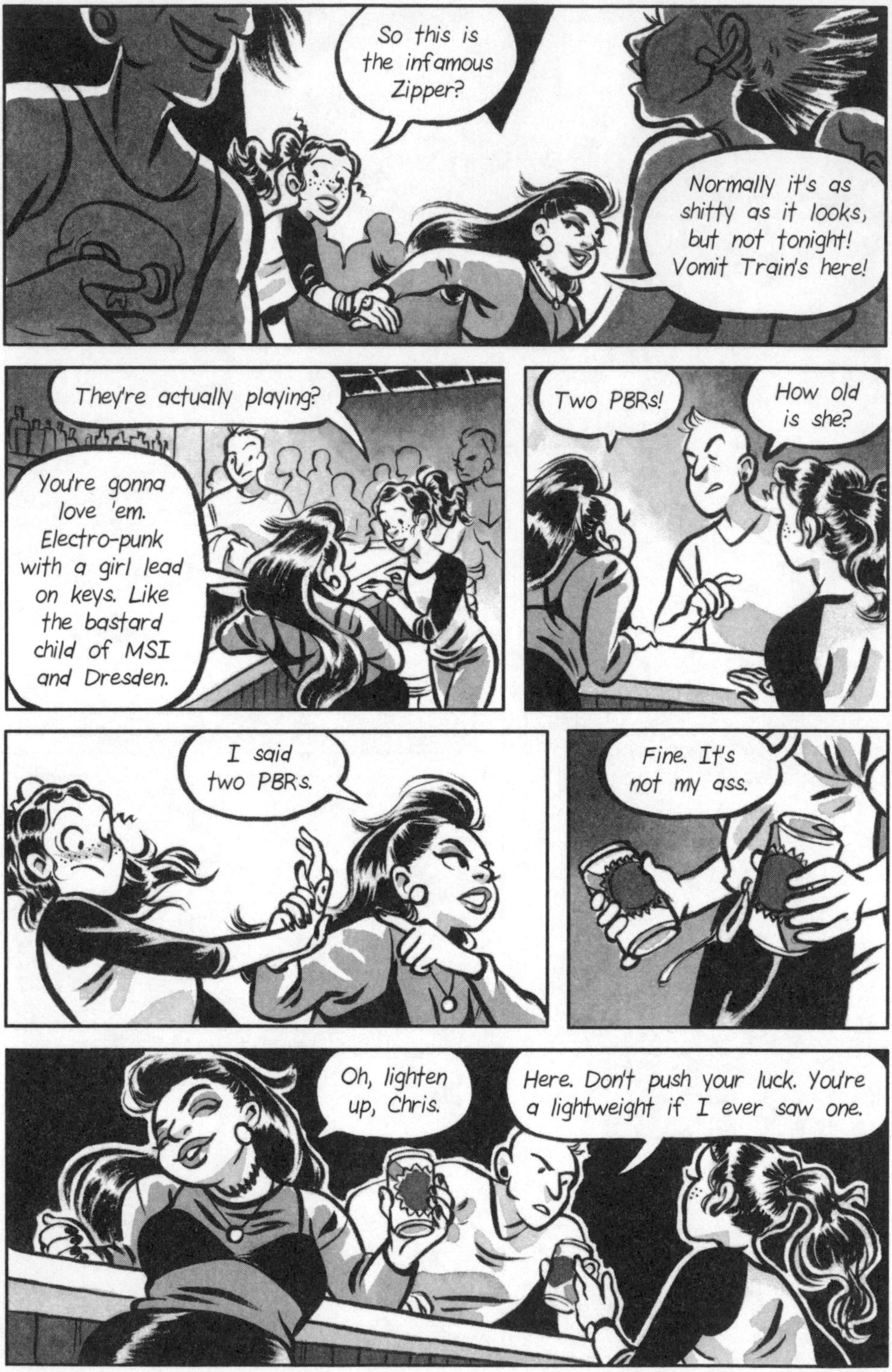
So this is the infamous Zipper?
Normally it's as shitty as it looks, but not tonight! Vomit Train's here!
They're actually playing?
You're gonna love 'em. Electro-punk with a girl lead on keys. Like the bastard child of MSI and Dresden.
Two PBRs!
How old is she?
I said two PBR's.
Fine. It's not my ass.
Oh, lighten up, Chris.
Here. Don't push your luck. You're a lightweight if I ever saw one.

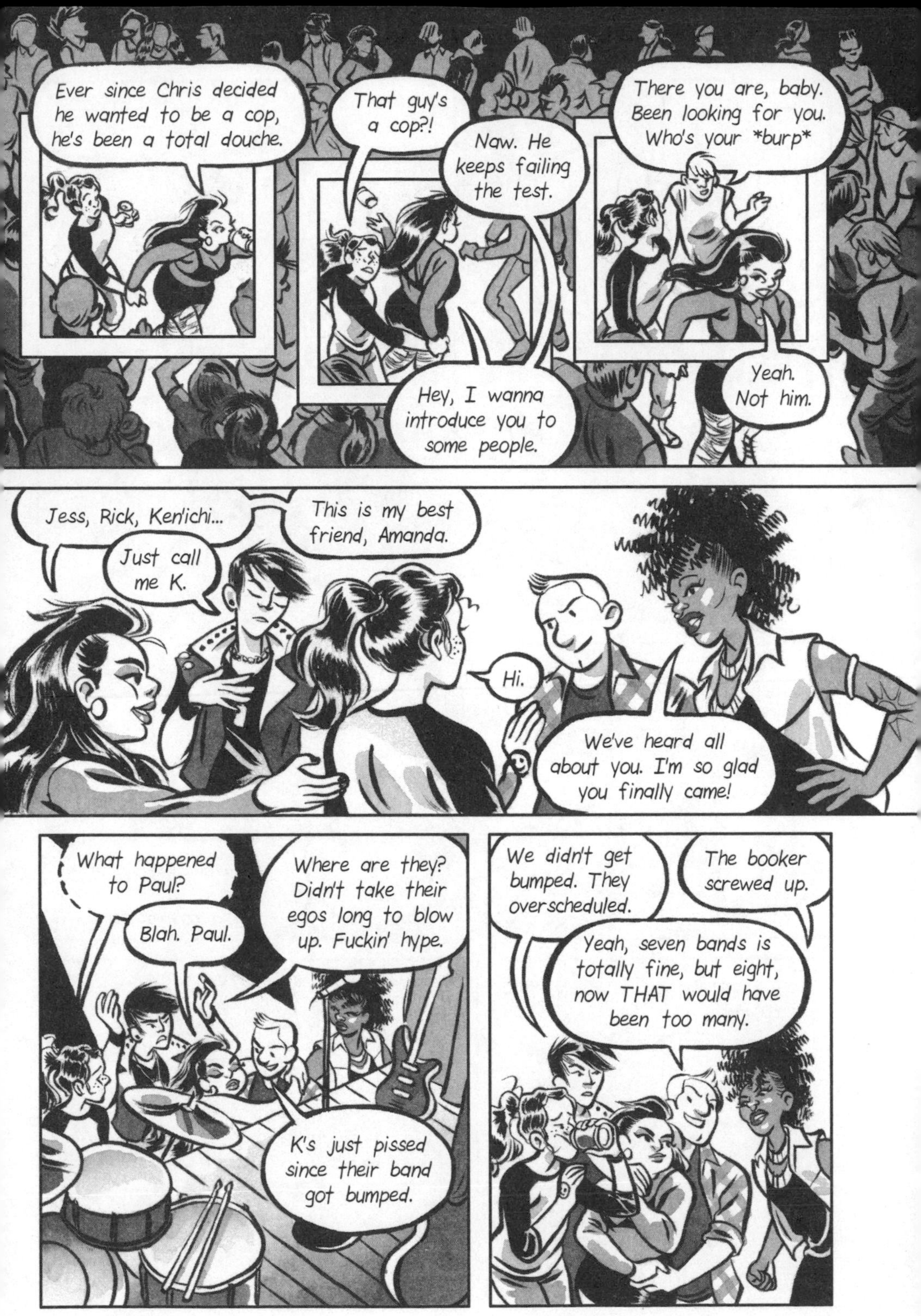
Ever since Chris decided he wanted to be a cop, he's been a total douche.
That guy's a cop?!
Naw. He keeps failing the test.
Hey, I wanna introduce you to some people.
There you are, baby. Been looking for you. Who's your *burp*
Yeah. Not him.
Jess, Rick, Ken'ichi...
Just call me K.
This is my best friend, Amanda.
Hi.
We've heard all about you. I'm so glad you finally came!
What happened to Paul?
Blah. Paul.
Where are they? Didn't take their egos long to blow up. Fuckin' hype.
K's just pissed since their band got bumped.
We didn't get bumped. They overscheduled.
The booker screwed up.
Yeah, seven bands is totally fine, but eight, now THAT would have been too many.

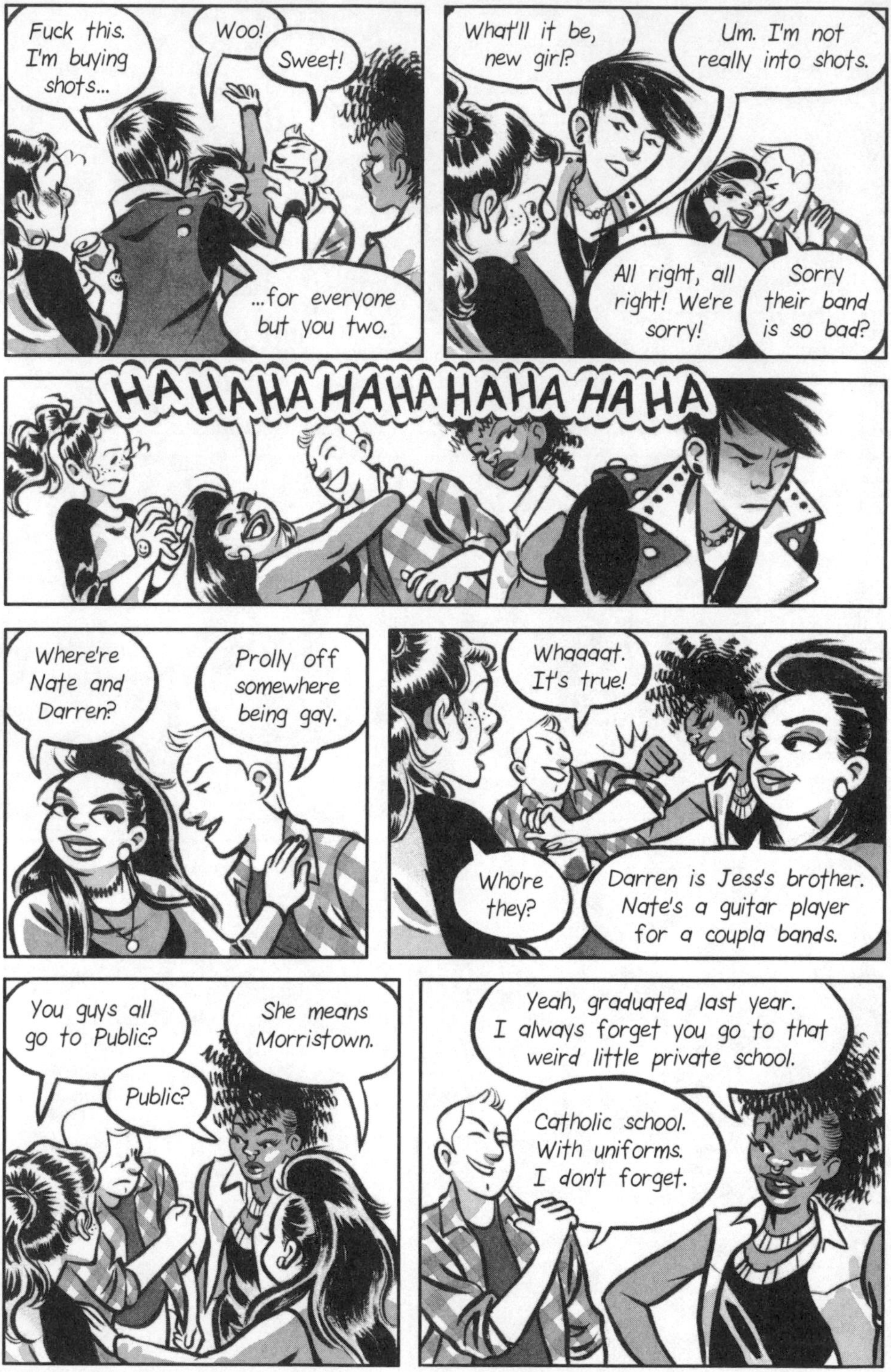
Fuck this. I'm buying shots...
Woo!
Sweet!
...for everyone but you two.
What'll it be, new girl?
Um. I'm not really into shots.
All right, all right! We're sorry!
Sorry their band is so bad?
HAHAHAHAHAHAHAHA HAHA
Where're Nate and Darren?
Prolly off somewhere being gay.
Whaaaat. It's true!
Who're they?
Darren is Jess's brother. Nate's a guitar player for a coupla bands.
You guys all go to Public?
Public?
She means Morristown.
Yeah, graduated last year. I always forget you go to that weird little private school.
Catholic school. With uniforms. I don't forget.

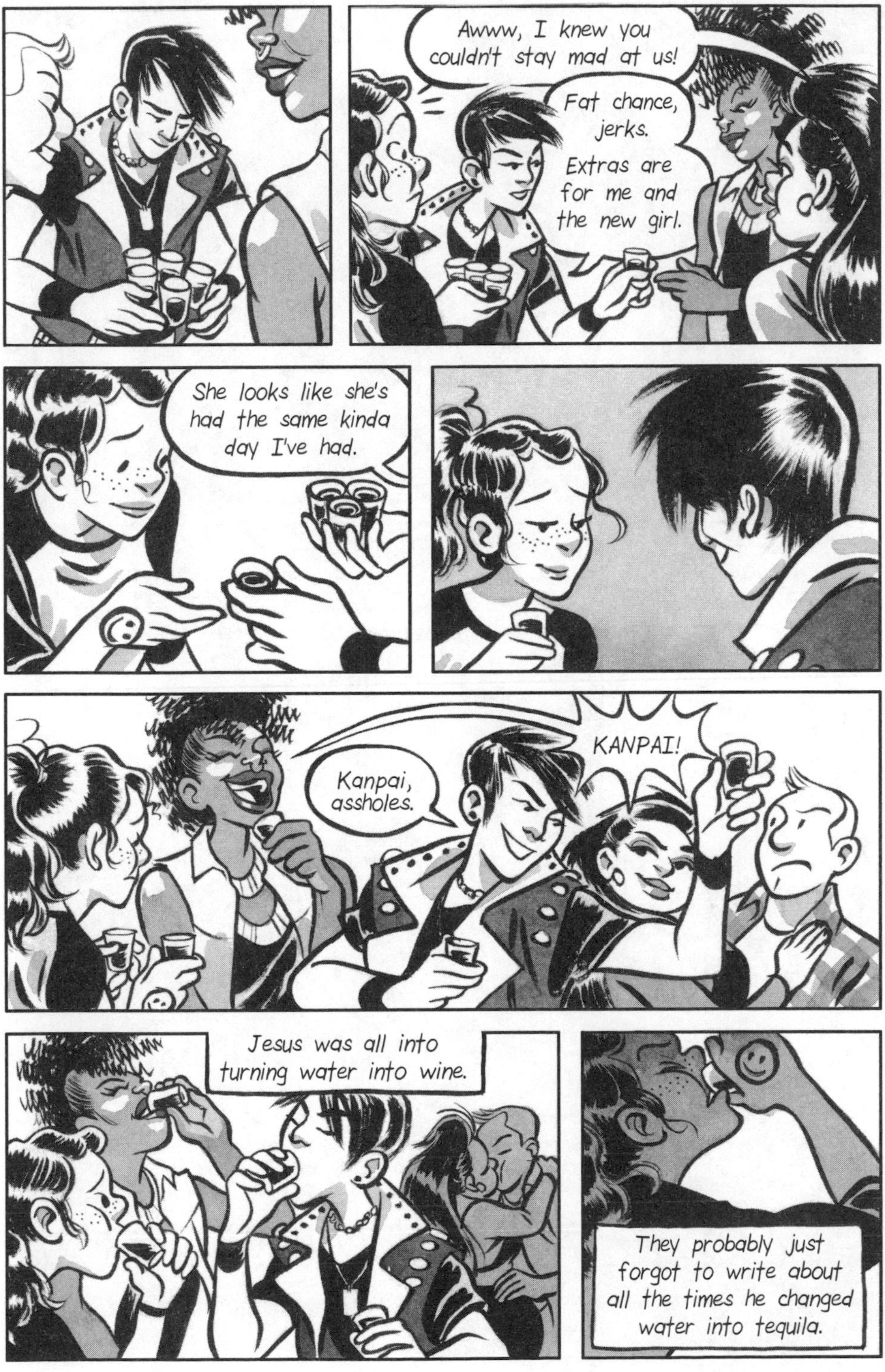
Awww, I knew you couldn't stay mad at us!
Fat chance, jerks.
Extras are for me and the new girl.
She looks like she's had the same kinda day I've had.
Kanpai, assholes.
KANPAI!
Jesus was all into turning water into wine.
They probably just forgot to write about all the times he changed water into tequila.

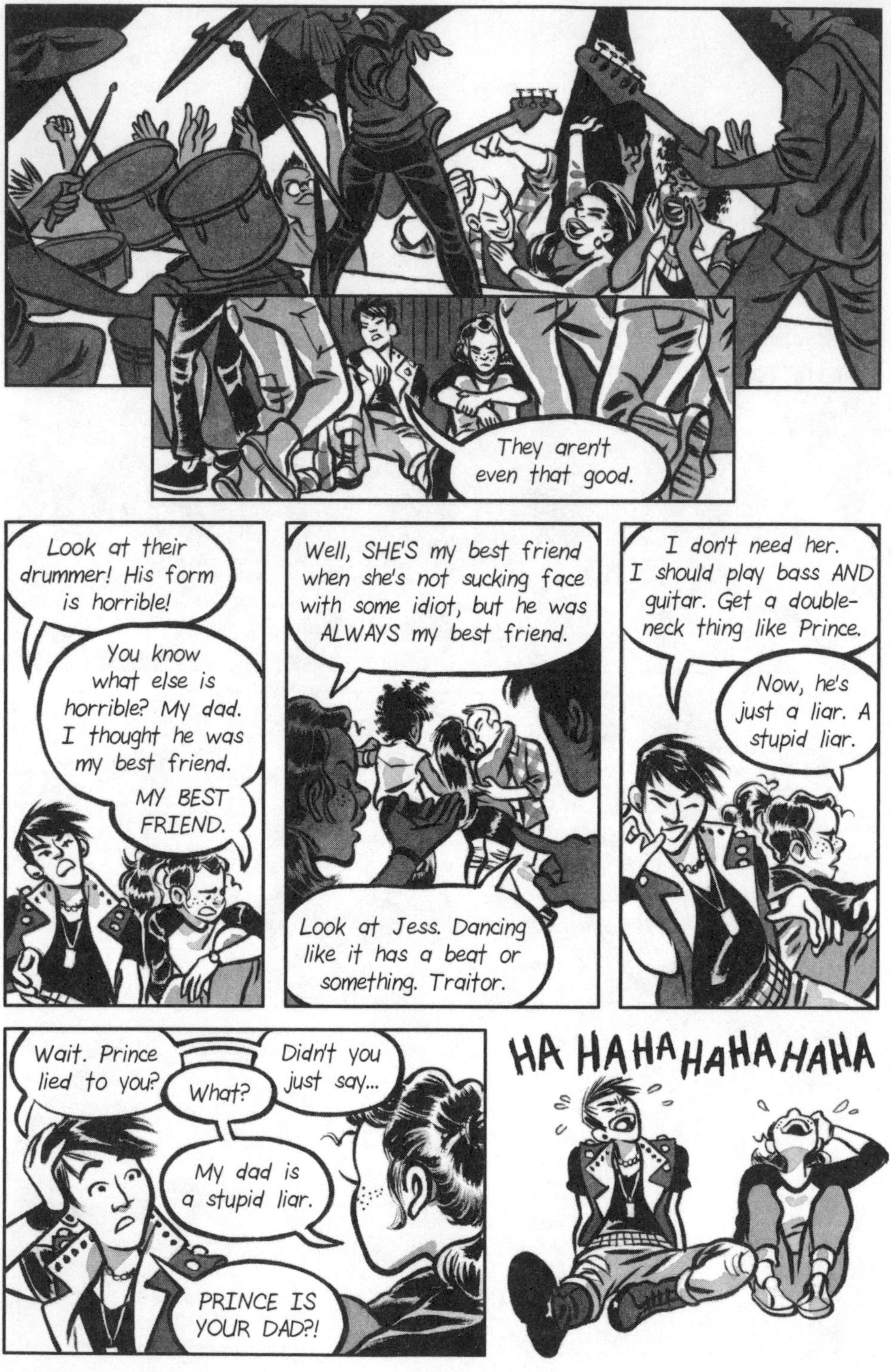
They aren't even that good.
Look at their drummer! His form is horrible!
You know what else is horrible? My dad. I thought he was my best friend.
MY BEST FRIEND.
Well, SHE'S my best friend when she's not sucking face with some idiot, but he was ALWAYS my best friend.
Look at Jess. Dancing like it has a beat or something. Traitor.
I don't need her. I should play bass AND guitar. Get a double-neck thing like Prince.
Now, he's just a liar. A stupid liar.
Wait. Prince lied to you?
What?
Didn't you just say...
My dad is a stupid liar.
PRINCE IS YOUR DAD?!
HA HA HA HA HA HA HA

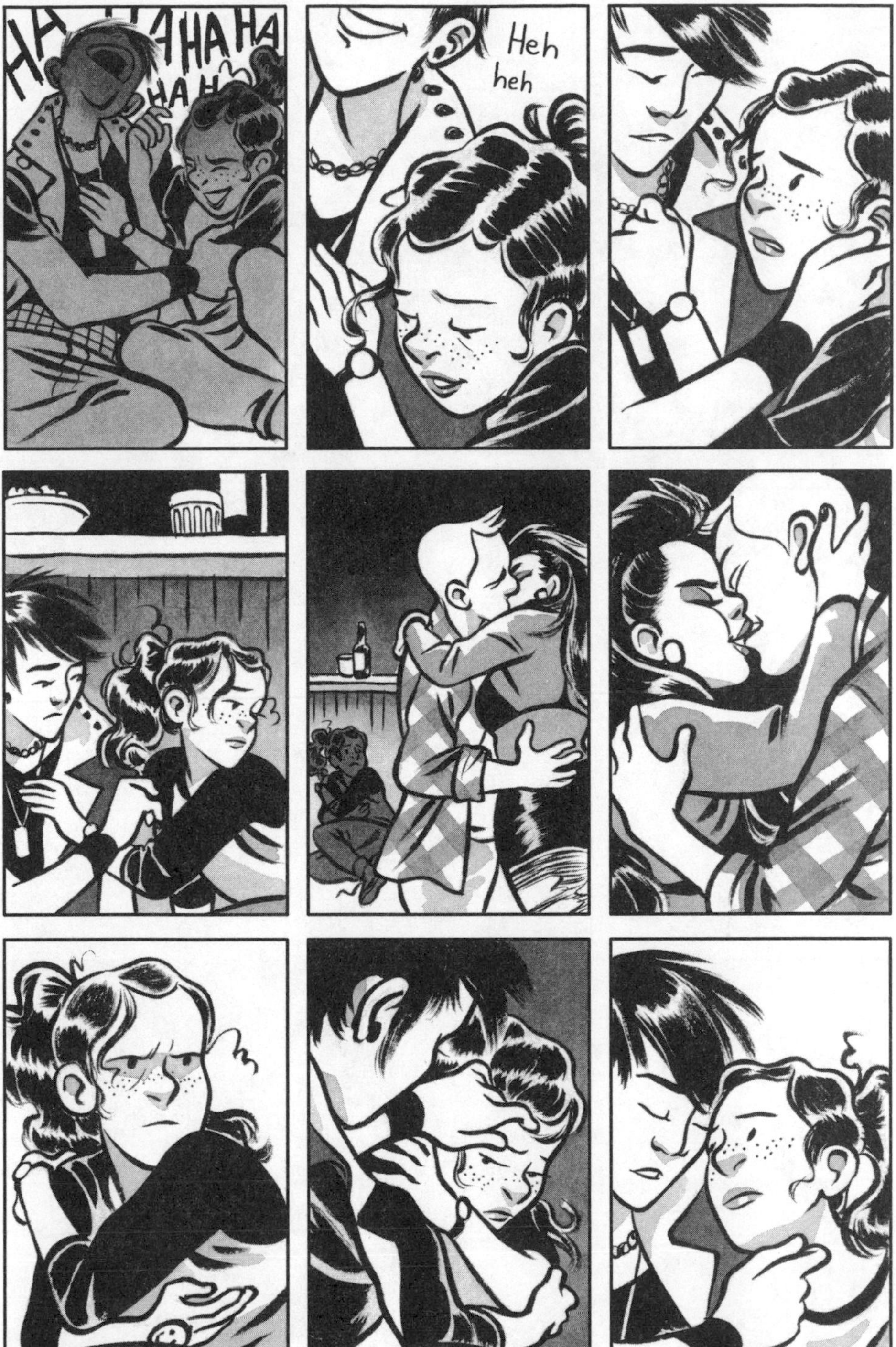
HAHAHAHA
HAH
Heh
heh

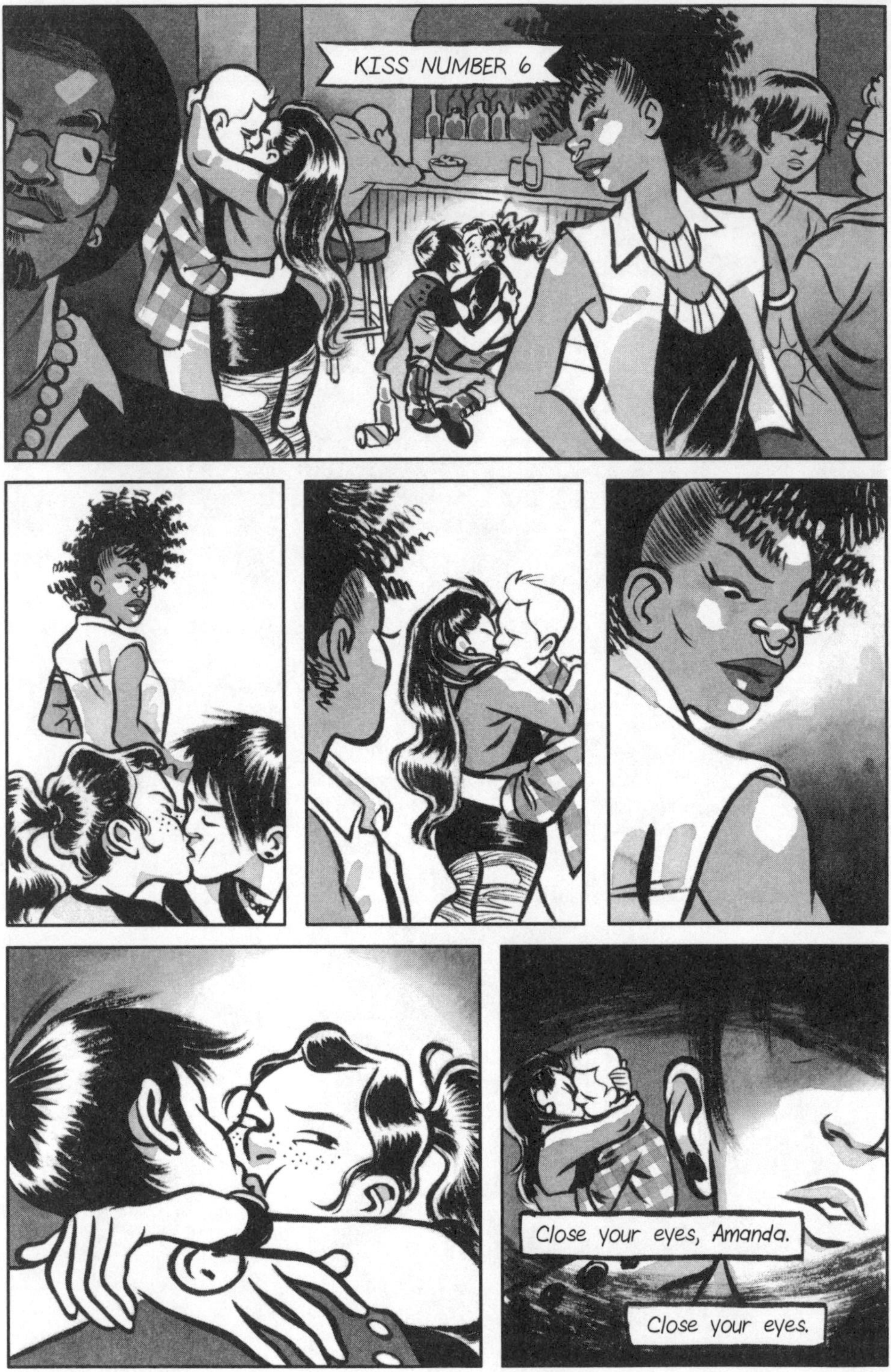
KISS NUMBER 6
Close your eyes, Amanda.
Close your eyes.

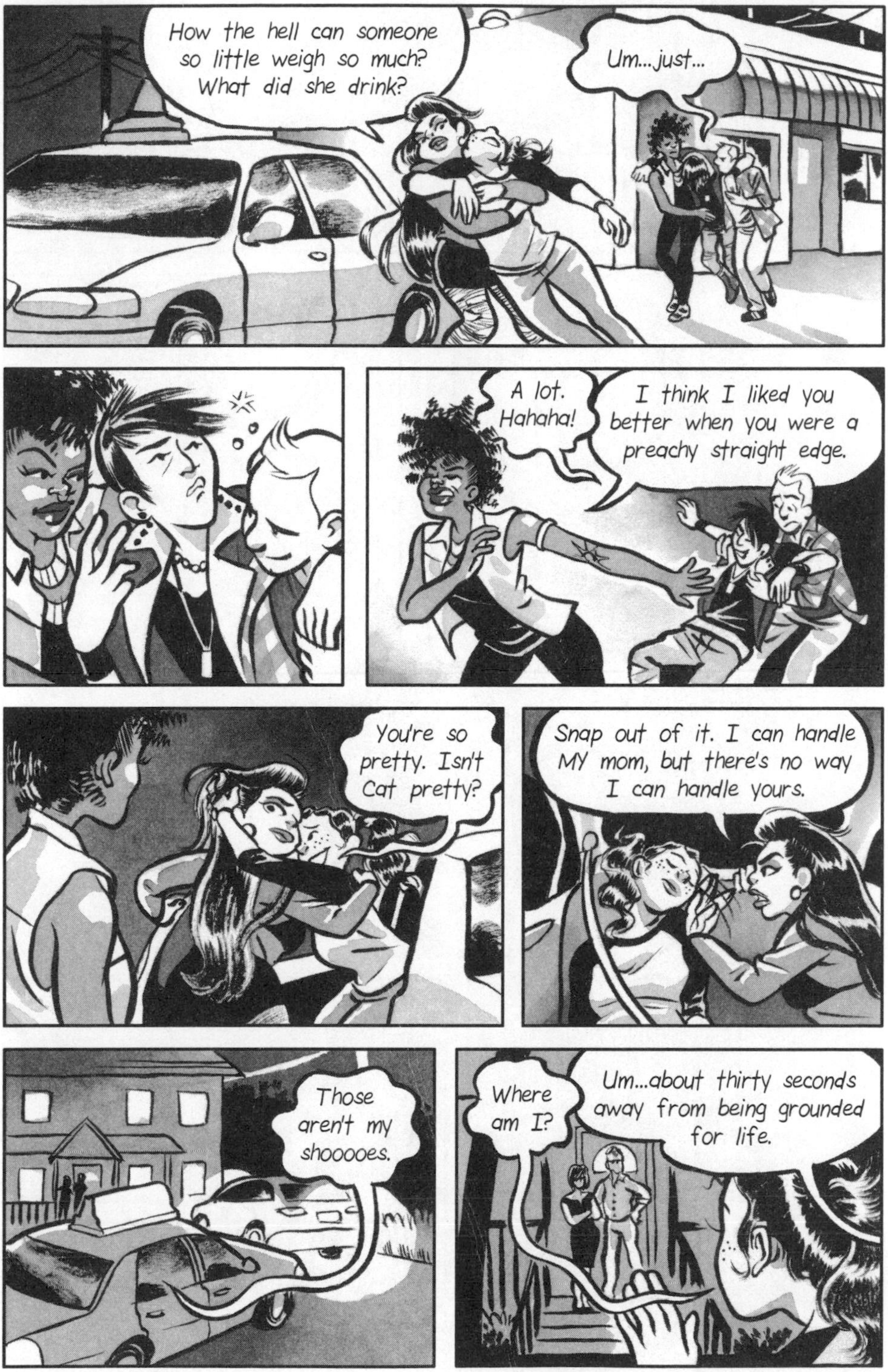
How the hell can someone so little weigh so much? What did she drink?
Um...just...
A lot. Hahaha!
I think I liked you better when you were a preachy straight edge.
You're so pretty. Isn't Cat pretty?
Snap out of it. I can handle MY mom, but there's no way I can handle yours.
Those aren't my shoooooes.
Where am I?
Um...about thirty seconds away from being grounded for life.

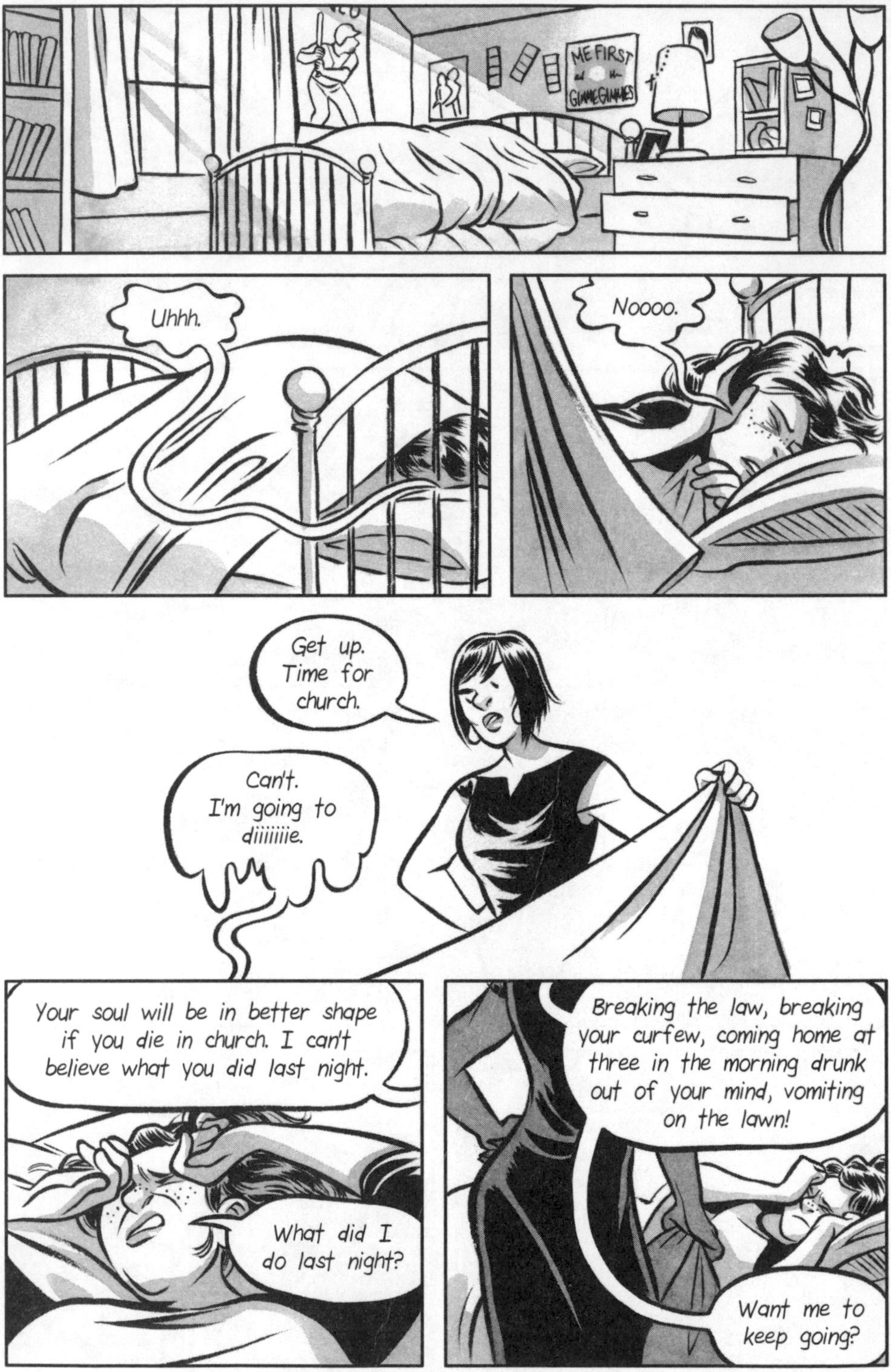
ME FIRST and the GIMME GIMMES
Uhhh.
Noooo.
Get up. Time for church.
Can't. I'm going to diiiiiiie.
Your soul will be in better shape if you die in church. I can't believe what you did last night.
What did I do last night?
Breaking the law, breaking your curfew, coming home at three in the morning drunk out of your mind, vomiting on the lawn!
Want me to keep going?

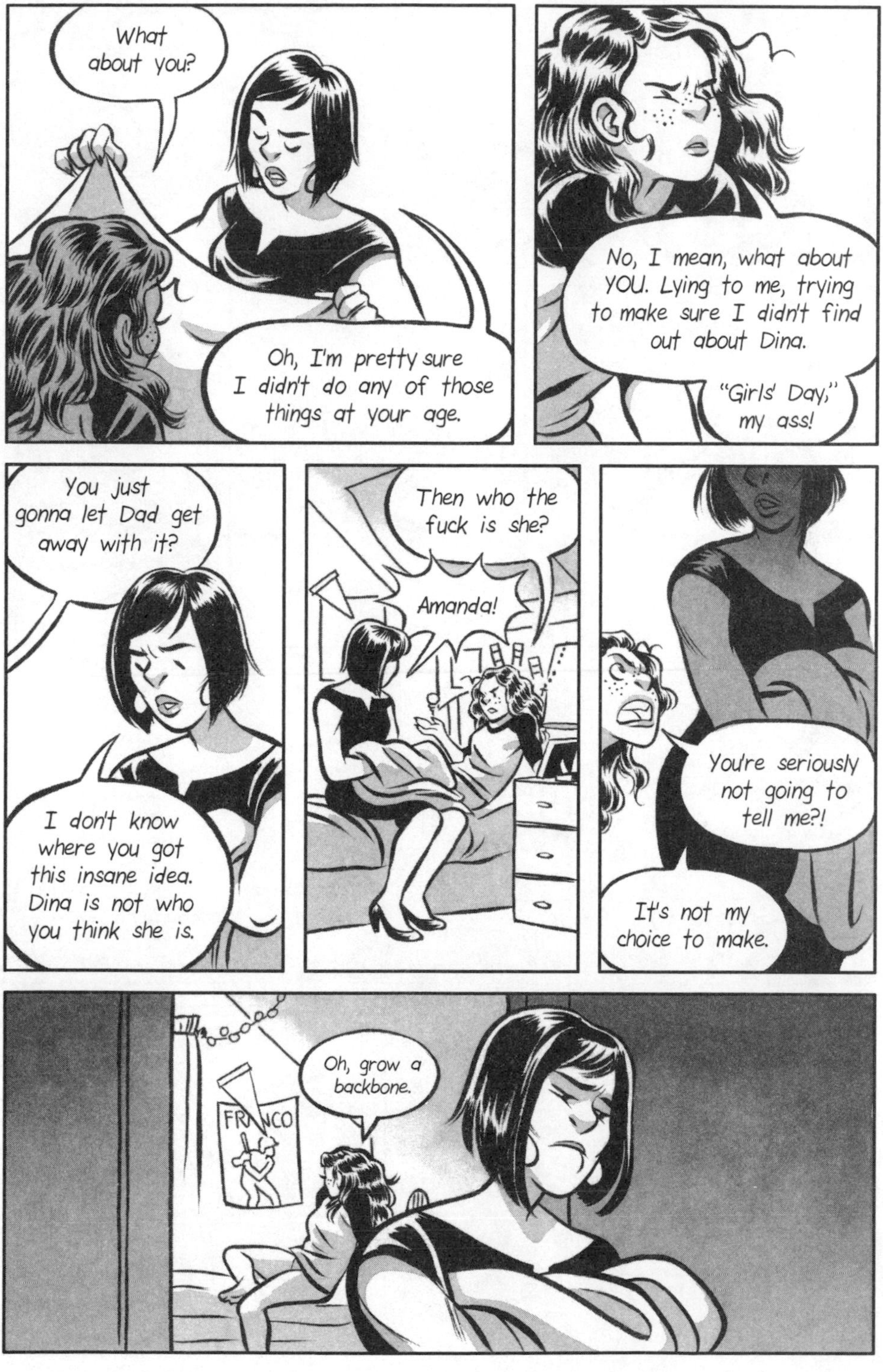
What about you?
Oh, I'm pretty sure I didn't do any of those things at your age.
No, I mean, what about YOU. Lying to me, trying to make sure I didn't find out about Dina.
"Girls' Day," my ass!
You just gonna let Dad get away with it?
I don't know where you got this insane idea. Dina is not who you think she is.
Then who the fuck is she?
Amanda!
You're seriously not going to tell me?!
It's not my choice to make.
Oh, grow a backbone.
FRANCO

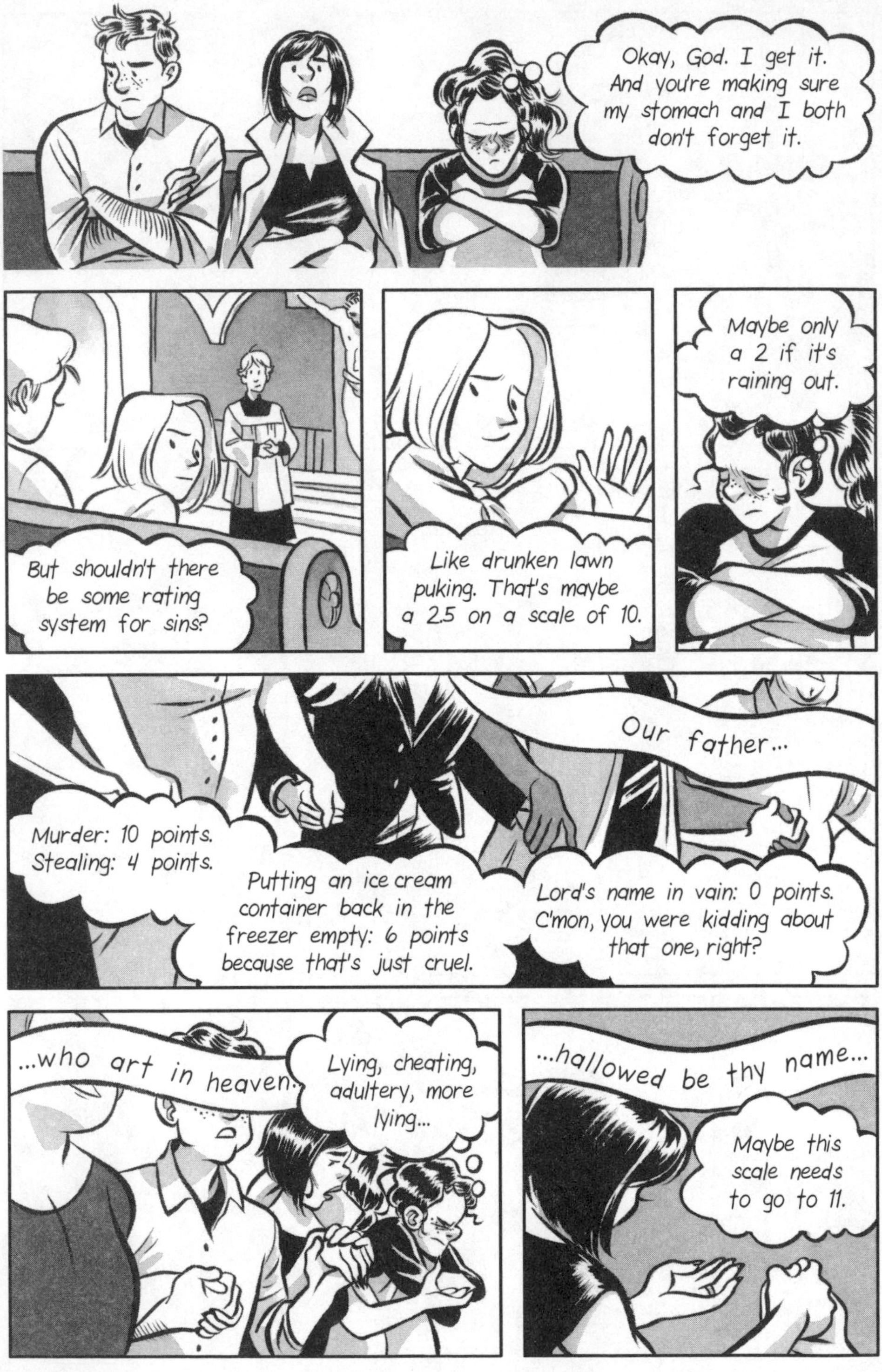
Okay, God. I get it. And you're making sure my stomach and I both don't forget it.
But shouldn't there be some rating system for sins?
Like drunken lawn puking. That's maybe a 2.5 on a scale of 10.
Maybe only a 2 if it's raining out.
Our father...
Murder: 10 points. Stealing: 4 points.
Putting an ice cream container back in the freezer empty: 6 points because that's just cruel.
Lord's name in vain: 0 points. C'mon, you were kidding about that one, right?
...who art in heaven...
Lying, cheating, adultery, more lying...
...hallowed be thy name...
Maybe this scale needs to go to 11.

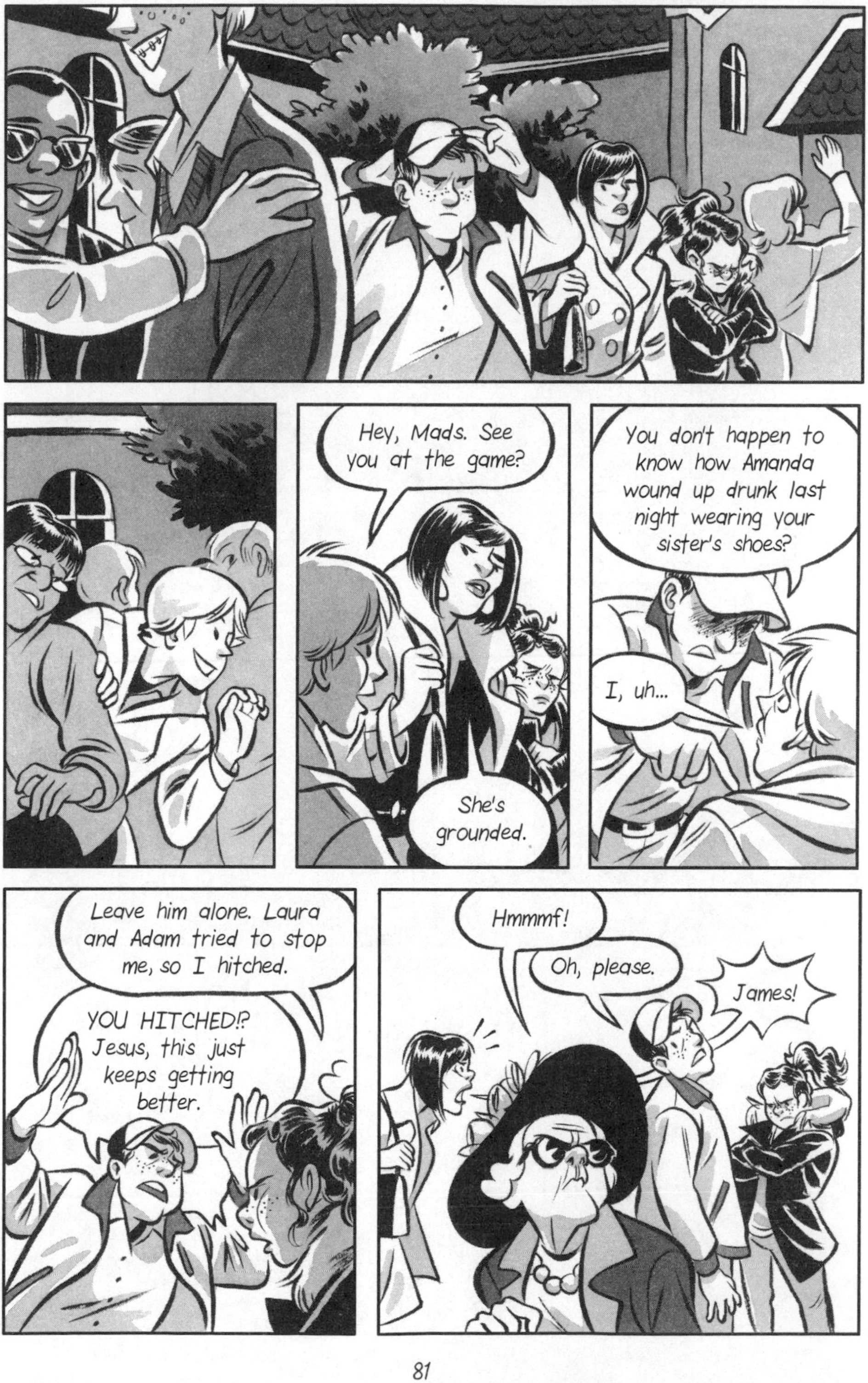
Hey, Mads. See you at the game?
She's grounded.
You don't happen to know how Amanda wound up drunk last night wearing your sister's shoes?
I, uh...
Leave him alone. Laura and Adam tried to stop me, so I hitched.
YOU HITCHED!? Jesus, this just keeps getting better.
Hmmmf!
Oh, please.
James!

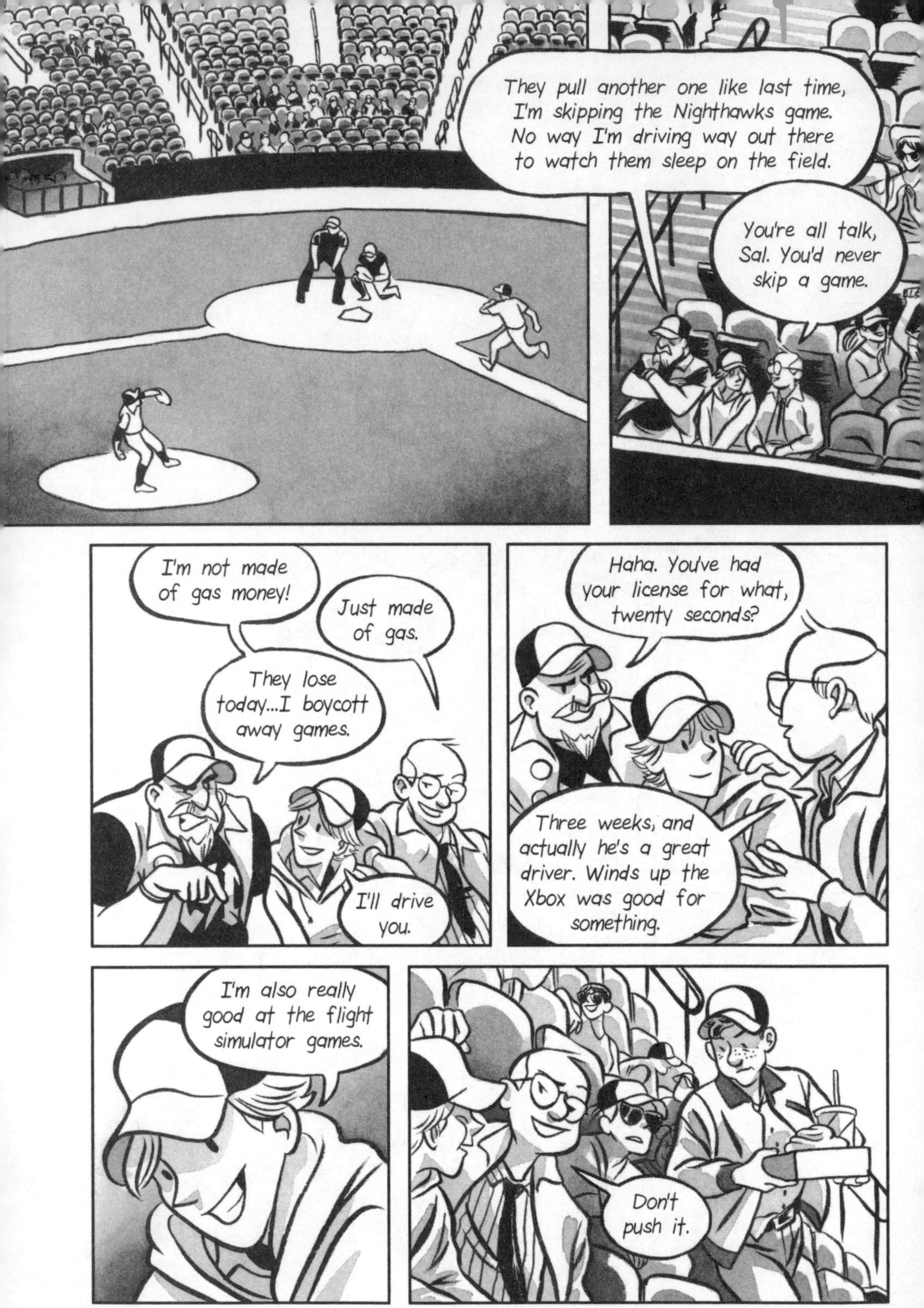
They pull another one like last time, I'm skipping the Nighthawks game. No way I'm driving way out there to watch them sleep on the field.
You're all talk, Sal. You'd never skip a game.
I'm not made of gas money!
Just made of gas.
They lose today...I boycott away games.
I'll drive you.
Haha. You've had your license for what, twenty seconds?
Three weeks, and actually he's a great driver. Winds up the Xbox was good for something.
I'm also really good at the flight simulator games.
Don't push it.

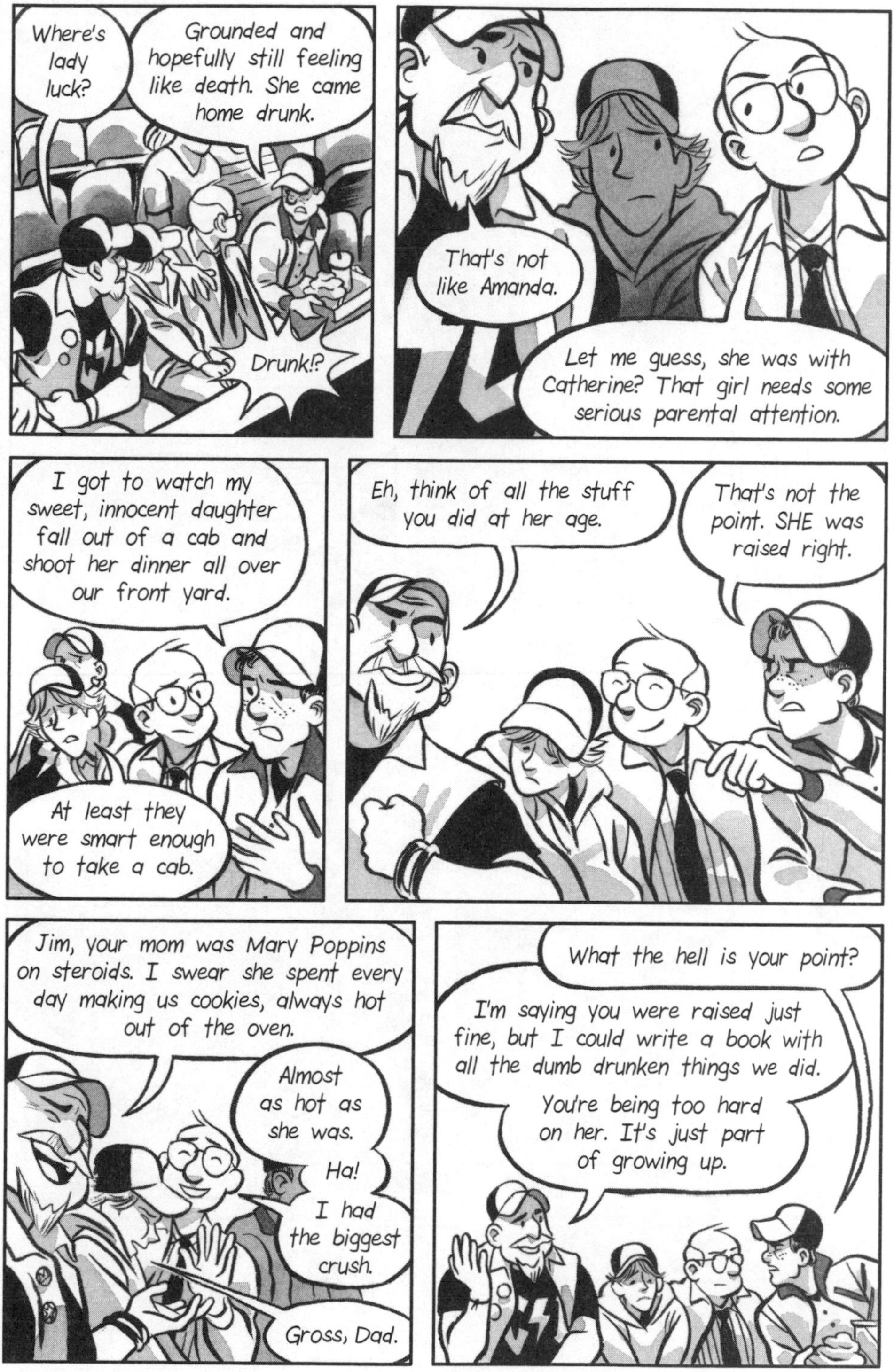
Where's lady luck?
Grounded and hopefully still feeling like death. She came home drunk.
Drunk!?
That's not like Amanda.
Let me guess, she was with Catherine? That girl needs some serious parental attention.
I got to watch my sweet, innocent daughter fall out of a cab and shoot her dinner all over our front yard.
At least they were smart enough to take a cab.
Eh, think of all the stuff you did at her age.
That's not the point. SHE was raised right.
Jim, your mom was Mary Poppins on steroids. I swear she spent every day making us cookies, always hot out of the oven.
Almost as hot as she was.
Ha!
I had the biggest crush.
Gross, Dad.
What the hell is your point?
I'm saying you were raised just fine, but I could write a book with all the dumb drunken things we did.
You're being too hard on her. It's just part of growing up.

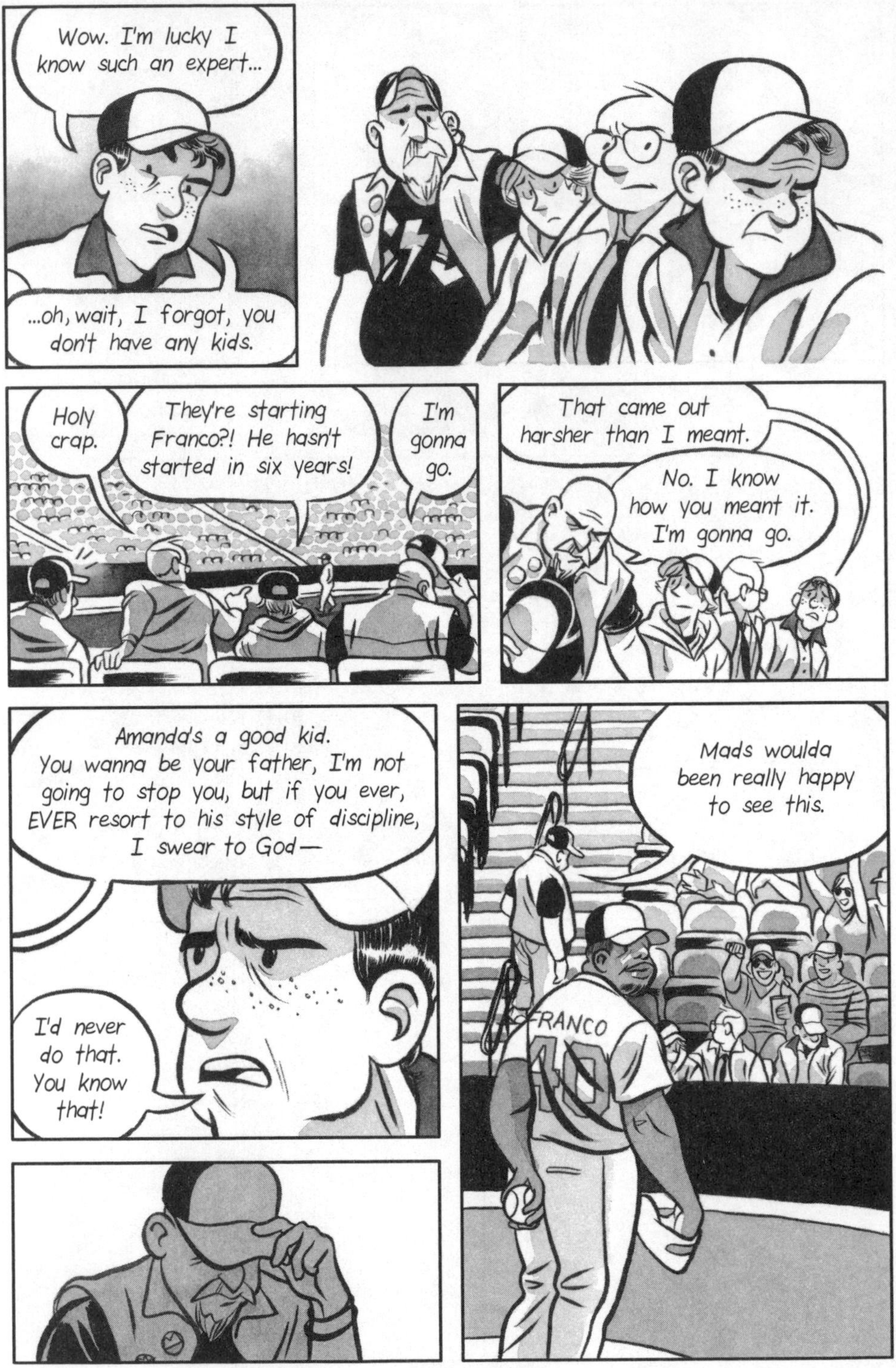

Wow. I'm lucky I know such an expert...
...oh, wait, I forgot, you don't have any kids.
Holy crap.
They're starting Franco?! He hasn't started in six years!
I'm gonna go.
That came out harsher than I meant.
No. I know how you meant it. I'm gonna go.
Amanda's a good kid. You wanna be your father, I'm not going to stop you, but if you ever, EVER resort to his style of discipline, I swear to God—
I'd never do that. You know that!
Mads woulda been really happy to see this.
FRANCO

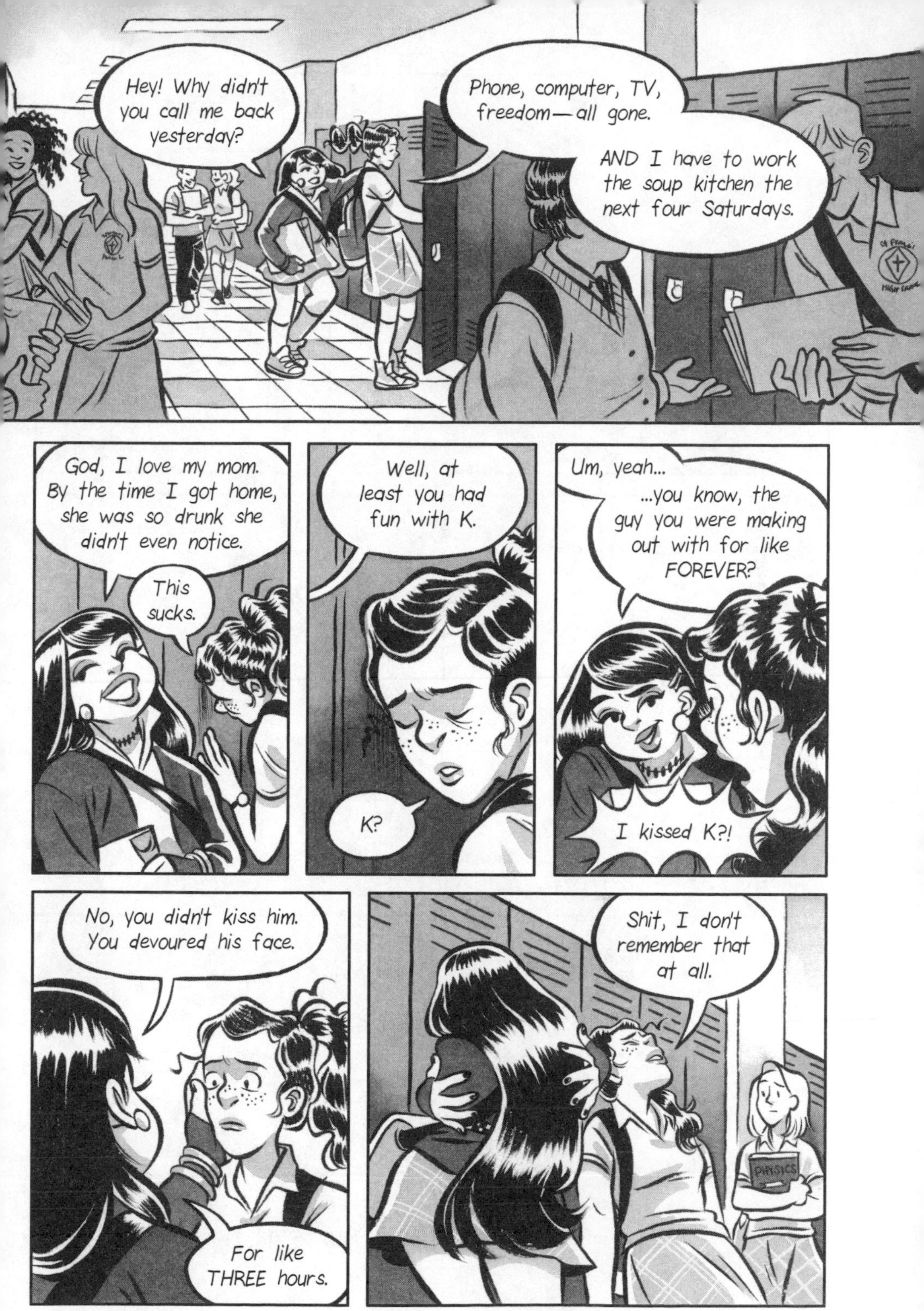
Hey! Why didn't you call me back yesterday?
Phone, computer, TV, freedom—all gone.
AND I have to work the soup kitchen the next four Saturdays.
God, I love my mom. By the time I got home, she was so drunk she didn't even notice.
This sucks.
Well, at least you had fun with K.
K?
Um, yeah...
...you know, the guy you were making out with for like FOREVER?
I kissed K?!
No, you didn't kiss him. You devoured his face.
For like THREE hours.
Shit, I don't remember that at all.
PHYSICS

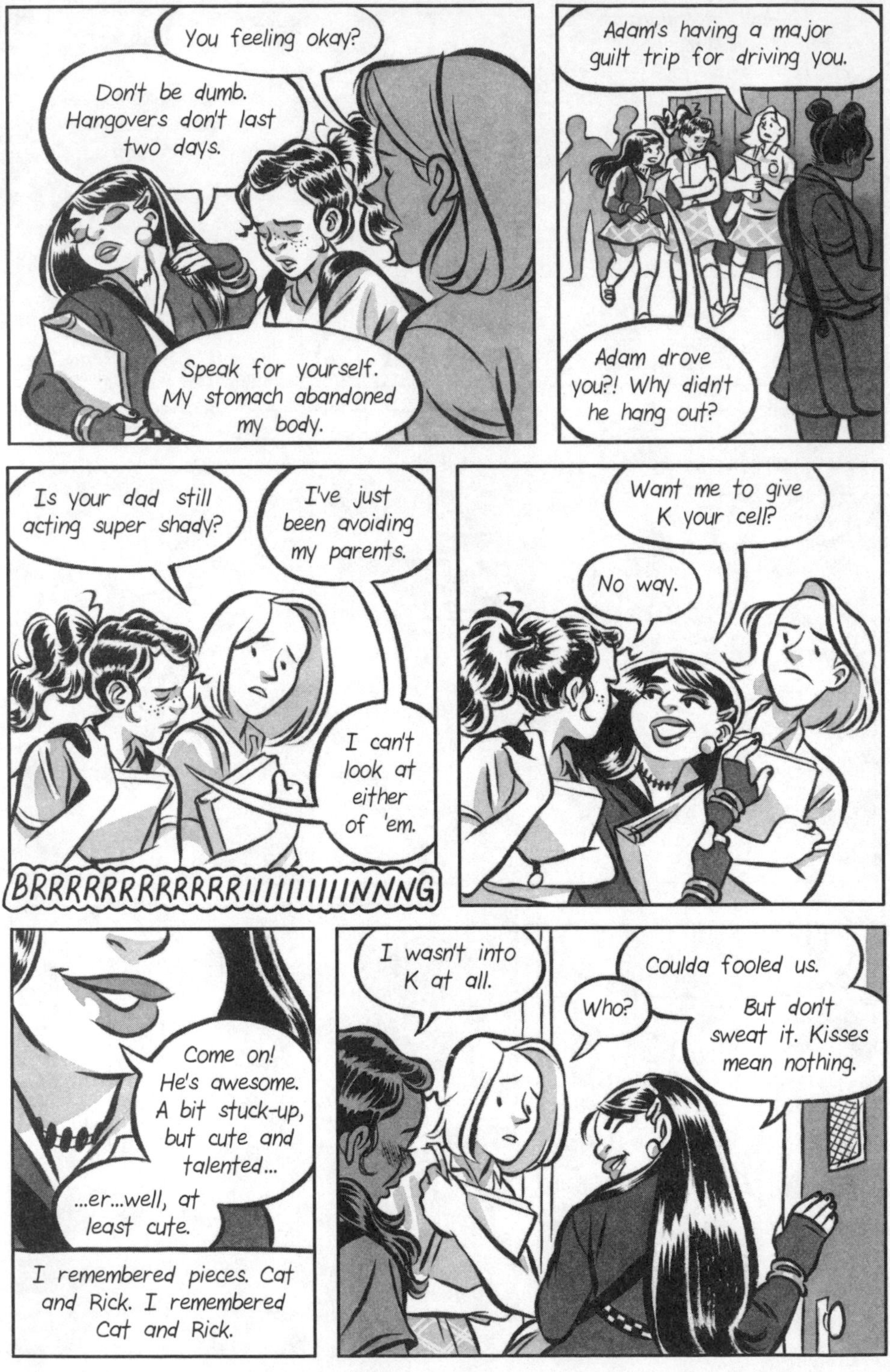
You feeling okay?
Don't be dumb. Hangovers don't last two days.
Speak for yourself. My stomach abandoned my body.
Adam's having a major guilt trip for driving you.
Adam drove you?! Why didn't he hang out?
Is your dad still acting super shady?
I've just been avoiding my parents.
I can't look at either of 'em.
BRRRRRRRRRRRRRIIIIIIIIIIINNNG
Want me to give K your cell?
No way.
Come on! He's awesome. A bit stuck-up, but cute and talented...
...er...well, at least cute.
I remembered pieces. Cat and Rick. I remembered Cat and Rick.
I wasn't into K at all.
Coulda fooled us.
Who?
But don't sweat it. Kisses mean nothing.

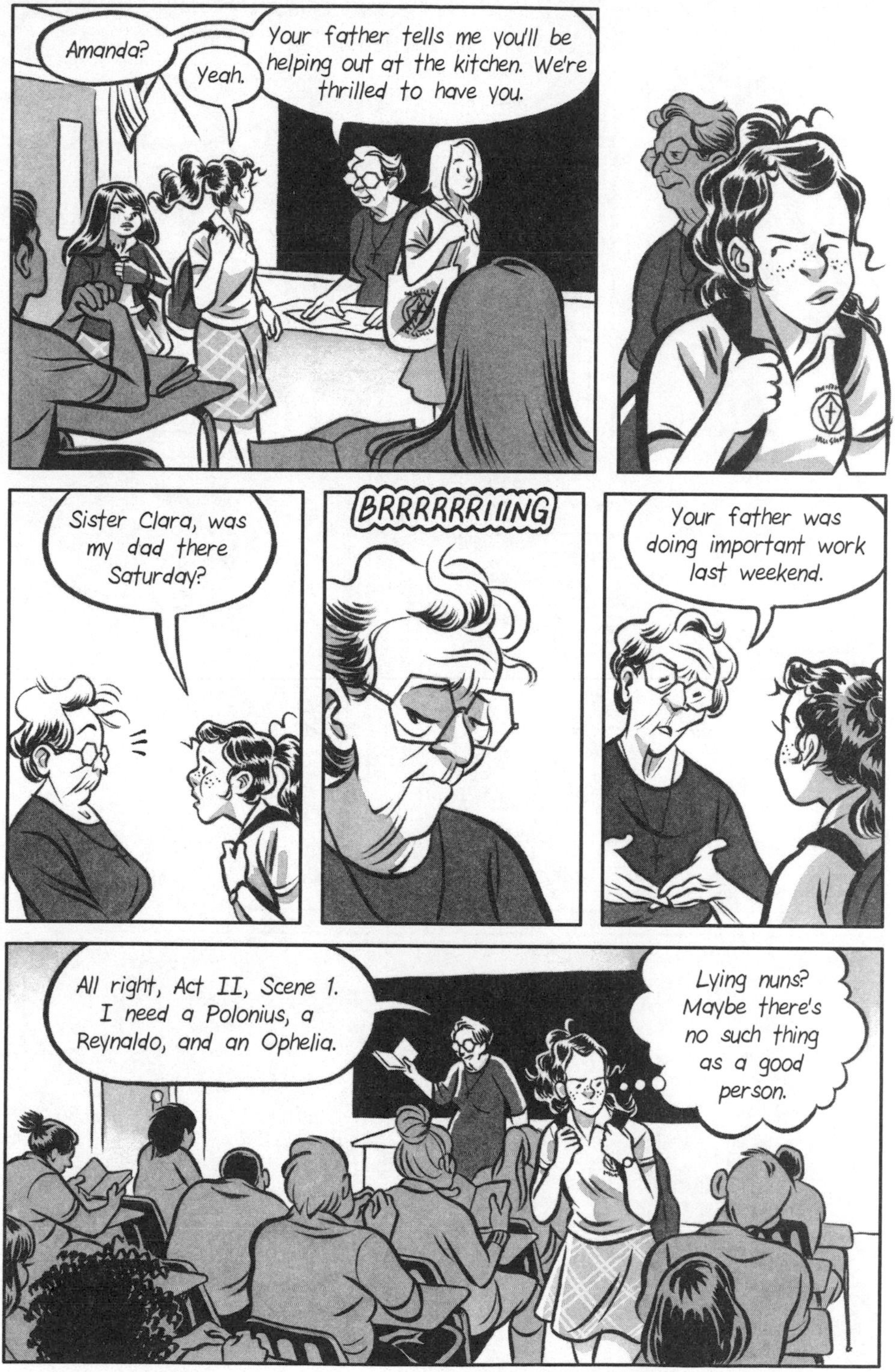
Amanda?
Yeah.
Your father tells me you'll be helping out at the kitchen. We're thrilled to have you.
Sister Clara, was my dad there Saturday?
BRRRRRRRIIING
Your father was doing important work last weekend.
All right, Act II, Scene 1. I need a Polonius, a Reynaldo, and an Ophelia.
Lying nuns? Maybe there's no such thing as a good person.

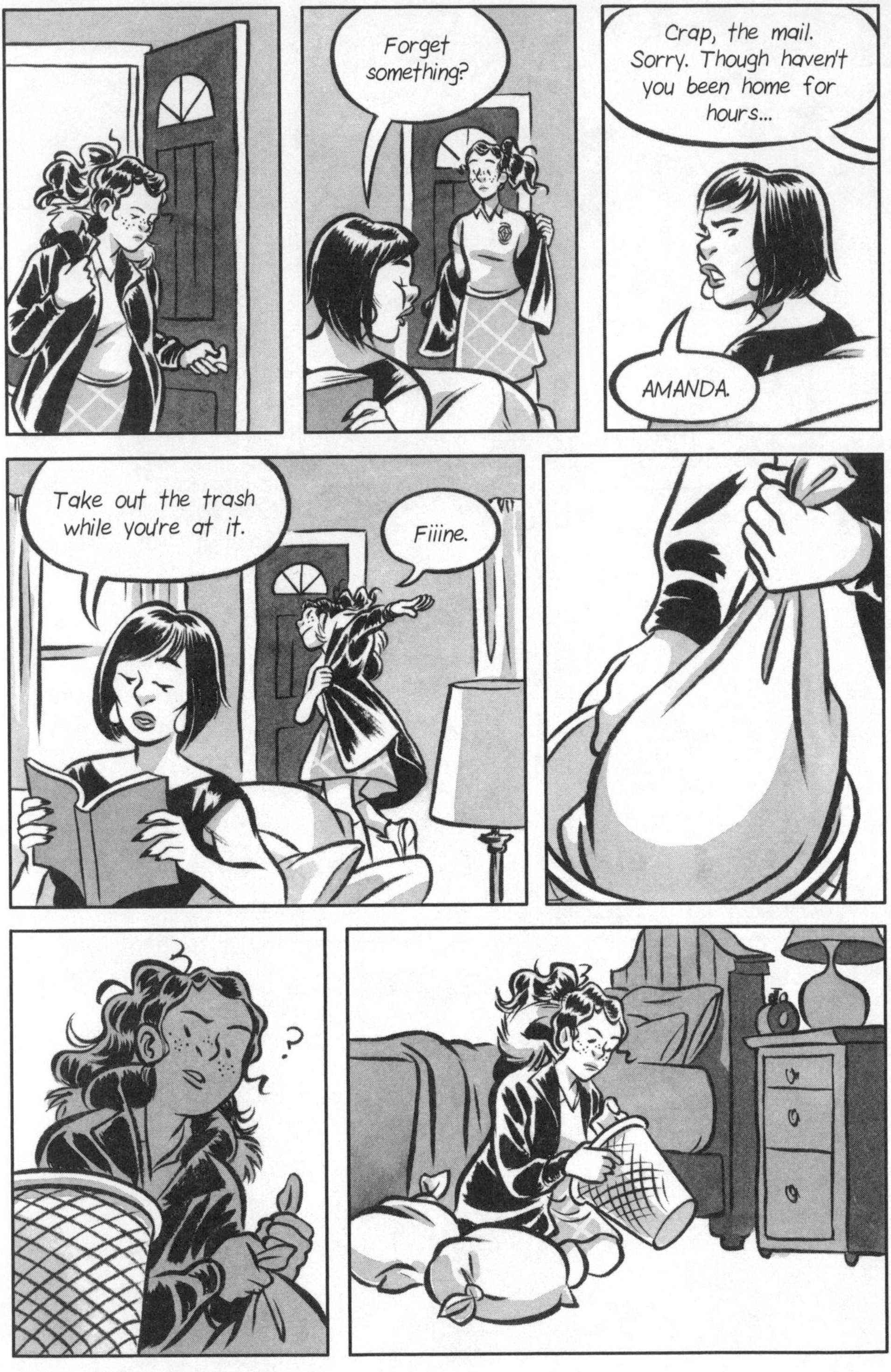
Forget something?
Crap, the mail. Sorry. Though haven't you been home for hours...
AMANDA.
Take out the trash while you're at it.
Fiiine.
?

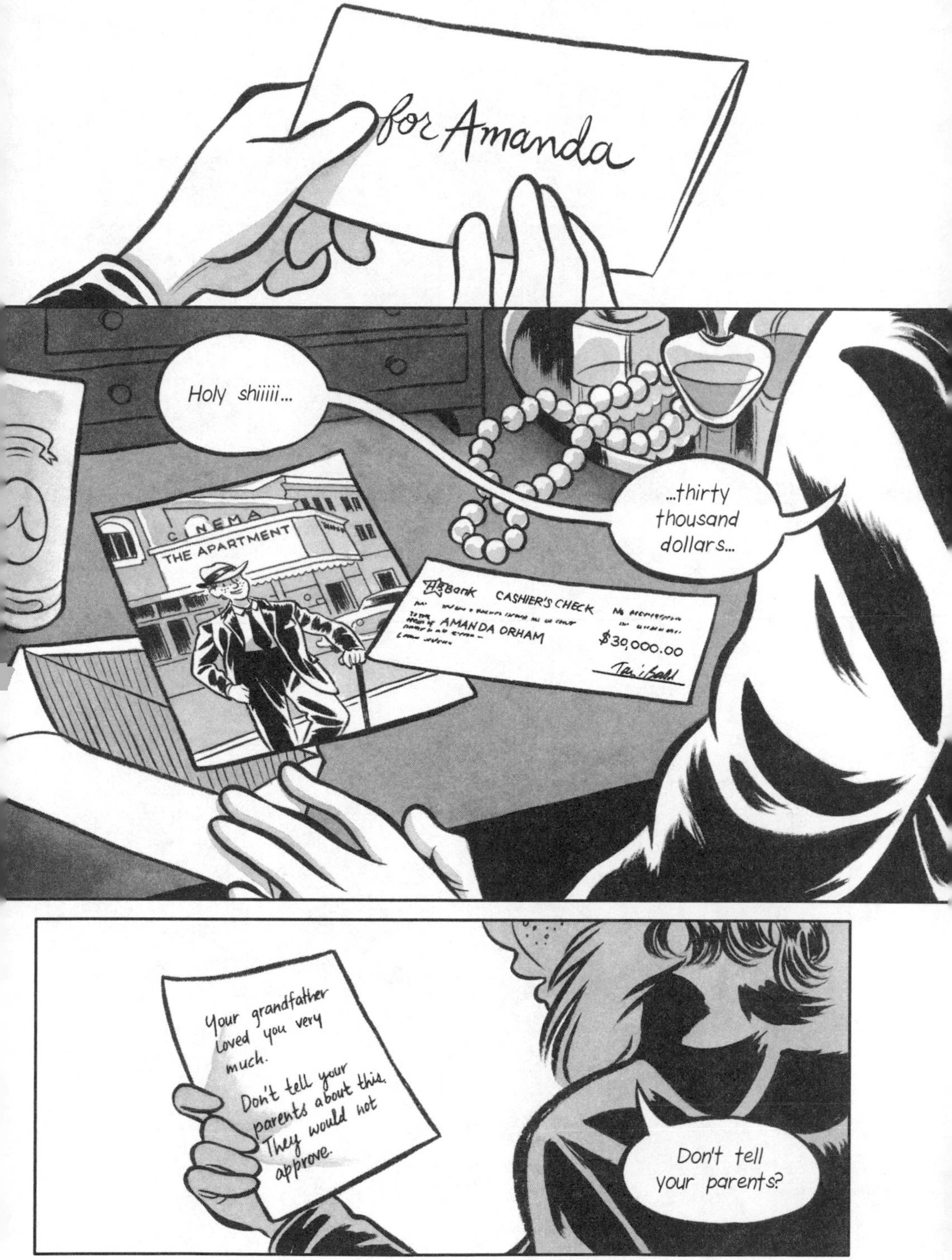
for Amanda
Holy shiiiii...
...thirty thousand dollars...
CINEMA
THE APARTMENT
Bank CASHIER'S CHECK
AMANDA ORHAM
$30,000.00
Your grandfather loved you very much.
Don't tell your parents about this. They would not approve.
Don't tell your parents?

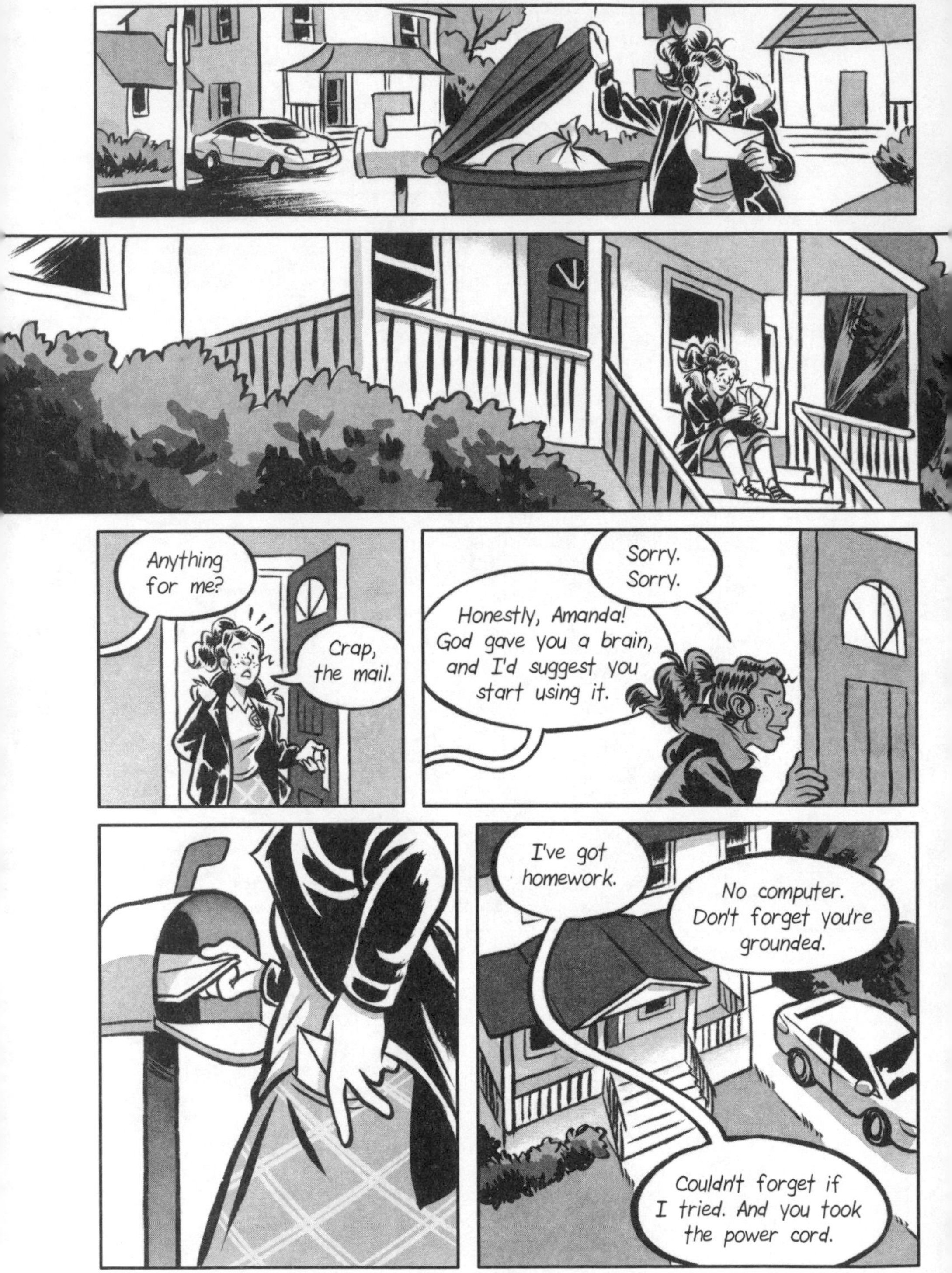
Anything for me?
Crap, the mail.
Sorry. Sorry.
Honestly, Amanda! God gave you a brain, and I'd suggest you start using it.
I've got homework.
No computer. Don't forget you're grounded.
Couldn't forget if I tried. And you took the power cord.

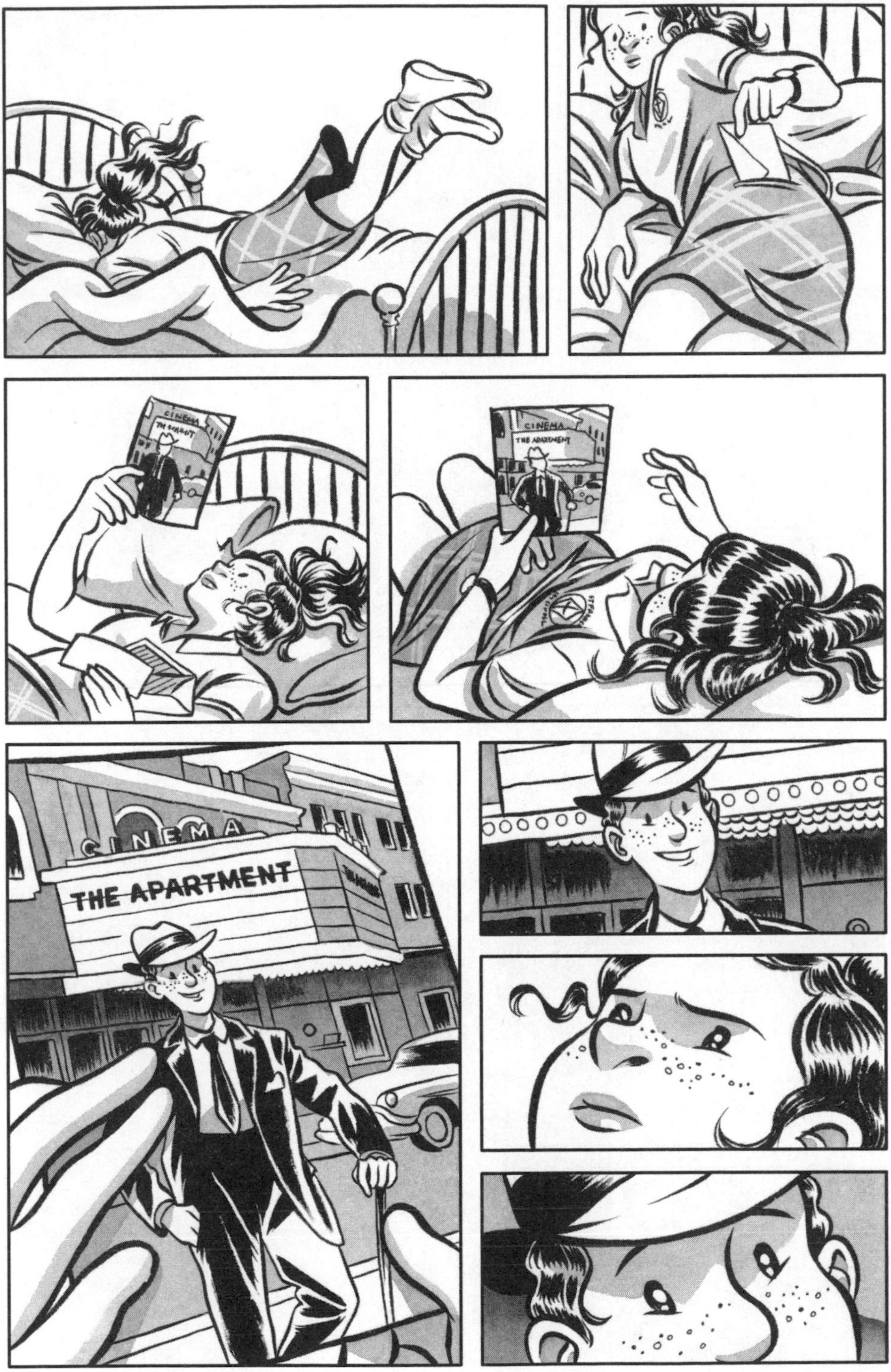
CINEMA
THE APARTMENT

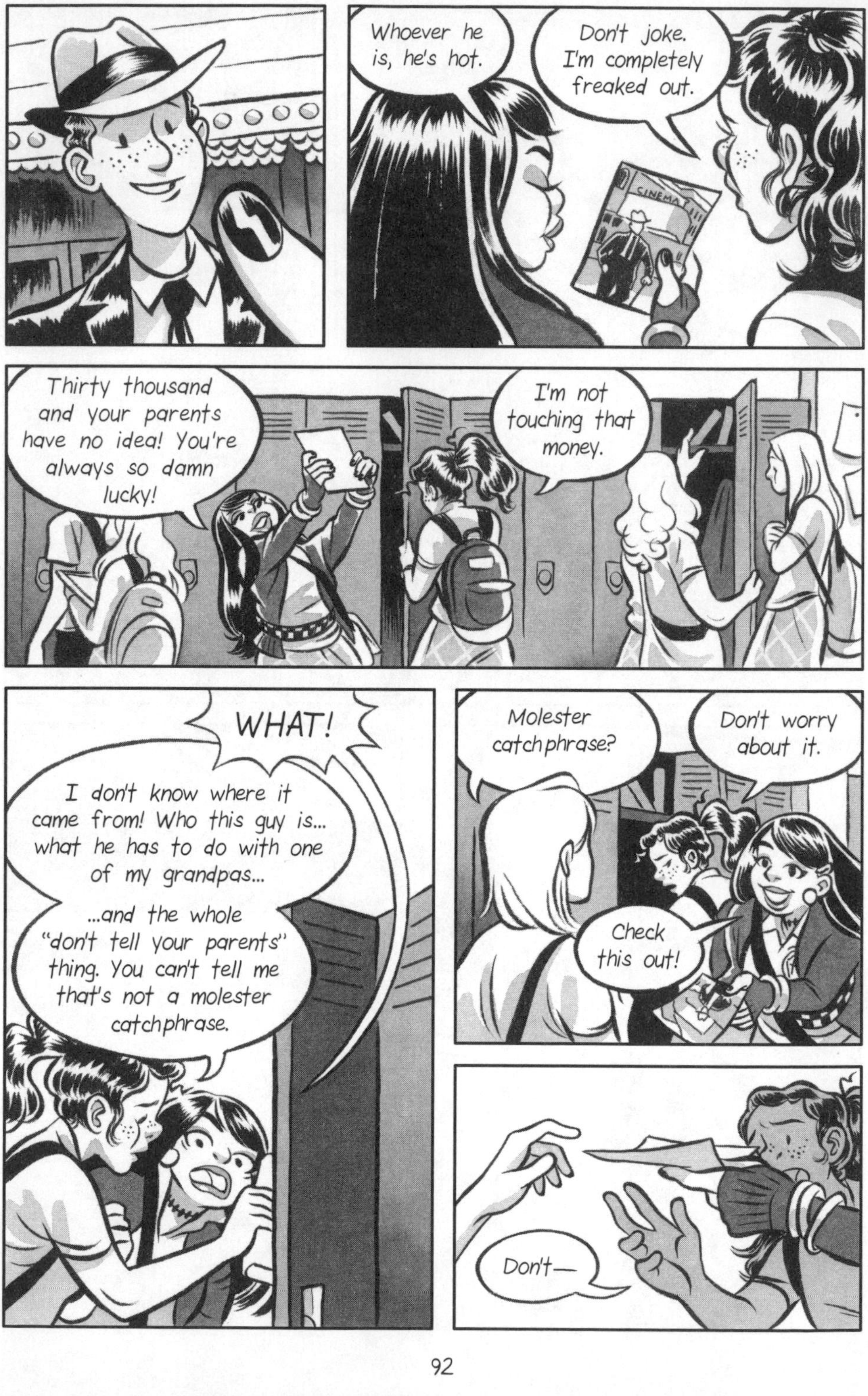
Whoever he is, he's hot.
Don't joke. I'm completely freaked out.
CINEMA
Thirty thousand and your parents have no idea! You're always so damn lucky!
I'm not touching that money.
WHAT!
I don't know where it came from! Who this guy is... what he has to do with one of my grandpas...
...and the whole "don't tell your parents" thing. You can't tell me that's not a molester catchphrase.
Molester catchphrase?
Don't worry about it.
Check this out!
Don't—

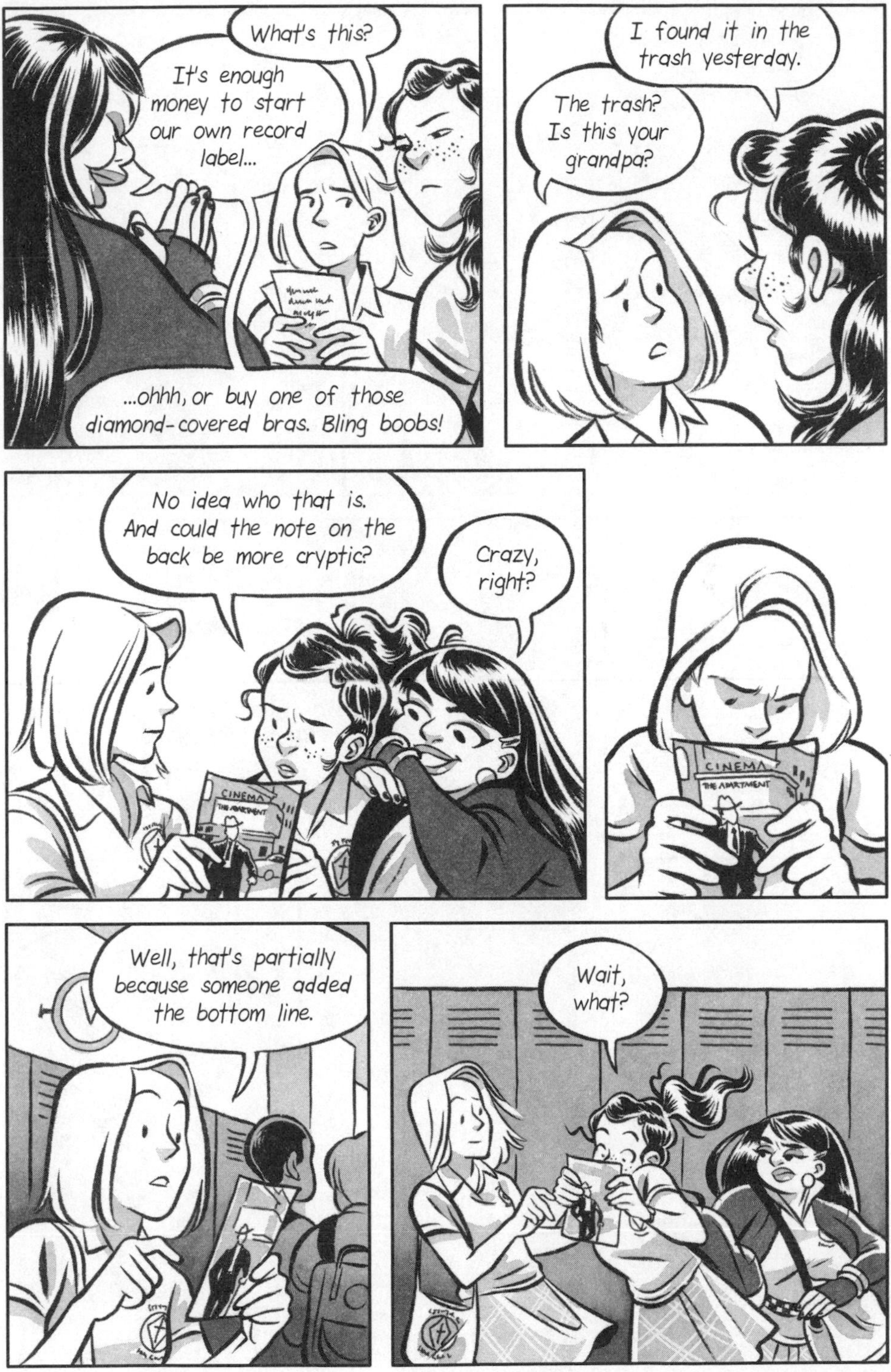
What's this?
It's enough money to start our own record label...
...ohhh, or buy one of those diamond-covered bras. Bling boobs!
I found it in the trash yesterday.
The trash? Is this your grandpa?
No idea who that is. And could the note on the back be more cryptic?
Crazy, right?
CINEMA
THE APARTMENT
CINEMA
THE APARTMENT
Well, that's partially because someone added the bottom line.
Wait, what?

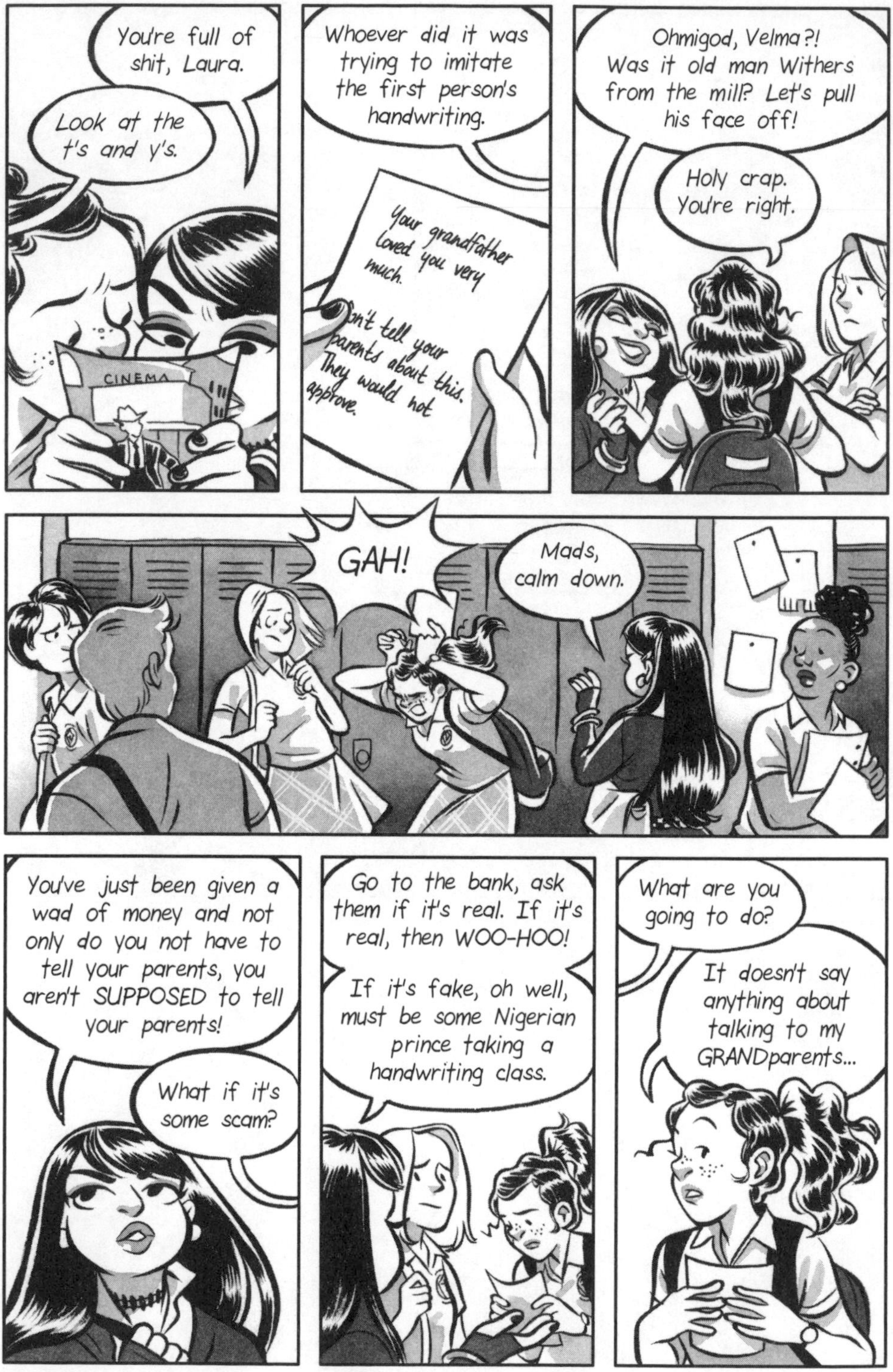
You're full of shit, Laura.
Look at the t's and y's.
Whoever did it was trying to imitate the first person's handwriting.
Your grandfather loved you very much.
...n't tell your parents about this. They would not approve.
Ohmigod, Velma?! Was it old man Withers from the mill? Let's pull his face off!
Holy crap. You're right.
GAH!
Mads, calm down.
You've just been given a wad of money and not only do you not have to tell your parents, you aren't SUPPOSED to tell your parents!
What if it's some scam?
Go to the bank, ask them if it's real. If it's real, then WOO-HOO!
If it's fake, oh well, must be some Nigerian prince taking a handwriting class.
What are you going to do?
It doesn't say anything about talking to my GRANDparents...

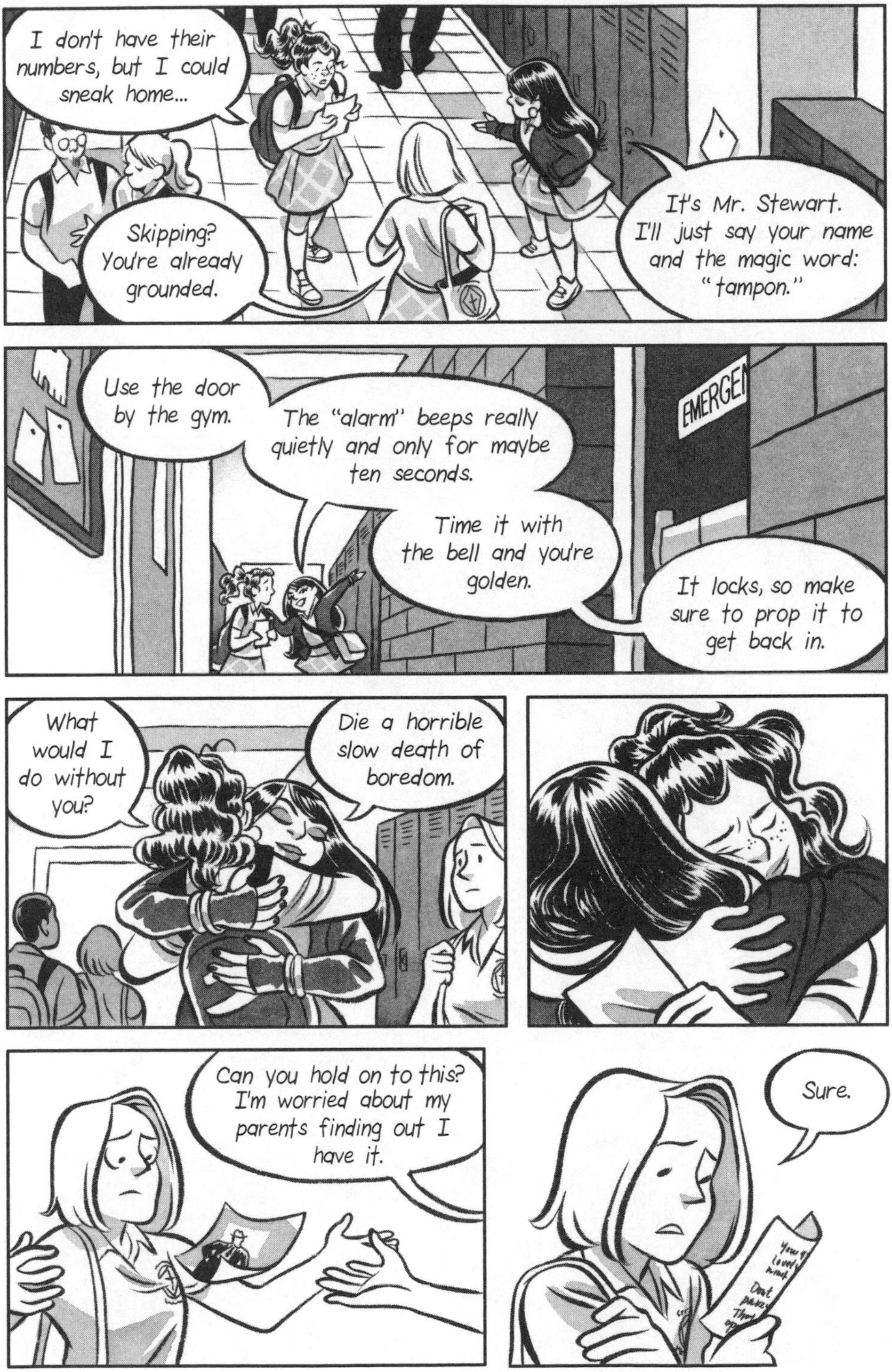
I don't have their numbers, but I could sneak home...
Skipping? You're already grounded.
It's Mr. Stewart. I'll just say your name and the magic word: "tampon."
Use the door by the gym.
The "alarm" beeps really quietly and only for maybe ten seconds.
Time it with the bell and you're golden.
It locks, so make sure to prop it to get back in.
EMERGEN
What would I do without you?
Die a horrible slow death of boredom.
Can you hold on to this? I'm worried about my parents finding out I have it.
Sure.

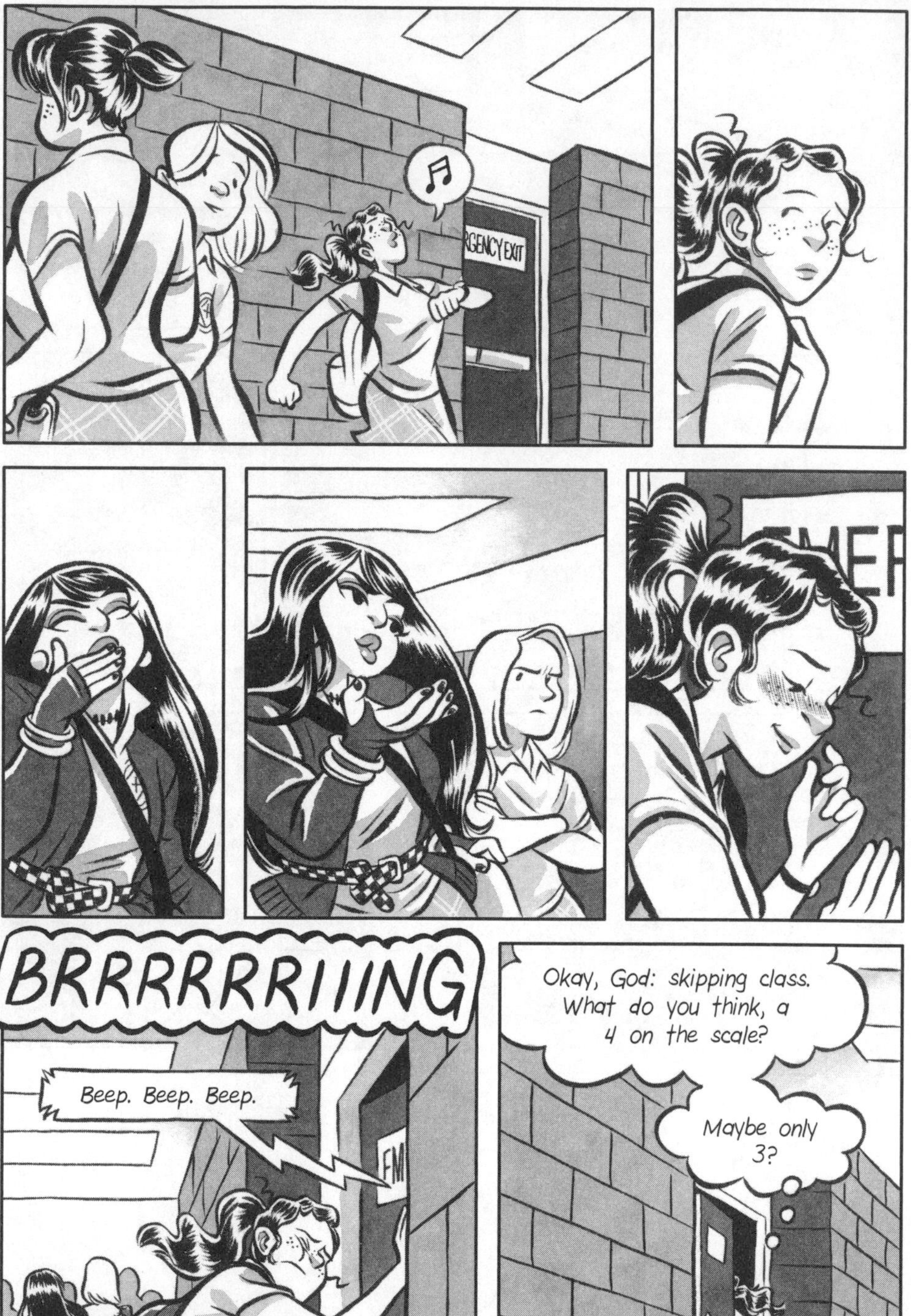
♫
RGENCY EXIT
EMER
BRRRRRRIIING
Beep. Beep. Beep.
EM
Okay, God: skipping class. What do you think, a 4 on the scale?
Maybe only 3?

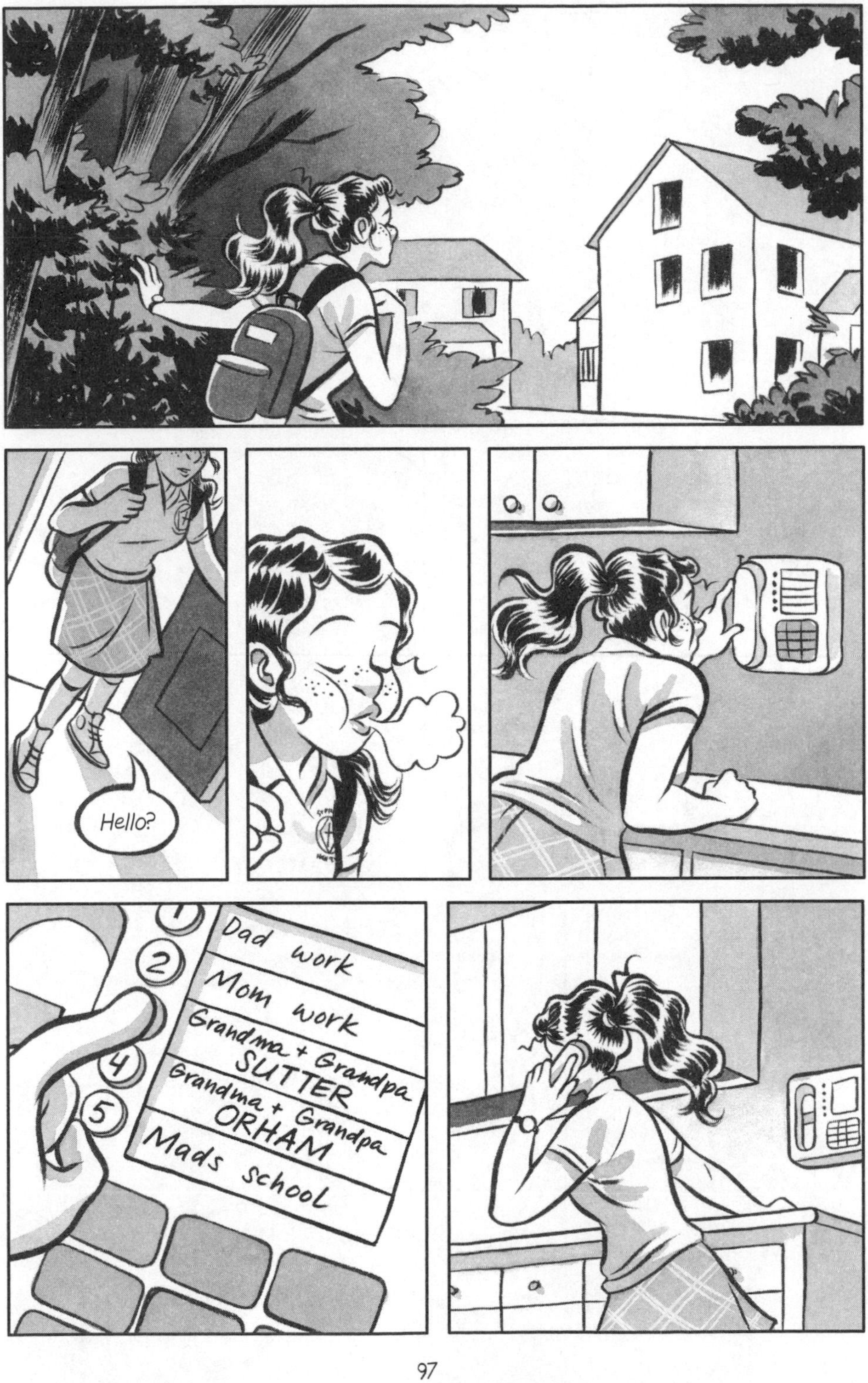
Hello?
Dad work
Mom work
Grandma + Grandpa SUTTER
Grandma + Grandpa ORHAM
Mads school

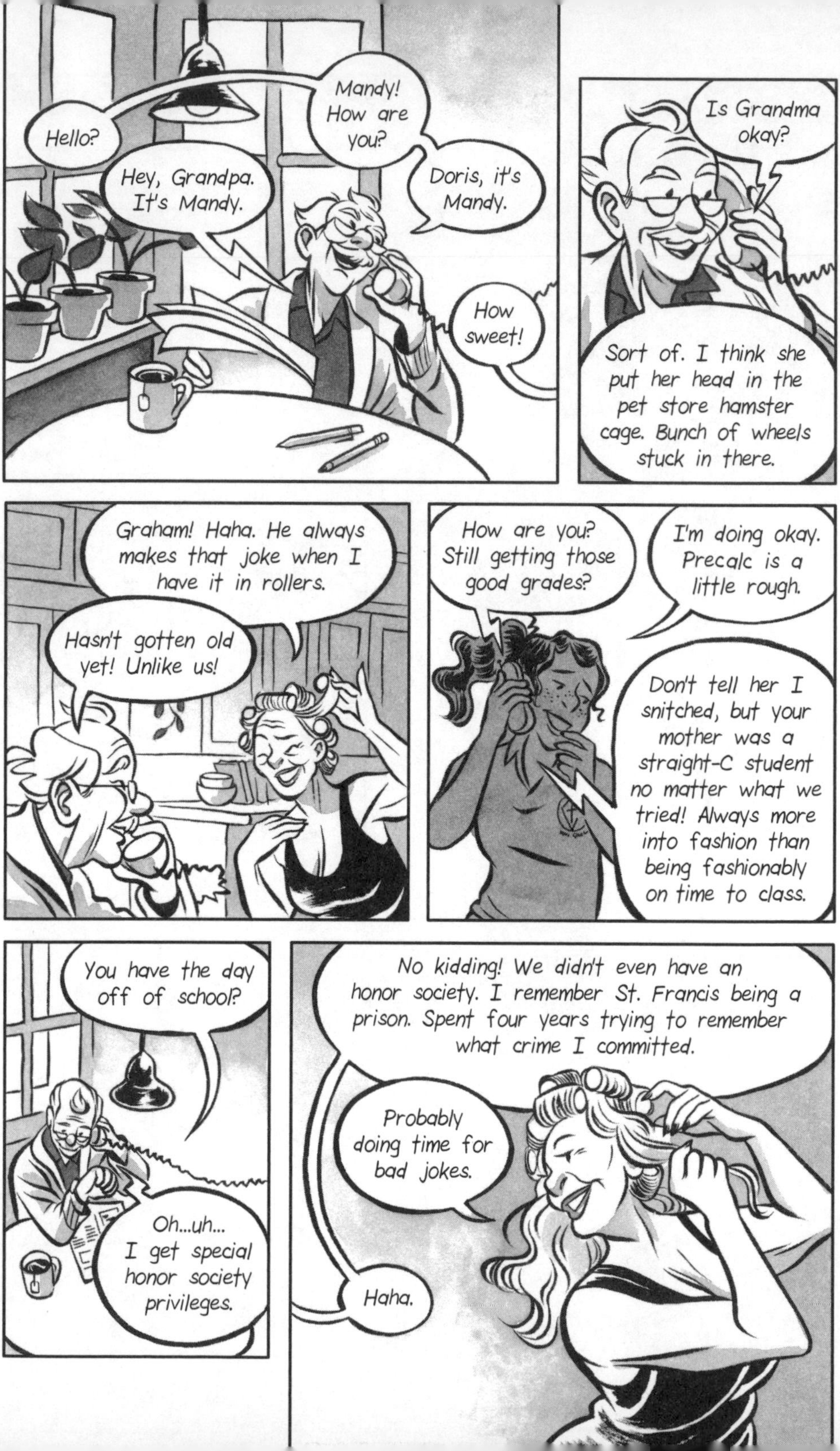
Hello?
Hey, Grandpa. It's Mandy.
Mandy! How are you?
Doris, it's Mandy.
How sweet!
Is Grandma okay?
Sort of. I think she put her head in the pet store hamster cage. Bunch of wheels stuck in there.
Graham! Haha. He always makes that joke when I have it in rollers.
Hasn't gotten old yet! Unlike us!
How are you? Still getting those good grades?
I'm doing okay. Precalc is a little rough.
Don't tell her I snitched, but your mother was a straight-C student no matter what we tried! Always more into fashion than being fashionably on time to class.
You have the day off of school?
Oh...uh... I get special honor society privileges.
No kidding! We didn't even have an honor society. I remember St. Francis being a prison. Spent four years trying to remember what crime I committed.
Probably doing time for bad jokes.
Haha.

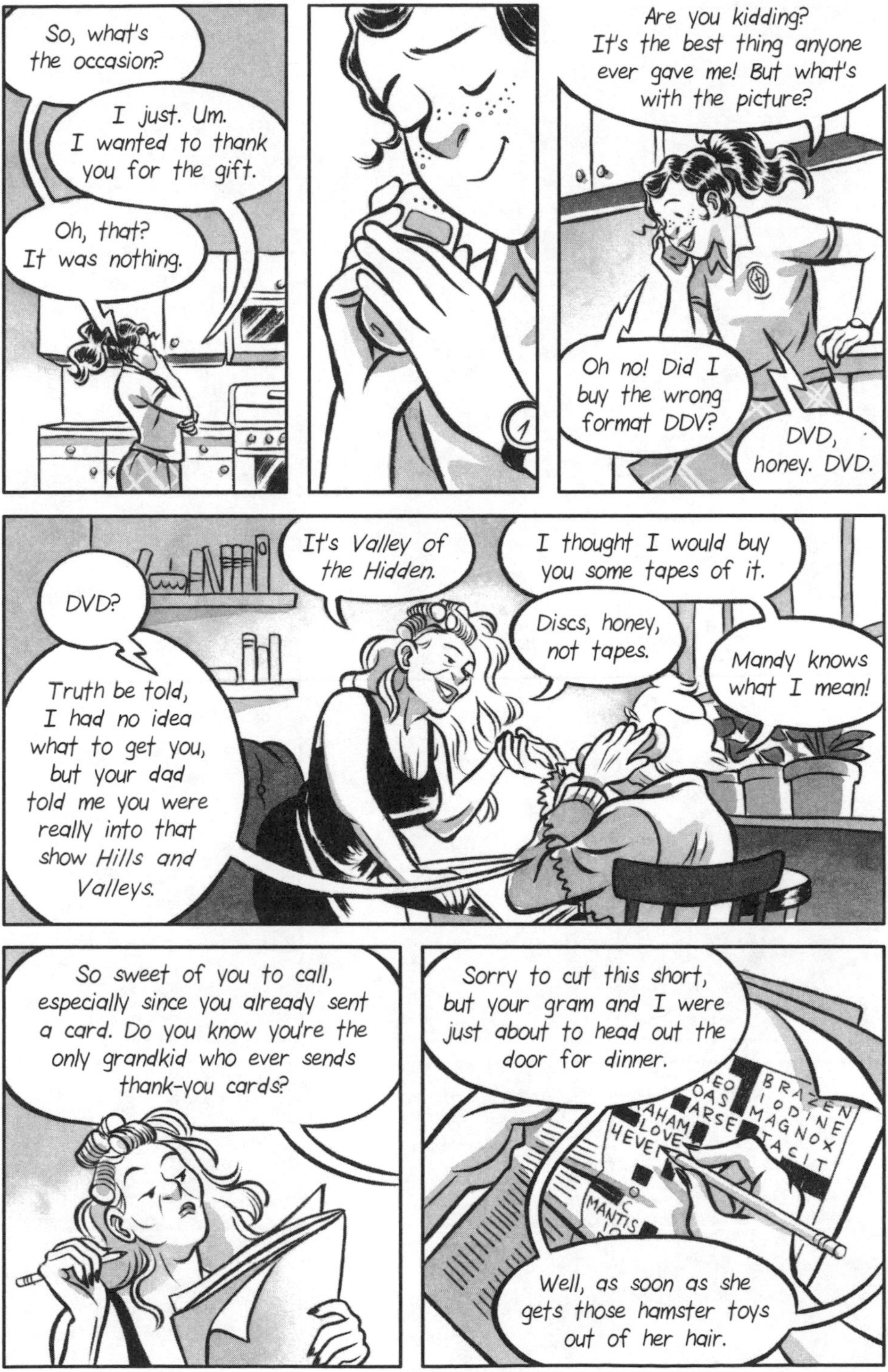
So, what's the occasion?
I just. Um. I wanted to thank you for the gift.
Oh, that? It was nothing.
Are you kidding? It's the best thing anyone ever gave me! But what's with the picture?
Oh no! Did I buy the wrong format DDV?
DVD, honey. DVD.
DVD?
Truth be told, I had no idea what to get you, but your dad told me you were really into that show *Hills and Valleys*.
It's *Valley of the Hidden*.
I thought I would buy you some tapes of it.
Discs, honey, not tapes.
Mandy knows what I mean!
So sweet of you to call, especially since you already sent a card. Do you know you're the only grandkid who ever sends thank-you cards?
Sorry to cut this short, but your gram and I were just about to head out the door for dinner.
BRAZEN
IODINE
MAGNOX
TACIT
Well, as soon as she gets those hamster toys out of her hair.

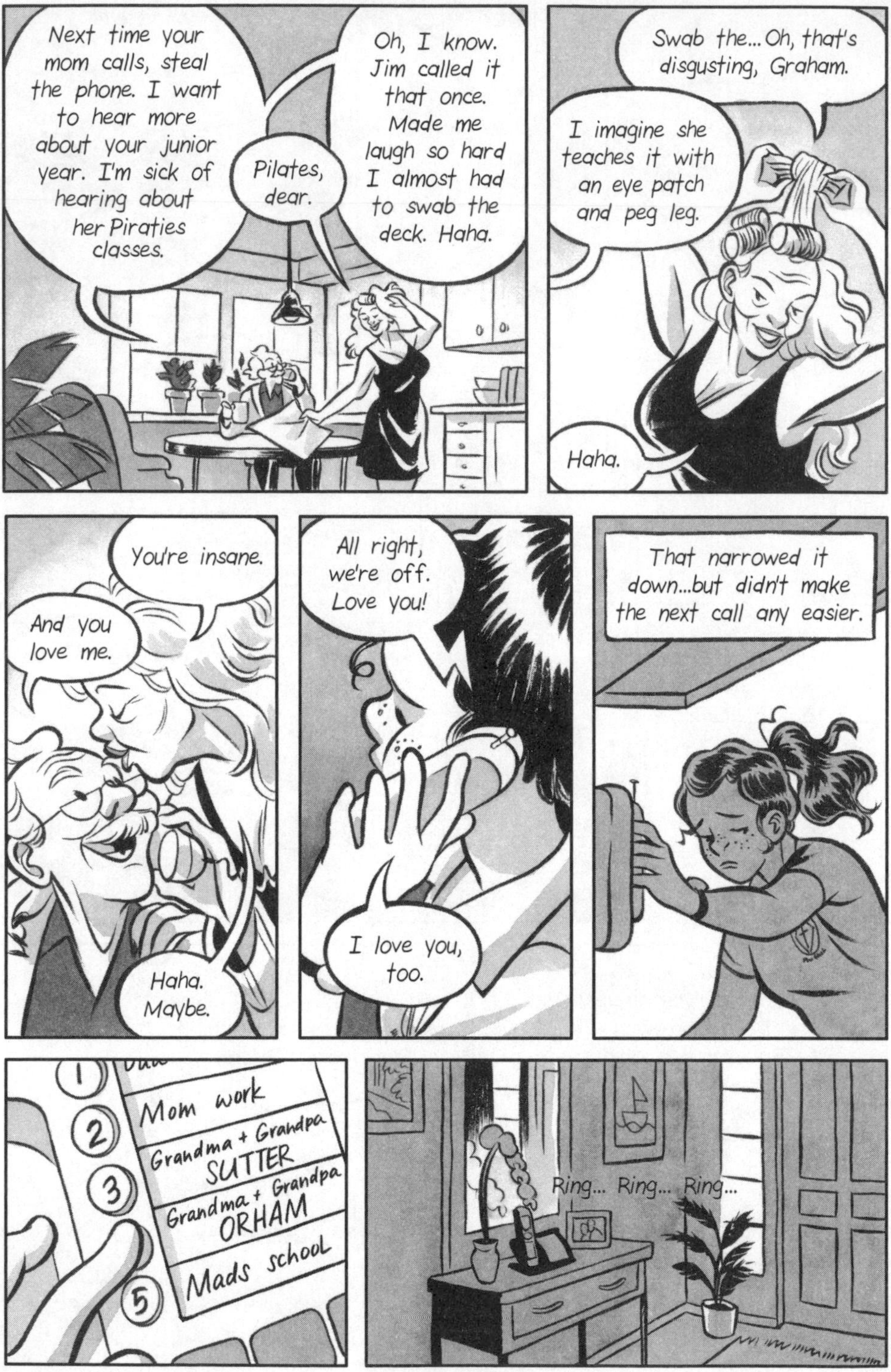
Next time your mom calls, steal the phone. I want to hear more about your junior year. I'm sick of hearing about her Piraties classes.
Pilates, dear.
Oh, I know. Jim called it that once. Made me laugh so hard I almost had to swab the deck. Haha.
Swab the... Oh, that's disgusting, Graham.
I imagine she teaches it with an eye patch and peg leg.
Haha.
You're insane.
And you love me.
Haha. Maybe.
All right, we're off. Love you!
I love you, too.
That narrowed it down...but didn't make the next call any easier.
1
Mom work
2
Grandma + Grandpa SUTTER
3
Grandma + Grandpa ORHAM
Mads school
5
Ring... Ring... Ring...

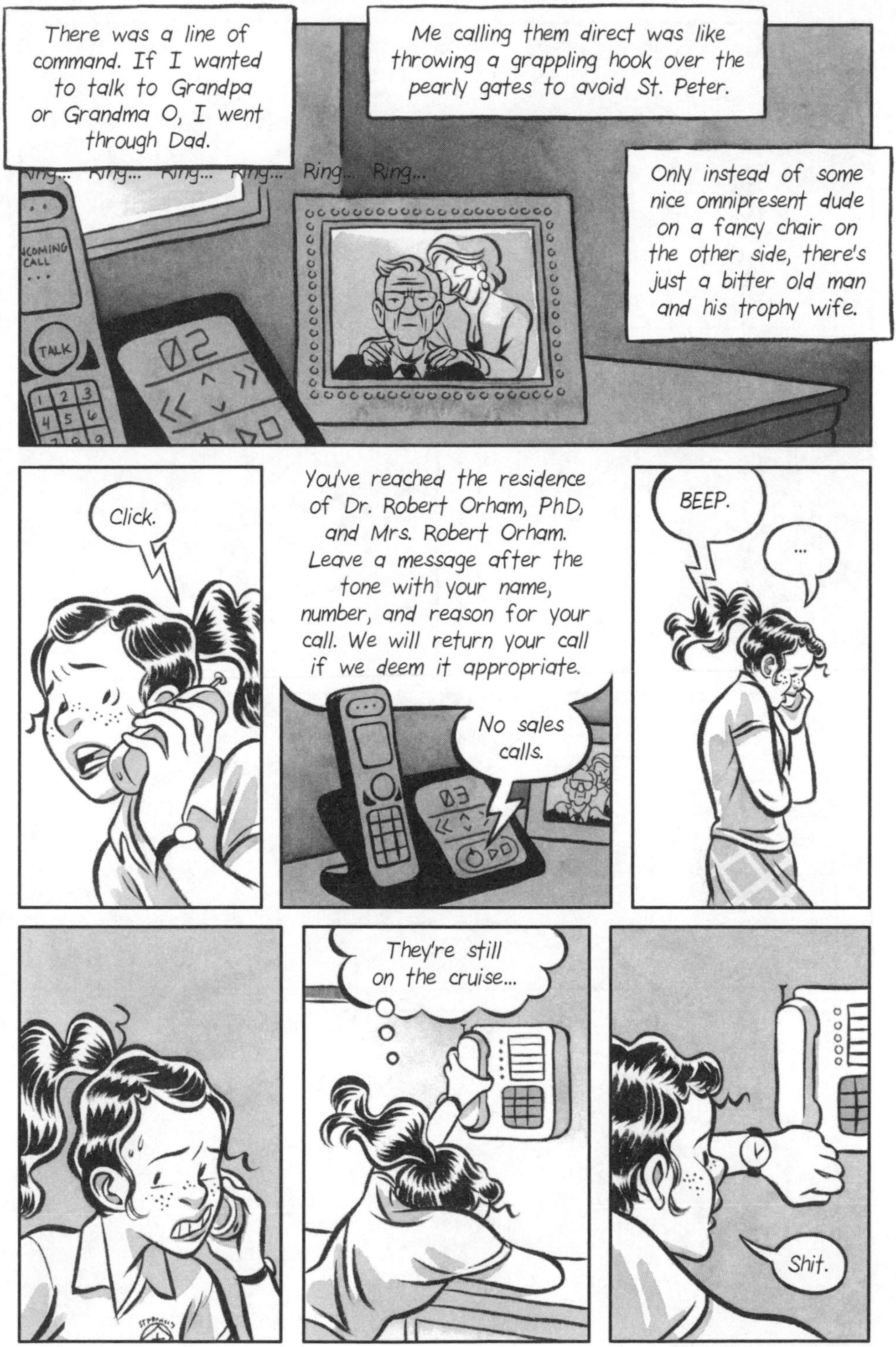
There was a line of command. If I wanted to talk to Grandpa or Grandma O, I went through Dad.
Me calling them direct was like throwing a grappling hook over the pearly gates to avoid St. Peter.
Ring... Ring... Ring... Ring... Ring... Ring...
Only instead of some nice omnipresent dude on a fancy chair on the other side, there's just a bitter old man and his trophy wife.
INCOMING CALL
TALK
02
Click.
You've reached the residence of Dr. Robert Orham, PhD, and Mrs. Robert Orham. Leave a message after the tone with your name, number, and reason for your call. We will return your call if we deem it appropriate.
No sales calls.
03
BEEP.
...
They're still on the cruise...
Shit.

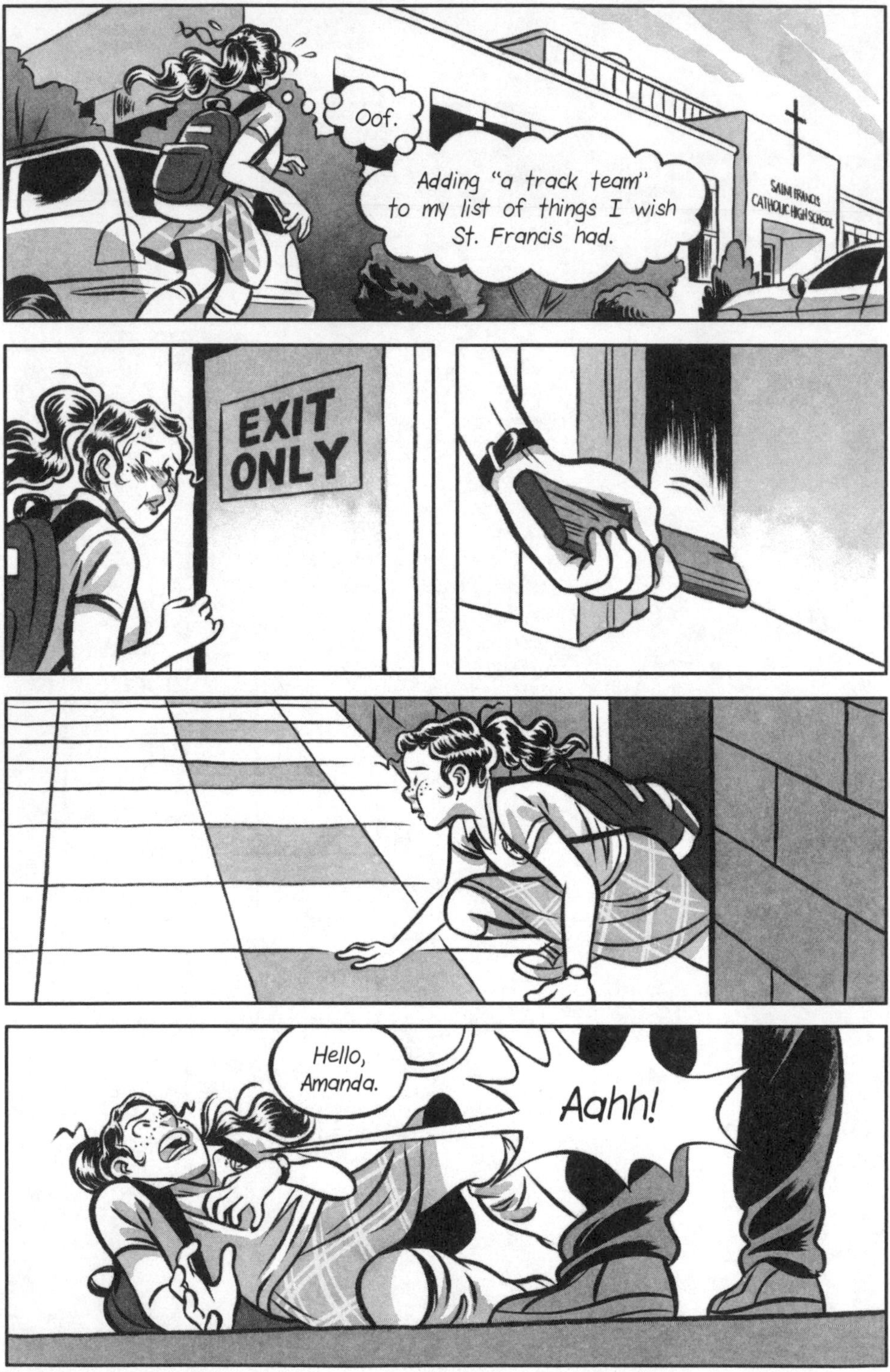

Oof.
Adding "a track team" to my list of things I wish St. Francis had.
SAINT FRANCIS CATHOLIC HIGH SCHOOL
EXIT ONLY
Hello, Amanda.
Aahh!

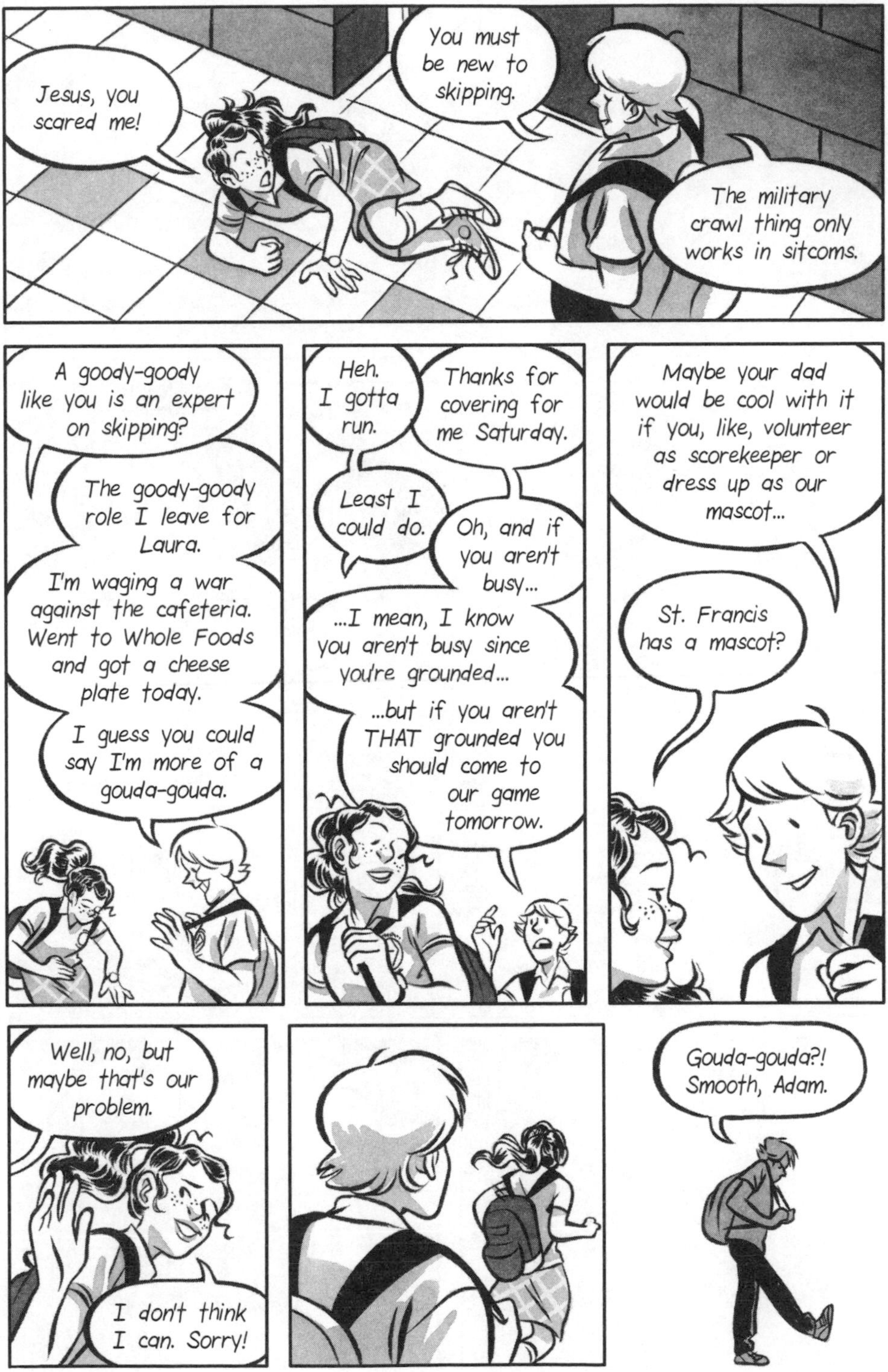
Jesus, you scared me!
You must be new to skipping.
The military crawl thing only works in sitcoms.
A goody-goody like you is an expert on skipping?
The goody-goody role I leave for Laura.
I'm waging a war against the cafeteria. Went to Whole Foods and got a cheese plate today.
I guess you could say I'm more of a gouda-gouda.
Heh. I gotta run.
Thanks for covering for me Saturday.
Least I could do.
Oh, and if you aren't busy...
...I mean, I know you aren't busy since you're grounded...
...but if you aren't THAT grounded you should come to our game tomorrow.
Maybe your dad would be cool with it if you, like, volunteer as scorekeeper or dress up as our mascot...
St. Francis has a mascot?
Well, no, but maybe that's our problem.
I don't think I can. Sorry!
Gouda-gouda?! Smooth, Adam.

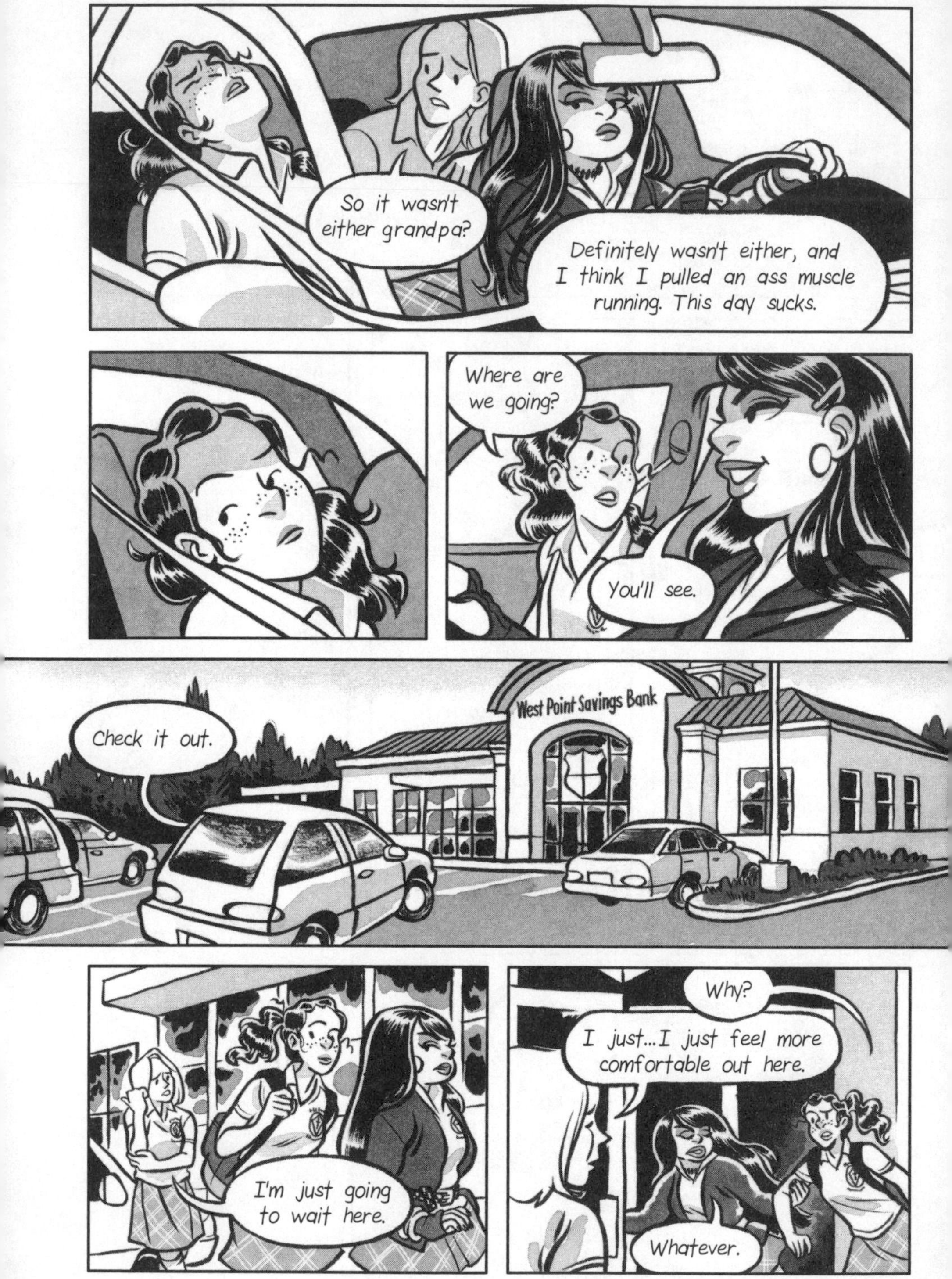
So it wasn't either grandpa?
Definitely wasn't either, and I think I pulled an ass muscle running. This day sucks.
Where are we going?
You'll see.
West Point Savings Bank
Check it out.
I'm just going to wait here.
Why?
I just...I just feel more comfortable out here.
Whatever.

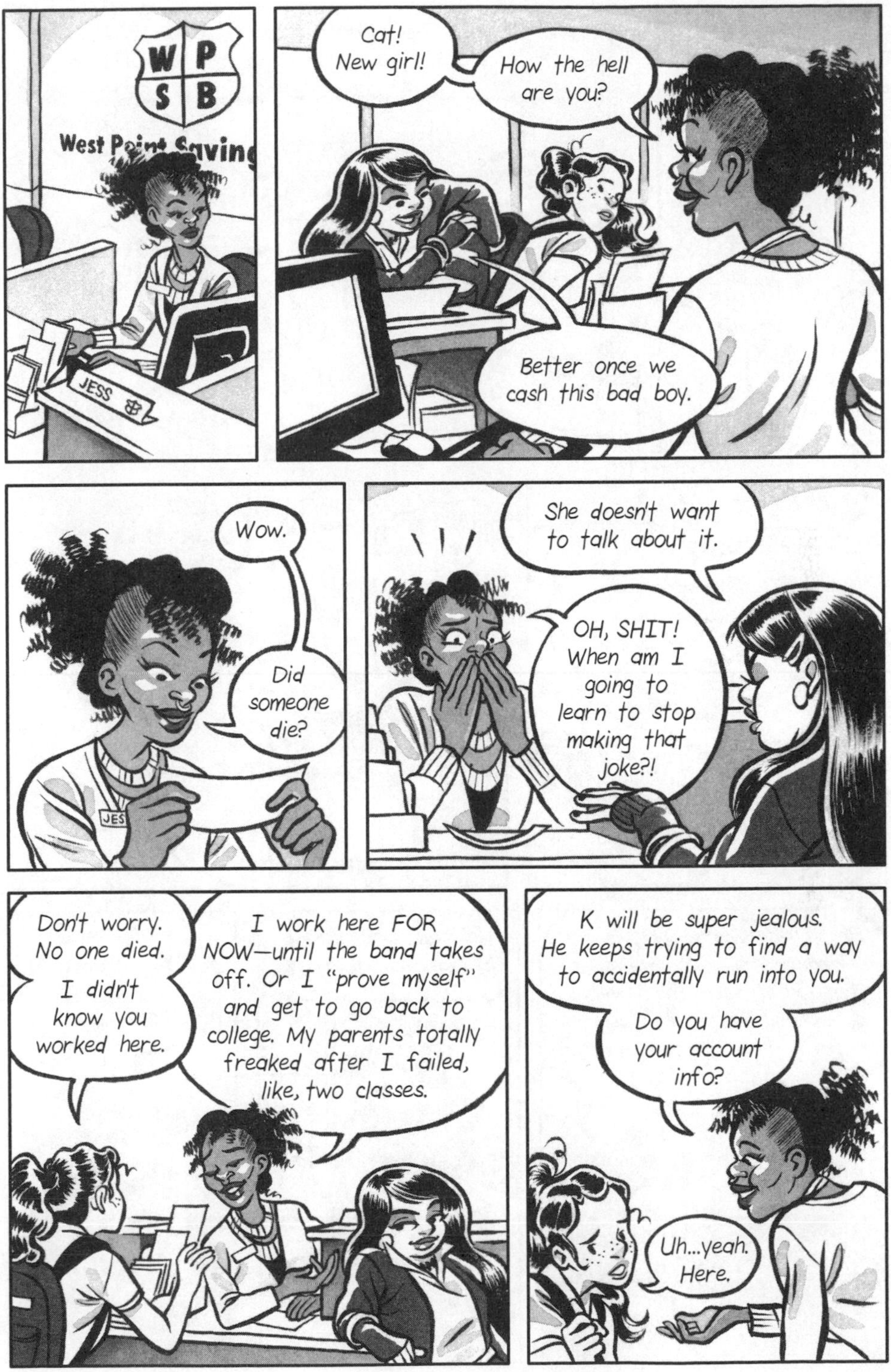
WPSB
West Point Saving
Cat! New girl!
How the hell are you?
JESS
Better once we cash this bad boy.
Wow.
Did someone die?
JES
She doesn't want to talk about it.
OH, SHIT! When am I going to learn to stop making that joke?!
Don't worry. No one died.
I didn't know you worked here.
I work here FOR NOW—until the band takes off. Or I "prove myself" and get to go back to college. My parents totally freaked after I failed, like, two classes.
K will be super jealous. He keeps trying to find a way to accidentally run into you.
Do you have your account info?
Uh...yeah. Here.

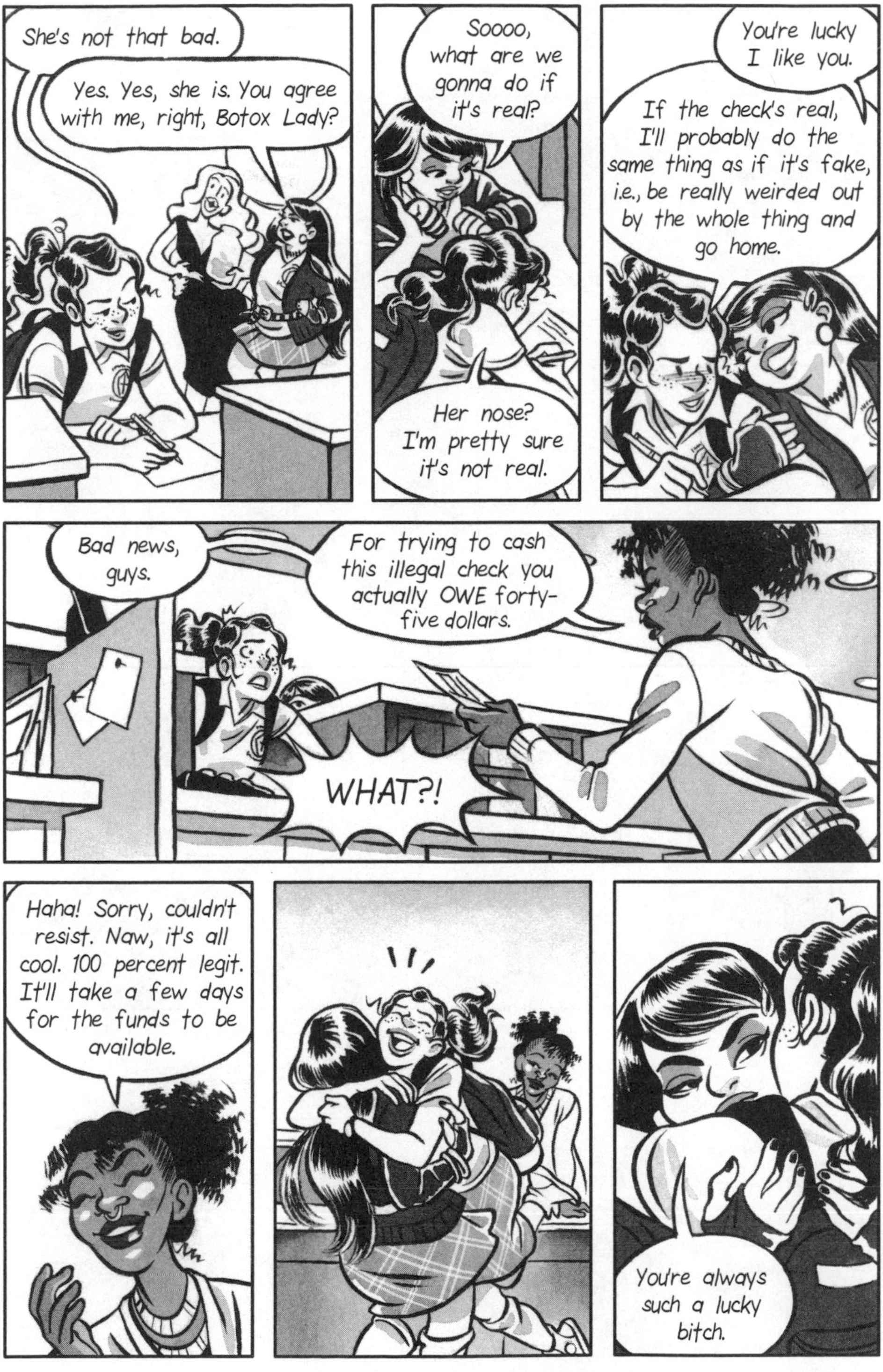

She's not that bad.
Yes. Yes, she is. You agree with me, right, Botox Lady?
Soooo, what are we gonna do if it's real?
Her nose? I'm pretty sure it's not real.
You're lucky I like you.
If the check's real, I'll probably do the same thing as if it's fake, i.e., be really weirded out by the whole thing and go home.
Bad news, guys.
For trying to cash this illegal check you actually OWE forty-five dollars.
WHAT?!
Haha! Sorry, couldn't resist. Naw, it's all cool. 100 percent legit. It'll take a few days for the funds to be available.
You're always such a lucky bitch.

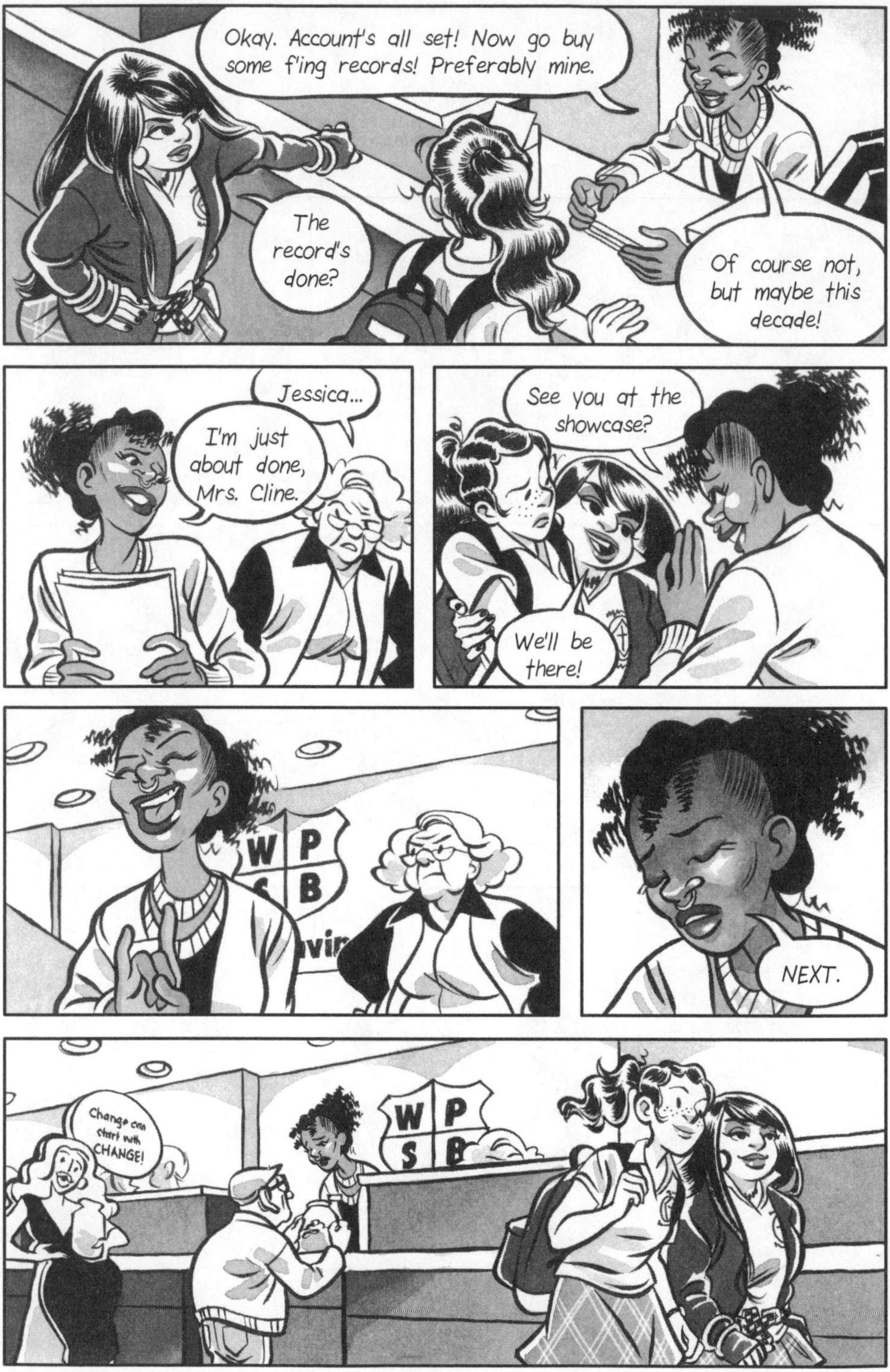
Okay. Account's all set! Now go buy some f'ing records! Preferably mine.
The record's done?
Of course not, but maybe this decade!
Jessica...
I'm just about done, Mrs. Cline.
See you at the showcase?
We'll be there!
NEXT.
Change can start with CHANGE!

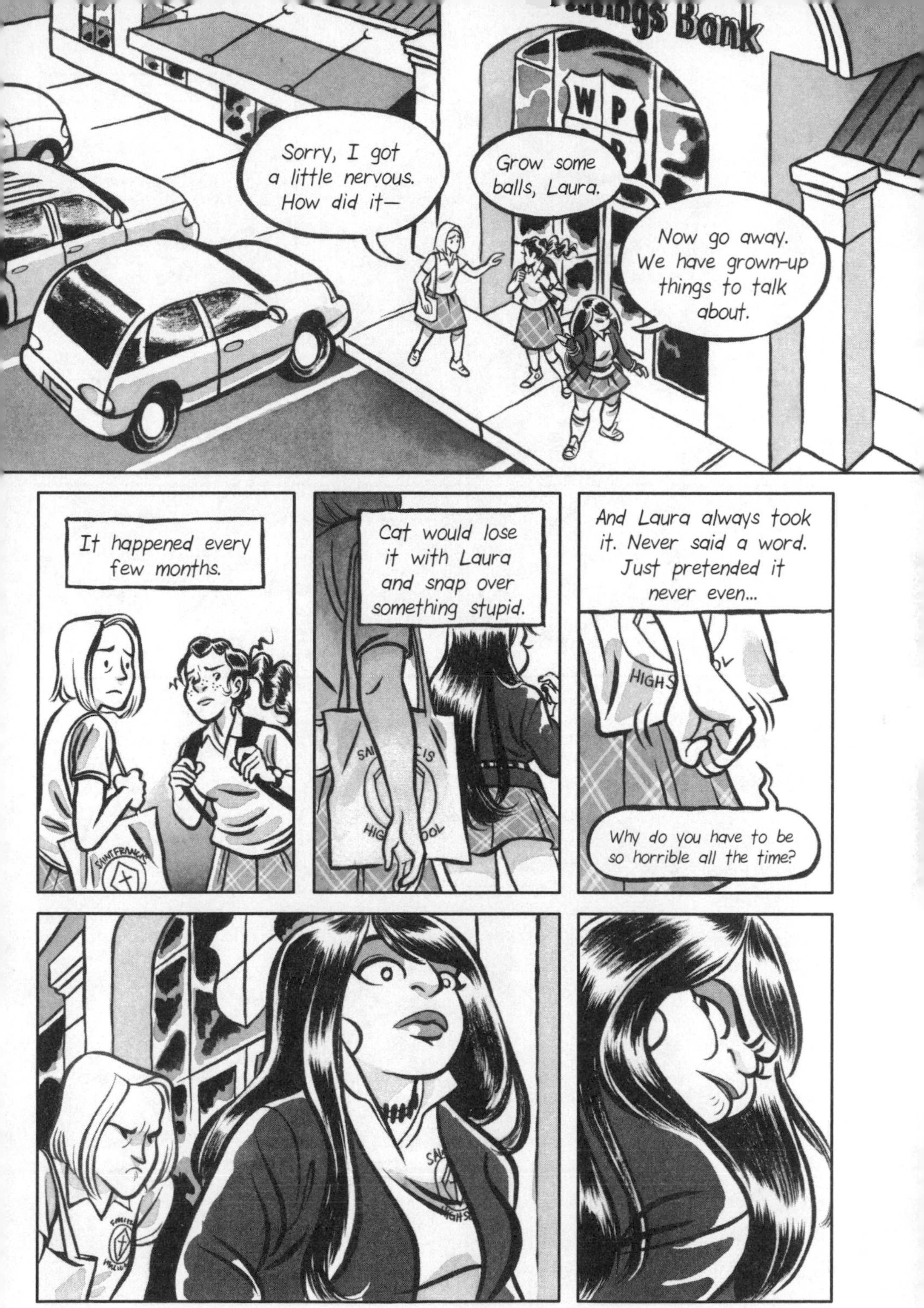
Savings Bank
WP
Sorry, I got a little nervous. How did it—
Grow some balls, Laura.
Now go away. We have grown-up things to talk about.
It happened every few months.
SAINT FRANCIS
Cat would lose it with Laura and snap over something stupid.
And Laura always took it. Never said a word. Just pretended it never even...
HIGH S
Why do you have to be so horrible all the time?

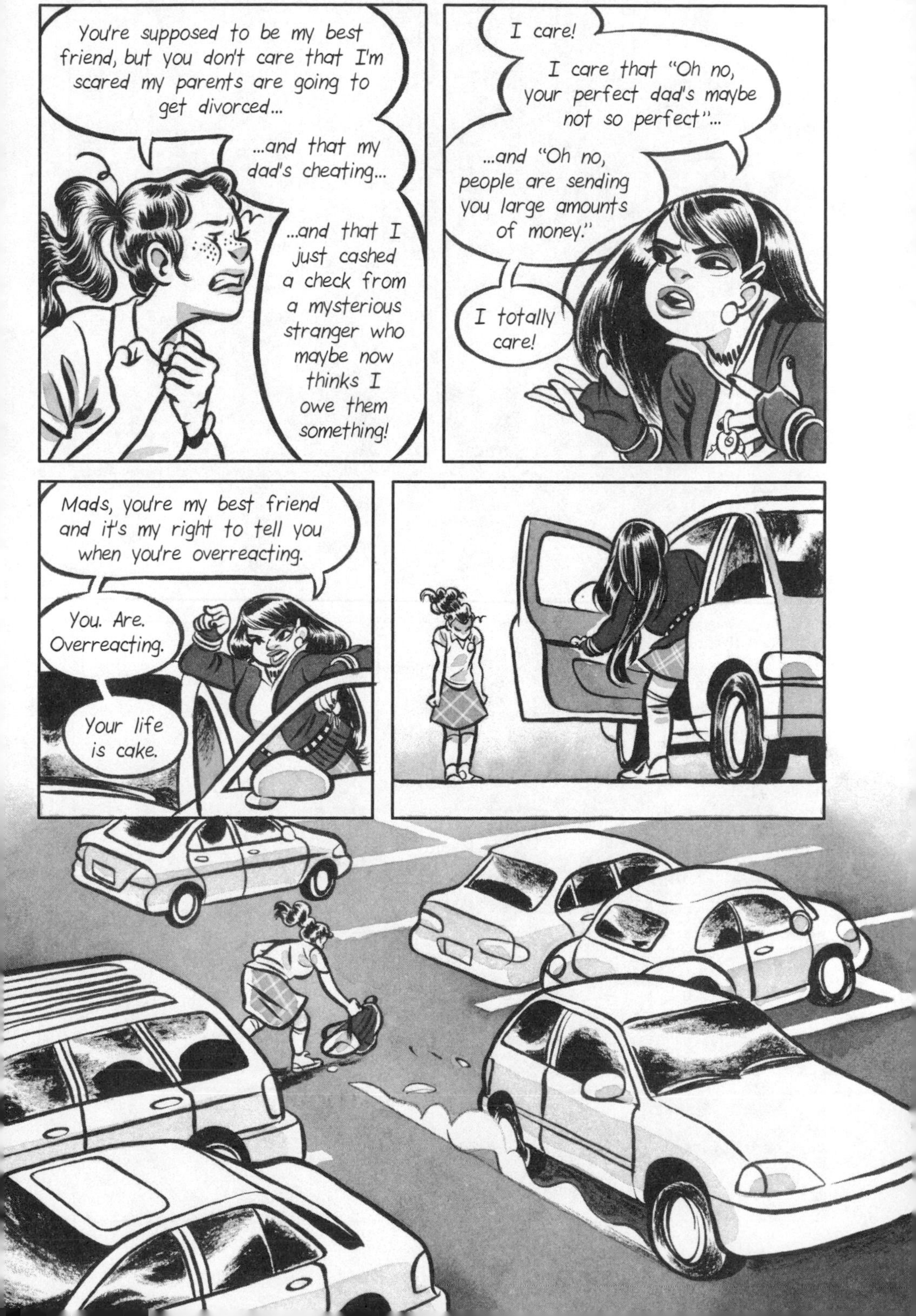
You're supposed to be my best friend, but you don't care that I'm scared my parents are going to get divorced...
...and that my dad's cheating...
...and that I just cashed a check from a mysterious stranger who maybe now thinks I owe them something!
I care!
I care that "Oh no, your perfect dad's maybe not so perfect"...
...and "Oh no, people are sending you large amounts of money."
I totally care!
Mads, you're my best friend and it's my right to tell you when you're overreacting.
You. Are. Overreacting.
Your life is cake.

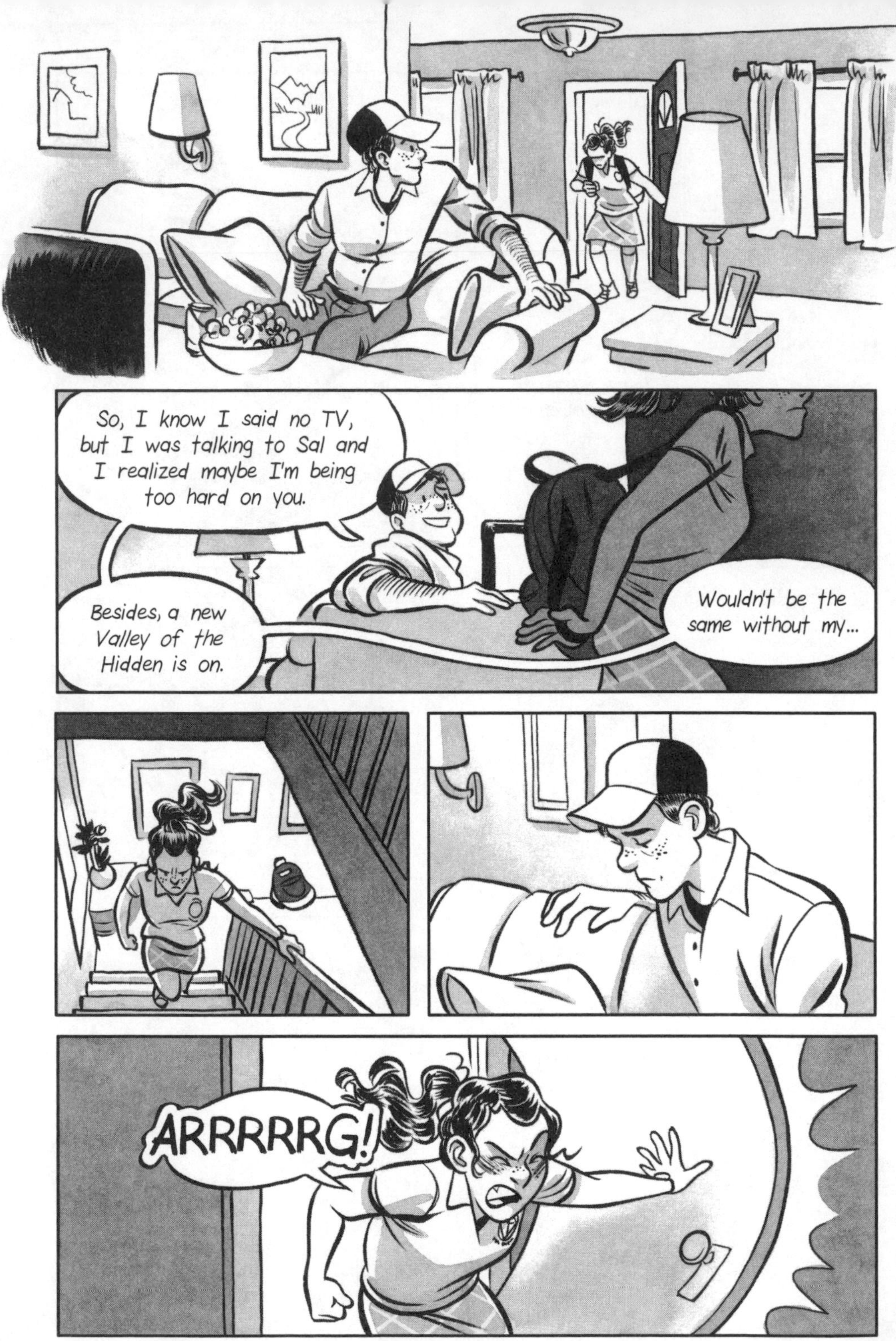
So, I know I said no TV, but I was talking to Sal and I realized maybe I'm being too hard on you.
Besides, a new Valley of the Hidden is on.
Wouldn't be the same without my...
ARRRRRG!

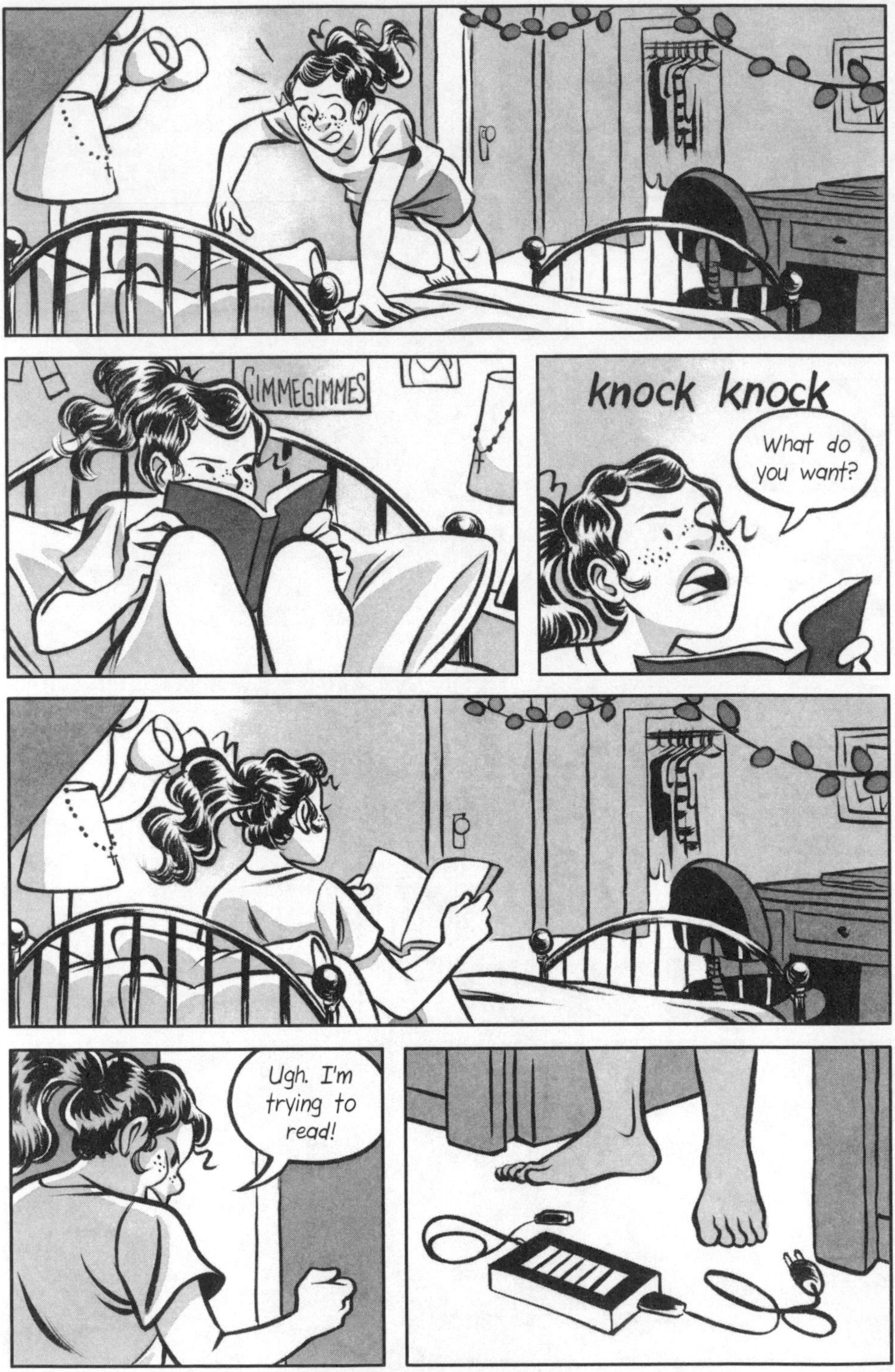
GIMMEGIMMES
knock knock
What do you want?
Ugh. I'm trying to read!

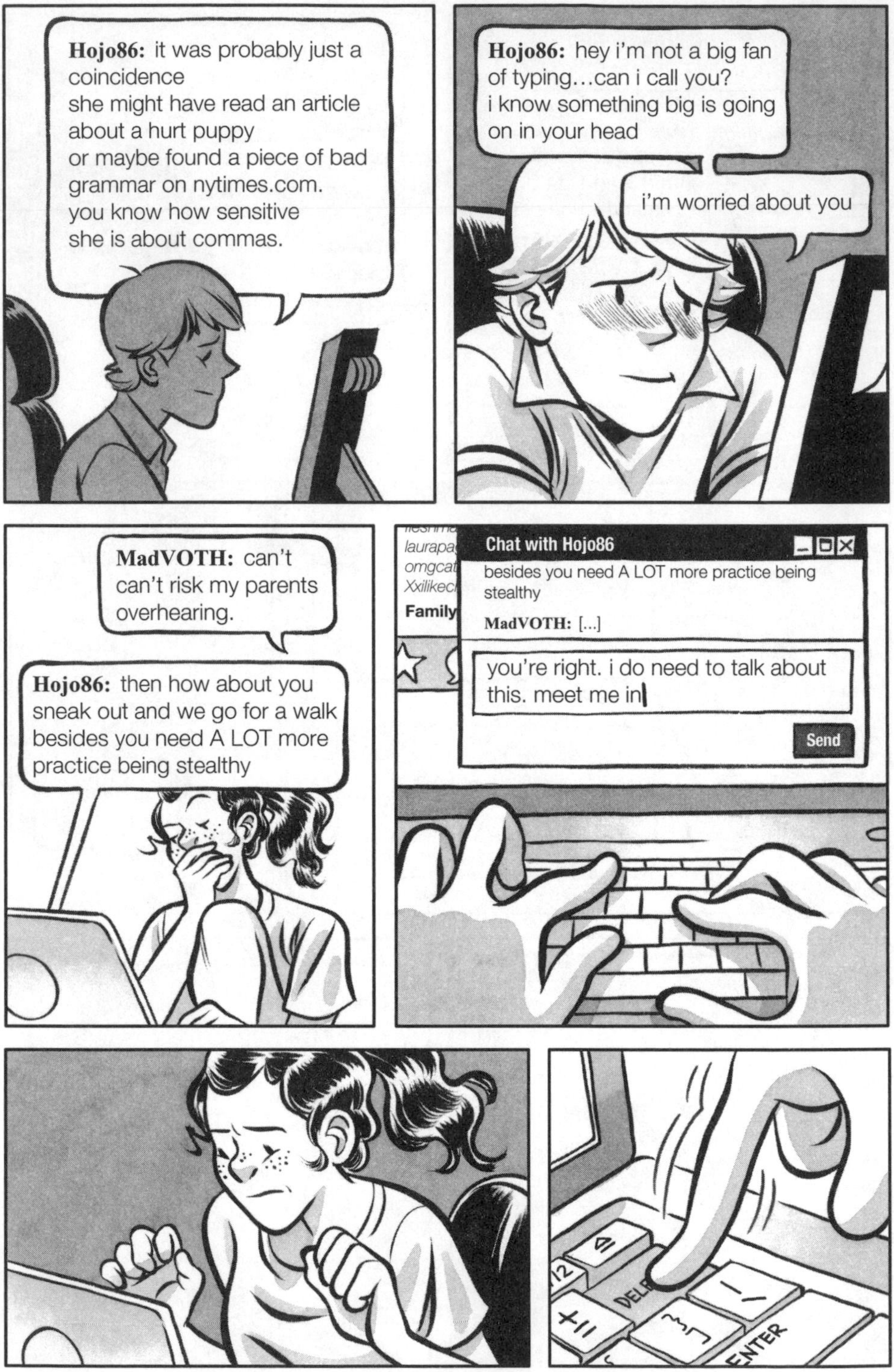
Hojo86: it was probably just a coincidence
she might have read an article about a hurt puppy
or maybe found a piece of bad grammar on nytimes.com.
you know how sensitive she is about commas.
Hojo86: hey i'm not a big fan of typing…can i call you?
i know something big is going on in your head
i'm worried about you
MadVOTH: can't
can't risk my parents overhearing.
Hojo86: then how about you sneak out and we go for a walk
besides you need A LOT more practice being stealthy
Family
Chat with Hojo86
besides you need A LOT more practice being stealthy
MadVOTH: [...]
you're right. i do need to talk about this. meet me in
Send
ENTER

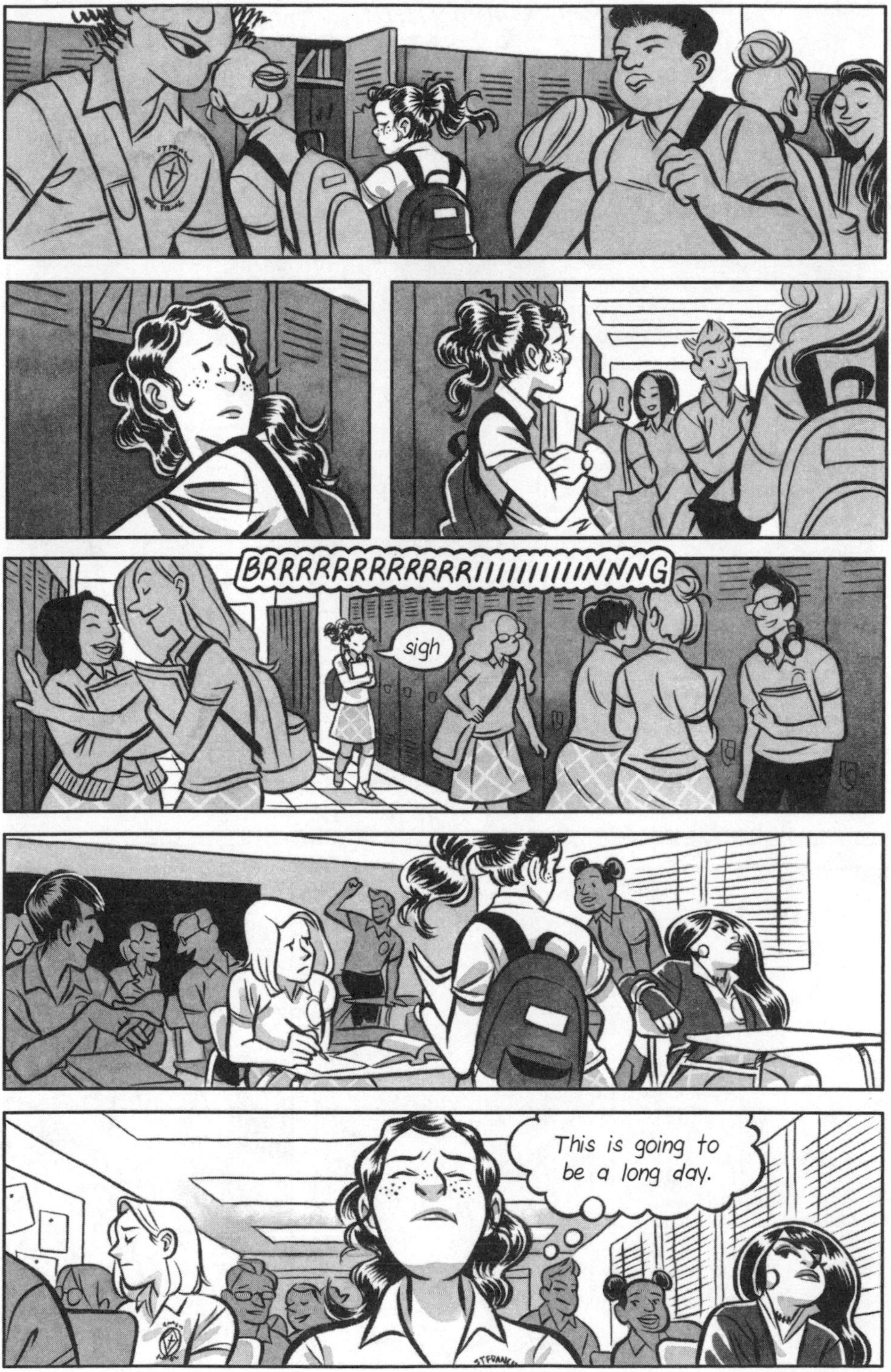
BRRRRRRRRRRRRRIIIIIIIIIIINNNG
sigh
This is going to be a long day.

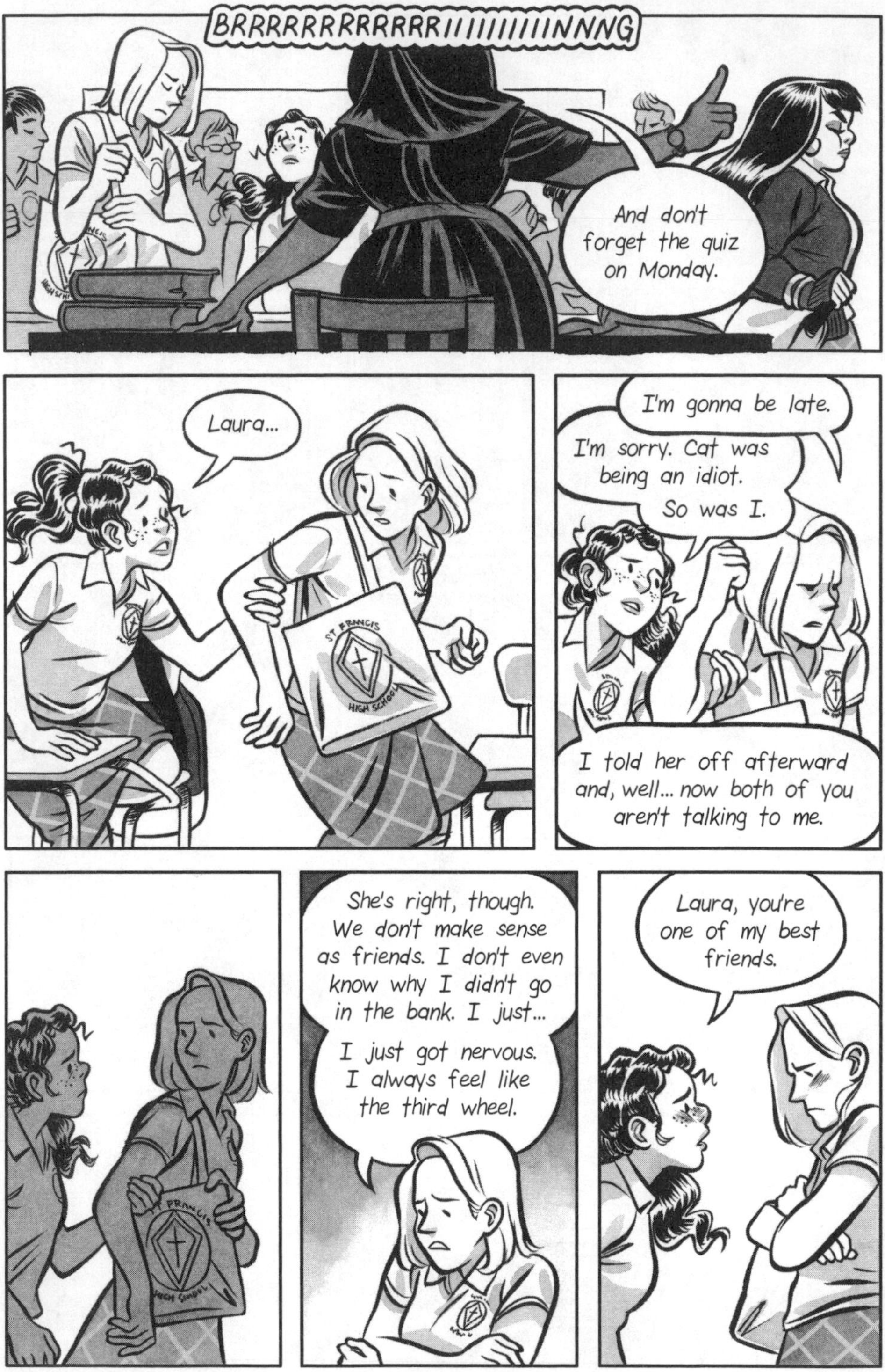
BRRRRRRRRRRRIIIIIIIIIIINNNG
And don't forget the quiz on Monday.
Laura...
I'm gonna be late.
I'm sorry. Cat was being an idiot.
So was I.
I told her off afterward and, well... now both of you aren't talking to me.
She's right, though. We don't make sense as friends. I don't even know why I didn't go in the bank. I just...
I just got nervous. I always feel like the third wheel.
Laura, you're one of my best friends.

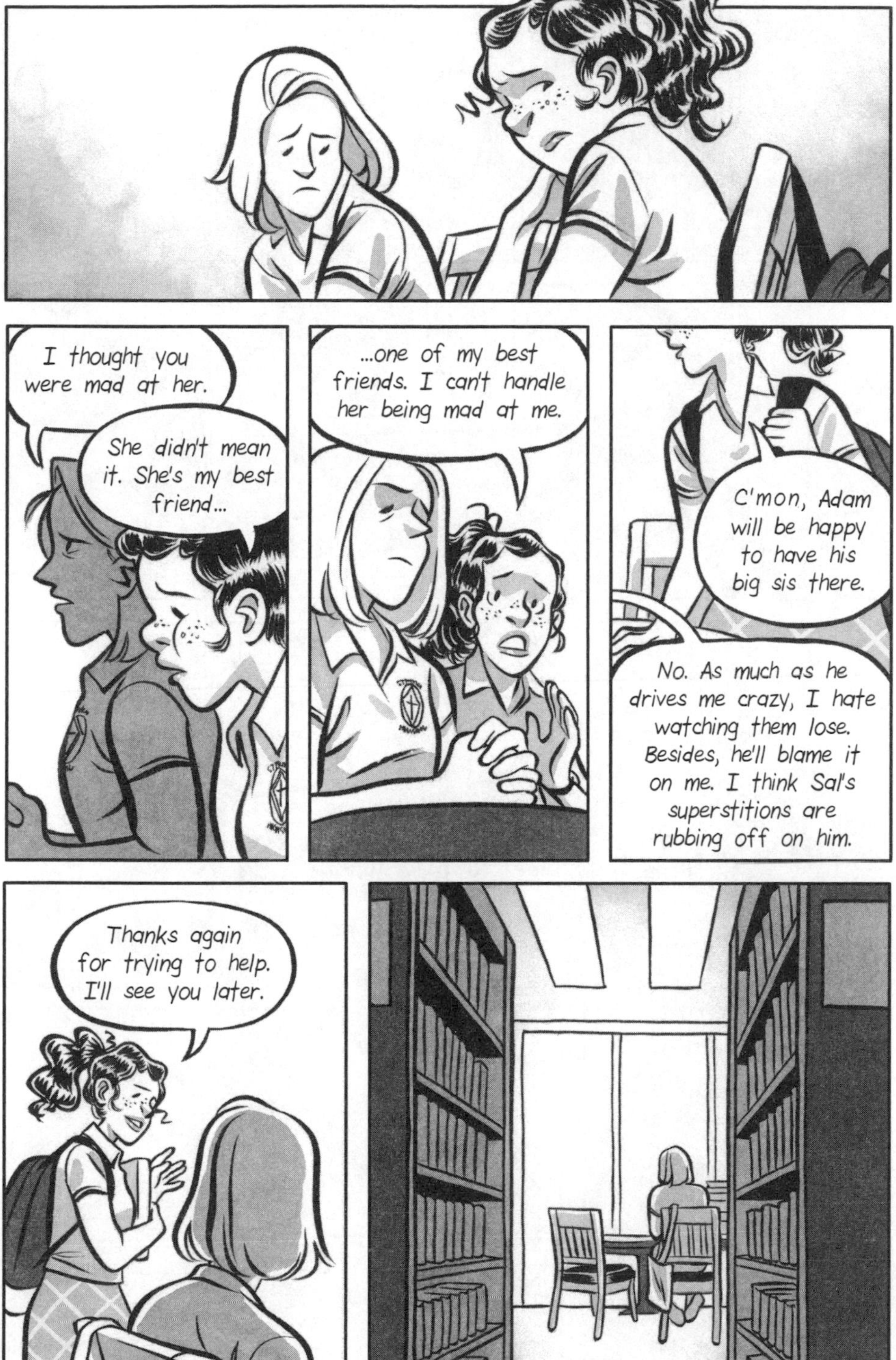
I thought you were mad at her.
She didn't mean it. She's my best friend...
...one of my best friends. I can't handle her being mad at me.
C'mon, Adam will be happy to have his big sis there.
No. As much as he drives me crazy, I hate watching them lose. Besides, he'll blame it on me. I think Sal's superstitions are rubbing off on him.
Thanks again for trying to help. I'll see you later.

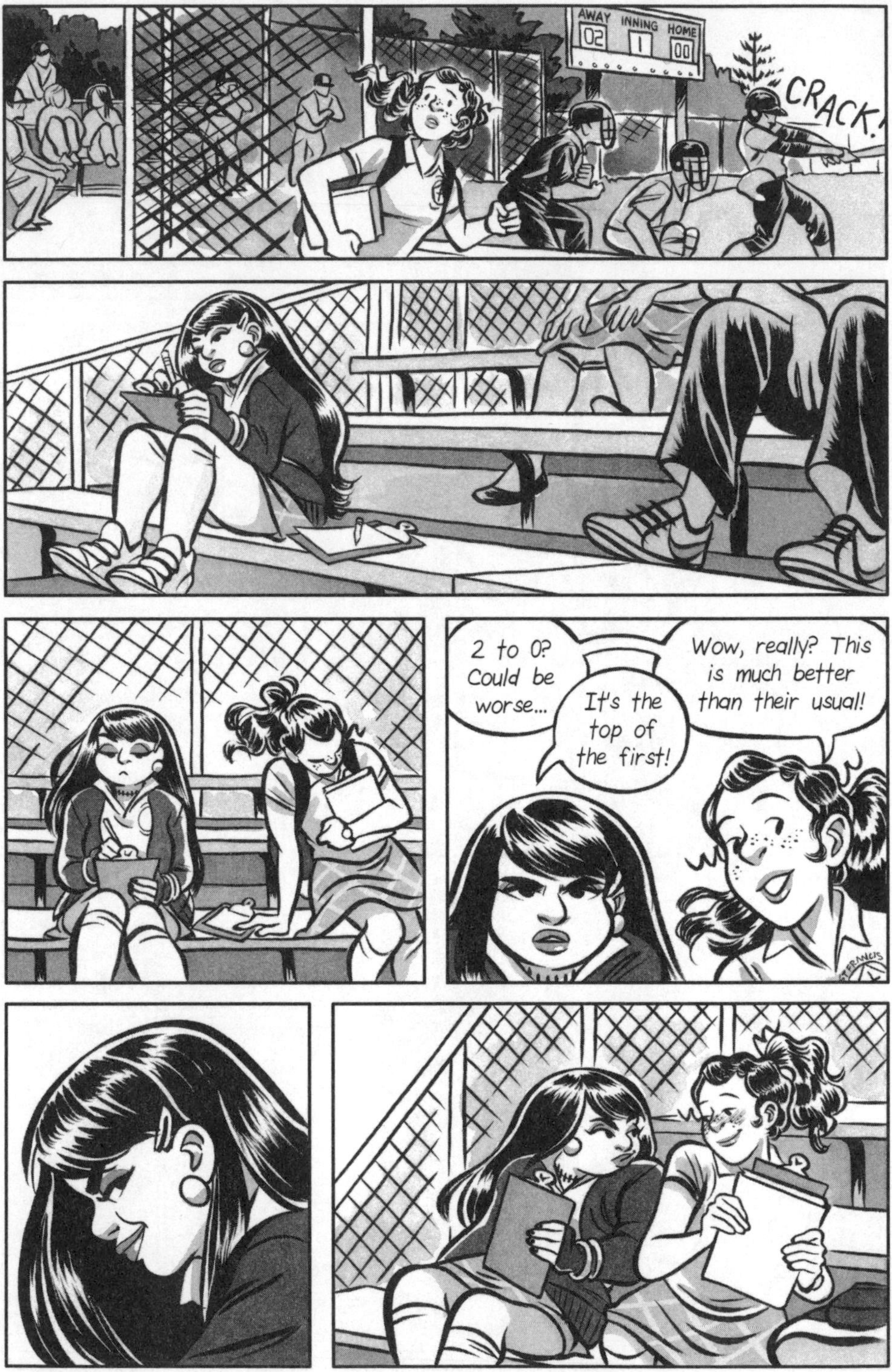
AWAY INNING HOME
02 1 00
CRACK!
2 to 0? Could be worse...
It's the top of the first!
Wow, really? This is much better than their usual!

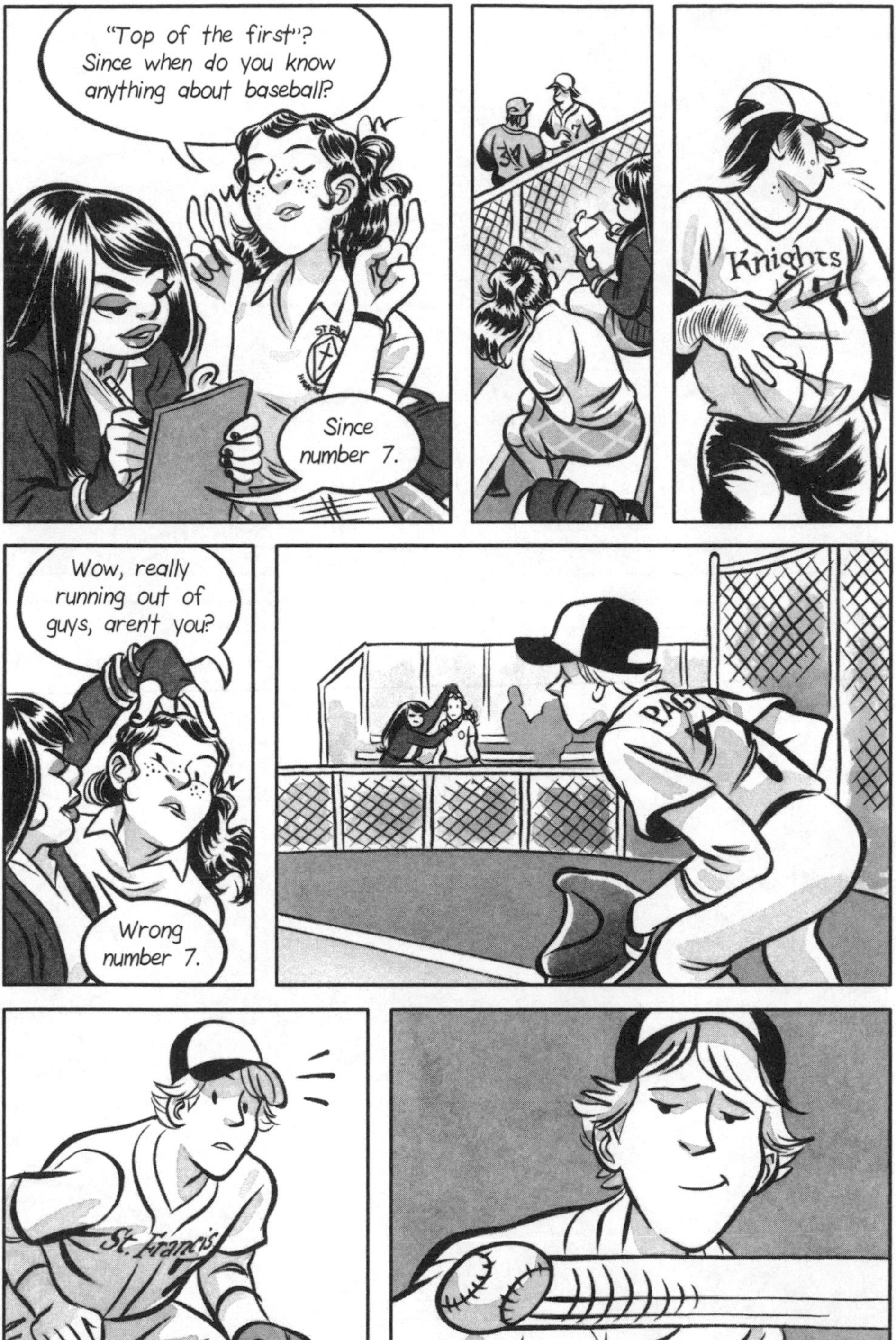
"Top of the first"? Since when do you know anything about baseball?
Since number 7.
Knights
Wow, really running out of guys, aren't you?
Wrong number 7.
St. Francis

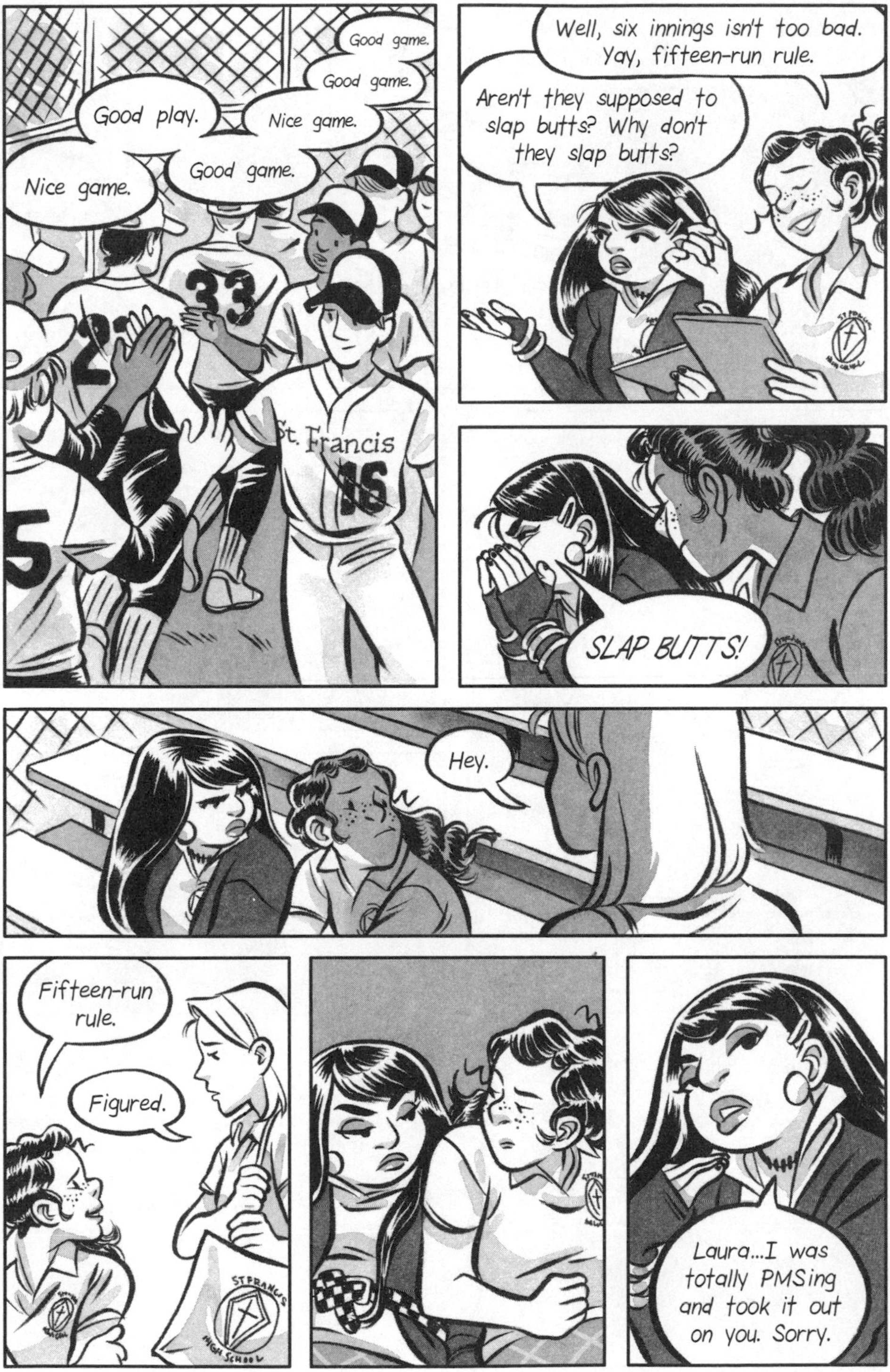
Good game.
Good game.
Good play.
Nice game.
Good game.
Nice game.
33
2
St. Francis
16
5
Well, six innings isn't too bad. Yay, fifteen-run rule.
Aren't they supposed to slap butts? Why don't they slap butts?
SLAP BUTTS!
Hey.
Fifteen-run rule.
Figured.
Laura...I was totally PMSing and took it out on you. Sorry.

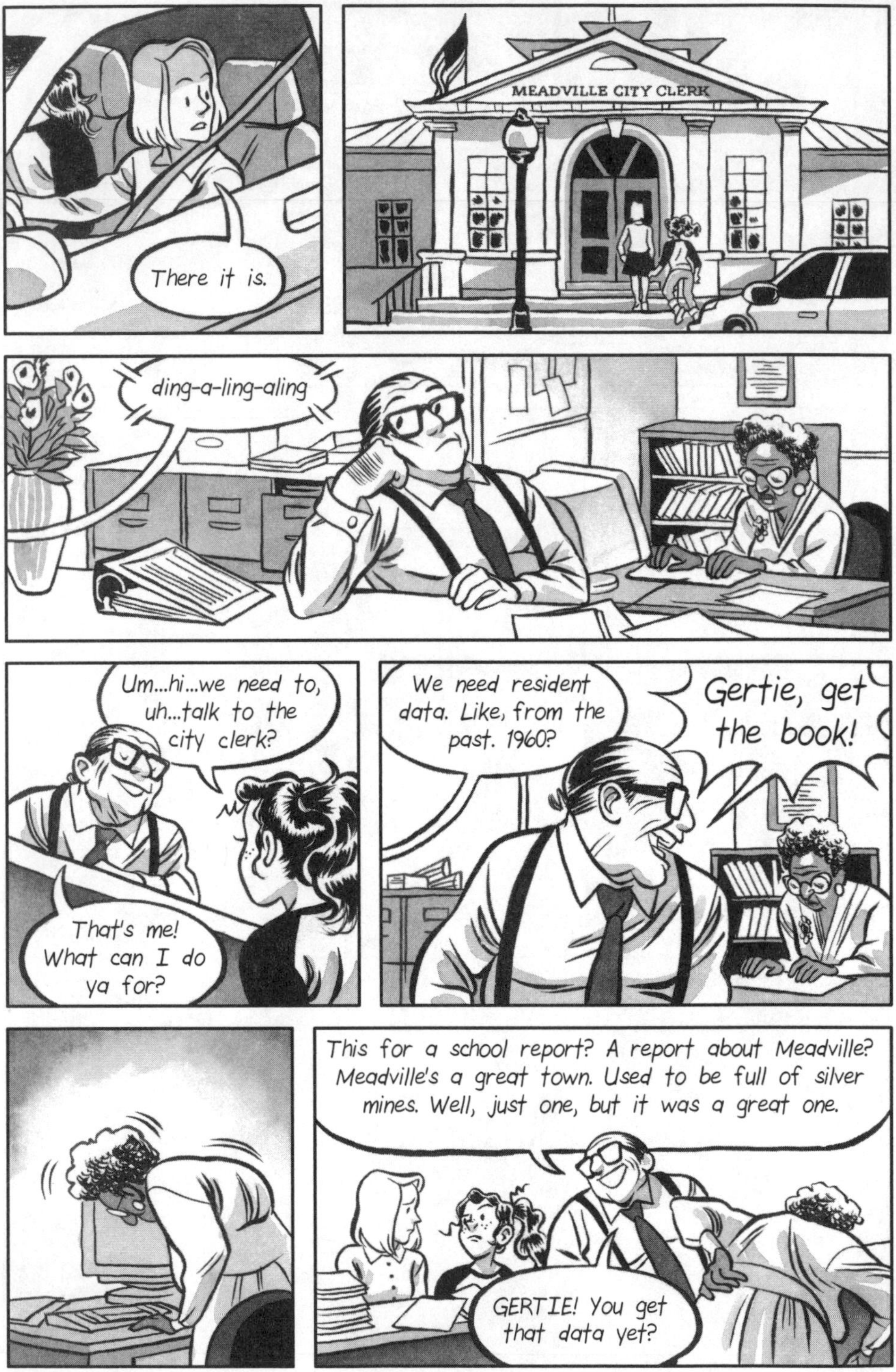
There it is.
MEADVILLE CITY CLERK
ding-a-ling-aling
Um...hi...we need to, uh...talk to the city clerk?
That's me! What can I do ya for?
We need resident data. Like, from the past. 1960?
Gertie, get the book!
This for a school report? A report about Meadville? Meadville's a great town. Used to be full of silver mines. Well, just one, but it was a great one.
GERTIE! You get that data yet?

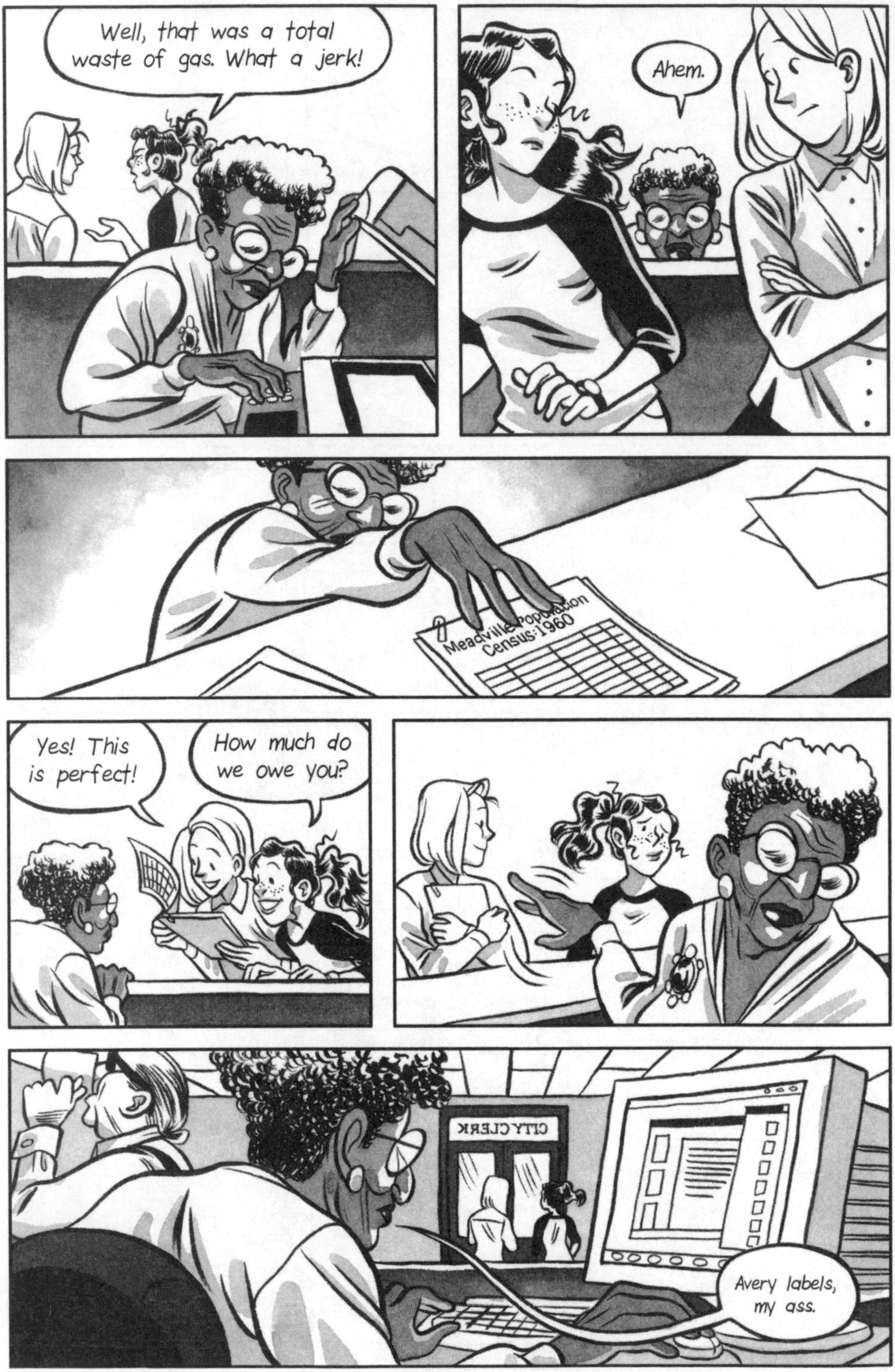
Well, that was a total waste of gas. What a jerk!
Ahem.
Meadville Population Census 1960
Yes! This is perfect!
How much do we owe you?
CITY CLERK
Avery labels, my ass.

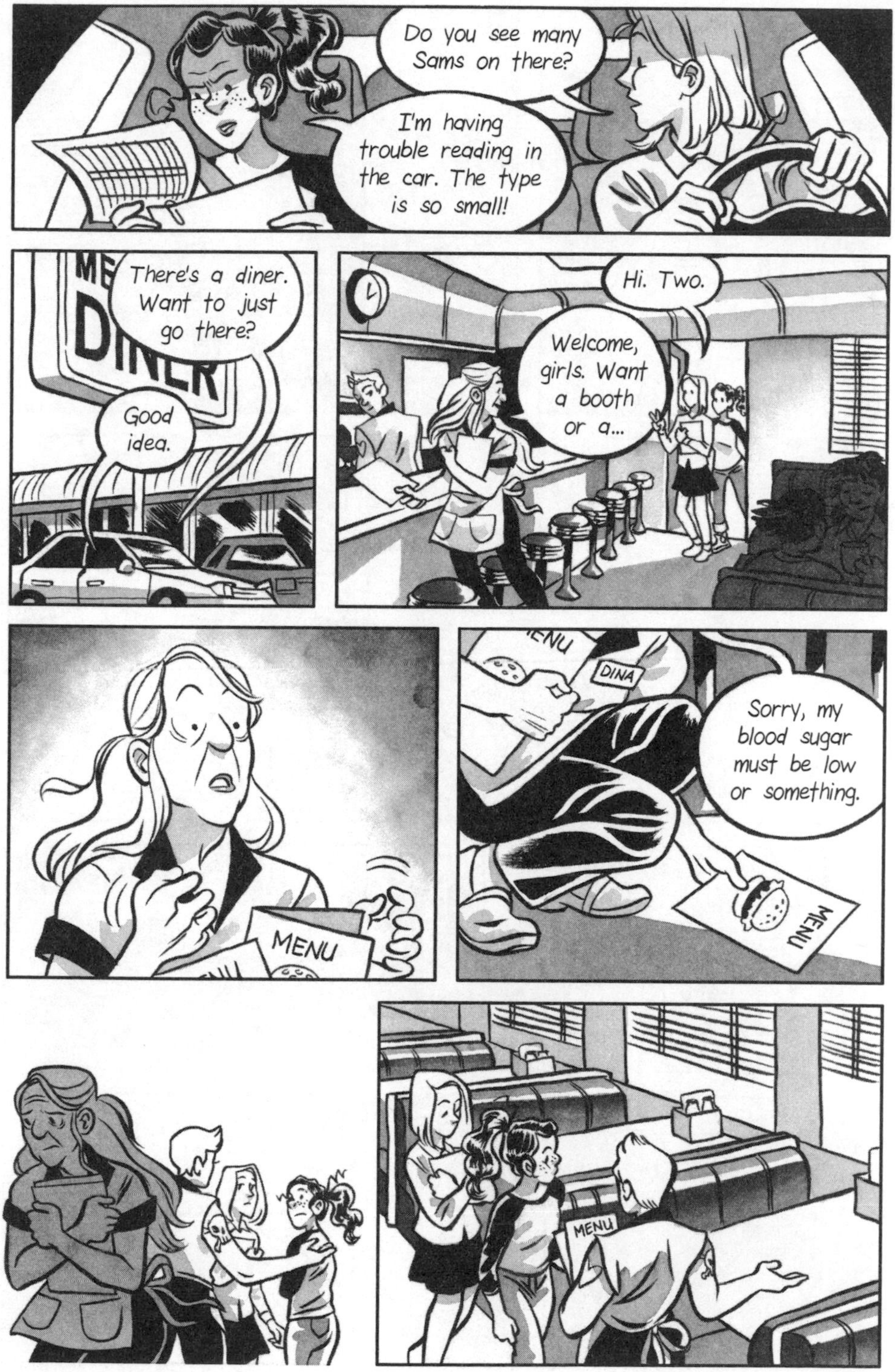
Do you see many Sams on there?
I'm having trouble reading in the car. The type is so small!
MENU
DINER
There's a diner. Want to just go there?
Good idea.
Hi. Two.
Welcome, girls. Want a booth or a...
MENU
DINA
Sorry, my blood sugar must be low or something.
MENU
MENU

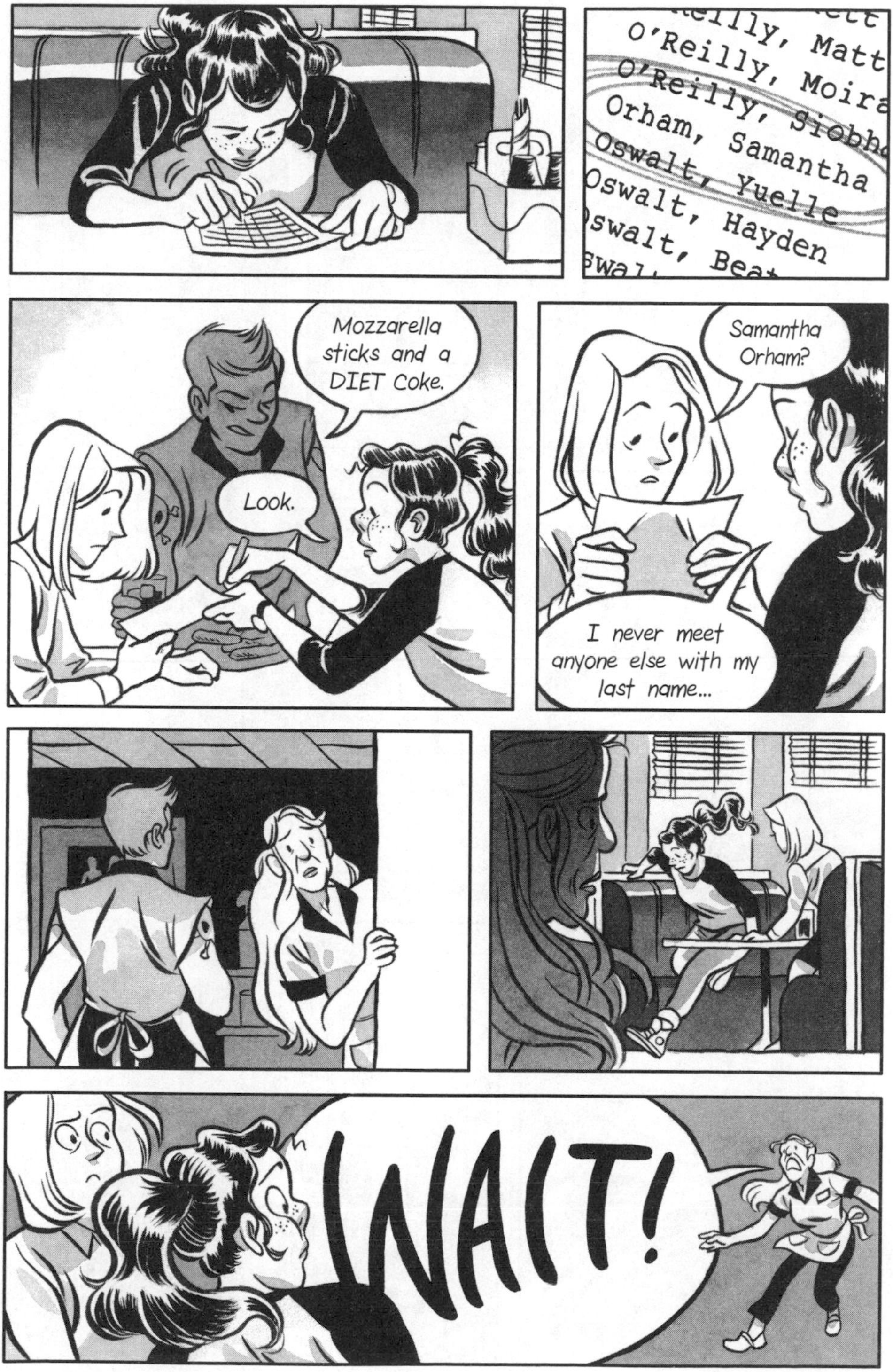
O'Reilly, Matt
O'Reilly, Moira
O'Reilly, Siobh
Orham, Samantha
Oswalt, Yuelle
Oswalt, Hayden
Oswalt, Beat
Mozzarella sticks and a DIET Coke.
Look.
Samantha Orham?
I never meet anyone else with my last name...
WAIT!

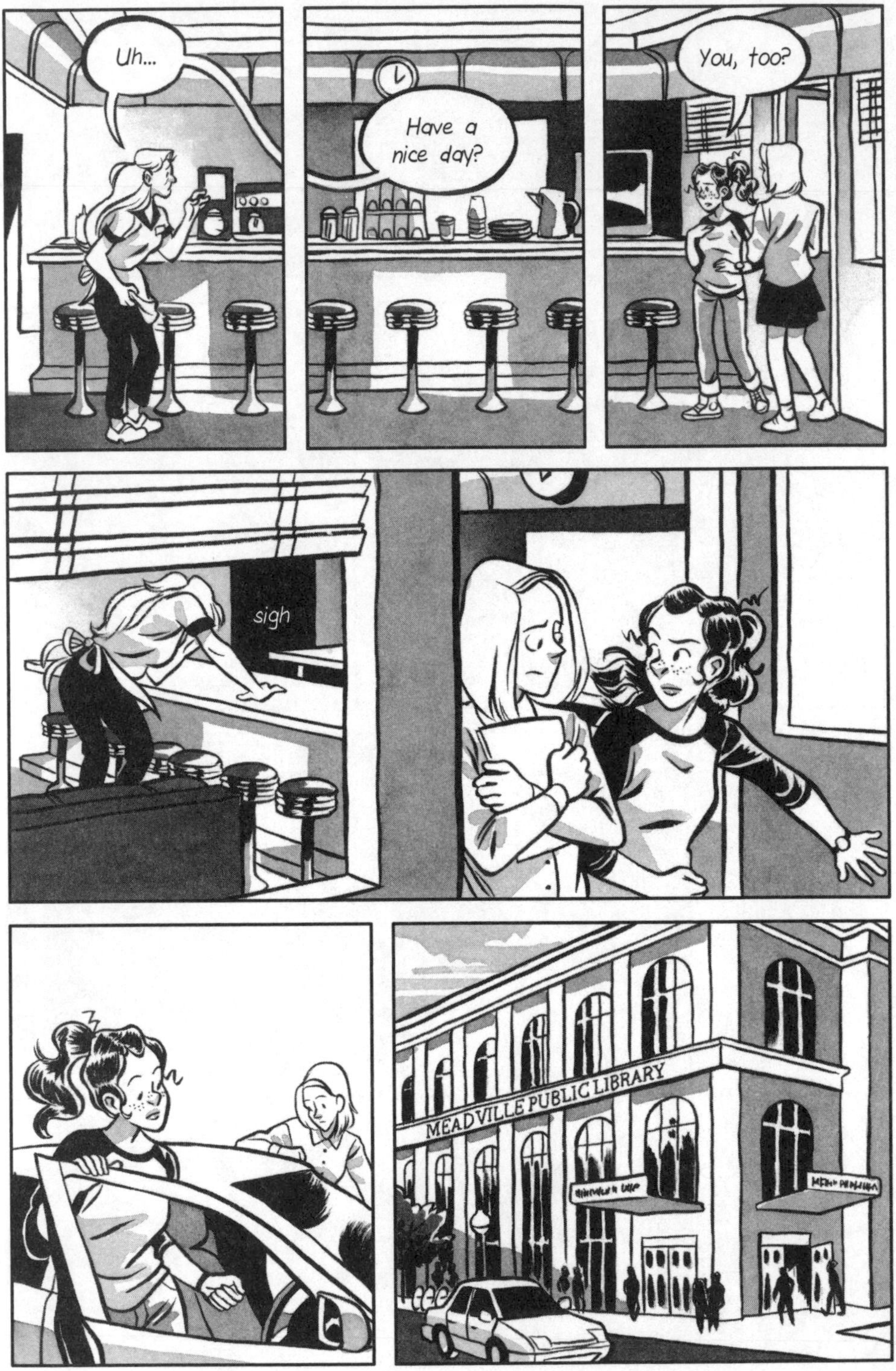
Uh...
Have a nice day?
You, too?
sigh
MEADVILLE PUBLIC LIBRARY

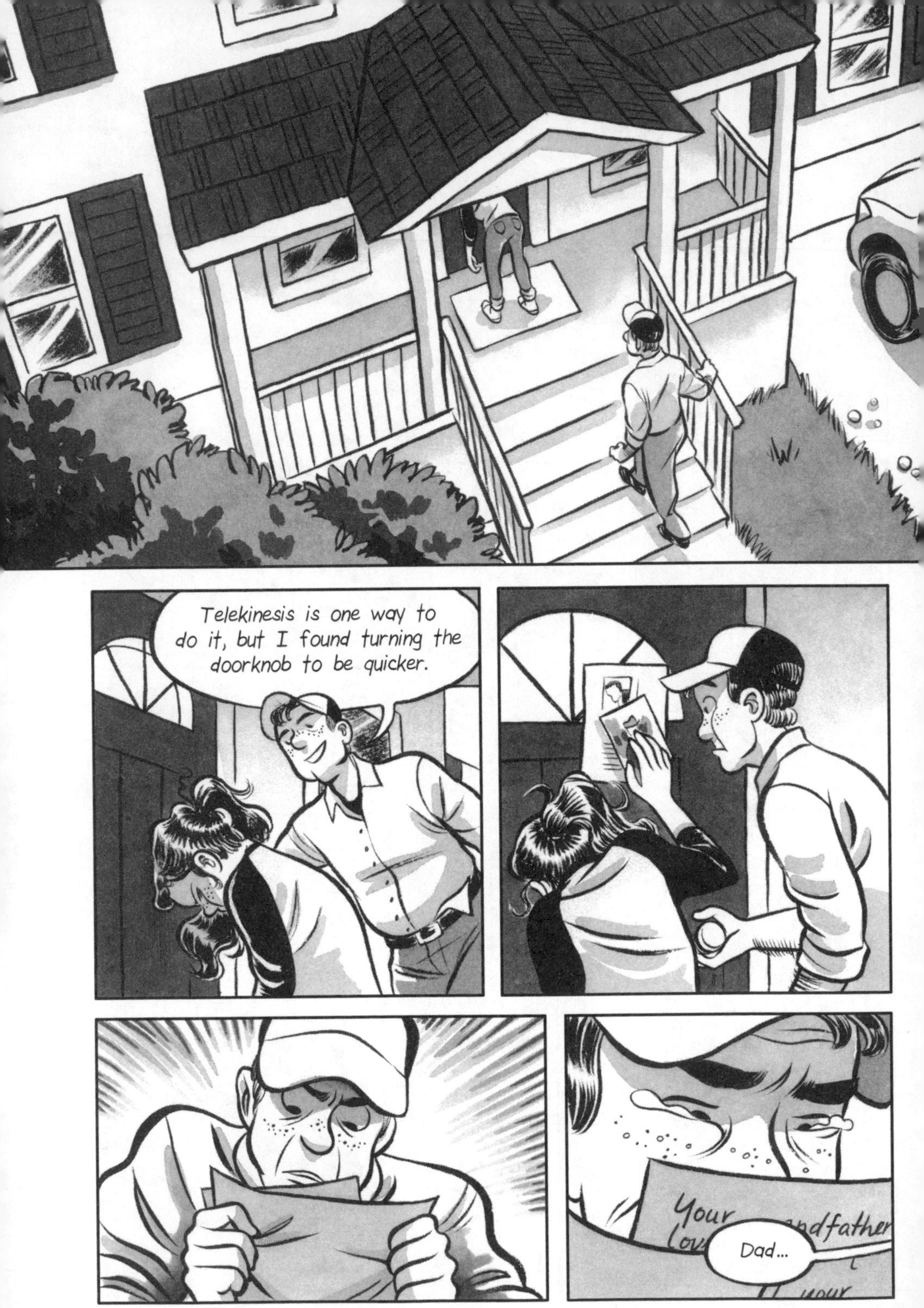
Telekinesis is one way to do it, but I found turning the doorknob to be quicker.
Your
Dad...
your

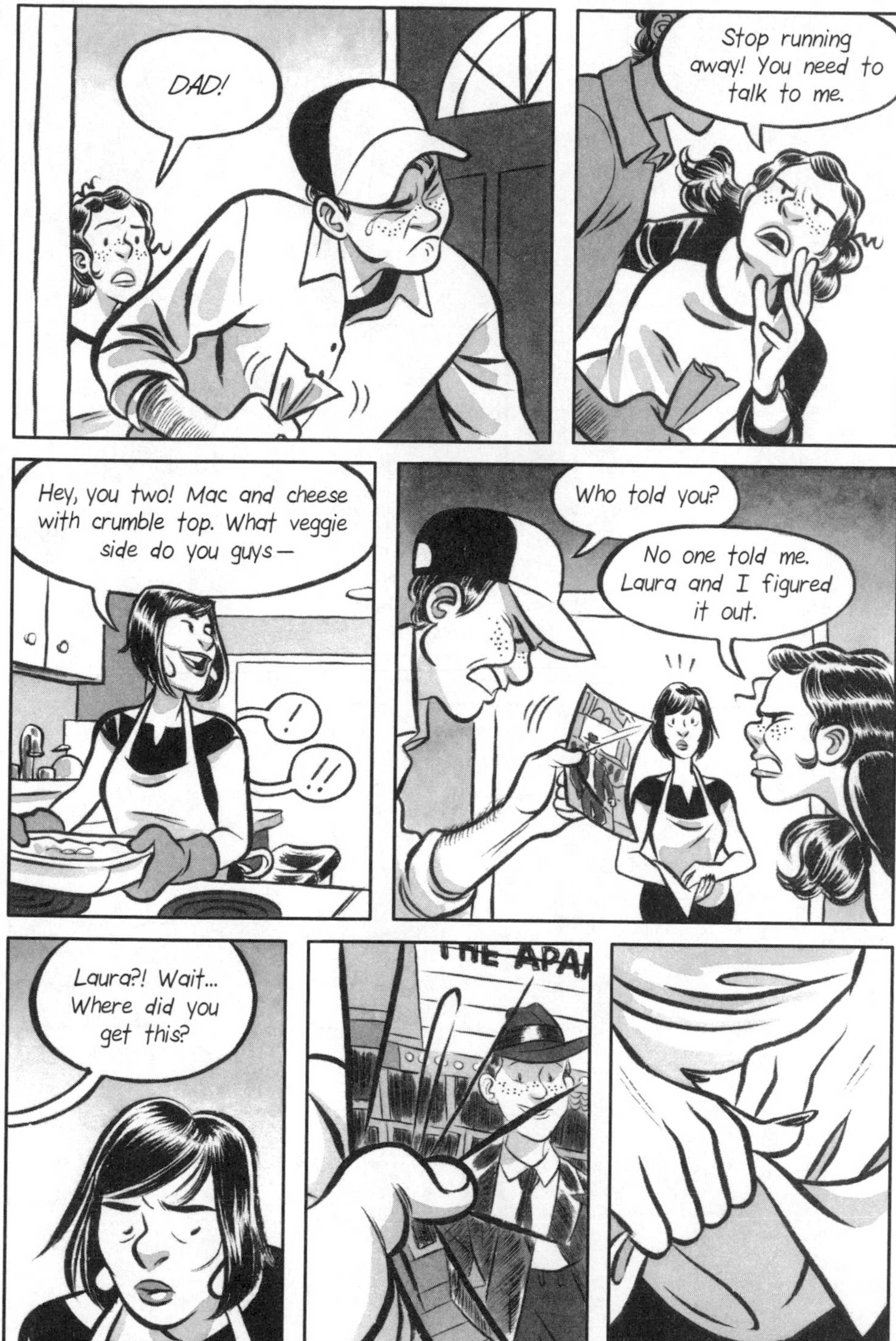
DAD!
Stop running away! You need to talk to me.
Hey, you two! Mac and cheese with crumble top. What veggie side do you guys—
!
!!
Who told you?
No one told me. Laura and I figured it out.
!!!
Laura?! Wait... Where did you get this?
THE APA

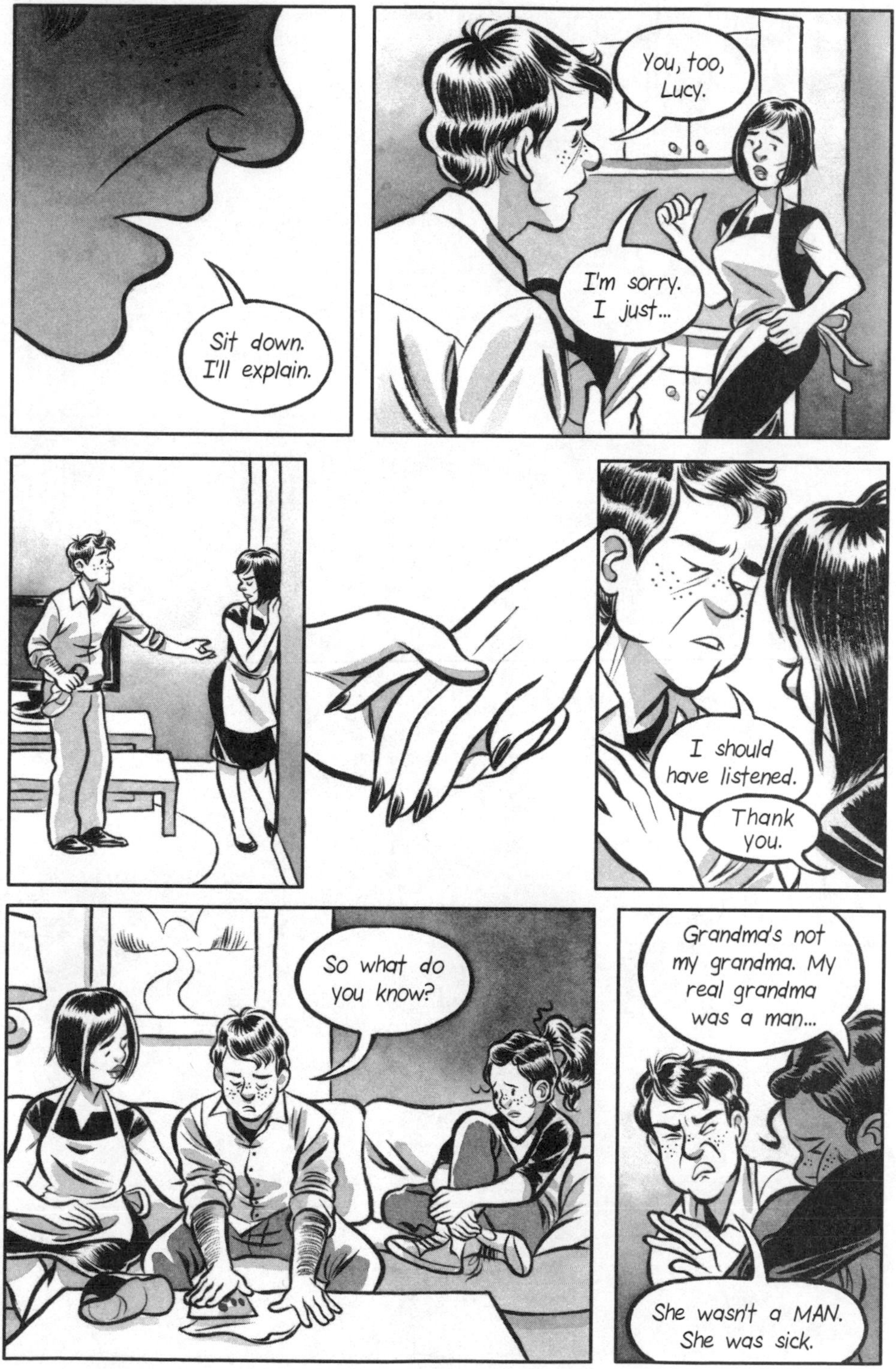
Sit down. I'll explain.
You, too, Lucy.
I'm sorry. I just...
I should have listened.
Thank you.
So what do you know?
Grandma's not my grandma. My real grandma was a man...
She wasn't a MAN. She was sick.

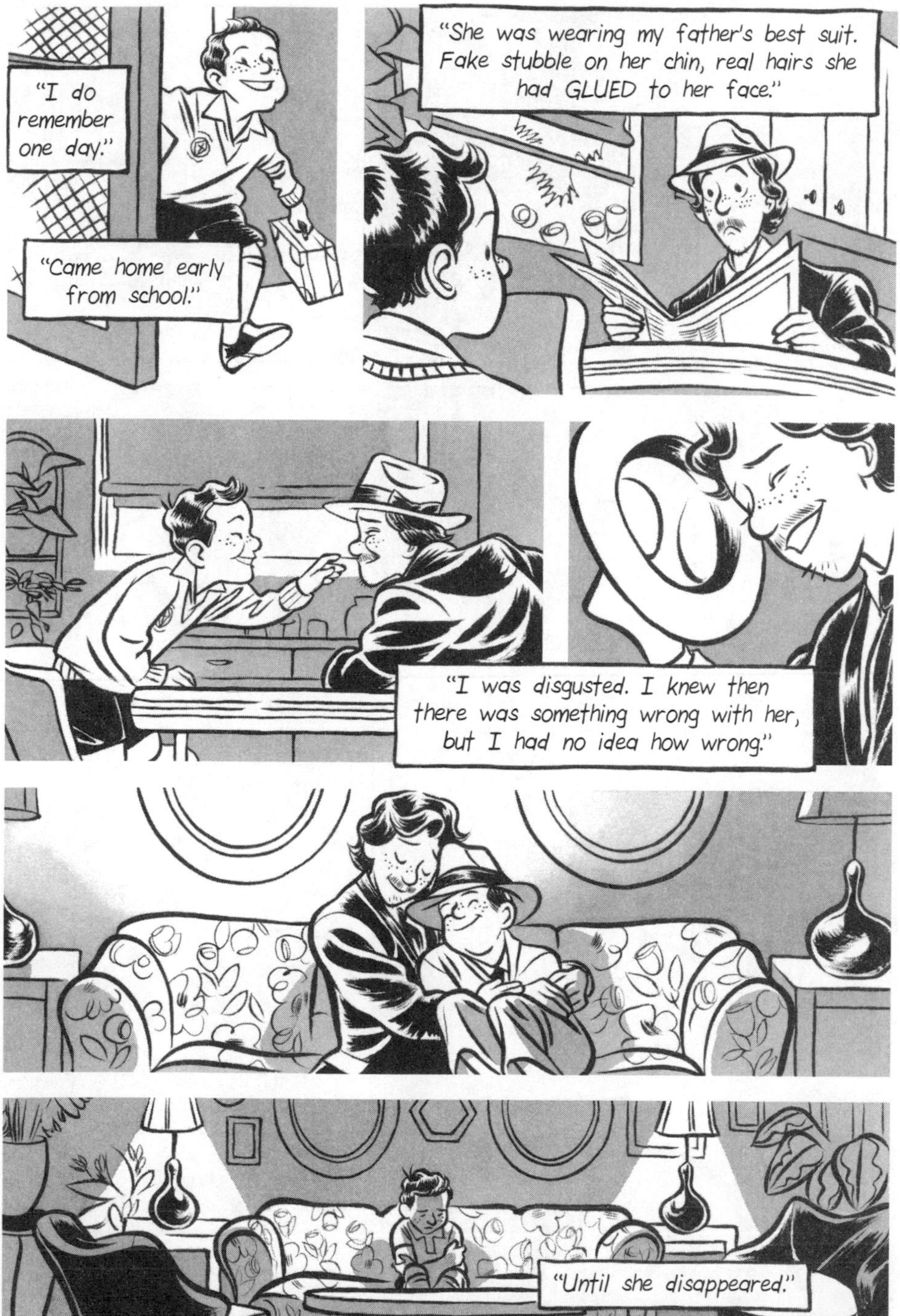
"I do remember one day."
"Came home early from school."
"She was wearing my father's best suit. Fake stubble on her chin, real hairs she had GLUED to her face."
"I was disgusted. I knew then there was something wrong with her, but I had no idea how wrong."
"Until she disappeared."

154

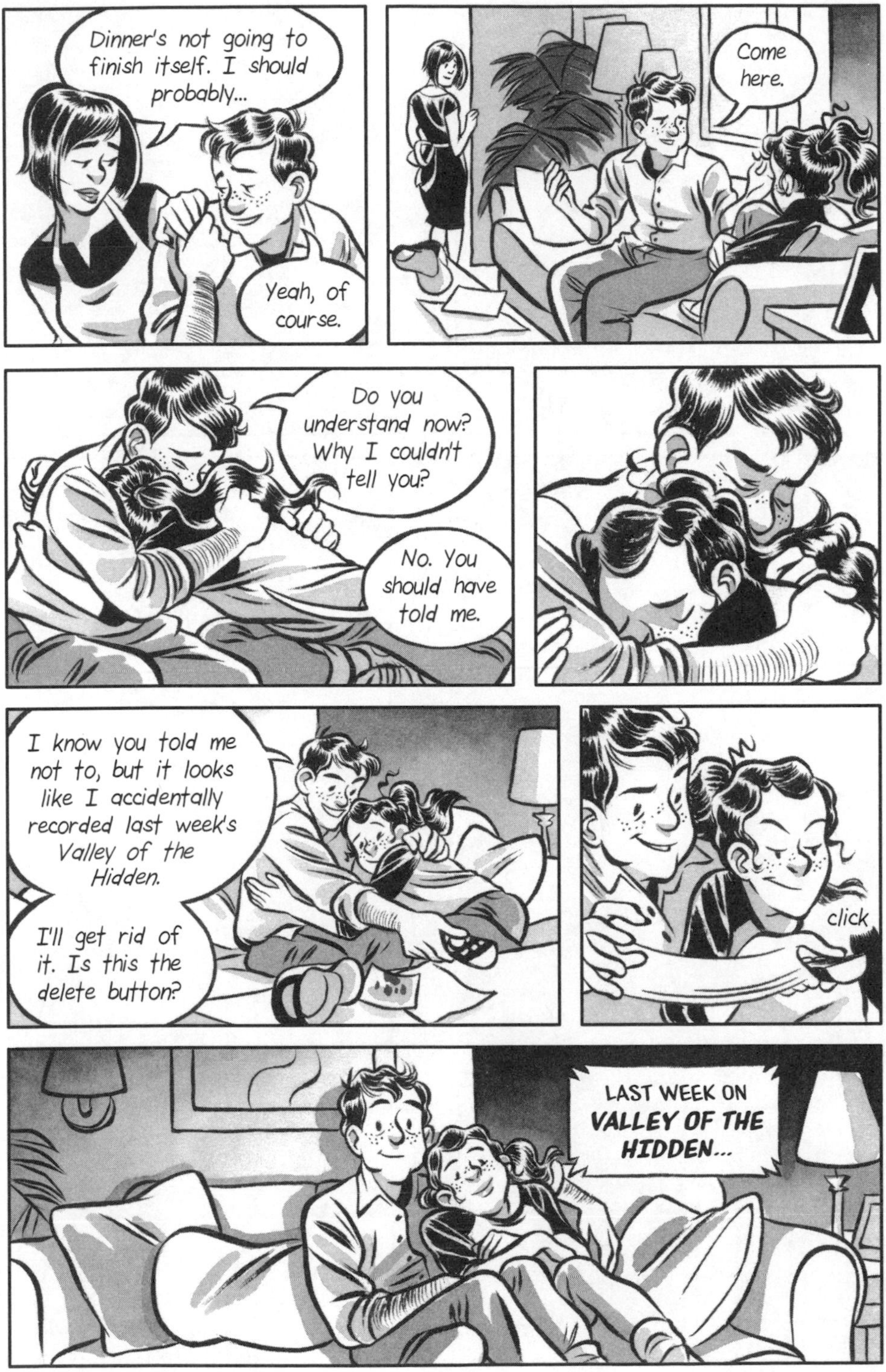
Dinner's not going to finish itself. I should probably...
Yeah, of course.
Come here.
Do you understand now? Why I couldn't tell you?
No. You should have told me.
I know you told me not to, but it looks like I accidentally recorded last week's Valley of the Hidden.
I'll get rid of it. Is this the delete button?
click
LAST WEEK ON VALLEY OF THE HIDDEN...

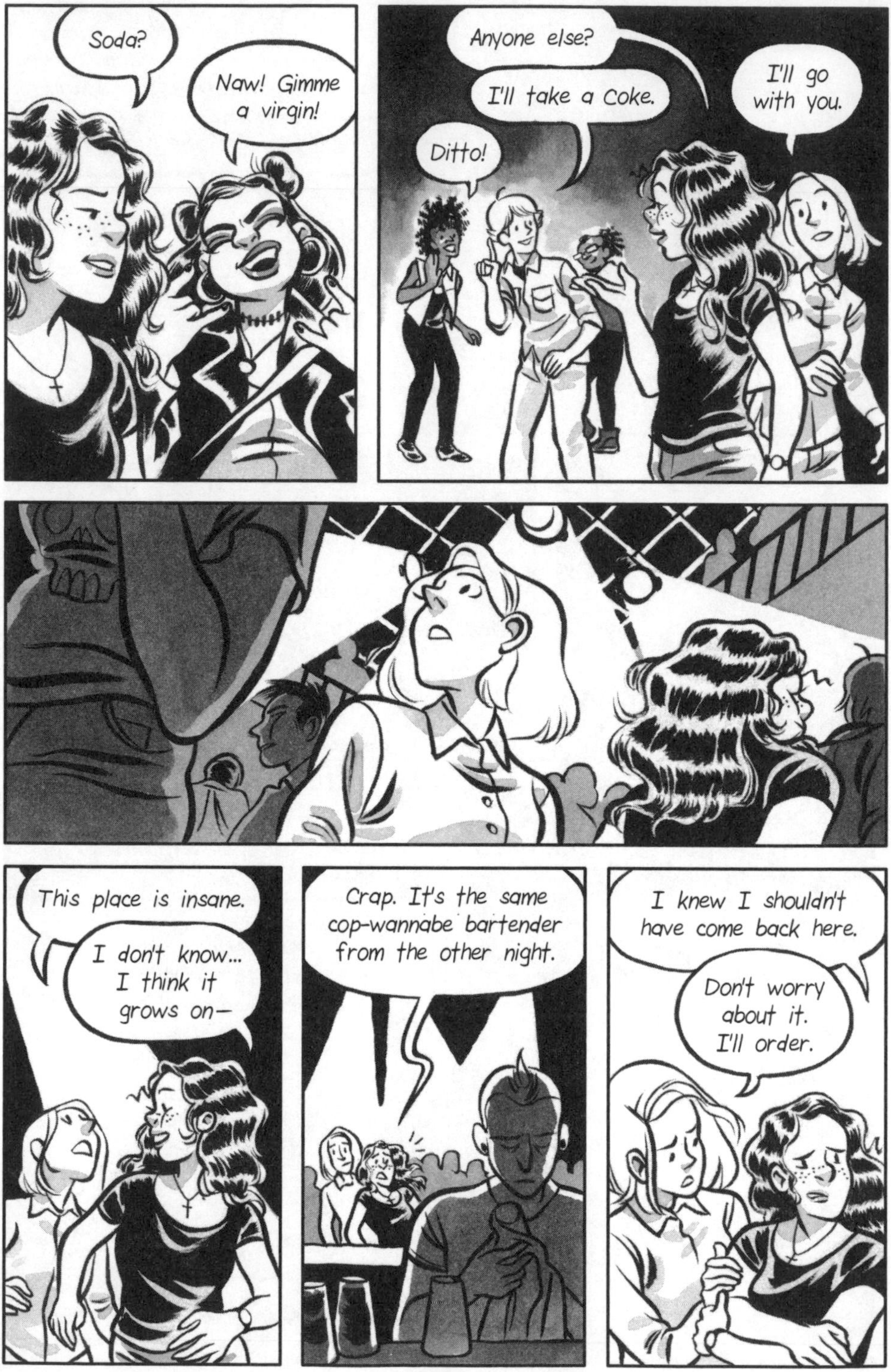
Soda?
Naw! Gimme a virgin!
Anyone else?
I'll take a Coke.
Ditto!
I'll go with you.
This place is insane.
I don't know... I think it grows on—
Crap. It's the same cop-wannabe bartender from the other night.
I knew I shouldn't have come back here.
Don't worry about it. I'll order.

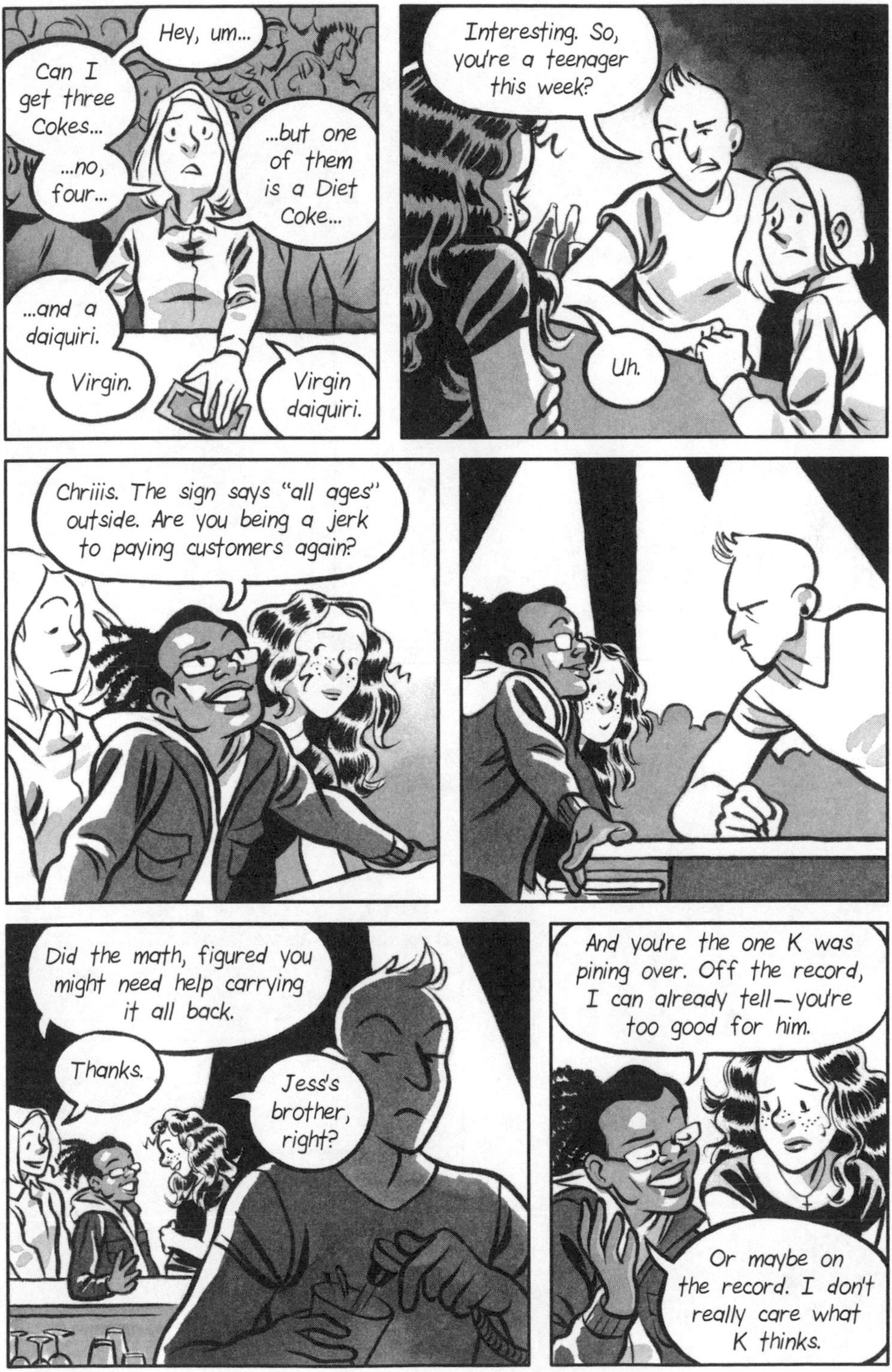
Hey, um...
Can I get three Cokes...
...no, four...
...but one of them is a Diet Coke...
...and a daiquiri.
Virgin.
Virgin daiquiri.
Interesting. So, you're a teenager this week?
Uh.
Chriiis. The sign says "all ages" outside. Are you being a jerk to paying customers again?
Did the math, figured you might need help carrying it all back.
Thanks.
Jess's brother, right?
And you're the one K was pining over. Off the record, I can already tell—you're too good for him.
Or maybe on the record. I don't really care what K thinks.

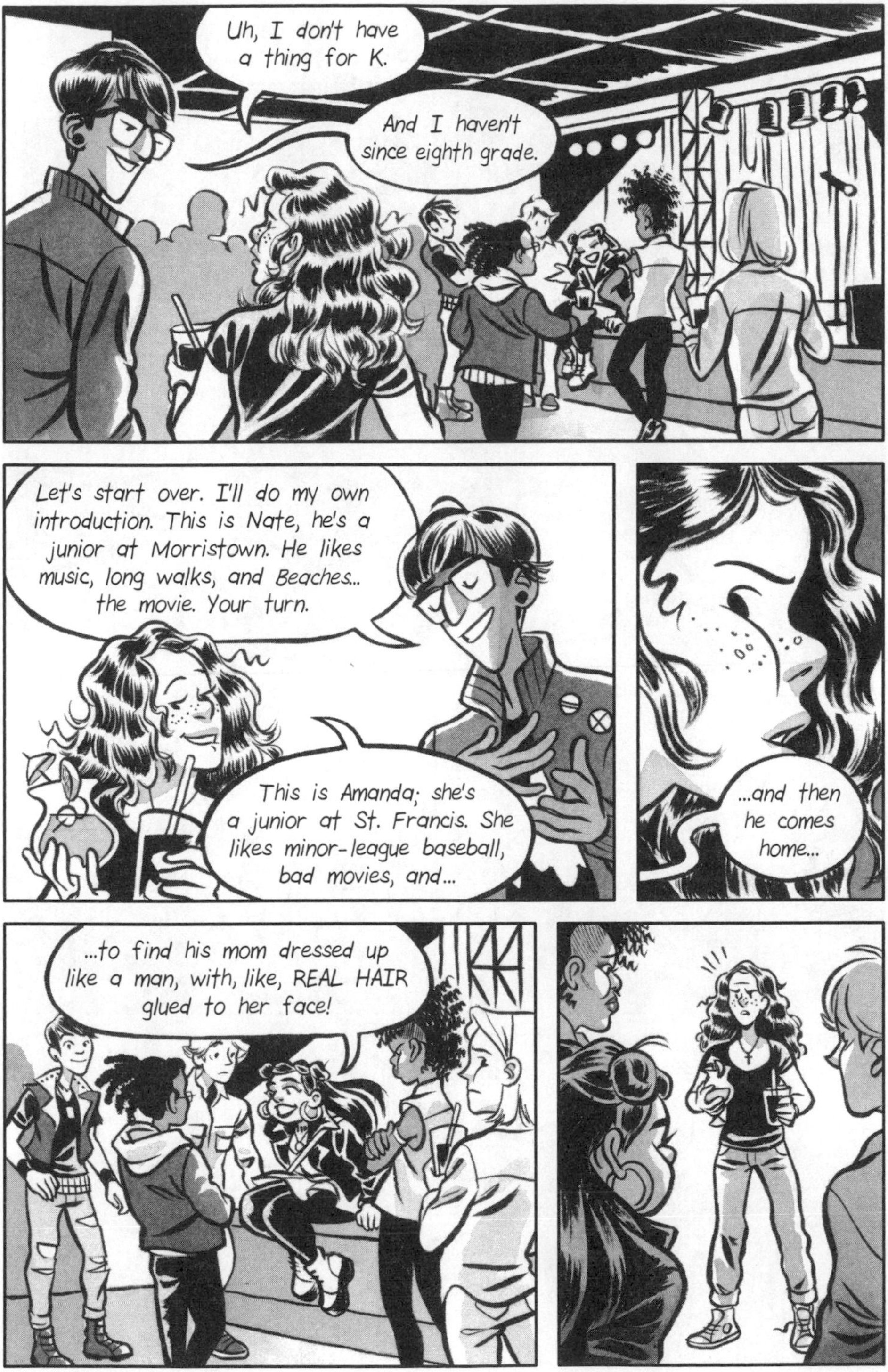
Uh, I don't have a thing for K.
And I haven't since eighth grade.
Let's start over. I'll do my own introduction. This is Nate, he's a junior at Morristown. He likes music, long walks, and *Beaches*... the movie. Your turn.
This is Amanda; she's a junior at St. Francis. She likes minor-league baseball, bad movies, and...
...and then he comes home...
...to find his mom dressed up like a man, with, like, REAL HAIR glued to her face!

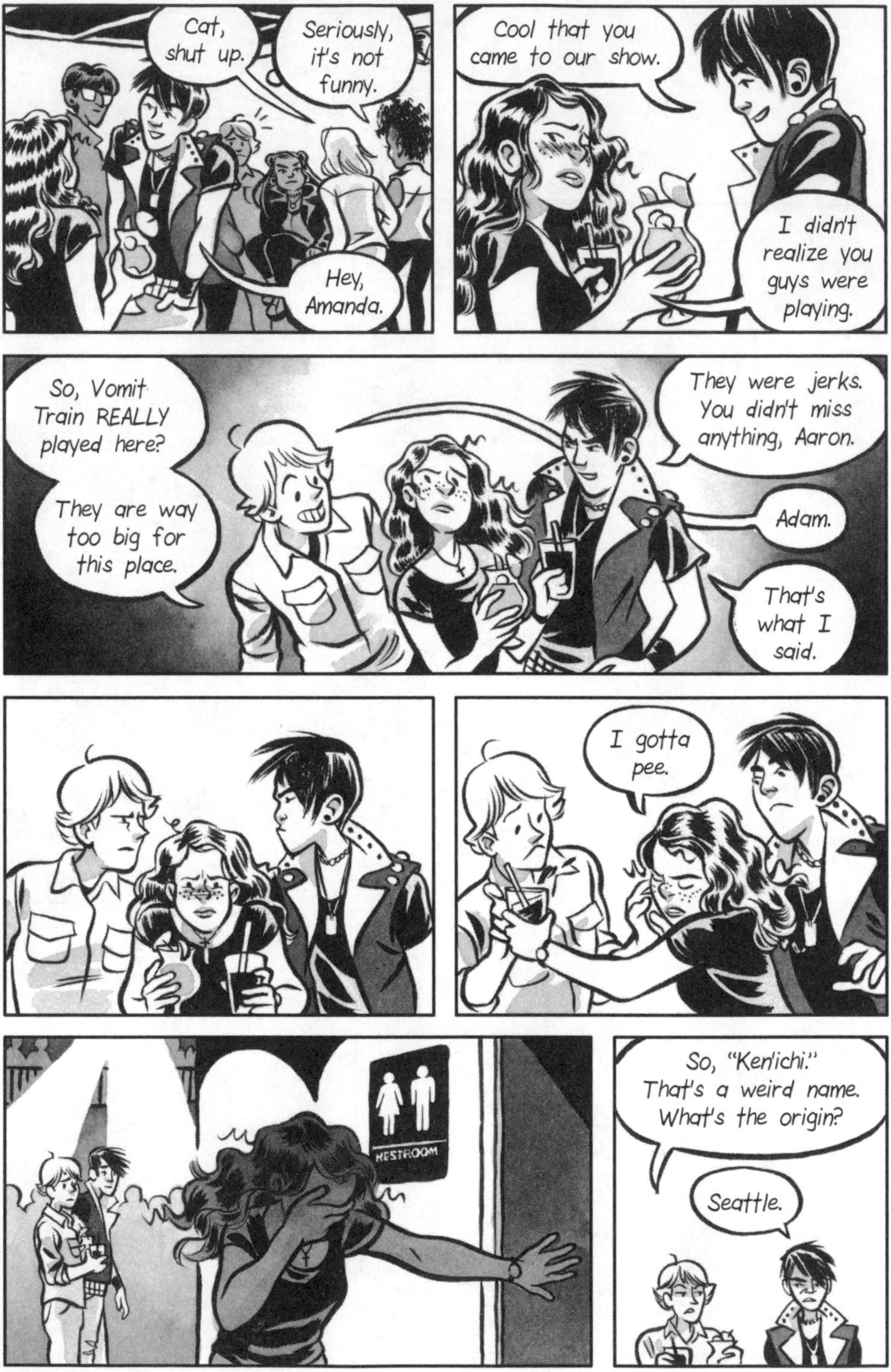
Cat, shut up.
Seriously, it's not funny.
Hey, Amanda.
Cool that you came to our show.
I didn't realize you guys were playing.
So, Vomit Train REALLY played here?
They are way too big for this place.
They were jerks. You didn't miss anything, Aaron.
Adam.
That's what I said.
I gotta pee.
RESTROOM
So, "Ken'ichi." That's a weird name. What's the origin?
Seattle.

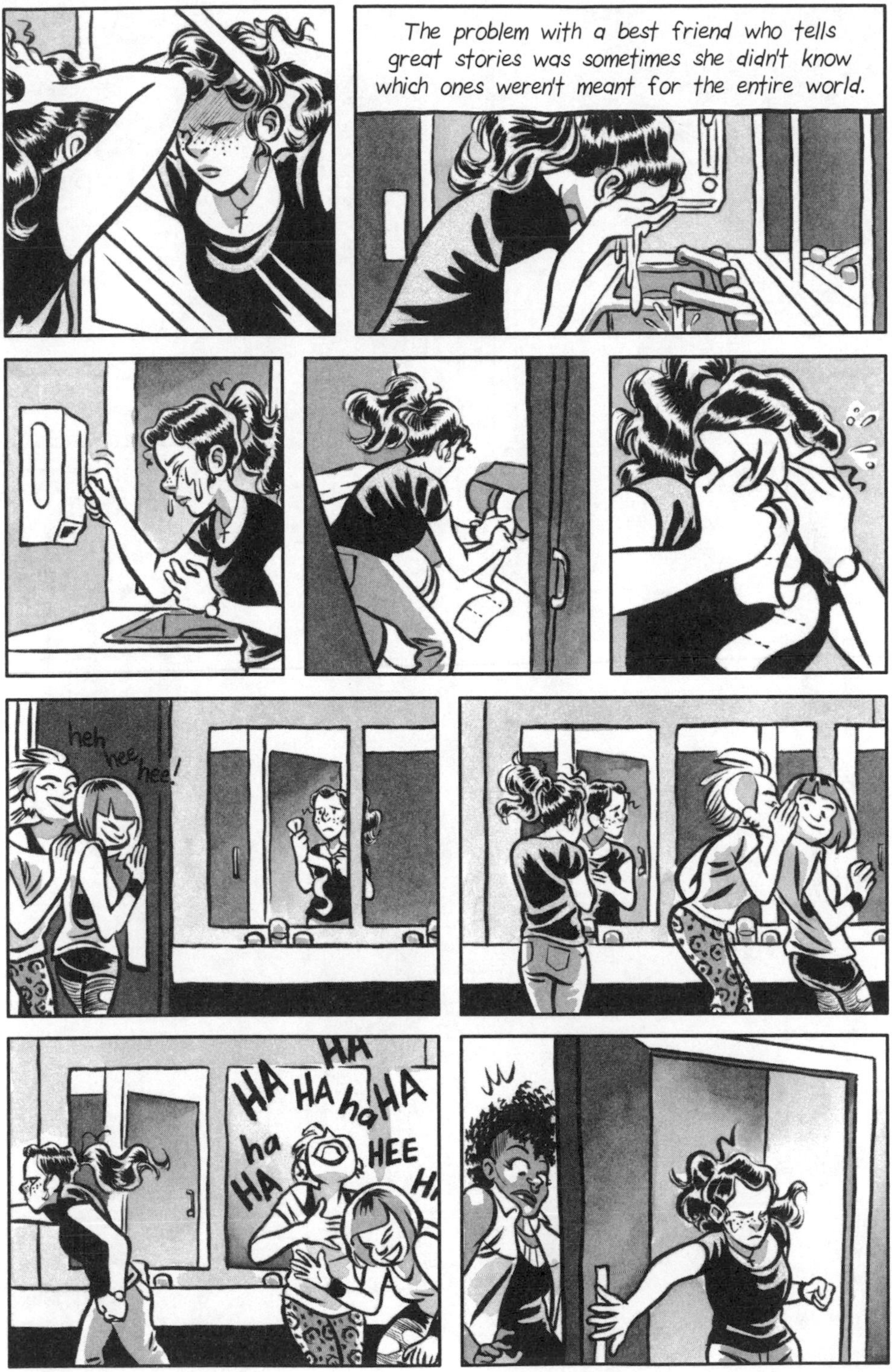
The problem with a best friend who tells great stories was sometimes she didn't know which ones weren't meant for the entire world.
heh hee hee!
HA HA HA ha HA ha HA HEE

169

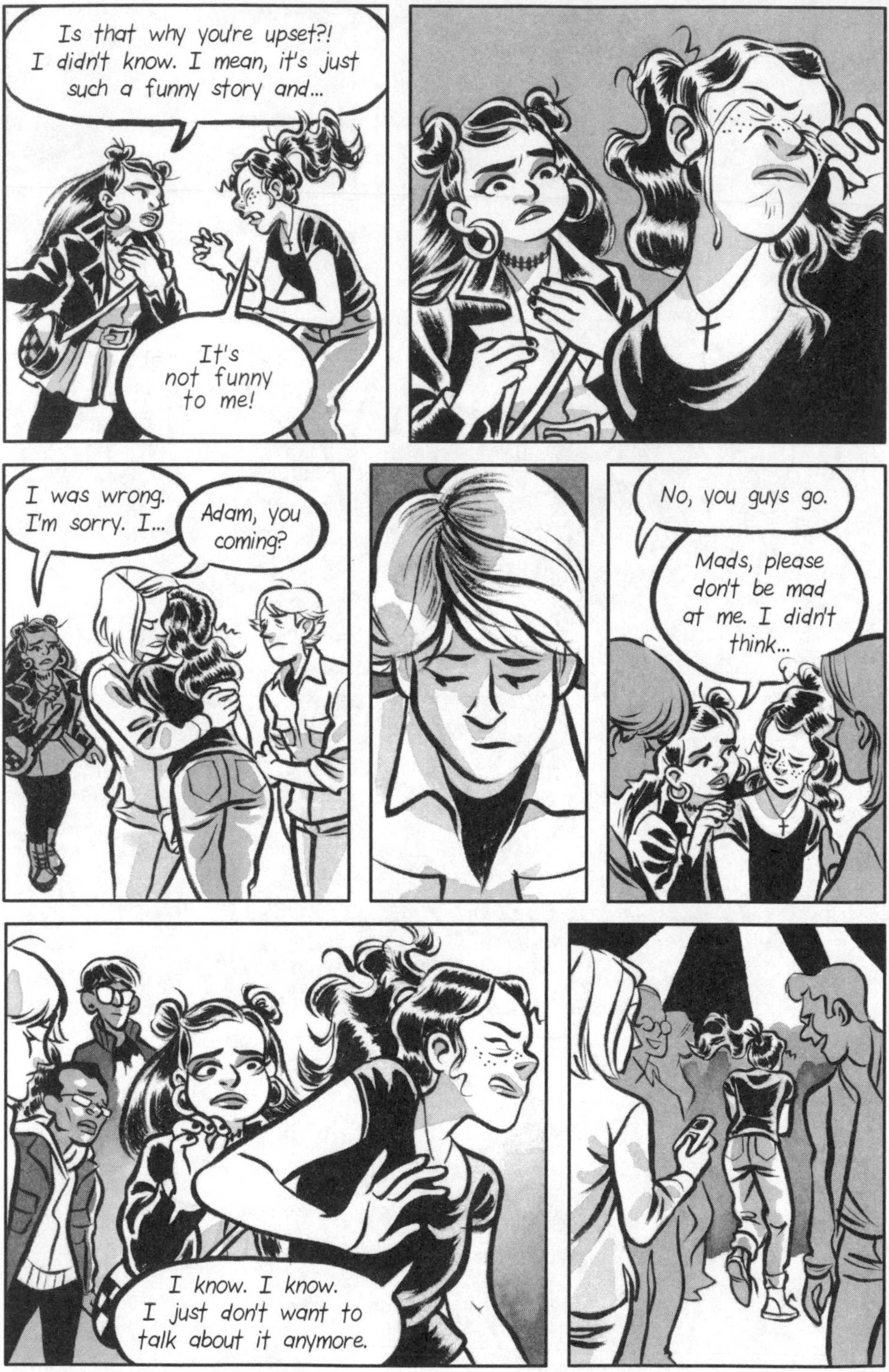
Is that why you're upset?! I didn't know. I mean, it's just such a funny story and...
It's not funny to me!
I was wrong. I'm sorry. I...
Adam, you coming?
No, you guys go.
Mads, please don't be mad at me. I didn't think...
I know. I know. I just don't want to talk about it anymore.

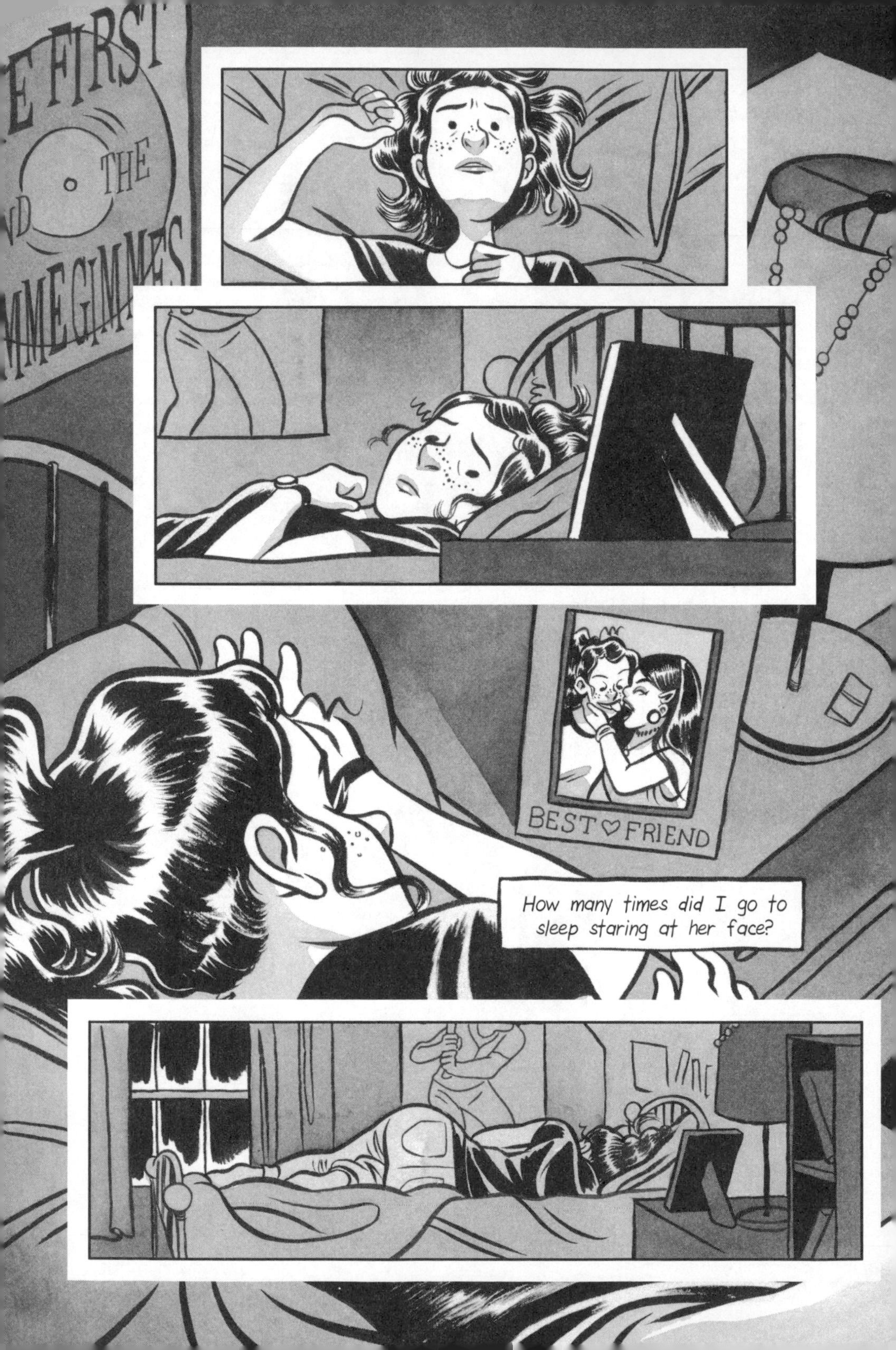
E FIRST
ND THE
MMEGIMMES
BEST♡FRIEND
How many times did I go to sleep staring at her face?

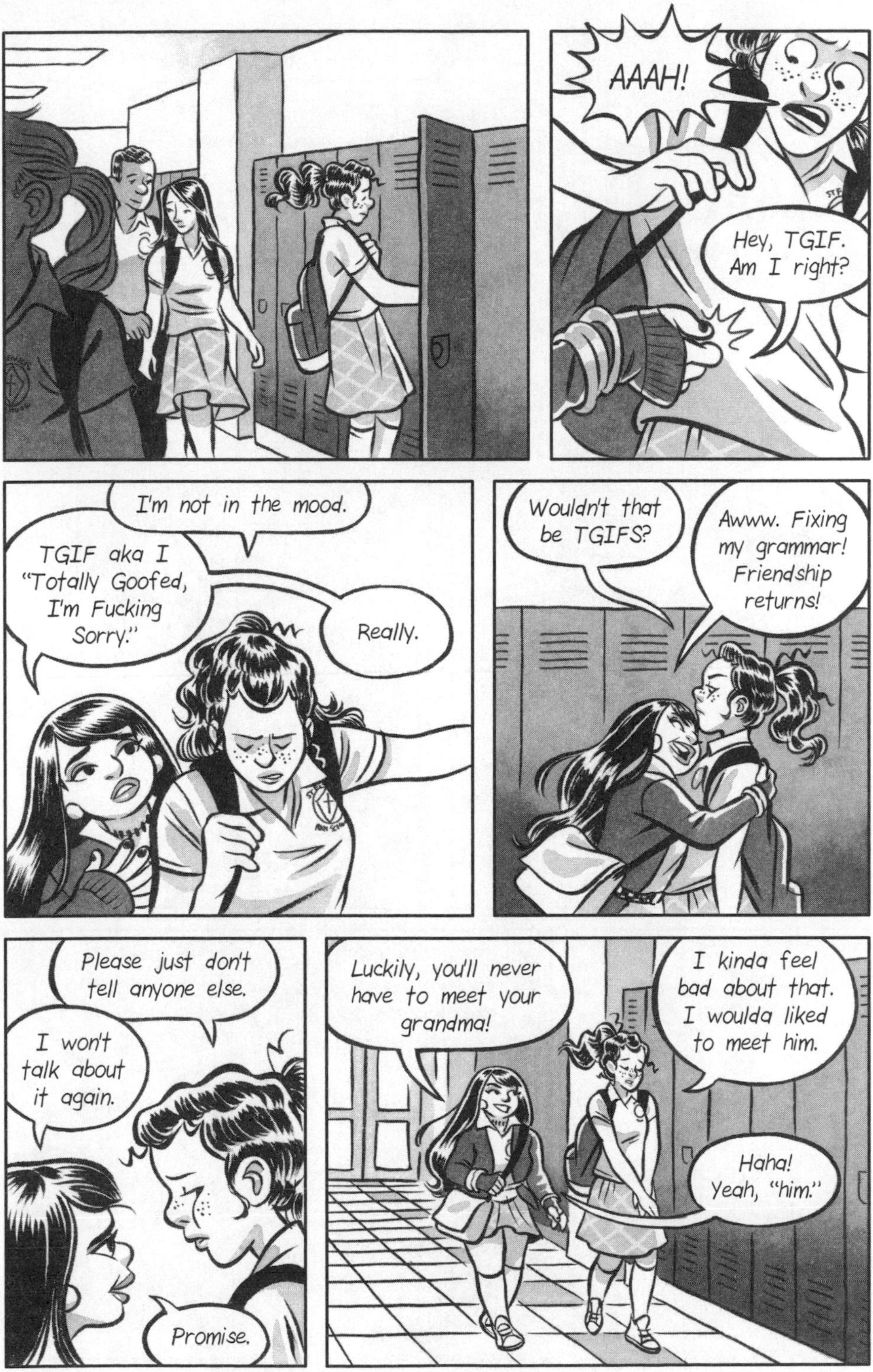
AAAH!
Hey, TGIF. Am I right?
I'm not in the mood.
TGIF aka I "Totally Goofed, I'm Fucking Sorry."
Really.
Wouldn't that be TGIFS?
Awww. Fixing my grammar! Friendship returns!
Please just don't tell anyone else.
I won't talk about it again.
Promise.
Luckily, you'll never have to meet your grandma!
I kinda feel bad about that. I woulda liked to meet him.
Haha! Yeah, "him."

179

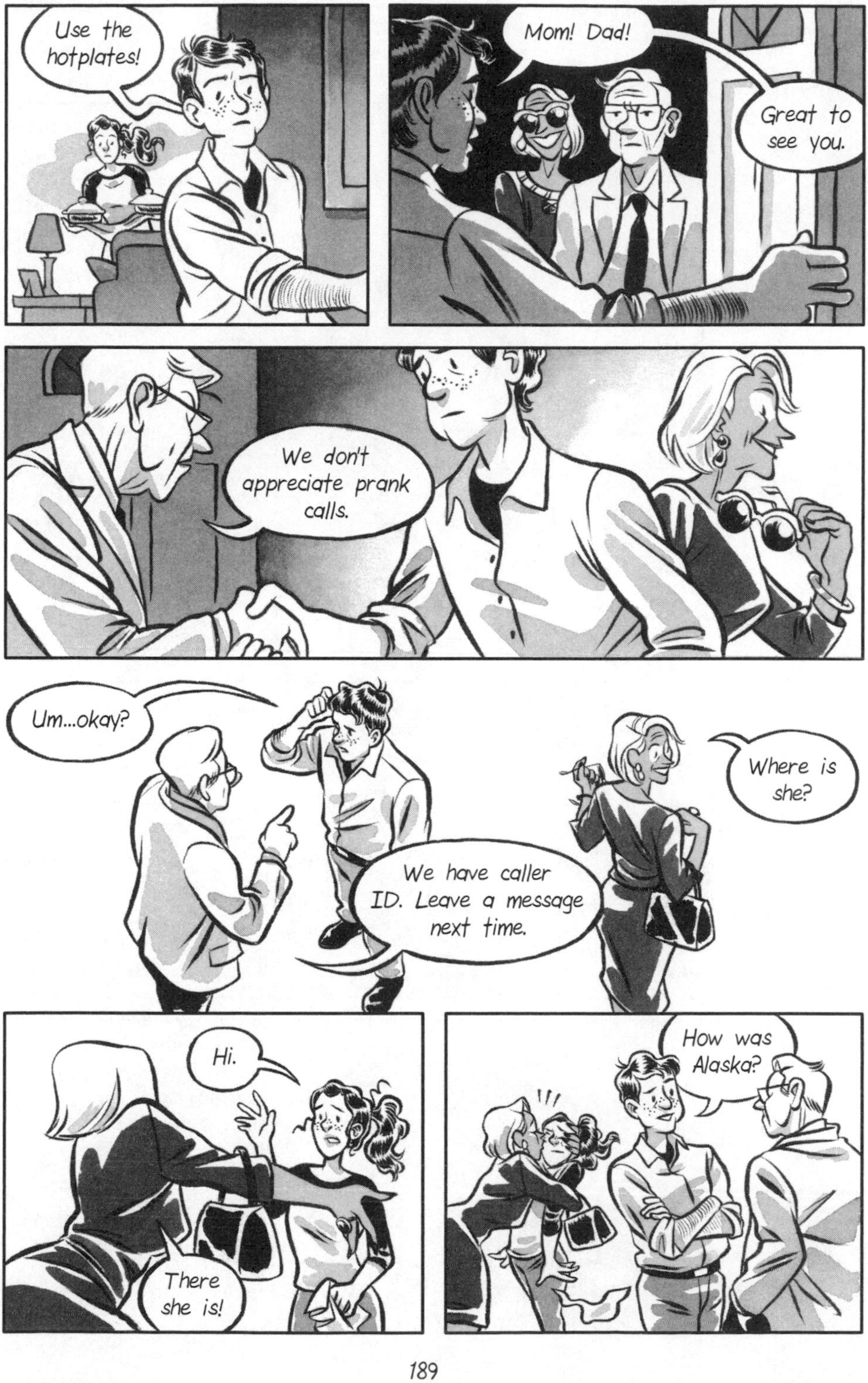
Use the hotplates!
Mom! Dad!
Great to see you.
We don't appreciate prank calls.
Um...okay?
Where is she?
We have caller ID. Leave a message next time.
Hi.
There she is!
How was Alaska?

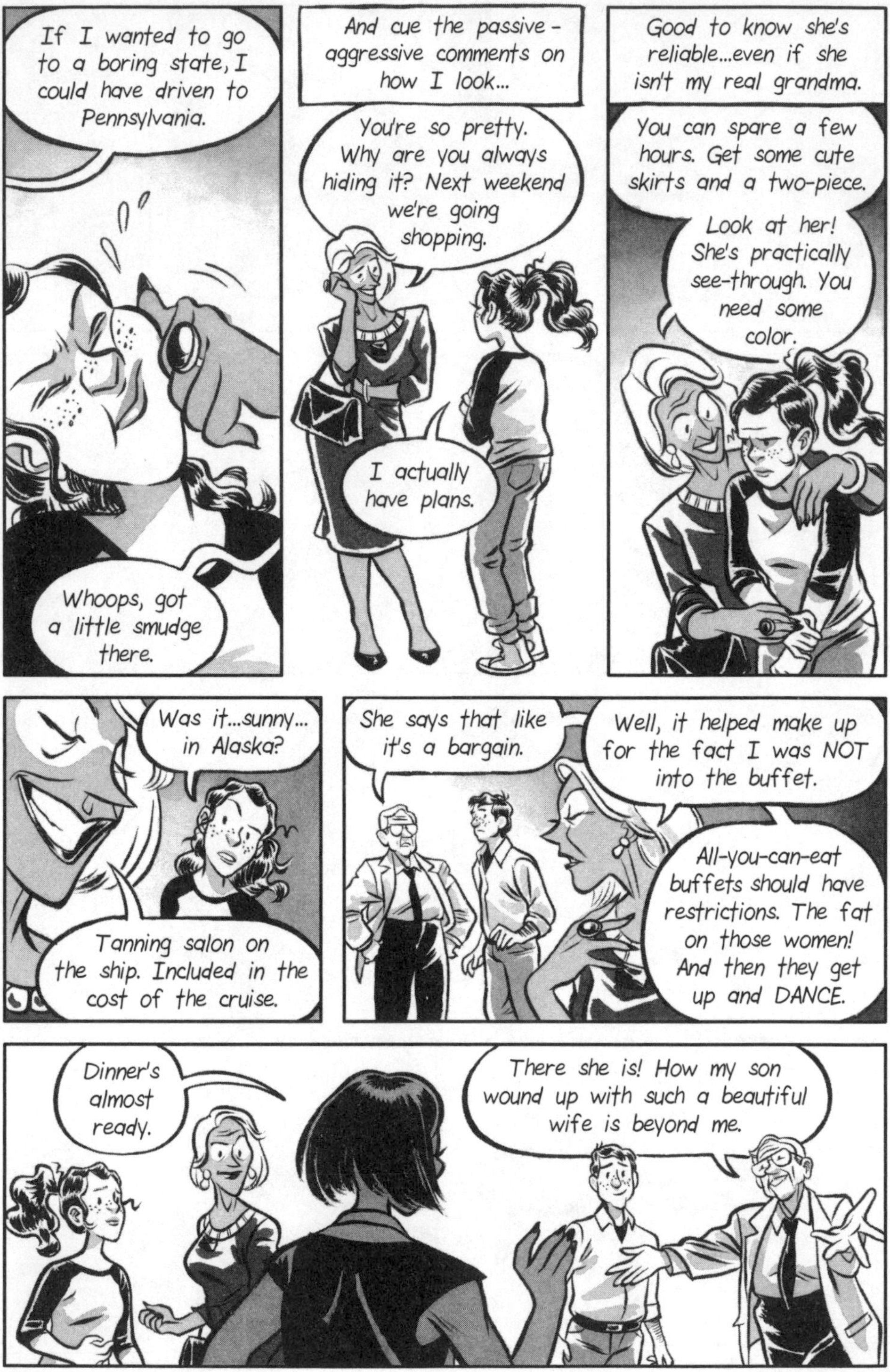

If I wanted to go to a boring state, I could have driven to Pennsylvania.
Whoops, got a little smudge there.
And cue the passive-aggressive comments on how I look...
You're so pretty. Why are you always hiding it? Next weekend we're going shopping.
I actually have plans.
Good to know she's reliable...even if she isn't my real grandma.
You can spare a few hours. Get some cute skirts and a two-piece.
Look at her! She's practically see-through. You need some color.
Was it...sunny... in Alaska?
Tanning salon on the ship. Included in the cost of the cruise.
She says that like it's a bargain.
Well, it helped make up for the fact I was NOT into the buffet.
All-you-can-eat buffets should have restrictions. The fat on those women! And then they get up and DANCE.
Dinner's almost ready.
There she is! How my son wound up with such a beautiful wife is beyond me.

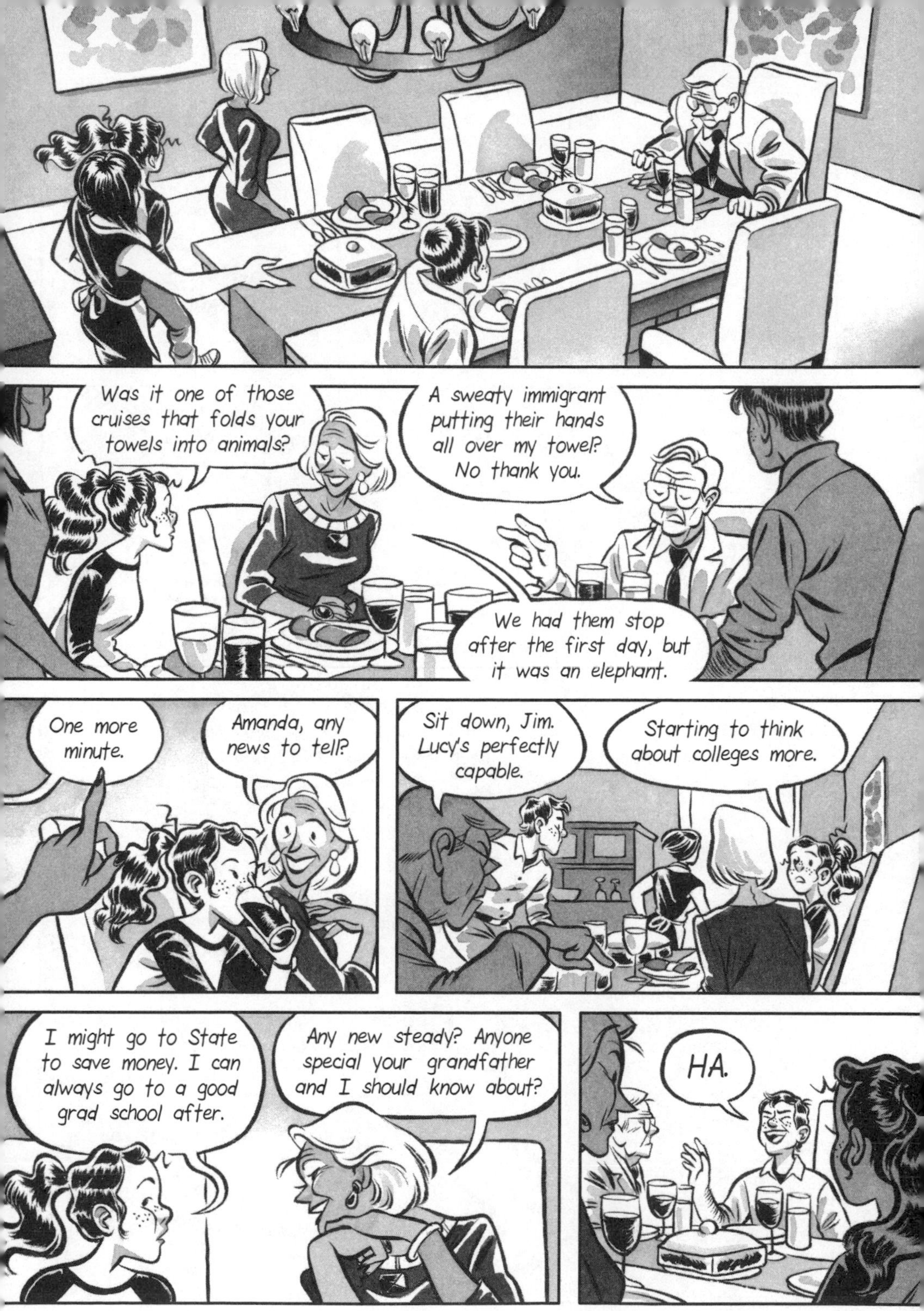
Was it one of those cruises that folds your towels into animals?
A sweaty immigrant putting their hands all over my towel? No thank you.
We had them stop after the first day, but it was an elephant.
One more minute.
Amanda, any news to tell?
Sit down, Jim. Lucy's perfectly capable.
Starting to think about colleges more.
I might go to State to save money. I can always go to a good grad school after.
Any new steady? Anyone special your grandfather and I should know about?
HA.

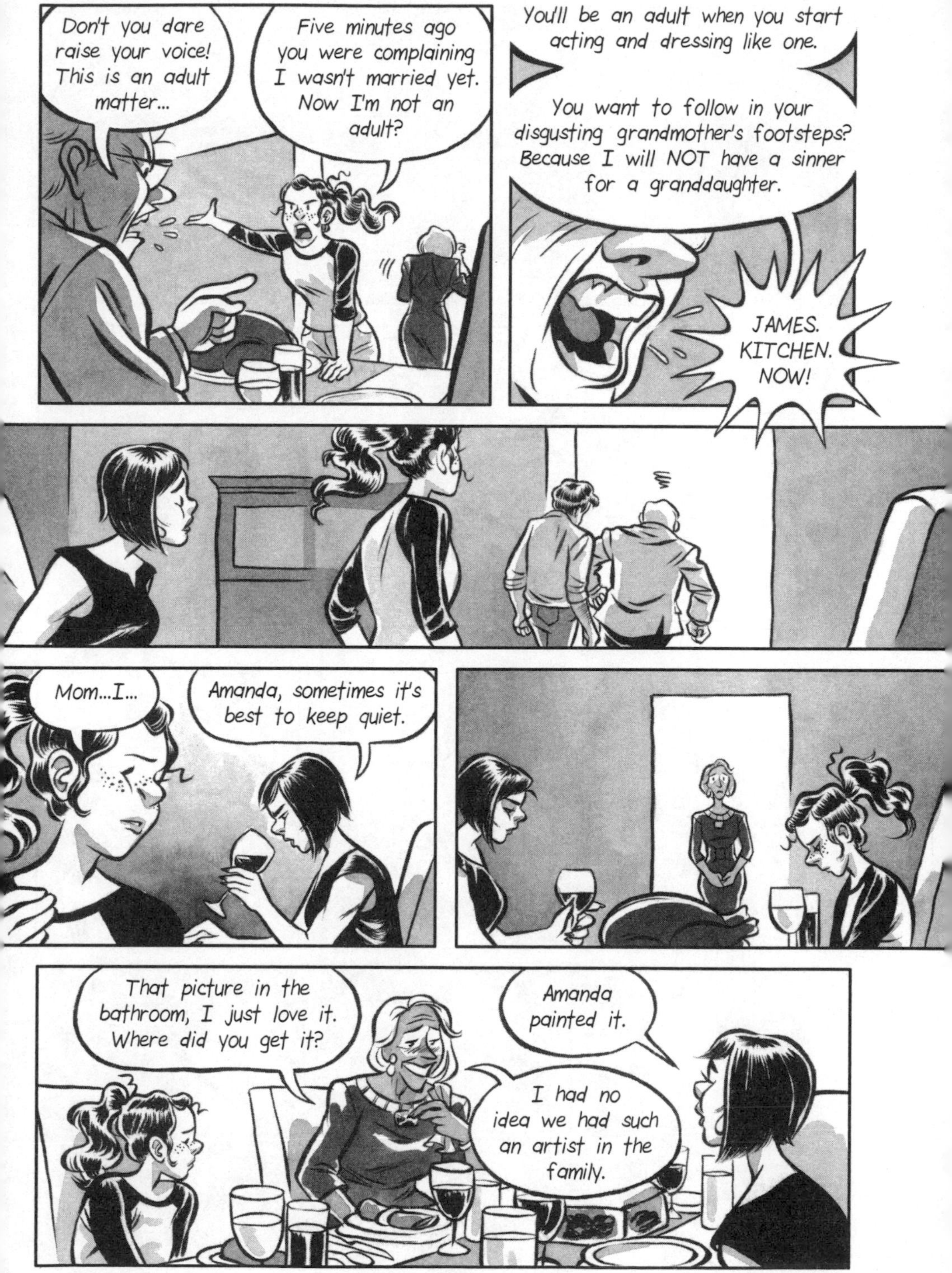
Don't you dare raise your voice! This is an adult matter...
Five minutes ago you were complaining I wasn't married yet. Now I'm not an adult?
You'll be an adult when you start acting and dressing like one.
You want to follow in your disgusting grandmother's footsteps? Because I will NOT have a sinner for a granddaughter.
JAMES. KITCHEN. NOW!
Mom...I...
Amanda, sometimes it's best to keep quiet.
That picture in the bathroom, I just love it. Where did you get it?
Amanda painted it.
I had no idea we had such an artist in the family.

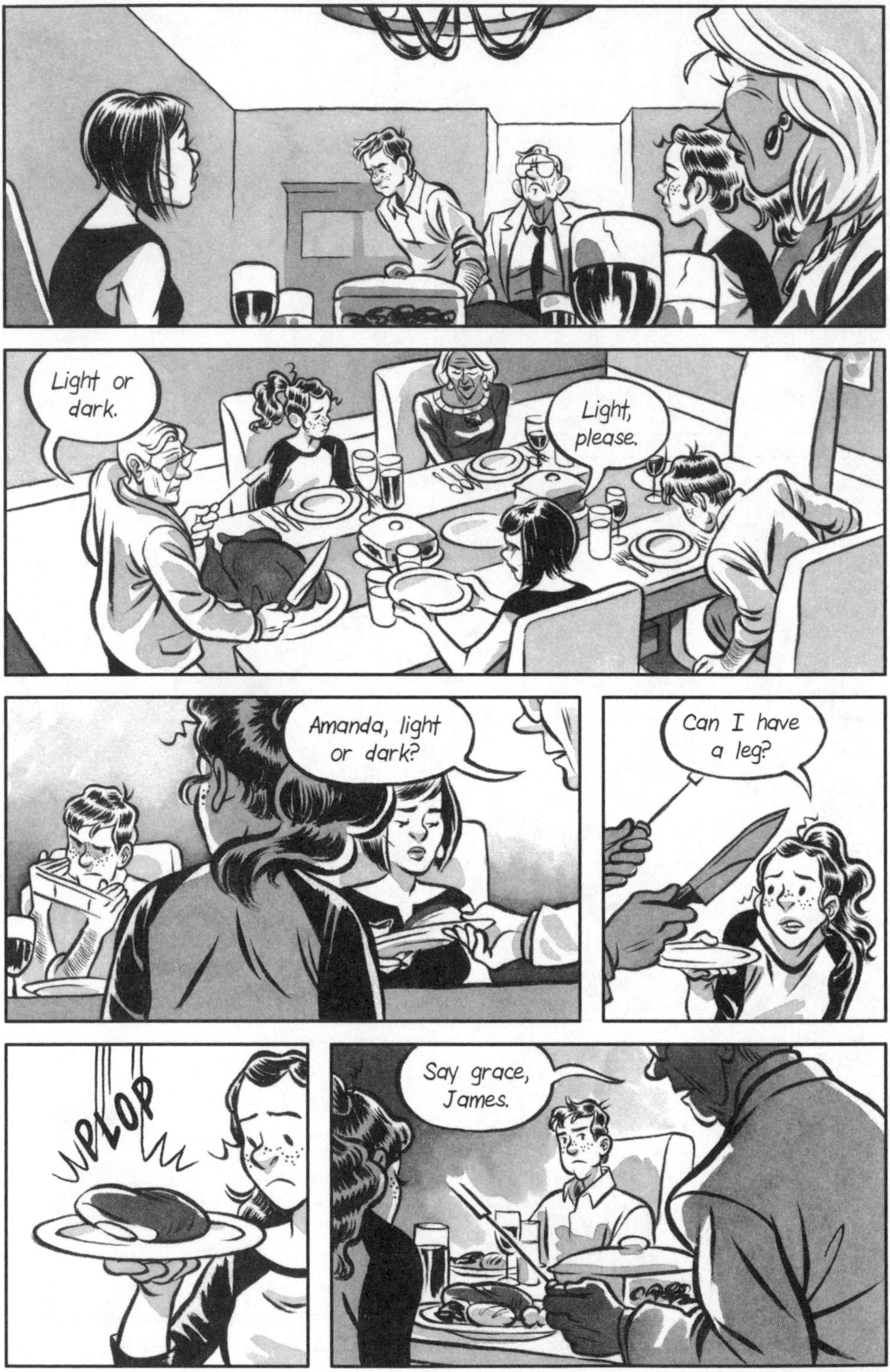
Light or dark.
Light, please.
Amanda, light or dark?
Can I have a leg?
PLOP
Say grace, James.

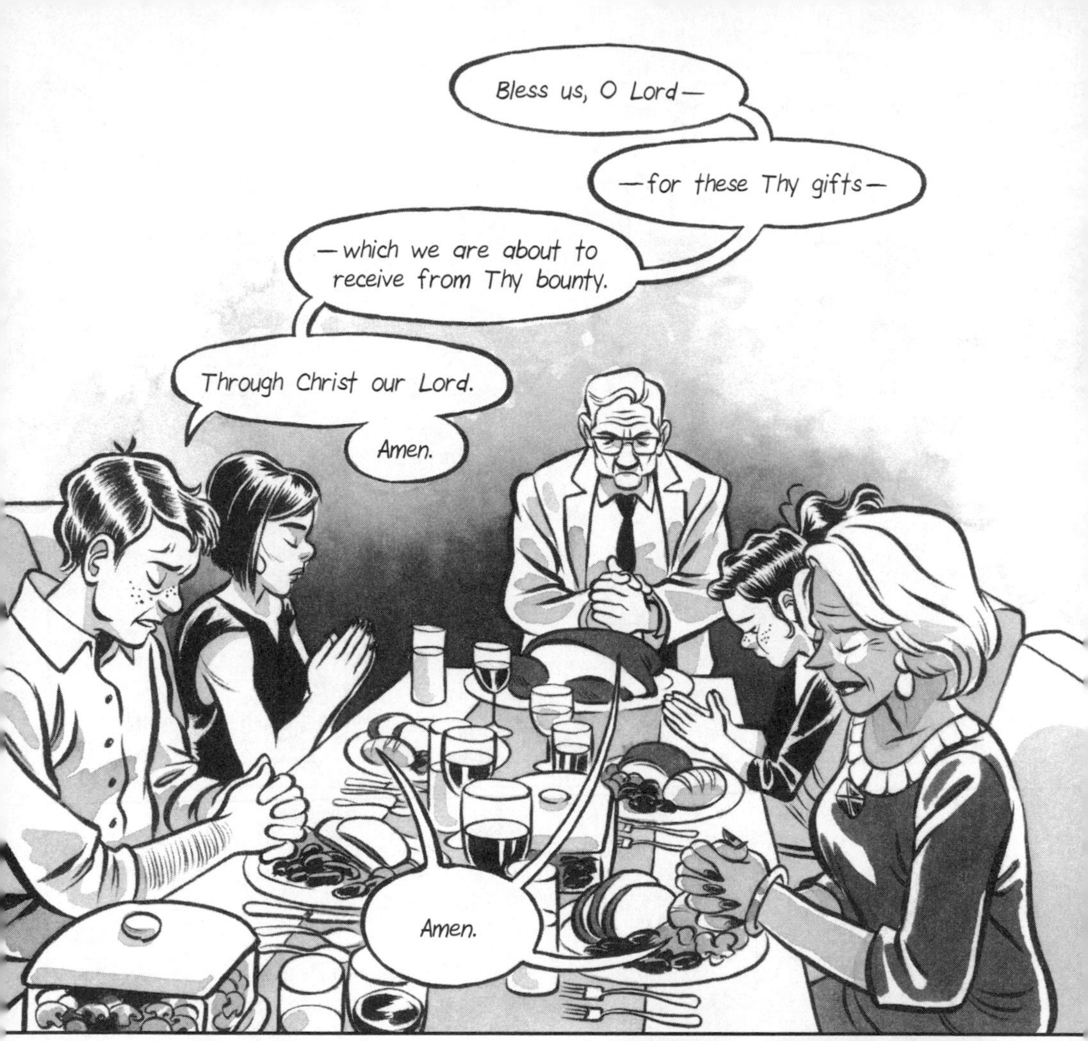
Bless us, O Lord—
—for these Thy gifts—
—which we are about to receive from Thy bounty.
Through Christ our Lord.
Amen.
Amen.

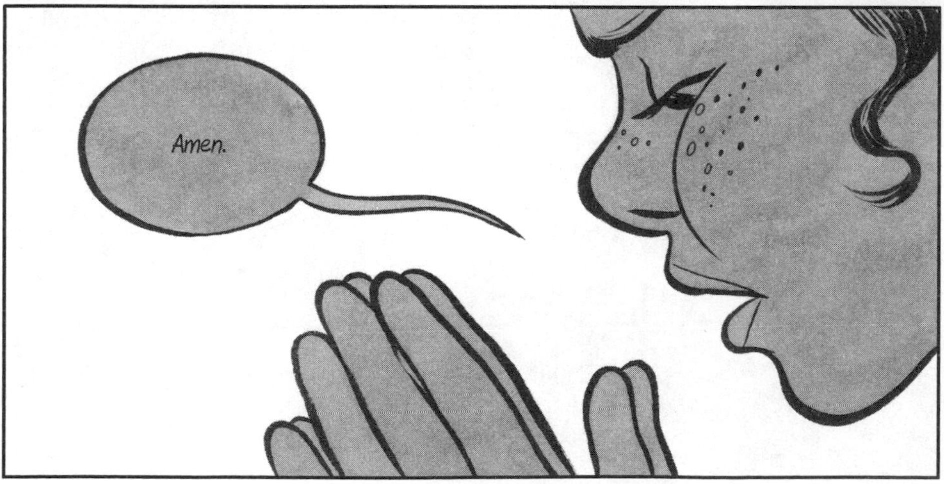
Amen.

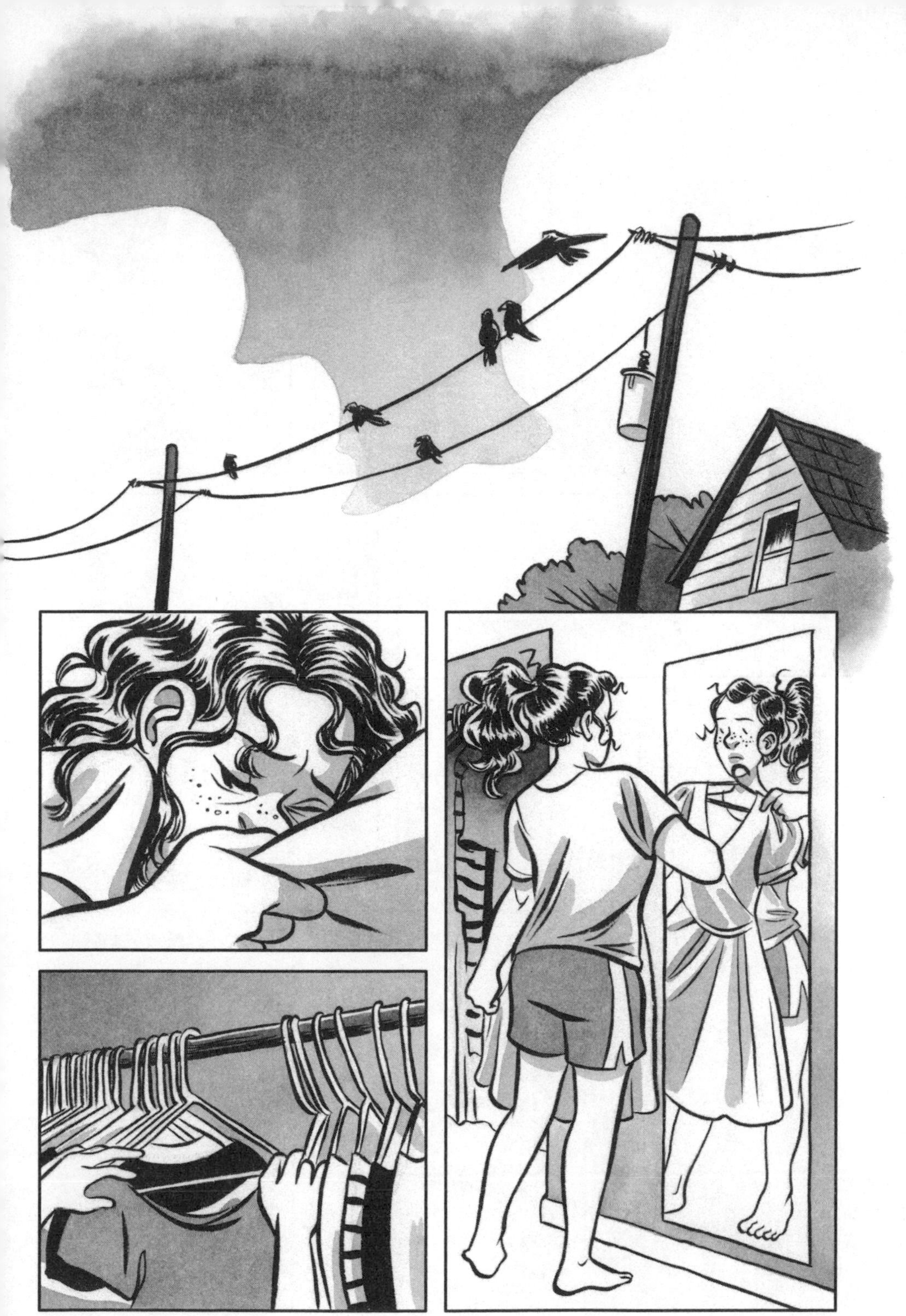

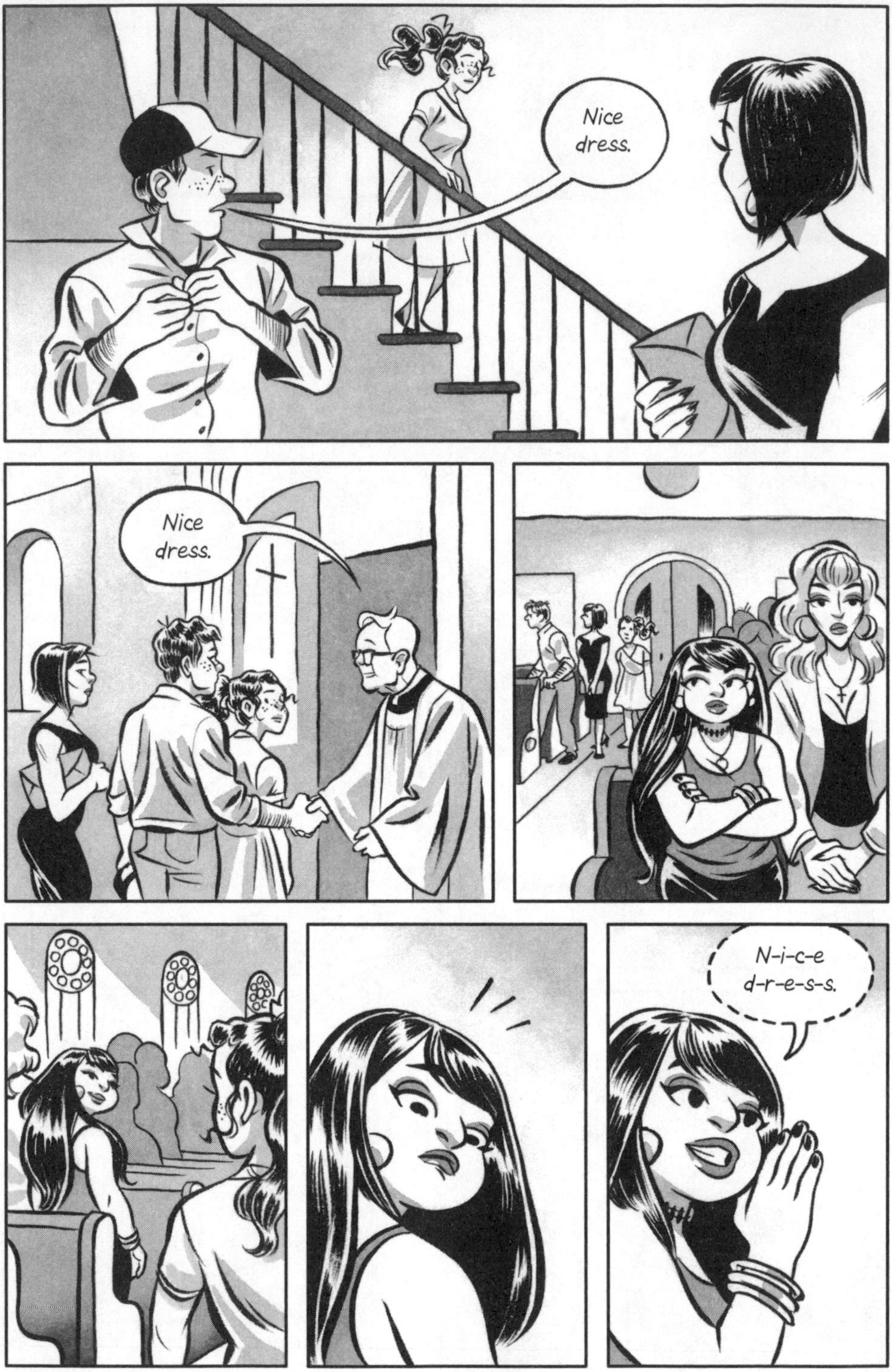

Nice dress.
Nice dress.
N-i-c-e d-r-e-s-s.

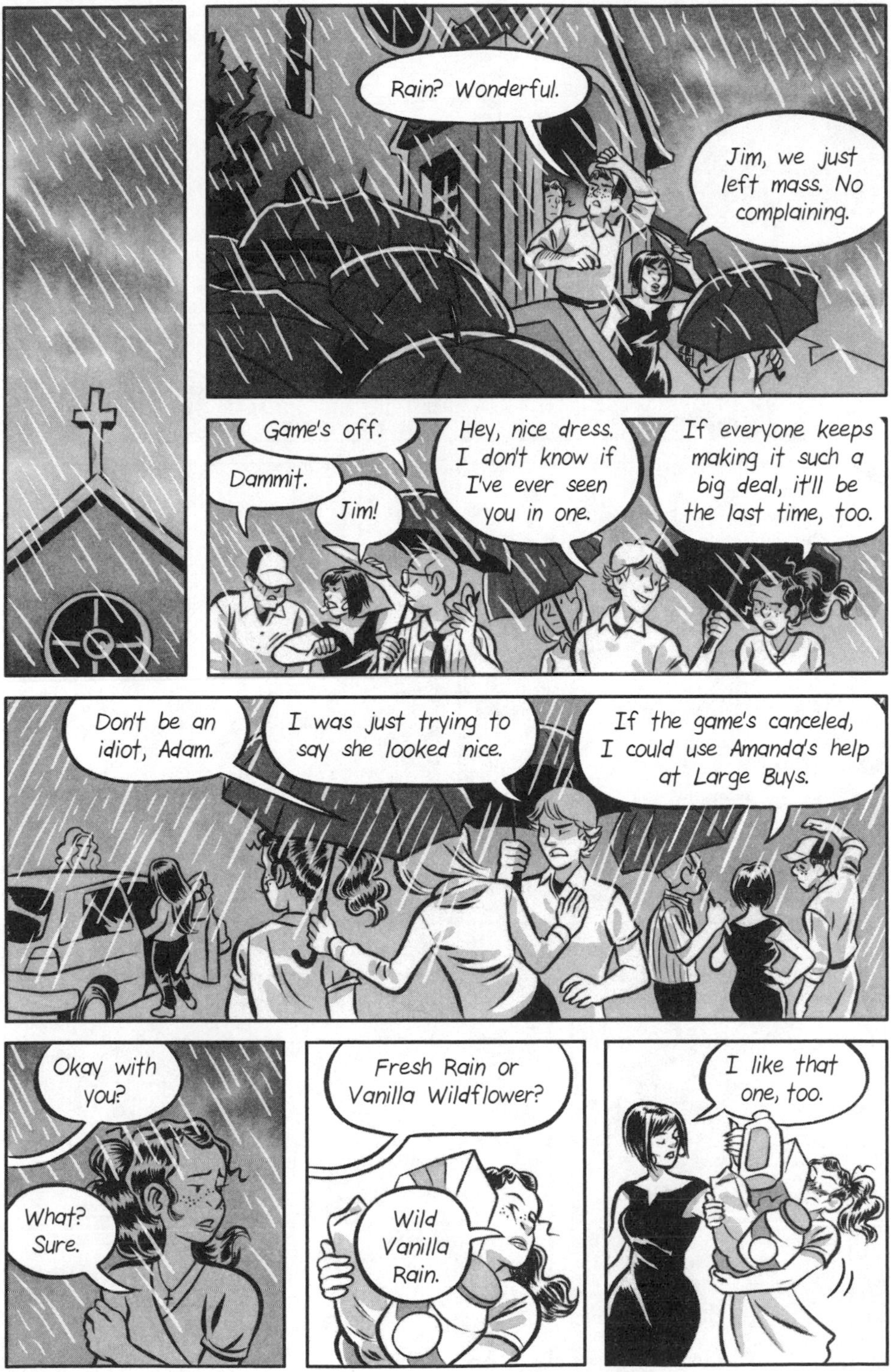
Rain? Wonderful.
Jim, we just left mass. No complaining.
Game's off.
Dammit.
Jim!
Hey, nice dress. I don't know if I've ever seen you in one.
If everyone keeps making it such a big deal, it'll be the last time, too.
Don't be an idiot, Adam.
I was just trying to say she looked nice.
If the game's canceled, I could use Amanda's help at Large Buys.
Okay with you?
What? Sure.
Fresh Rain or Vanilla Wildflower?
Wild Vanilla Rain.
I like that one, too.

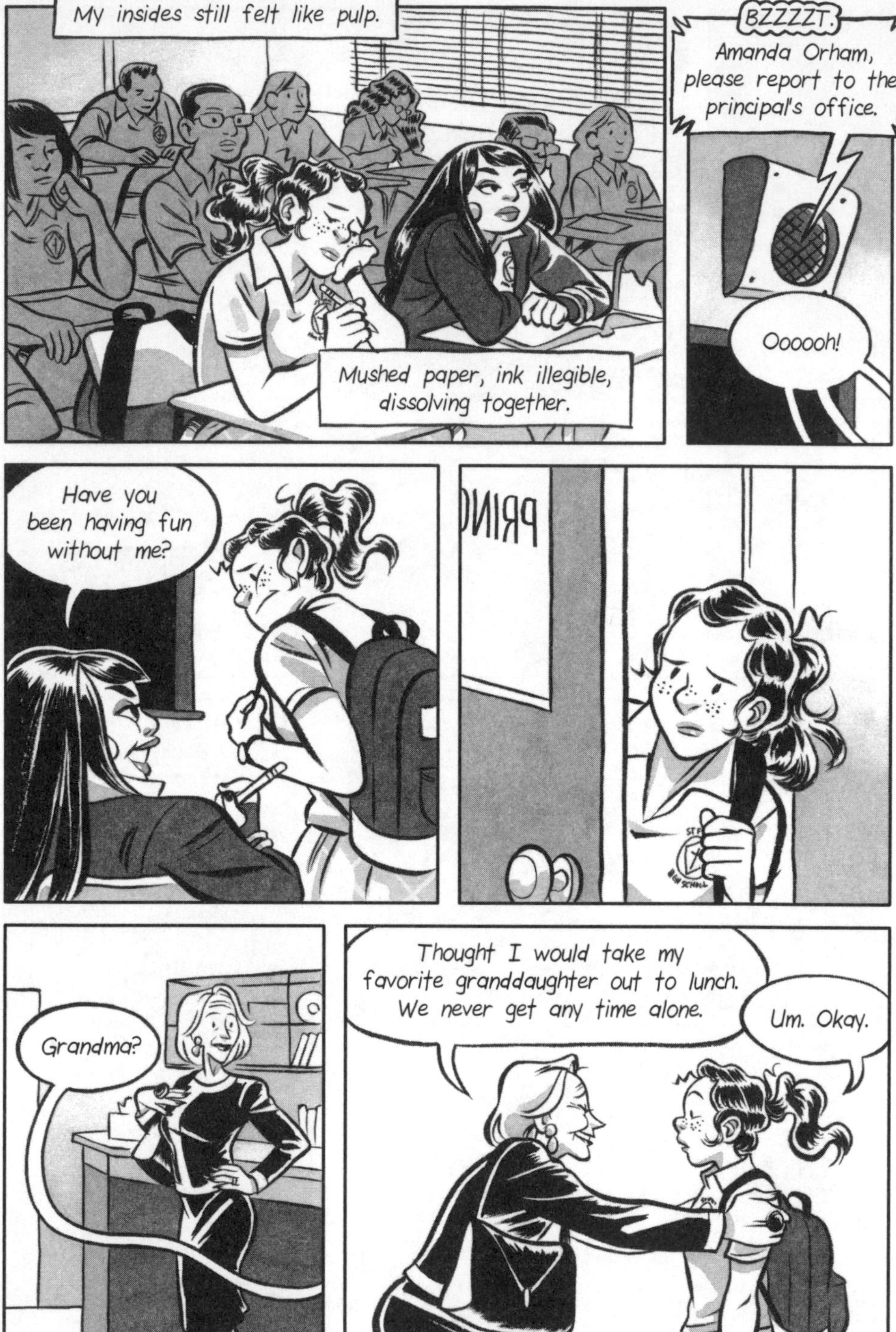
My insides still felt like pulp.
Mushed paper, ink illegible, dissolving together.
BZZZZT.
Amanda Orham, please report to the principal's office.
Oooooh!
Have you been having fun without me?
PRINC
Grandma?
Thought I would take my favorite granddaughter out to lunch. We never get any time alone.
Um. Okay.

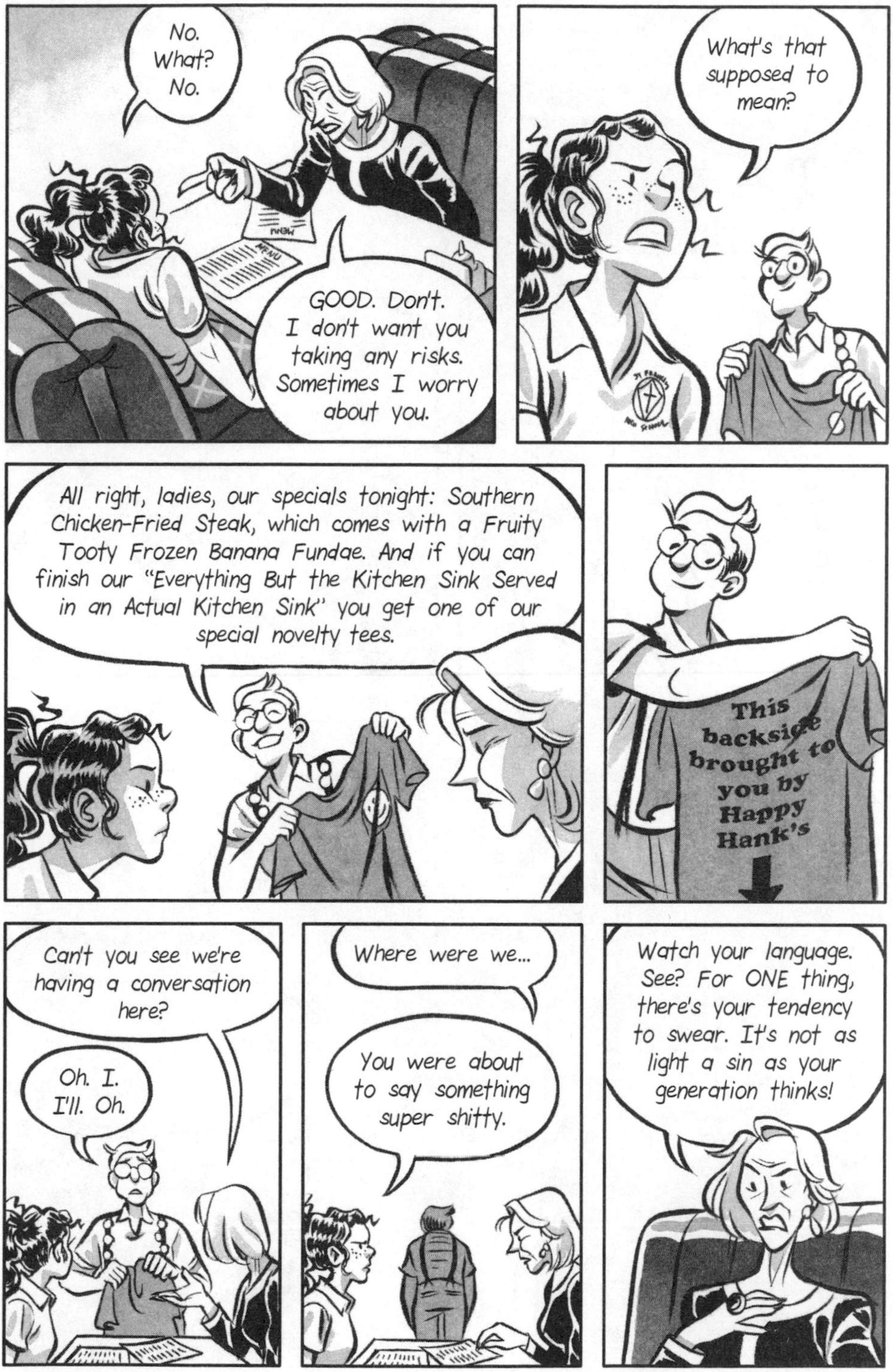

No.
What?
No.
GOOD. Don't. I don't want you taking any risks. Sometimes I worry about you.
What's that supposed to mean?
All right, ladies, our specials tonight: Southern Chicken-Fried Steak, which comes with a Fruity Tooty Frozen Banana Fundae. And if you can finish our "Everything But the Kitchen Sink Served in an Actual Kitchen Sink" you get one of our special novelty tees.
This backside brought to you by Happy Hank's
Can't you see we're having a conversation here?
Oh. I. I'll. Oh.
Where were we...
You were about to say something super shitty.
Watch your language. See? For ONE thing, there's your tendency to swear. It's not as light a sin as your generation thinks!

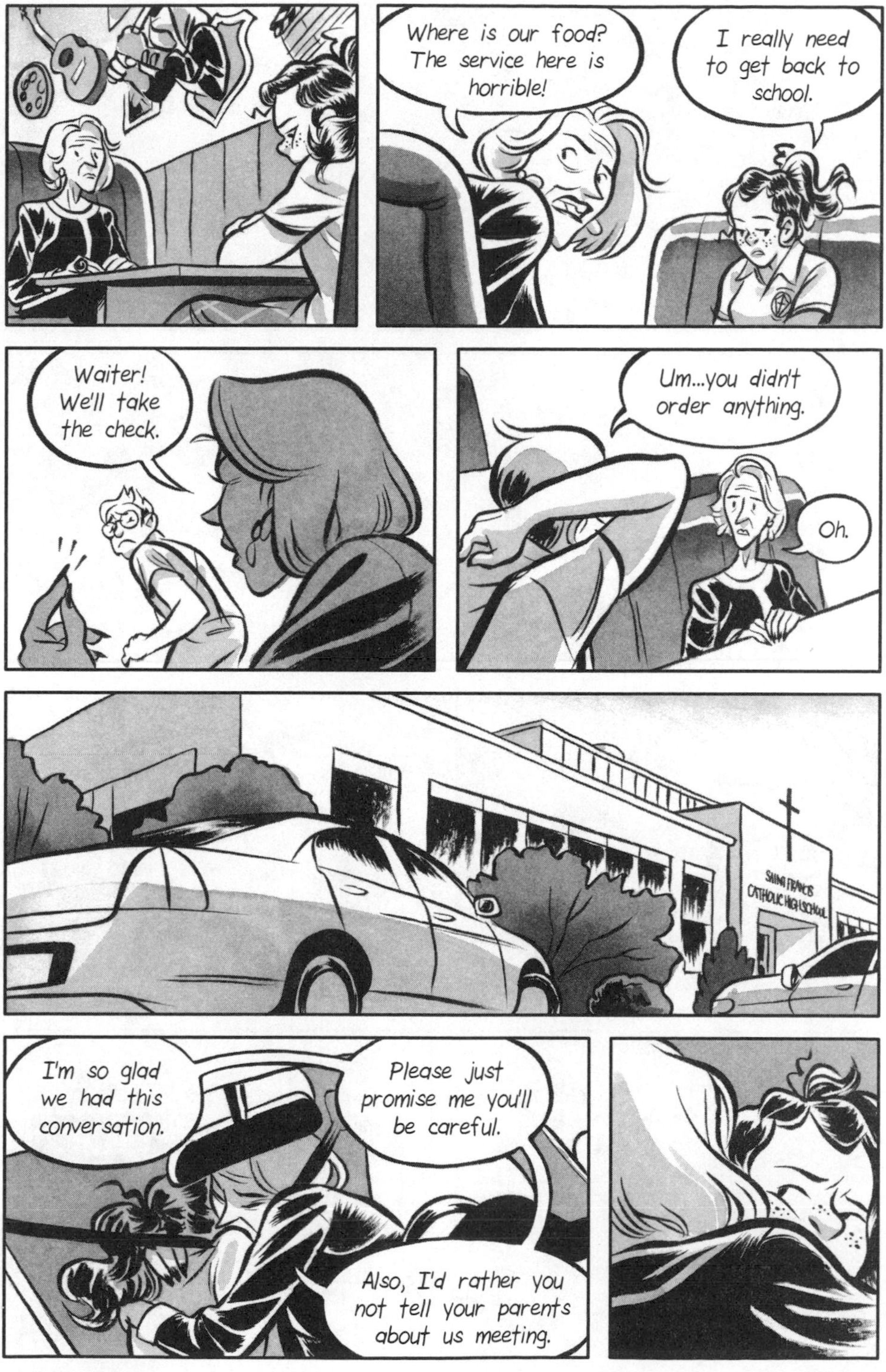
Where is our food? The service here is horrible!
I really need to get back to school.
Waiter! We'll take the check.
Um...you didn't order anything.
Oh.
SAINT FRANCIS CATHOLIC HIGH SCHOOL
I'm so glad we had this conversation.
Please just promise me you'll be careful.
Also, I'd rather you not tell your parents about us meeting.

211

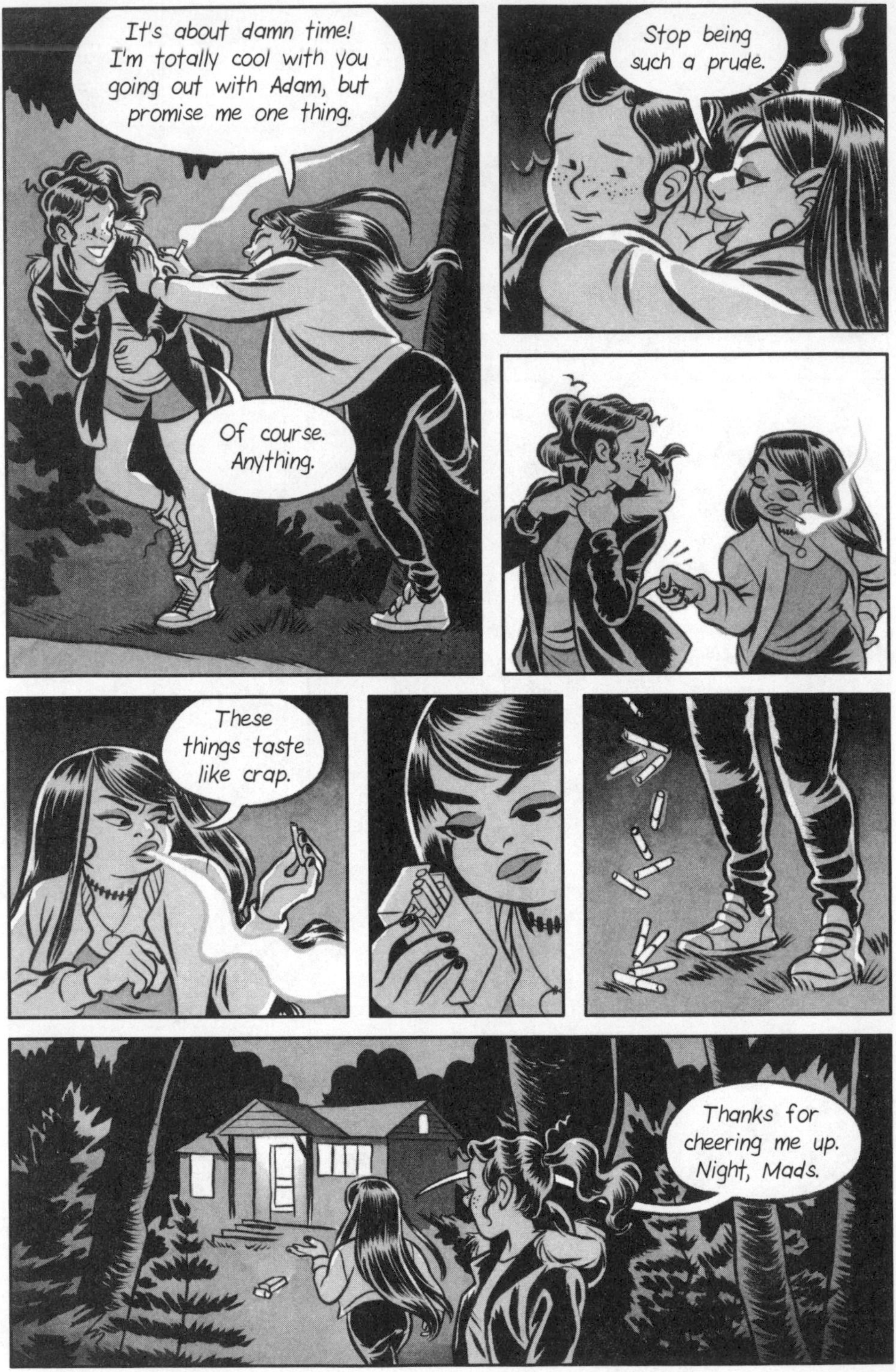
It's about damn time! I'm totally cool with you going out with Adam, but promise me one thing.
Of course. Anything.
Stop being such a prude.
These things taste like crap.
Thanks for cheering me up. Night, Mads.

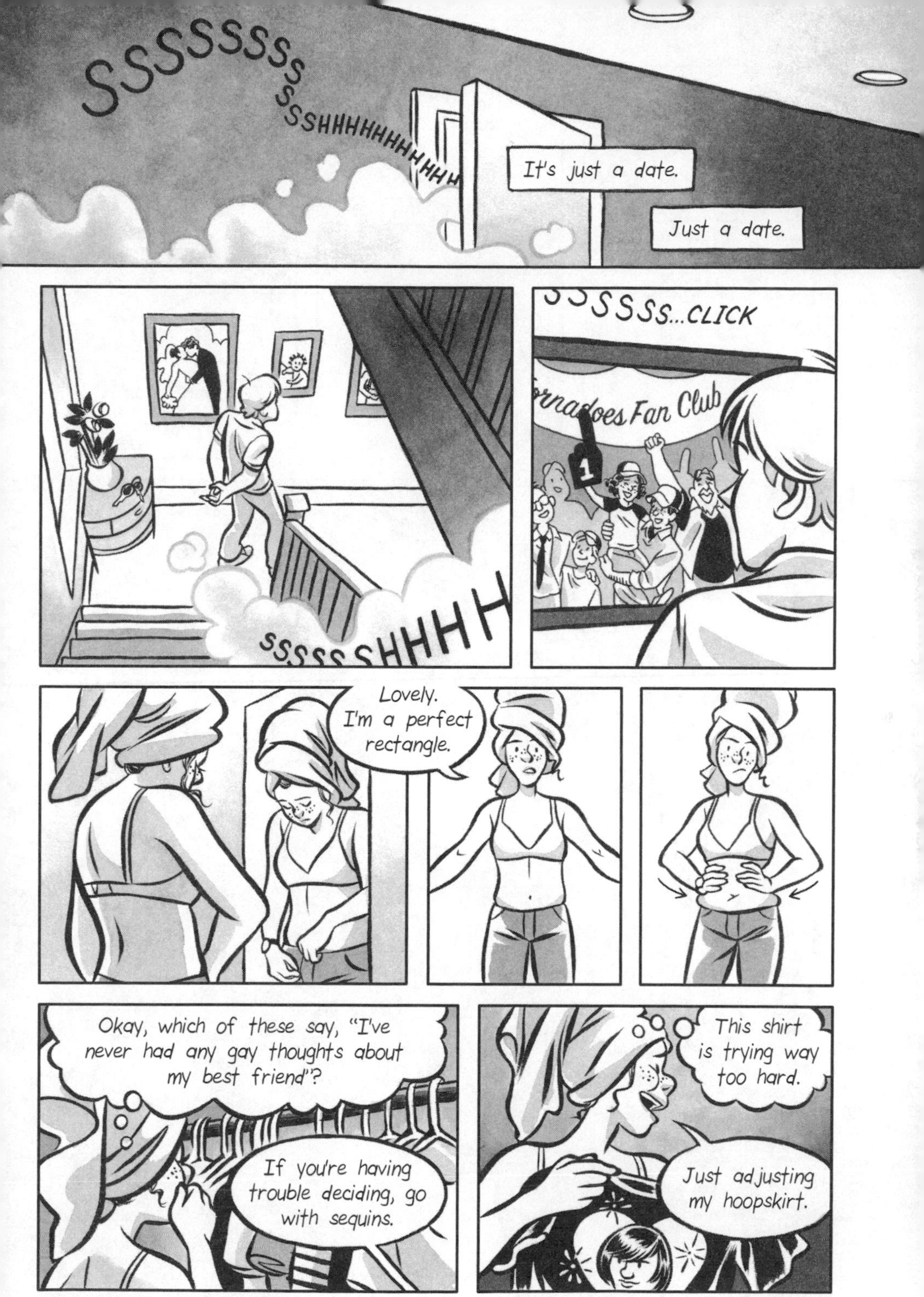
SSSSSSSSSSSHHHHHHHHHHH
It's just a date.
Just a date.
SSSSSHHHHH
SSSSSS...CLICK
Tornadoes Fan Club
1
Lovely. I'm a perfect rectangle.
Okay, which of these say, "I've never had any gay thoughts about my best friend"?
If you're having trouble deciding, go with sequins.
This shirt is trying way too hard.
Just adjusting my hoopskirt.

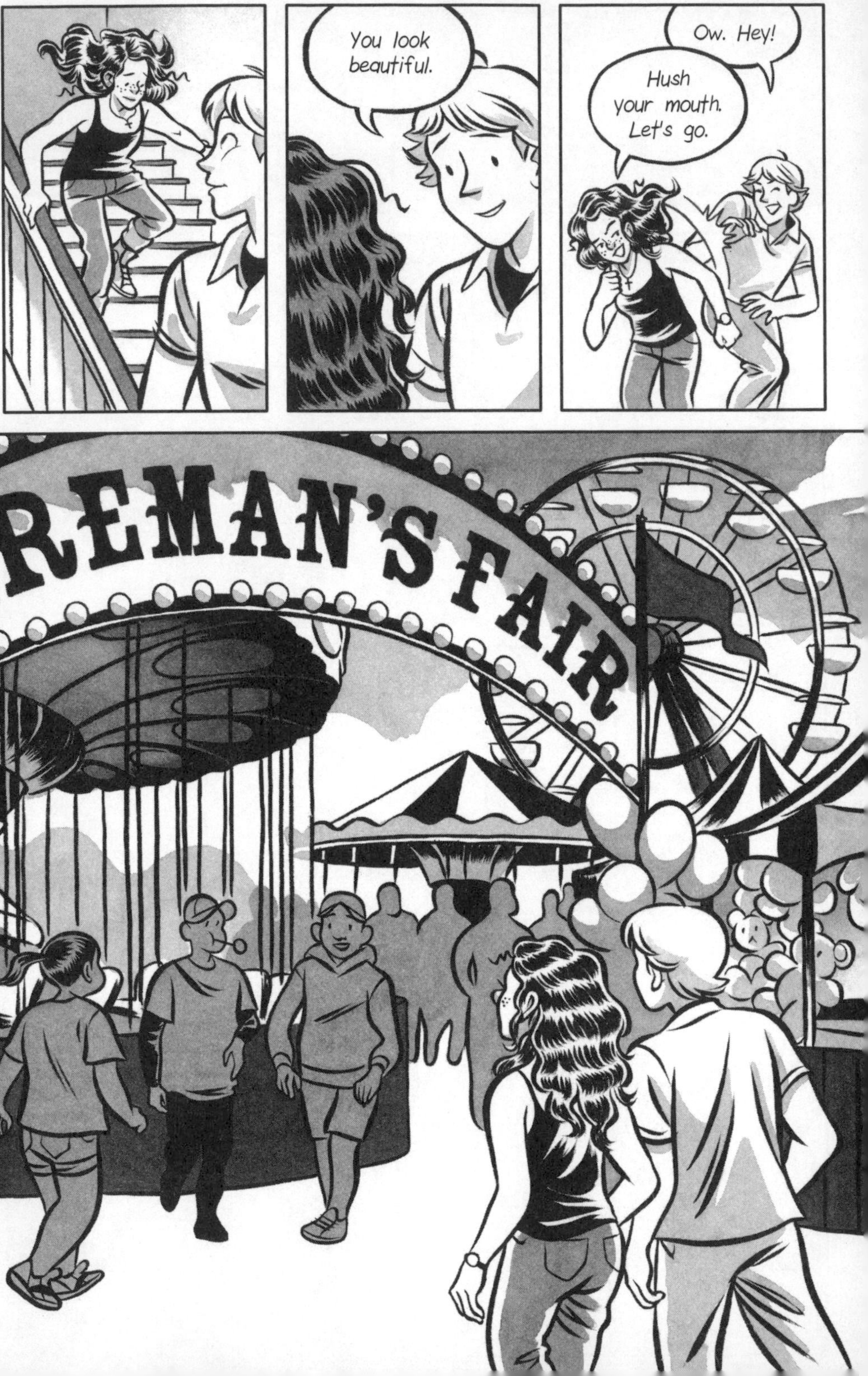
You look beautiful.
Hush your mouth. Let's go.
Ow. Hey!
IREMAN'S FAIR

225

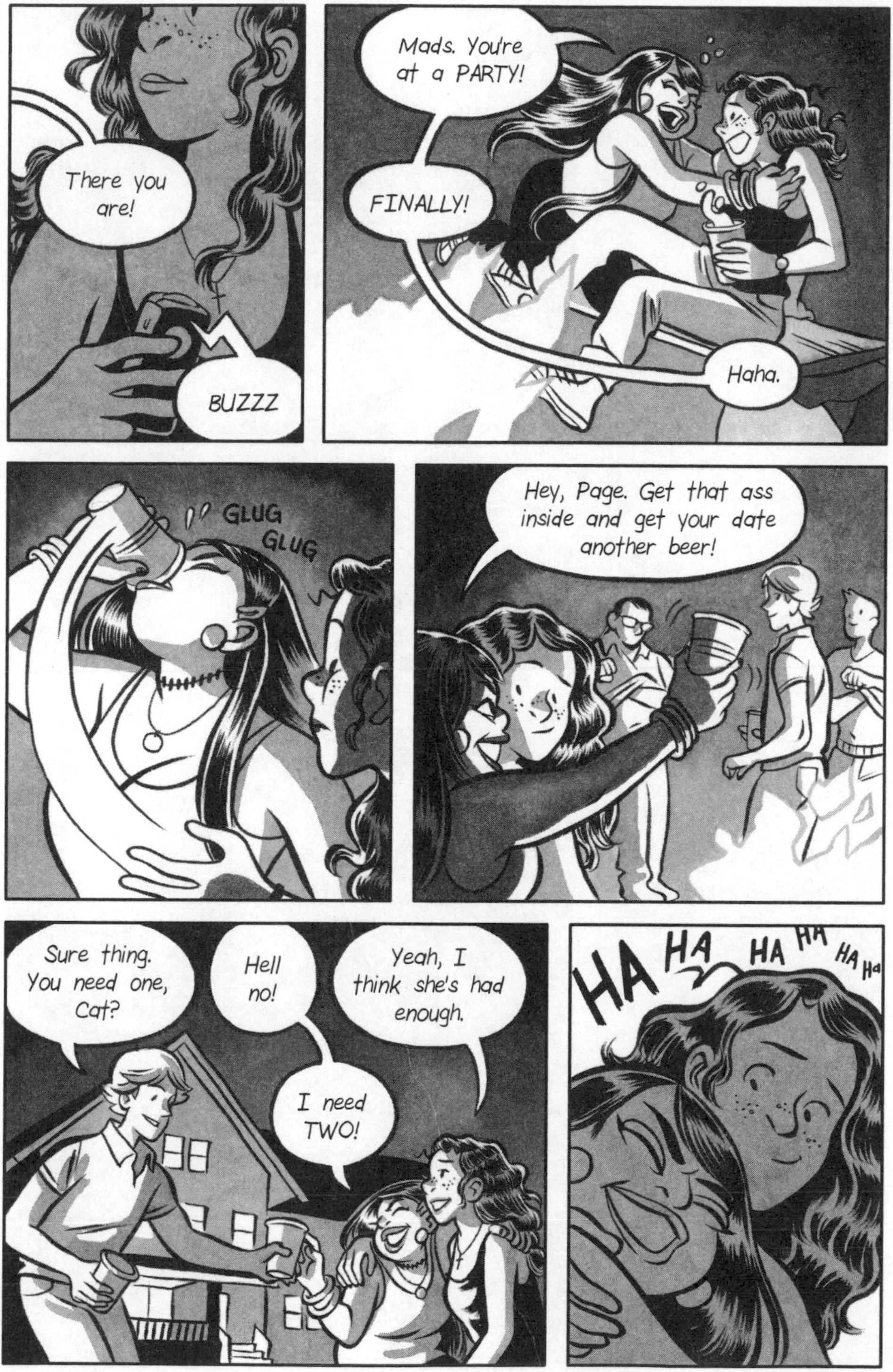
There you are!
BUZZZ
Mads. You're at a PARTY!
FINALLY!
Haha.
GLUG GLUG
Hey, Page. Get that ass inside and get your date another beer!
Sure thing. You need one, Cat?
Hell no!
I need TWO!
Yeah, I think she's had enough.
HA HA HA HA HA Ha

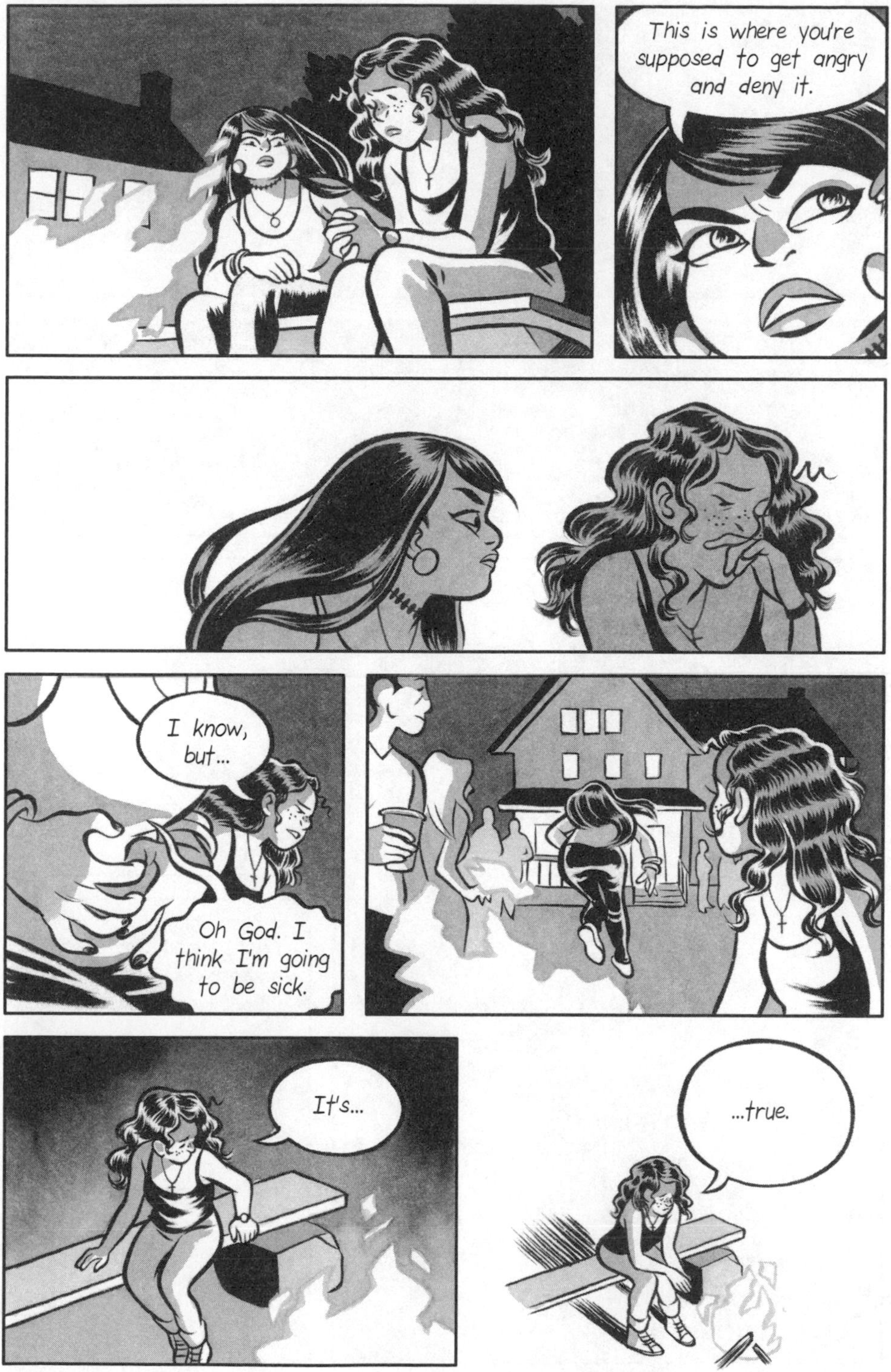
This is where you're supposed to get angry and deny it.
I know, but...
Oh God. I think I'm going to be sick.
It's...
...true.

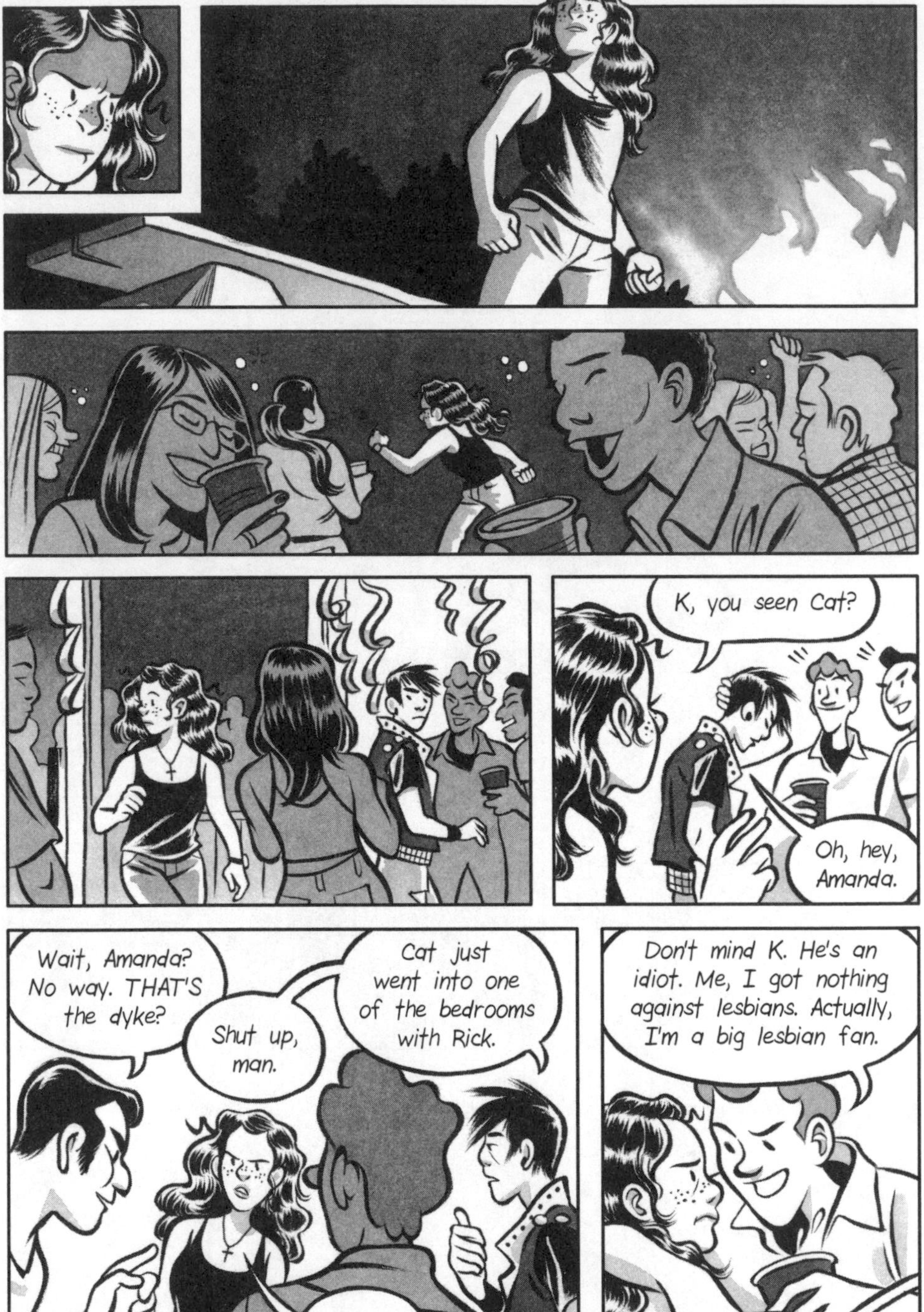
K, you seen Cat?
Oh, hey, Amanda.
Wait, Amanda? No way. THAT'S the dyke?
Shut up, man.
Cat just went into one of the bedrooms with Rick.
Wait. What?
Don't mind K. He's an idiot. Me, I got nothing against lesbians. Actually, I'm a big lesbian fan.
I said, shut the fuck up!

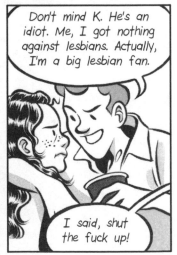

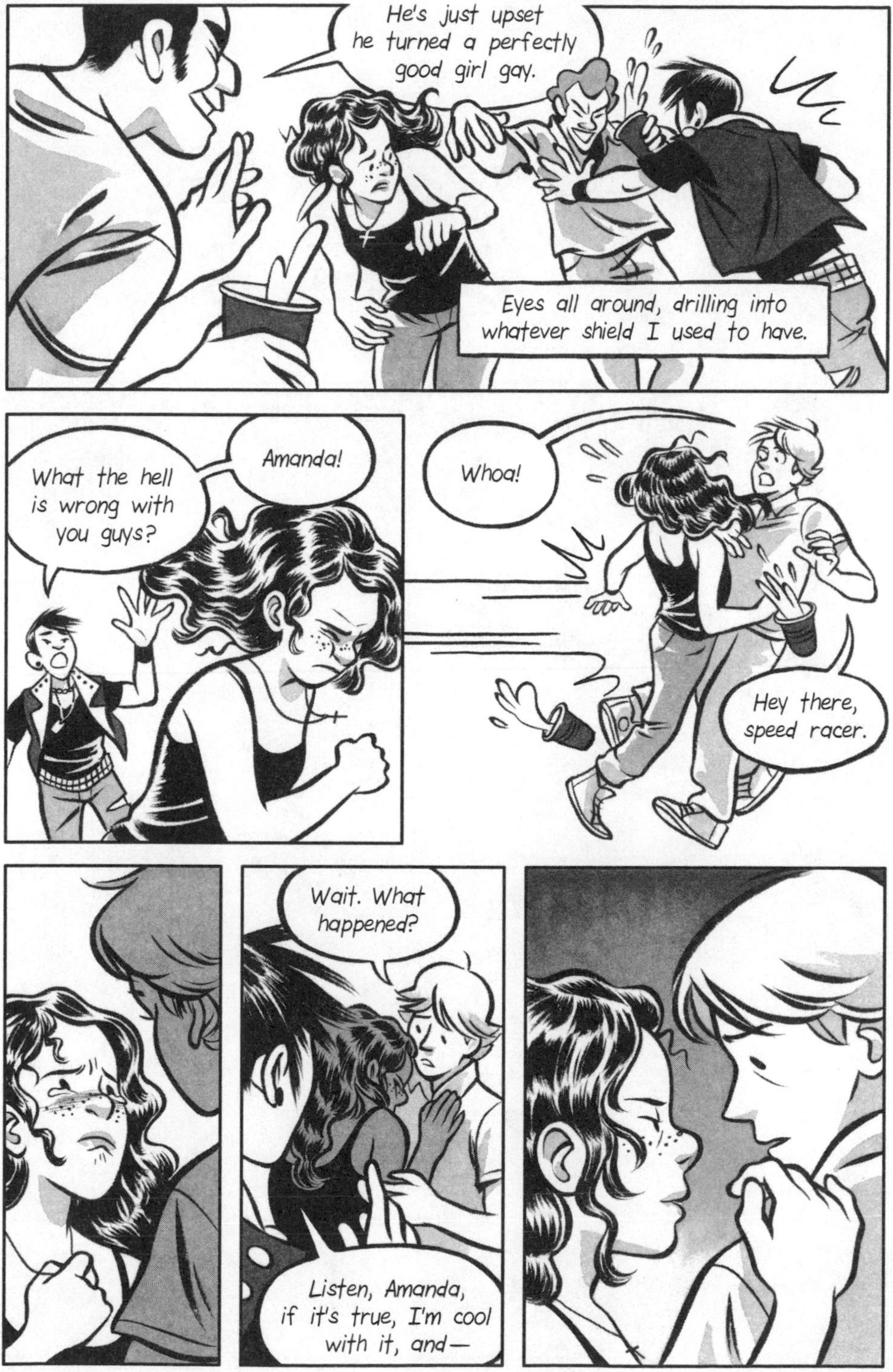
He's just upset he turned a perfectly good girl gay.
Eyes all around, drilling into whatever shield I used to have.
What the hell is wrong with you guys?
Amanda!
Whoa!
Hey there, speed racer.
Wait. What happened?
Listen, Amanda, if it's true, I'm cool with it, and—

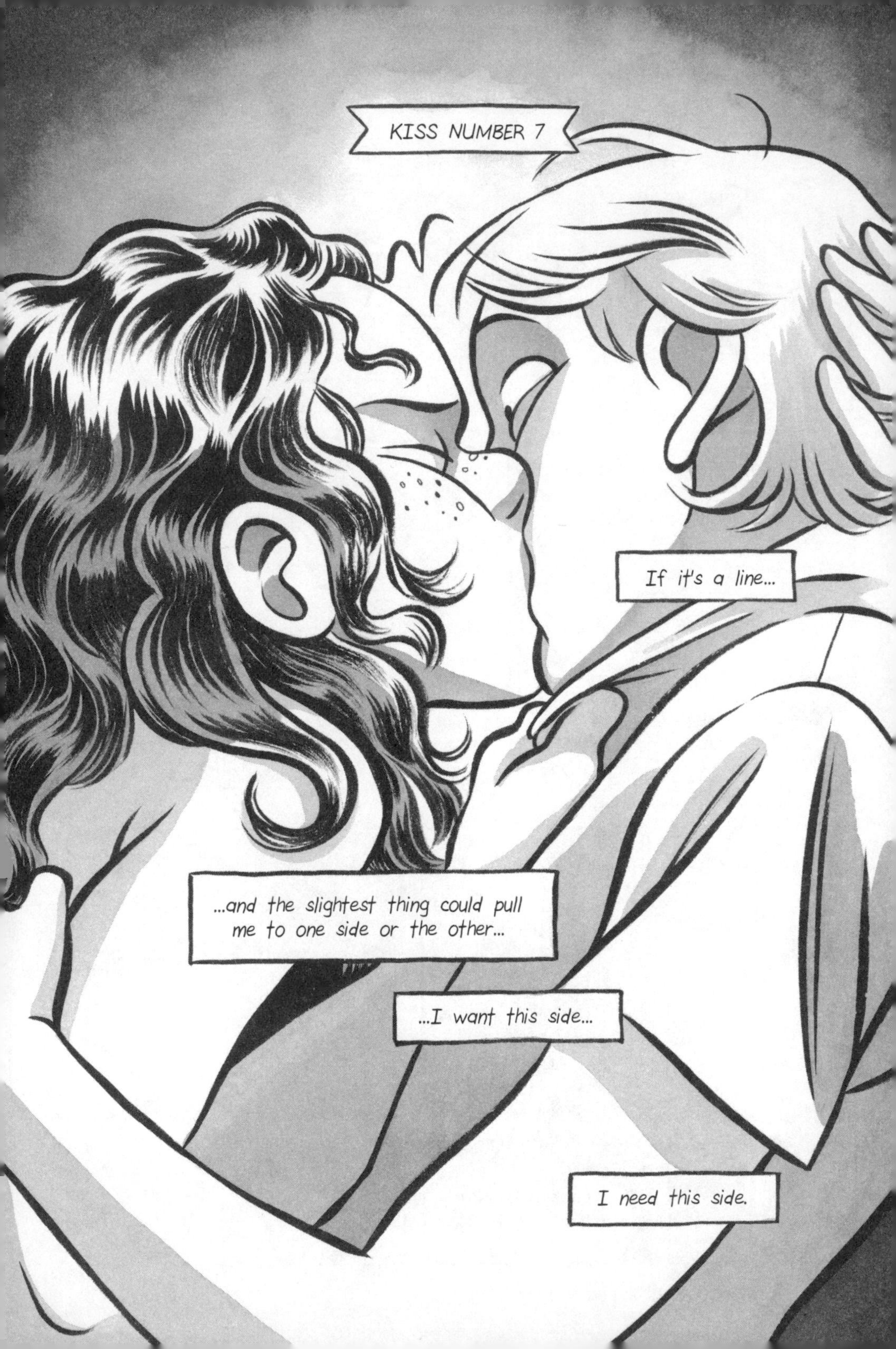
KISS NUMBER 7
If it's a line...
...and the slightest thing could pull me to one side or the other...
...I want this side...
I need this side.

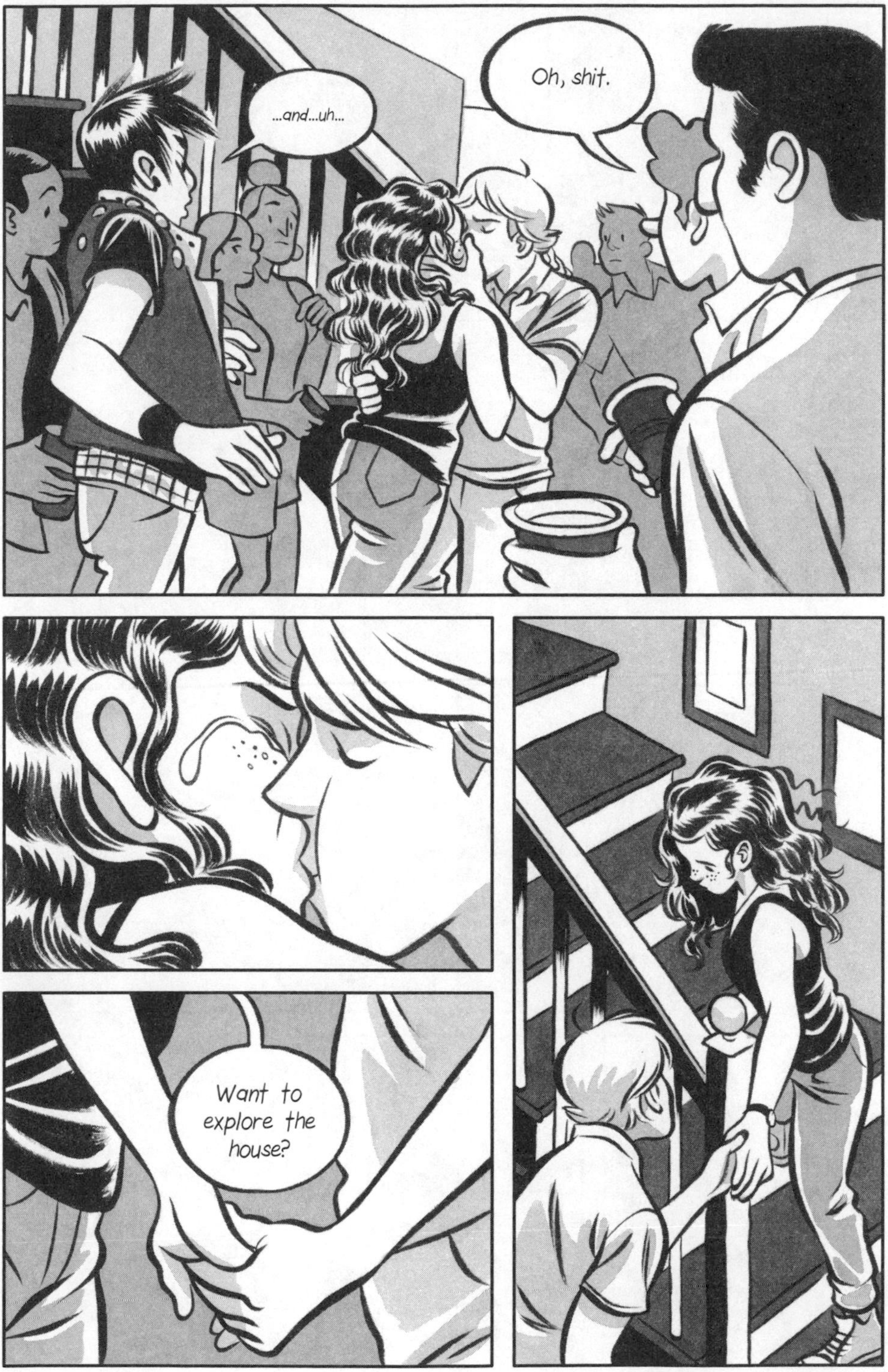
...and...uh...
Oh, shit.
Want to explore the house?

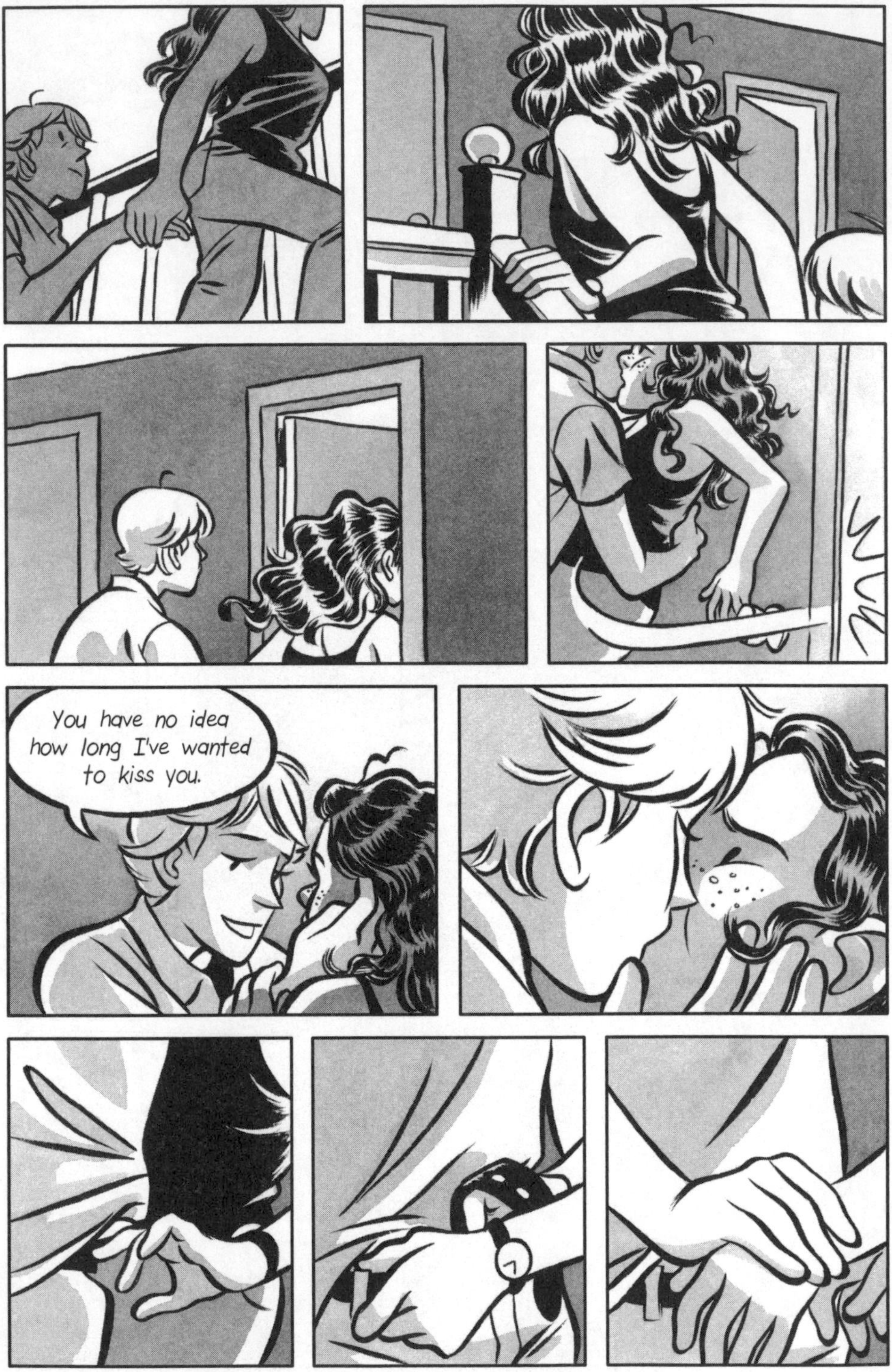
You have no idea how long I've wanted to kiss you.

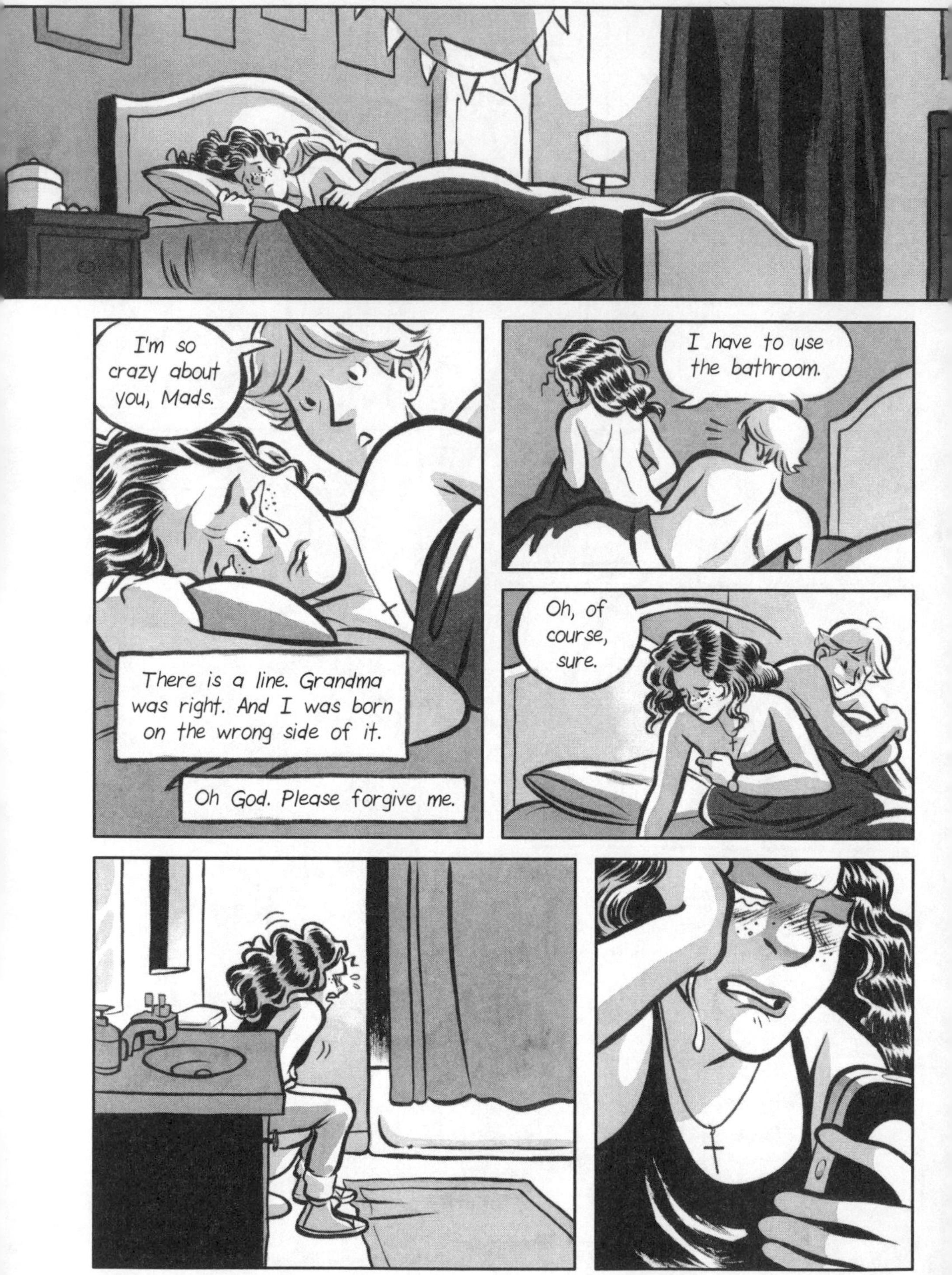
I'm so crazy about you, Mads.
There is a line. Grandma was right. And I was born on the wrong side of it.
Oh God. Please forgive me.
I have to use the bathroom.
Oh, of course, sure.

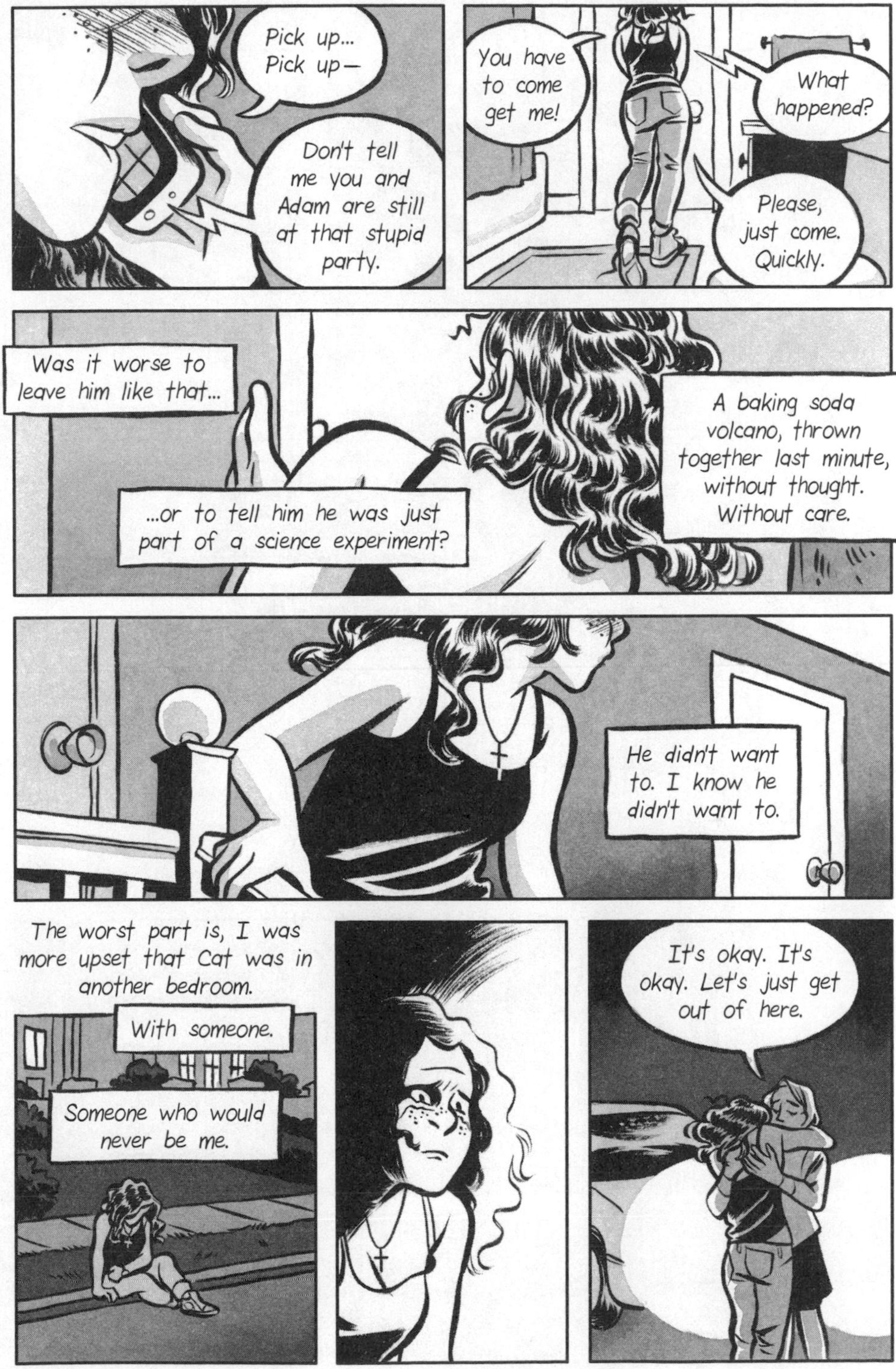
Pick up... Pick up—
Don't tell me you and Adam are still at that stupid party.
You have to come get me!
What happened?
Please, just come. Quickly.
Was it worse to leave him like that...
...or to tell him he was just part of a science experiment?
A baking soda volcano, thrown together last minute, without thought. Without care.
He didn't want to. I know he didn't want to.
The worst part is, I was more upset that Cat was in another bedroom.
With someone.
Someone who would never be me.
It's okay. It's okay. Let's just get out of here.

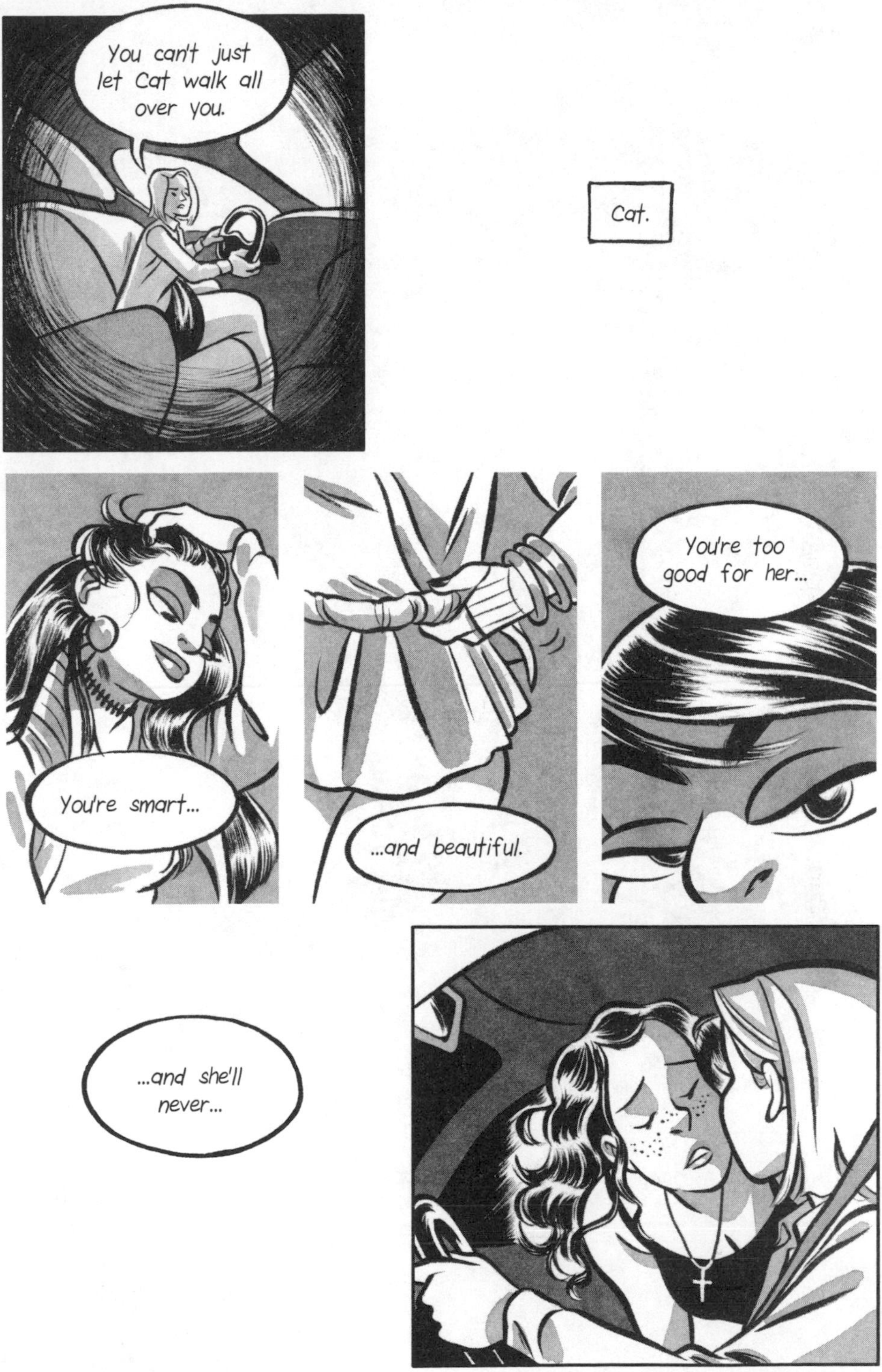
You can't just let Cat walk all over you.
Cat.
You're smart...
...and beautiful.
You're too good for her...
...and she'll never...

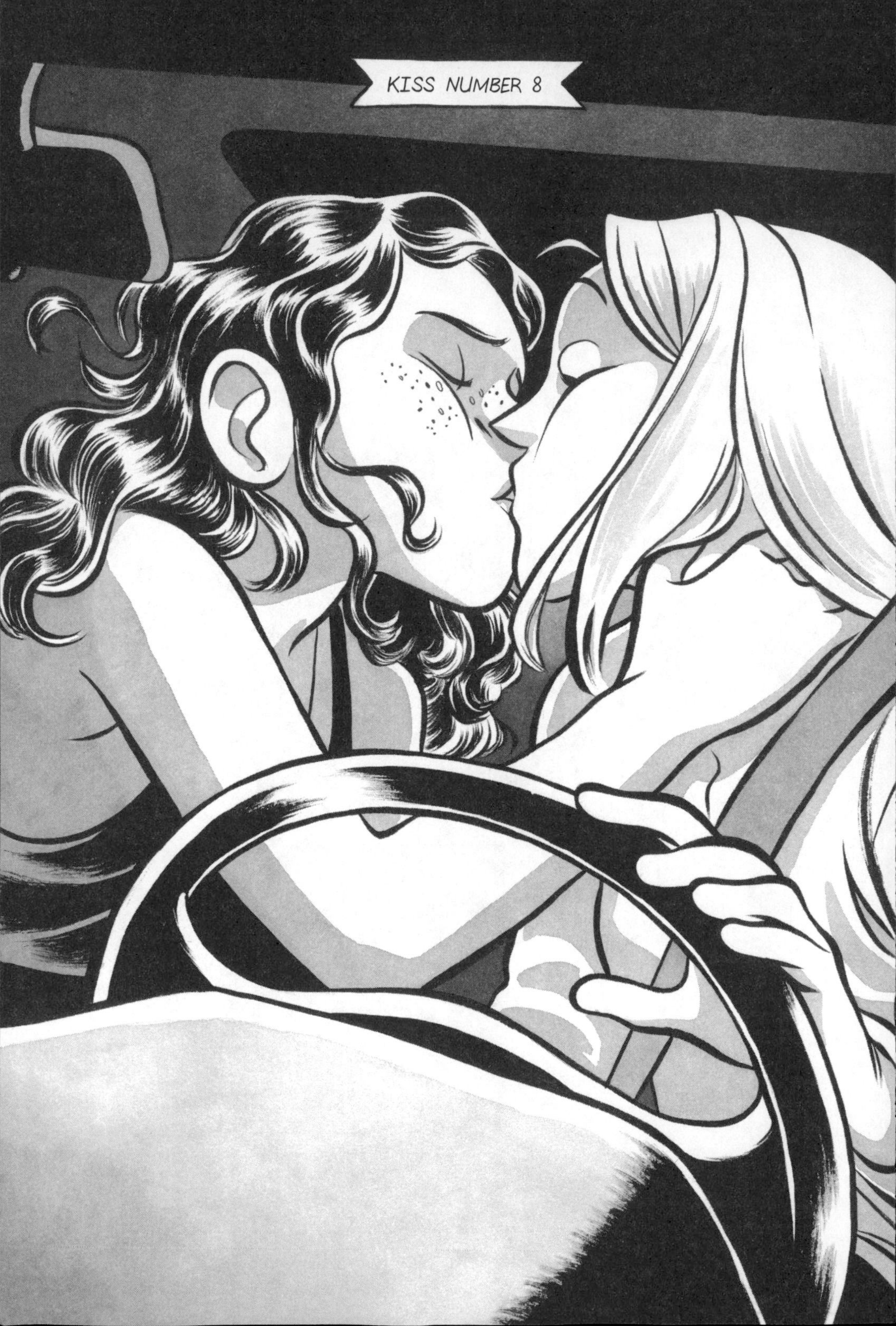
KISS NUMBER 8

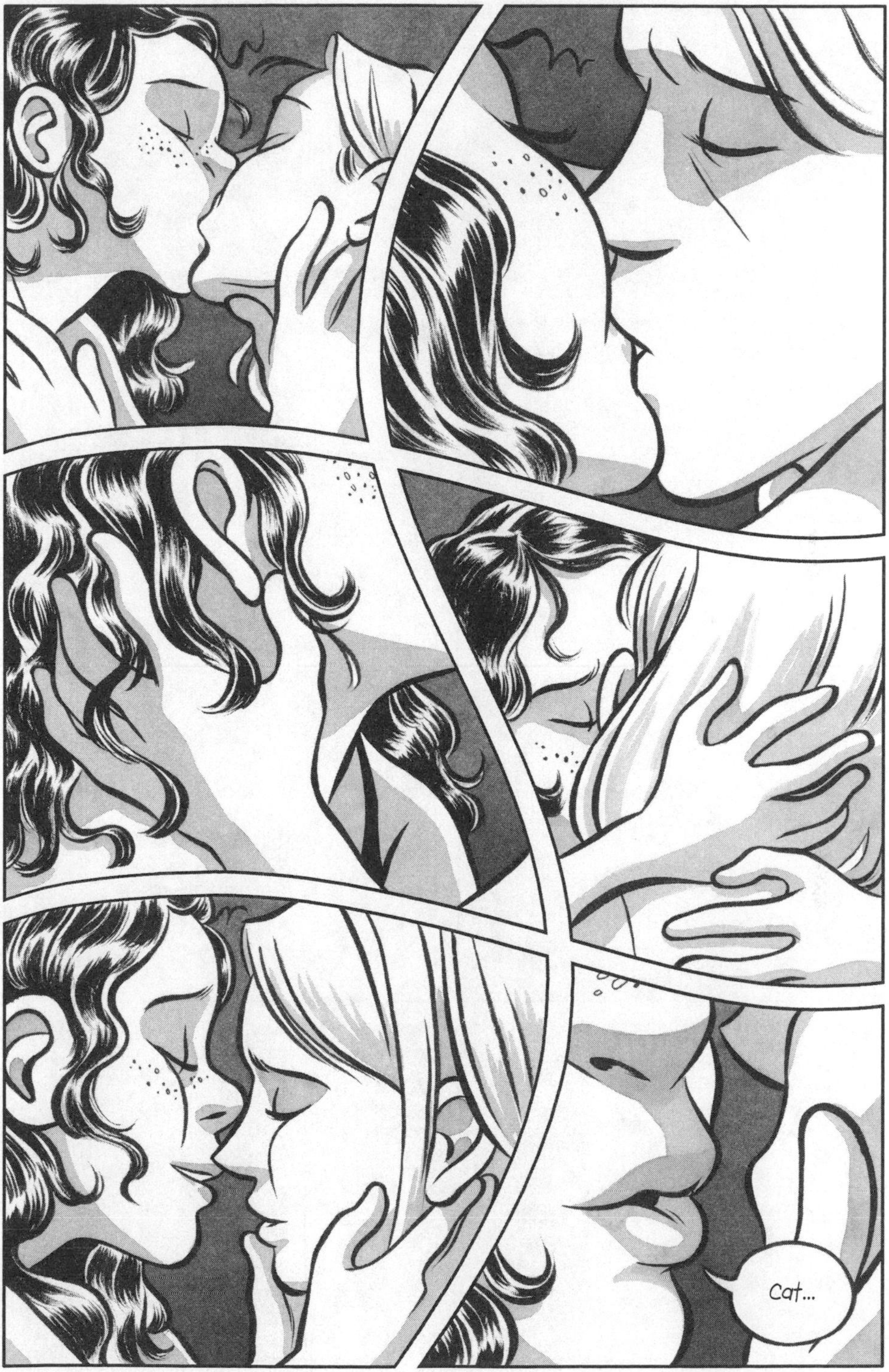
Cat...

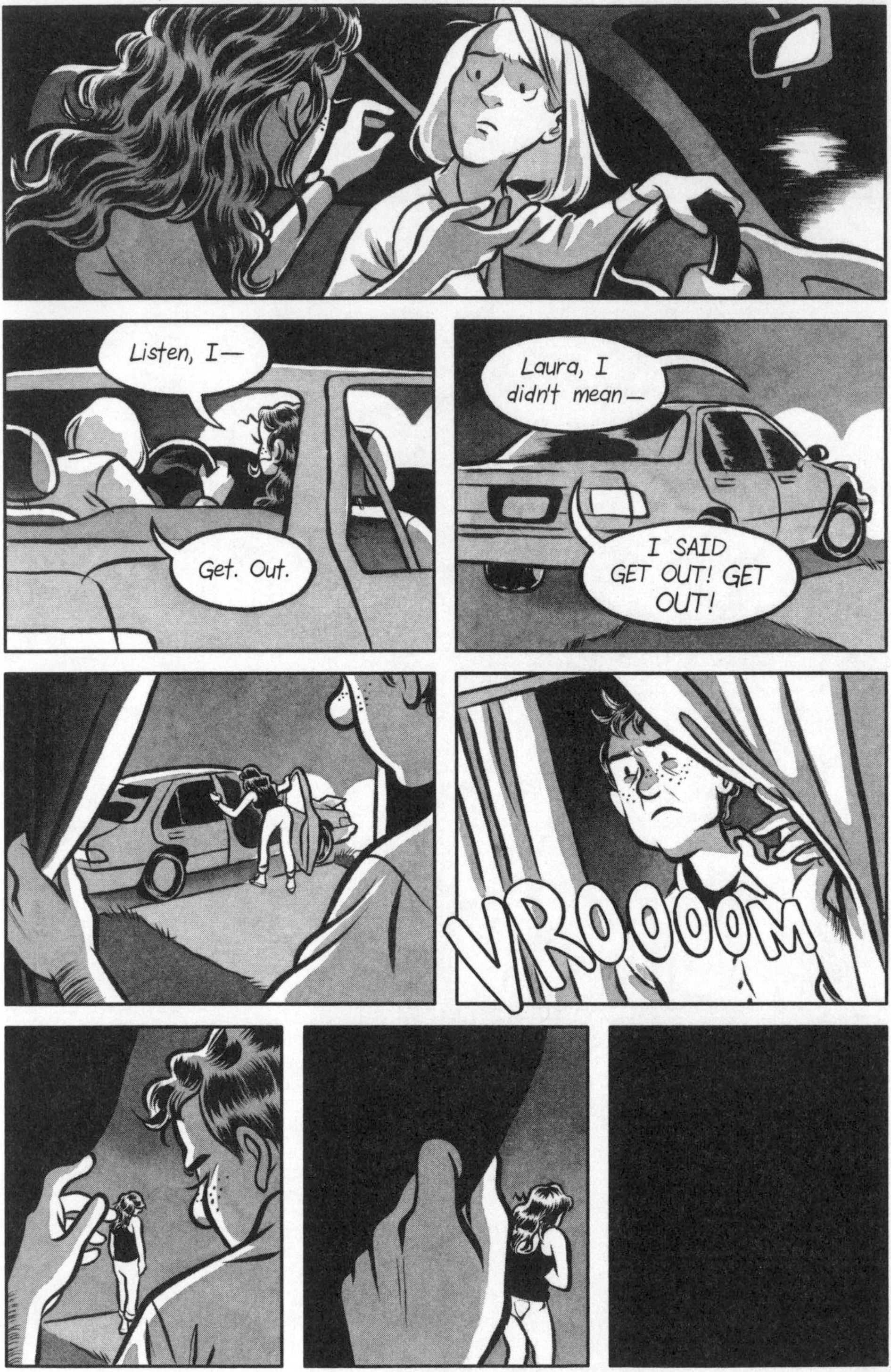
Listen, I—
Get. Out.
Laura, I didn't mean—
I SAID GET OUT! GET OUT!
VROOOOM

243

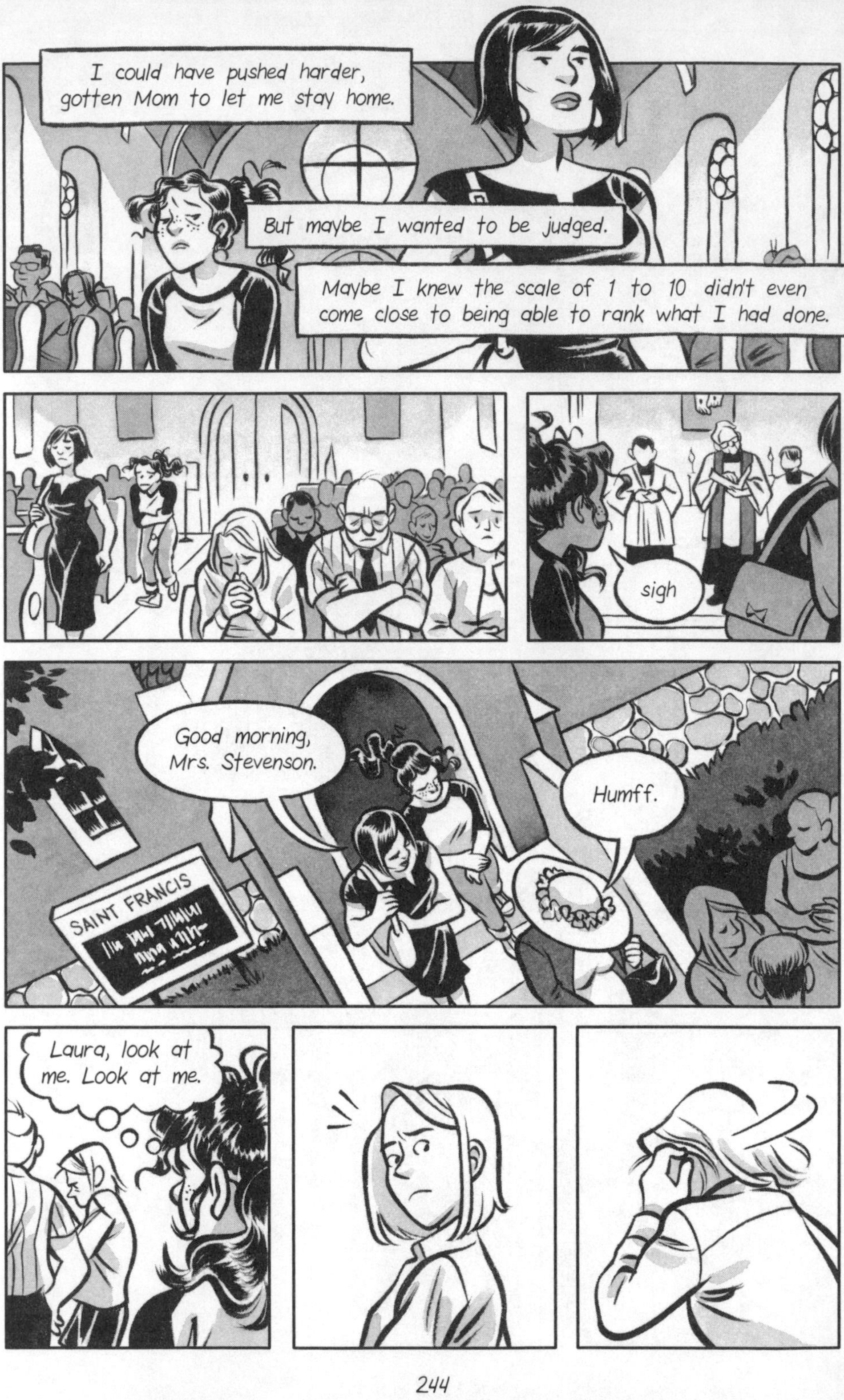
I could have pushed harder, gotten Mom to let me stay home.
But maybe I wanted to be judged.
Maybe I knew the scale of 1 to 10 didn't even come close to being able to rank what I had done.
sigh
Good morning, Mrs. Stevenson.
Humff.
SAINT FRANCIS
Laura, look at me. Look at me.

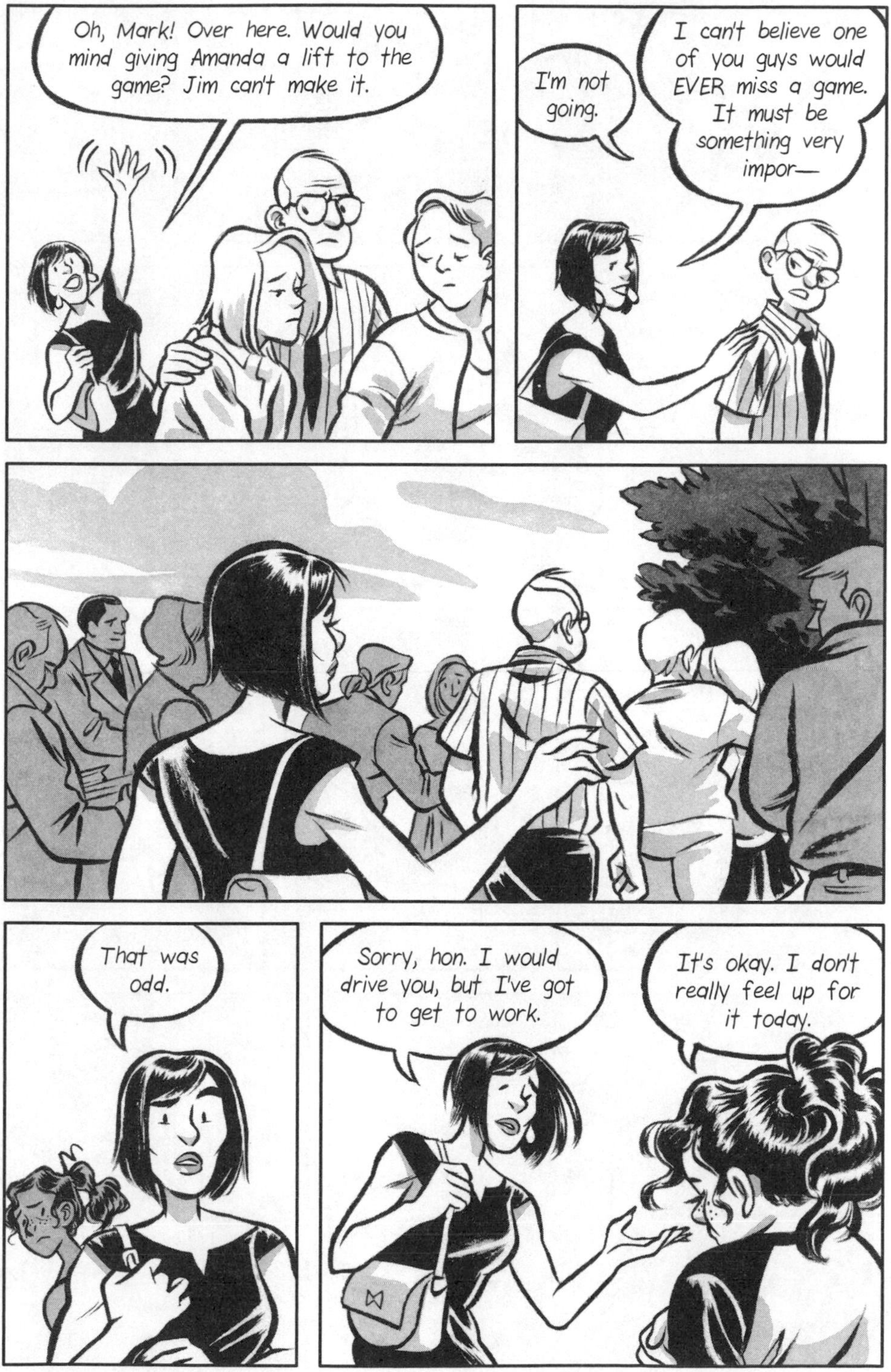
Oh, Mark! Over here. Would you mind giving Amanda a lift to the game? Jim can't make it.
I'm not going.
I can't believe one of you guys would EVER miss a game. It must be something very impor—
That was odd.
Sorry, hon. I would drive you, but I've got to get to work.
It's okay. I don't really feel up for it today.

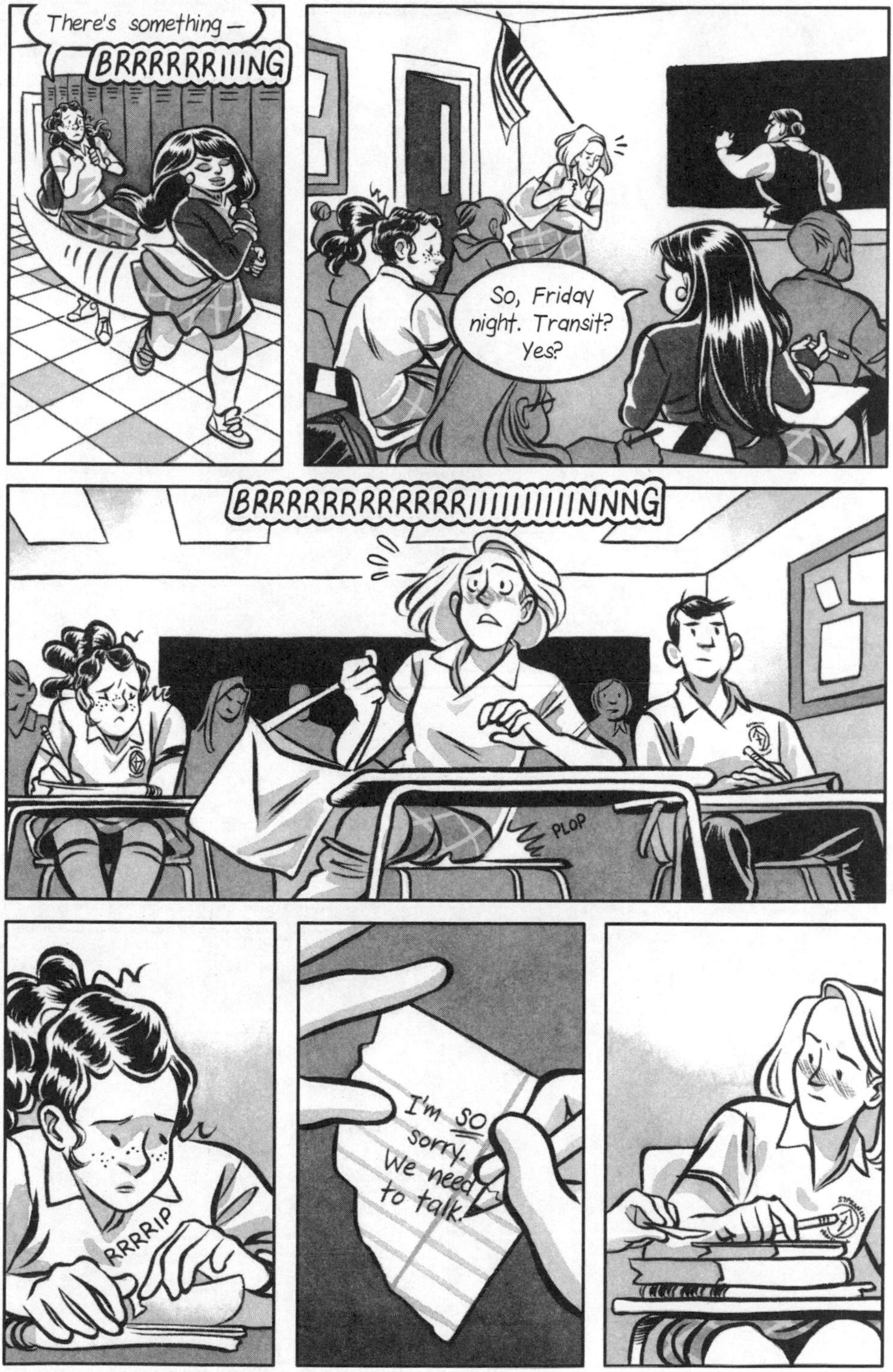
There's something—
BRRRRRRRIIIING
So, Friday night. Transit? Yes?
BRRRRRRRRRRRRRIIIIIIIIIIINNNG
PLOP
RRRRIP
I'm SO sorry. We need to talk.

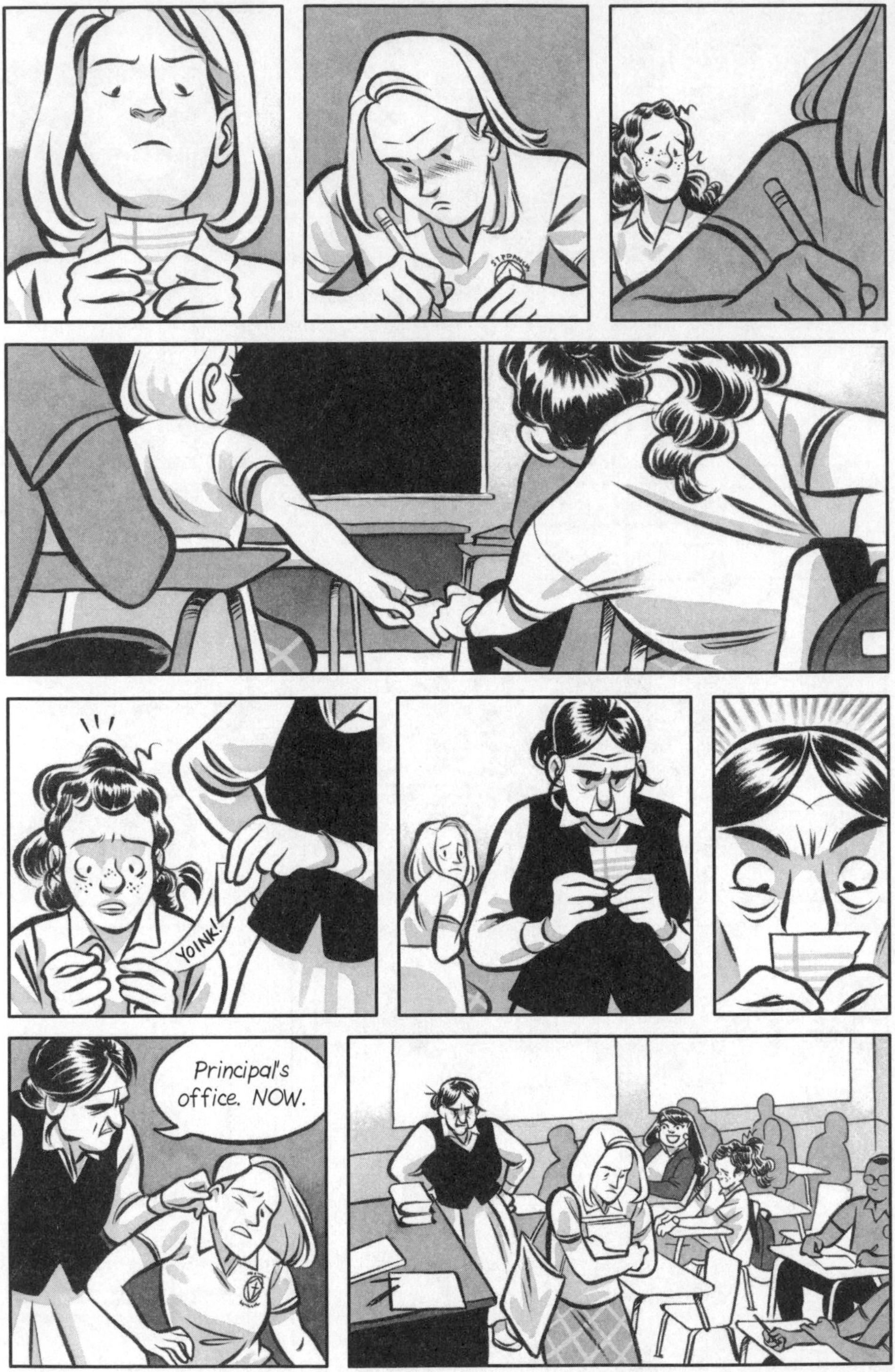

YOINK!
Principal's office. NOW.

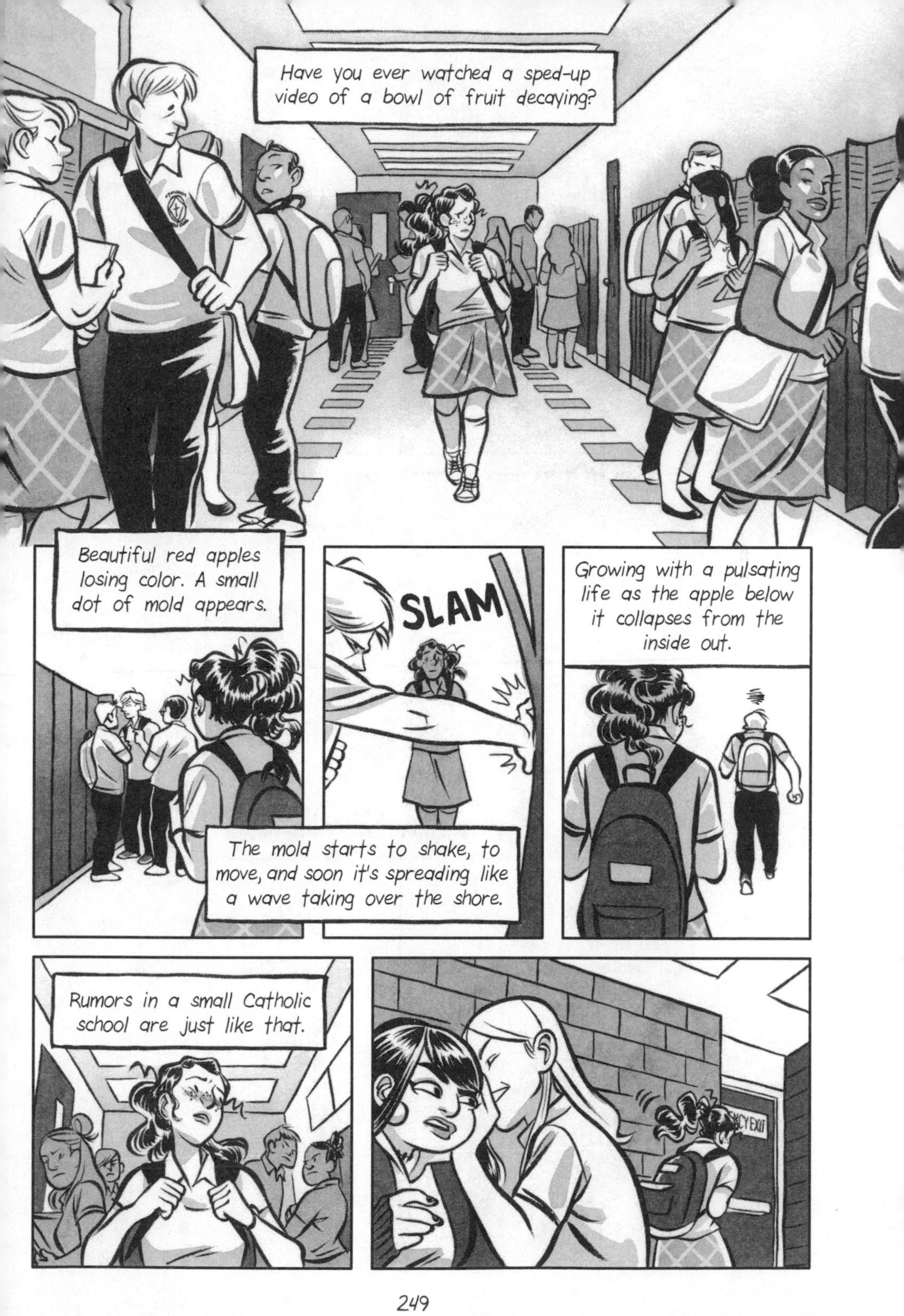
Have you ever watched a sped-up video of a bowl of fruit decaying?
Beautiful red apples losing color. A small dot of mold appears.
SLAM
The mold starts to shake, to move, and soon it's spreading like a wave taking over the shore.
Growing with a pulsating life as the apple below it collapses from the inside out.
Rumors in a small Catholic school are just like that.

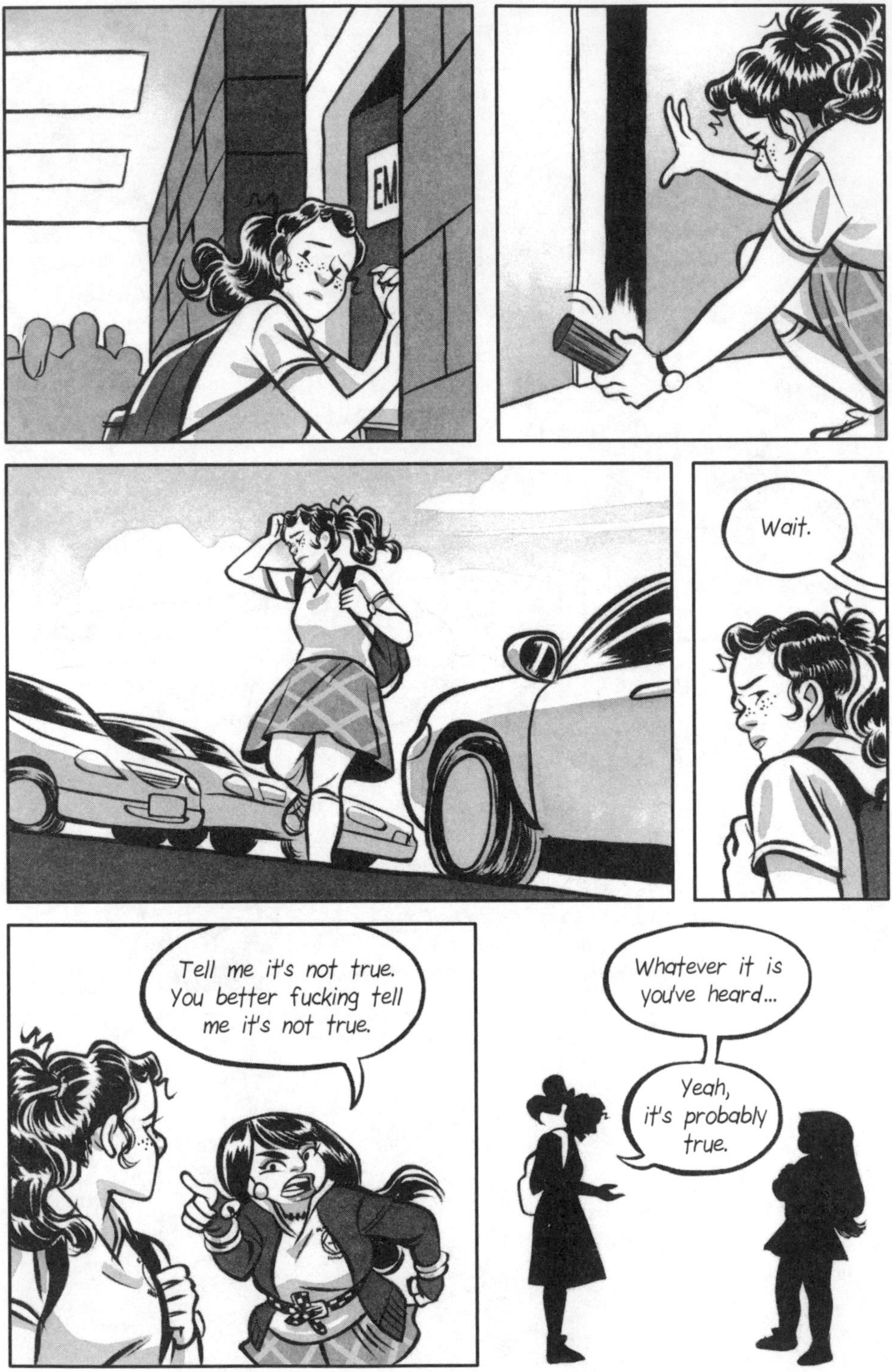
EM
Wait.
Tell me it's not true. You better fucking tell me it's not true.
Whatever it is you've heard...
Yeah, it's probably true.

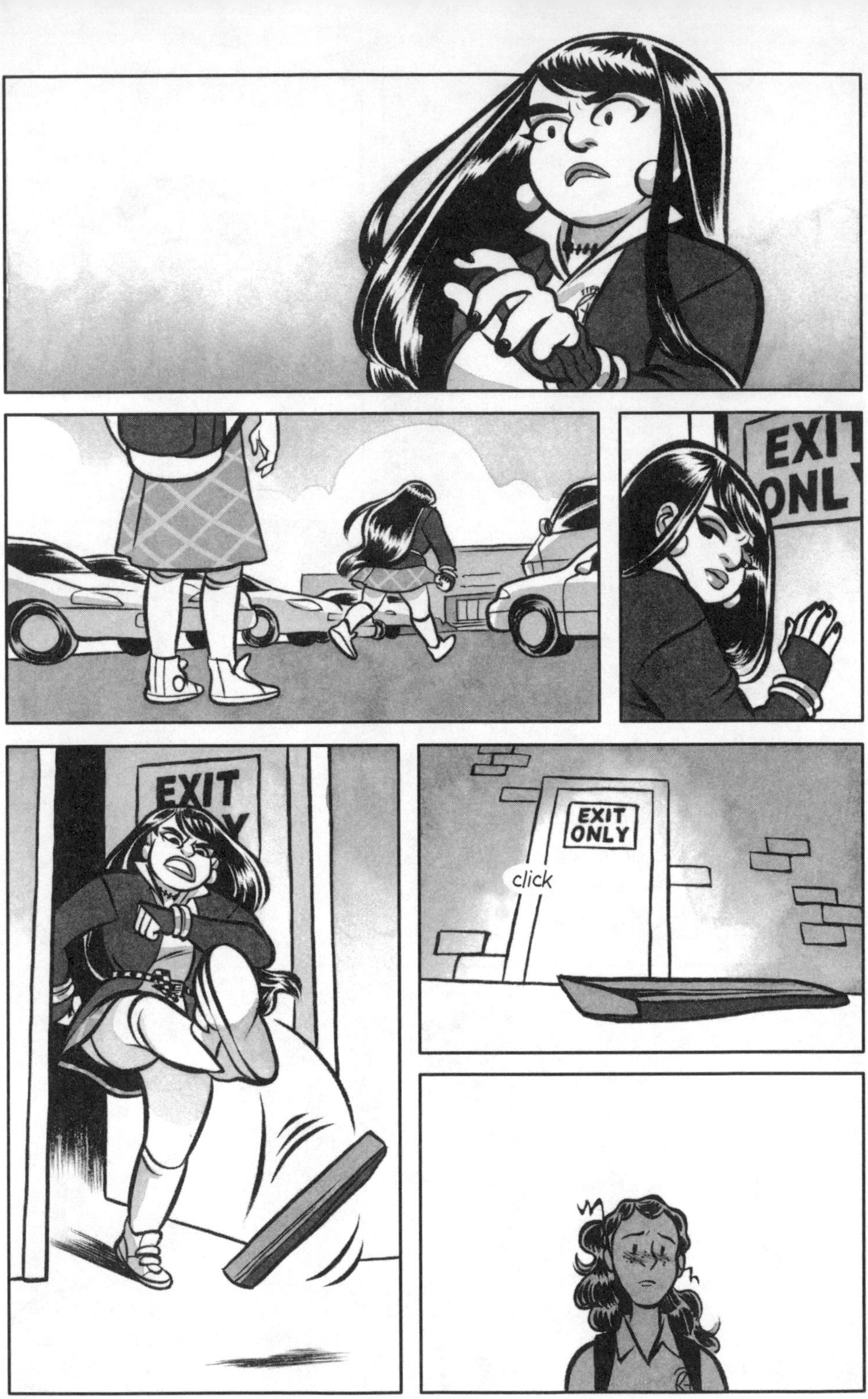
EXIT ONLY
EXIT
EXIT ONLY
click

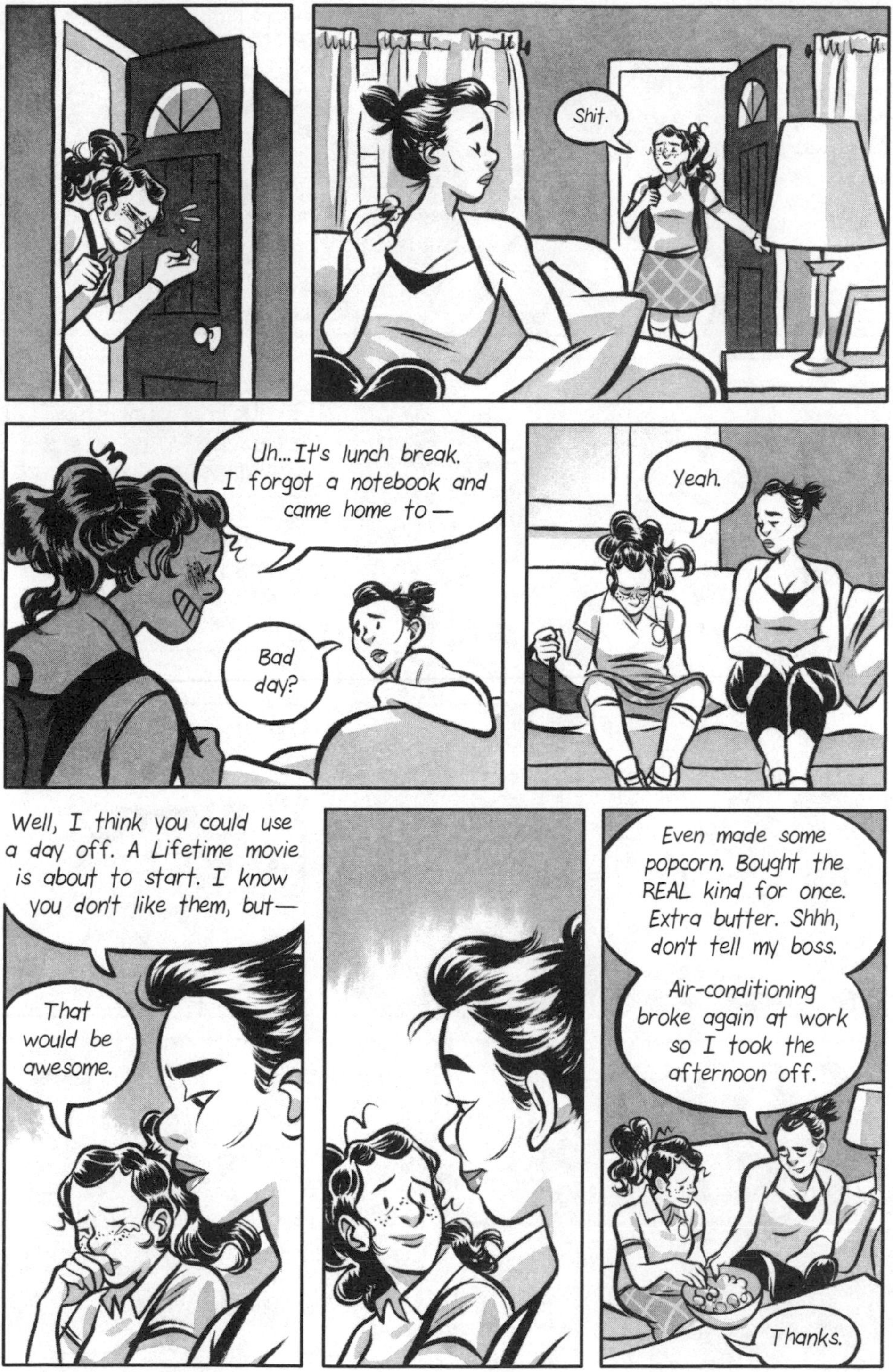
Shit.
Uh...It's lunch break. I forgot a notebook and came home to—
Bad day?
Yeah.
Well, I think you could use a day off. A Lifetime movie is about to start. I know you don't like them, but—
That would be awesome.
Even made some popcorn. Bought the REAL kind for once. Extra butter. Shhh, don't tell my boss.
Air-conditioning broke again at work so I took the afternoon off.
Thanks.

254

255

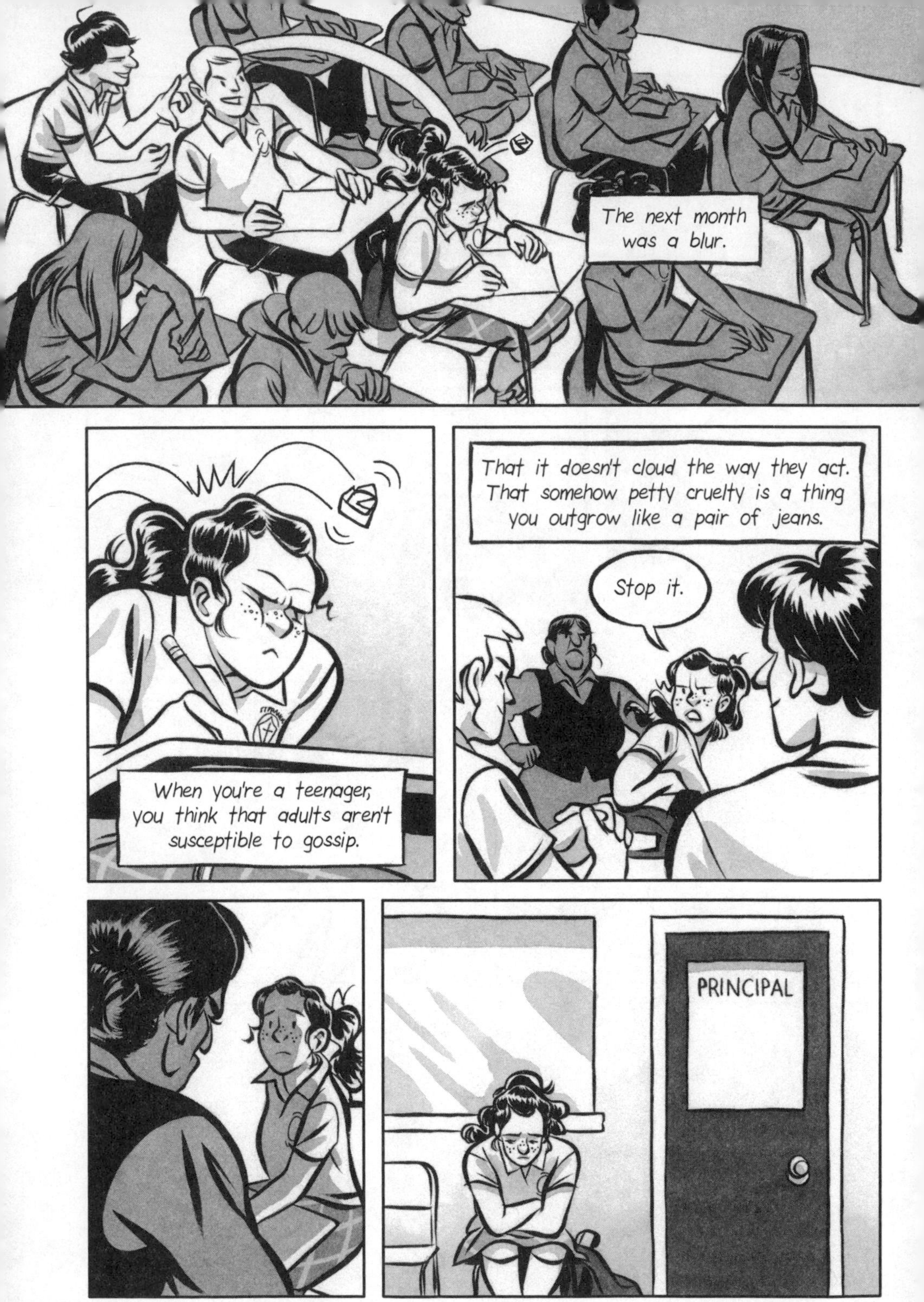
The next month was a blur.
When you're a teenager, you think that adults aren't susceptible to gossip.
That it doesn't cloud the way they act. That somehow petty cruelty is a thing you outgrow like a pair of jeans.
Stop it.
PRINCIPAL

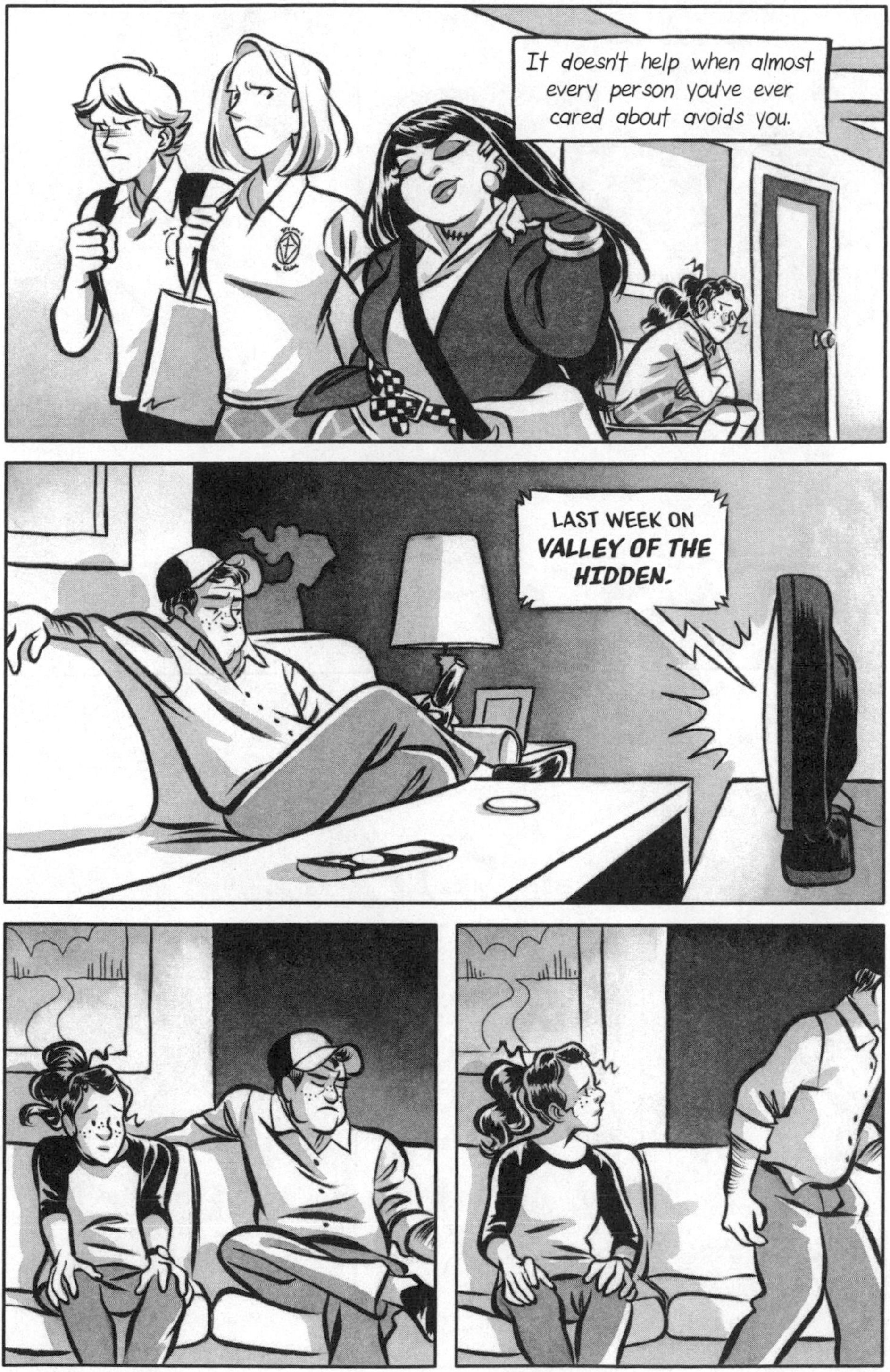
It doesn't help when almost every person you've ever cared about avoids you.
LAST WEEK ON VALLEY OF THE HIDDEN.

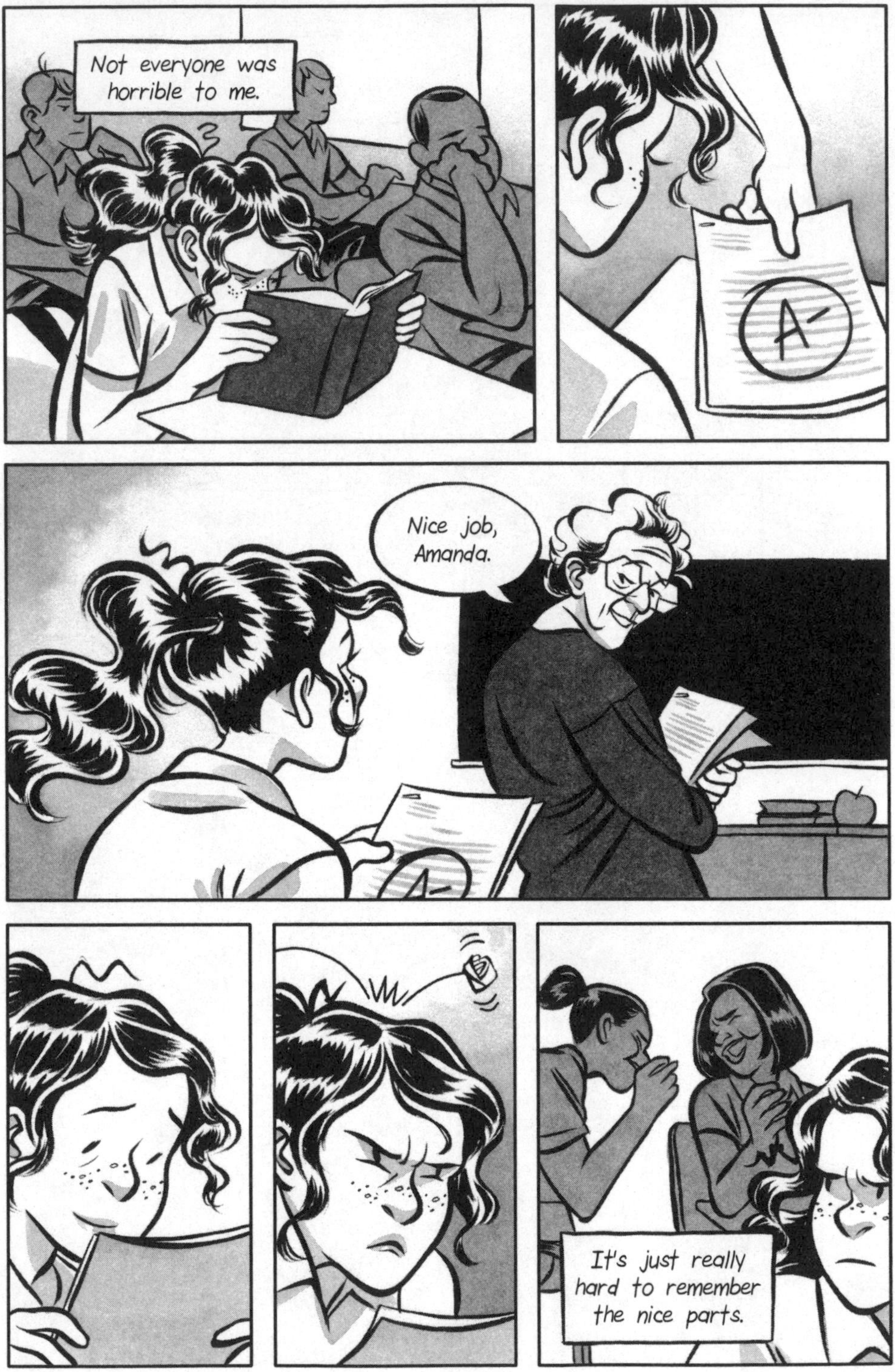
Not everyone was horrible to me.
Nice job, Amanda.
It's just really hard to remember the nice parts.

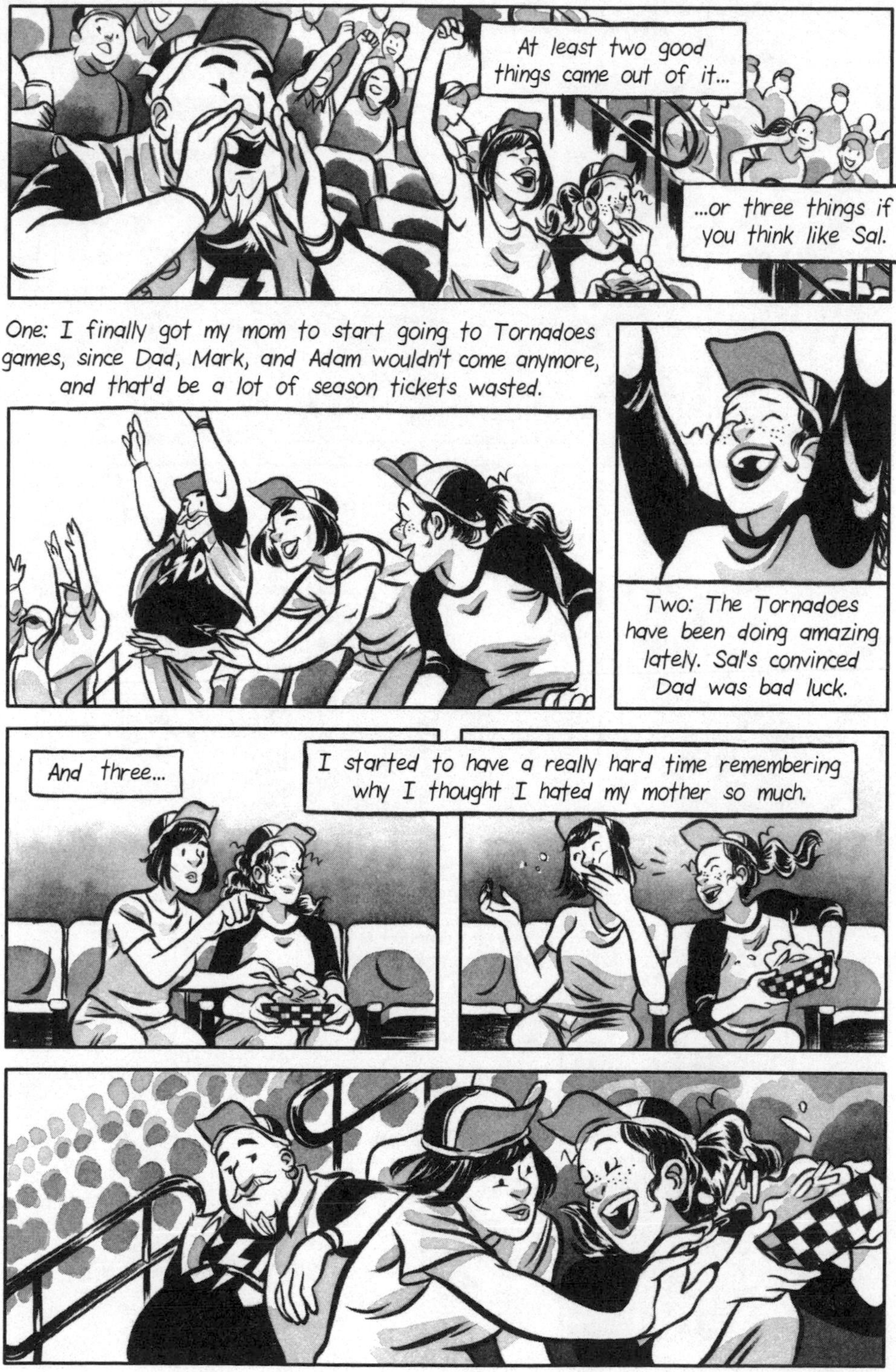
At least two good things came out of it...
...or three things if you think like Sal.
One: I finally got my mom to start going to Tornadoes games, since Dad, Mark, and Adam wouldn't come anymore, and that'd be a lot of season tickets wasted.
Two: The Tornadoes have been doing amazing lately. Sal's convinced Dad was bad luck.
And three...
I started to have a really hard time remembering why I thought I hated my mother so much.

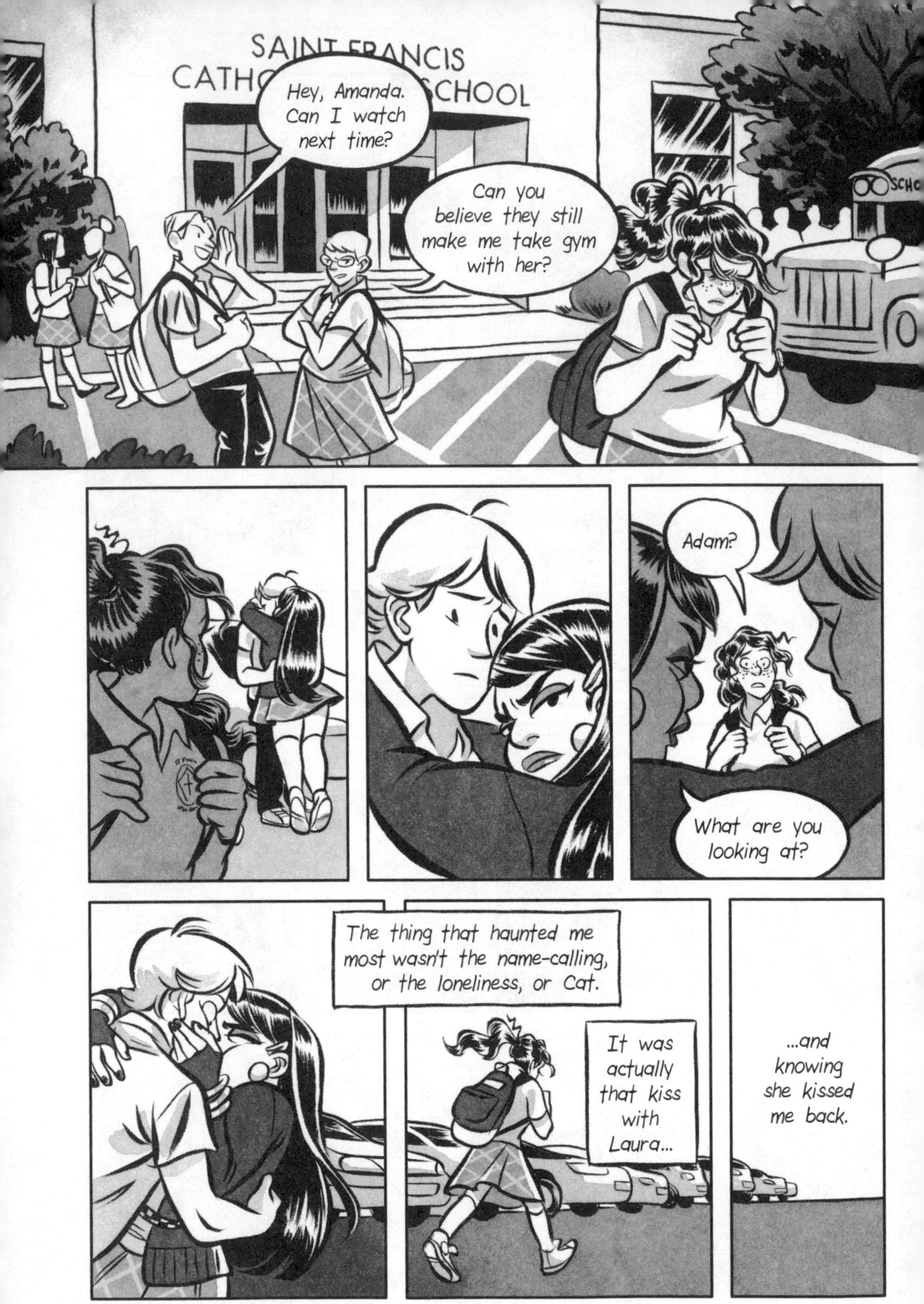
SAINT FRANCIS
CATHO SCHOOL
Hey, Amanda. Can I watch next time?
Can you believe they still make me take gym with her?
SCHO
Adam?
What are you looking at?
The thing that haunted me most wasn't the name-calling, or the loneliness, or Cat.
It was actually that kiss with Laura...
...and knowing she kissed me back.

261

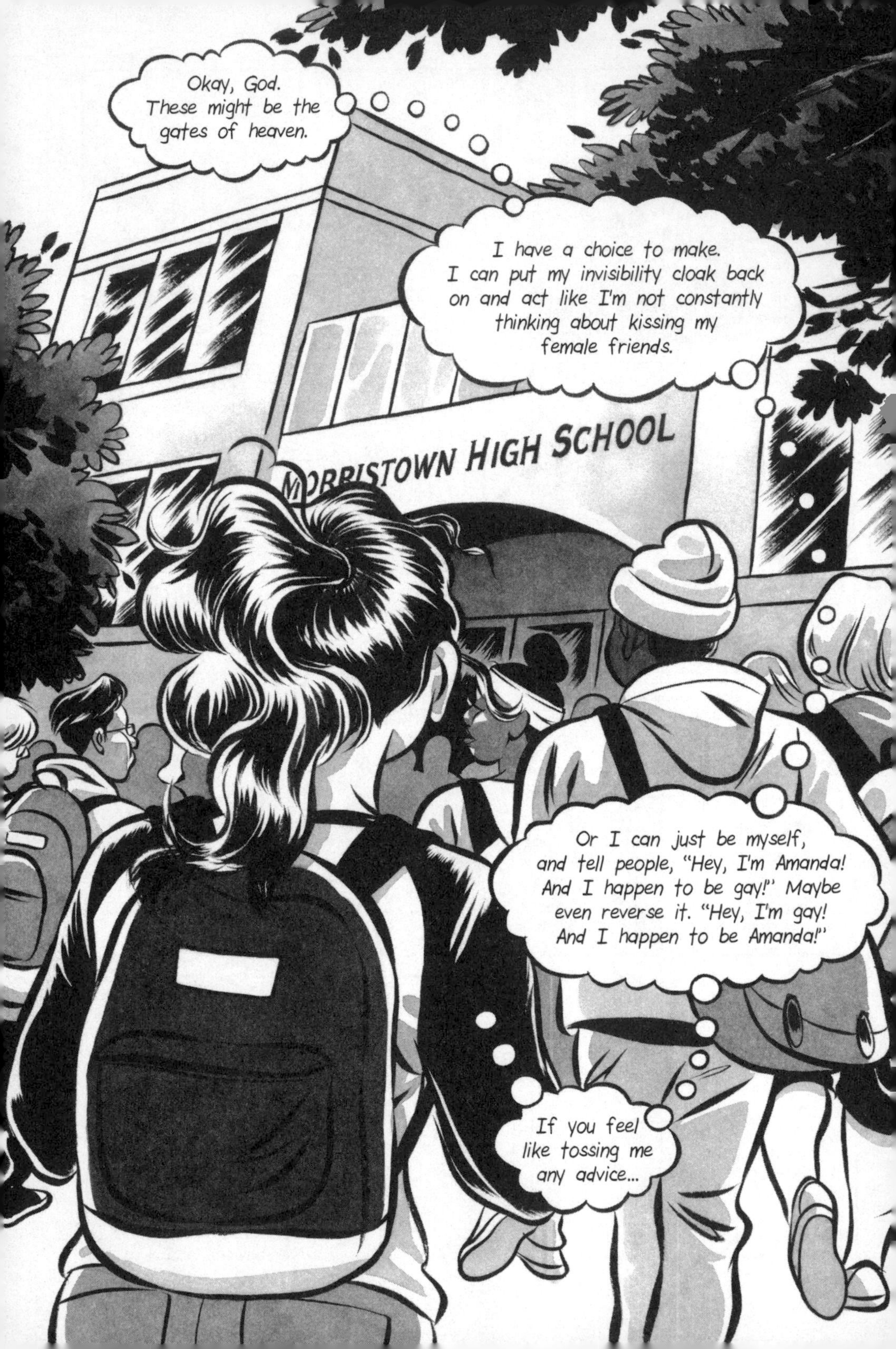
Okay, God. These might be the gates of heaven.
I have a choice to make. I can put my invisibility cloak back on and act like I'm not constantly thinking about kissing my female friends.
MORRISTOWN HIGH SCHOOL
Or I can just be myself, and tell people, "Hey, I'm Amanda! And I happen to be gay!" Maybe even reverse it. "Hey, I'm gay! And I happen to be Amanda!"
If you feel like tossing me any advice...

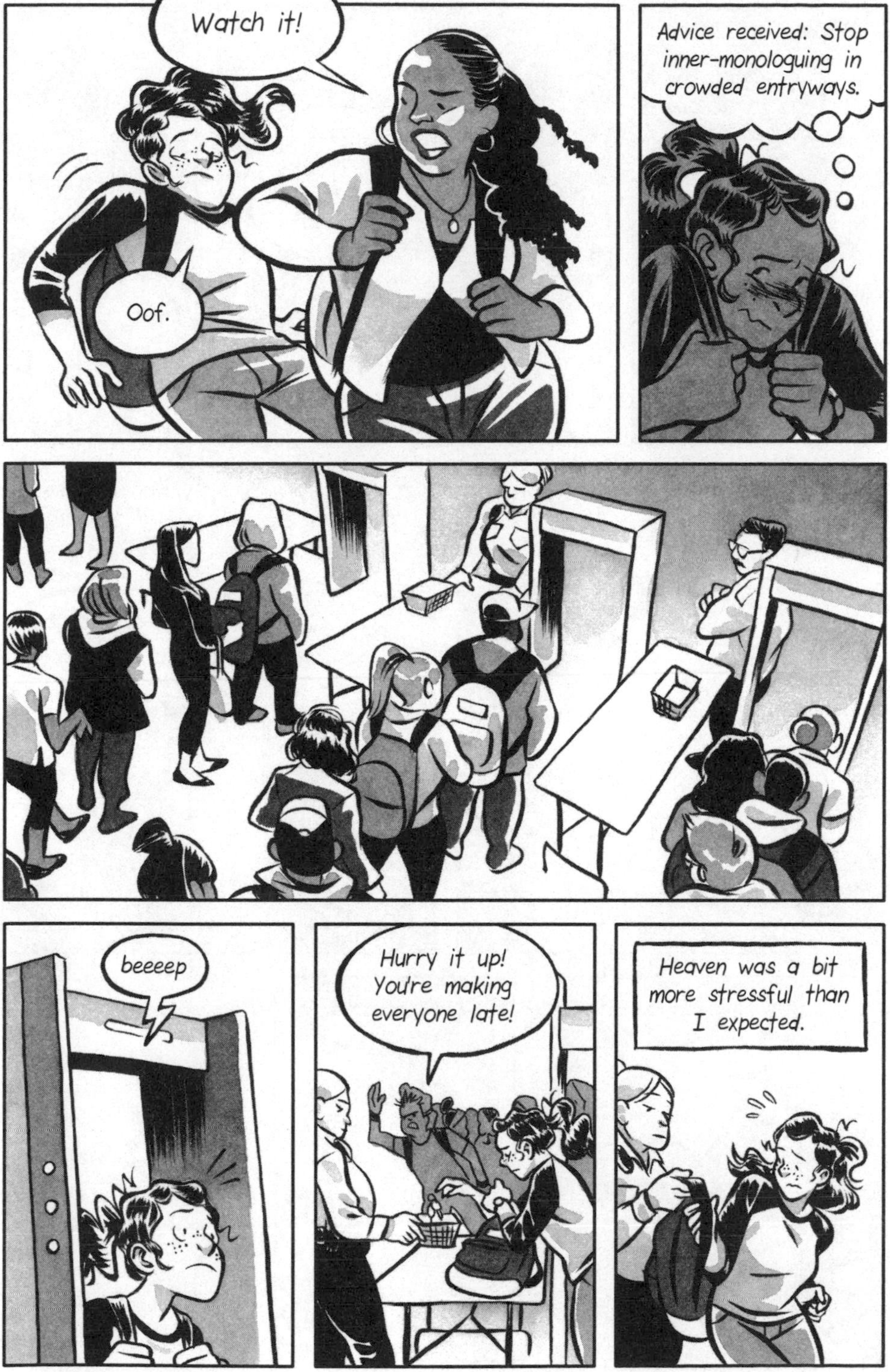
Watch it!
Oof.
Advice received: Stop inner-monologuing in crowded entryways.
beeeep
Hurry it up! You're making everyone late!
Heaven was a bit more stressful than I expected.

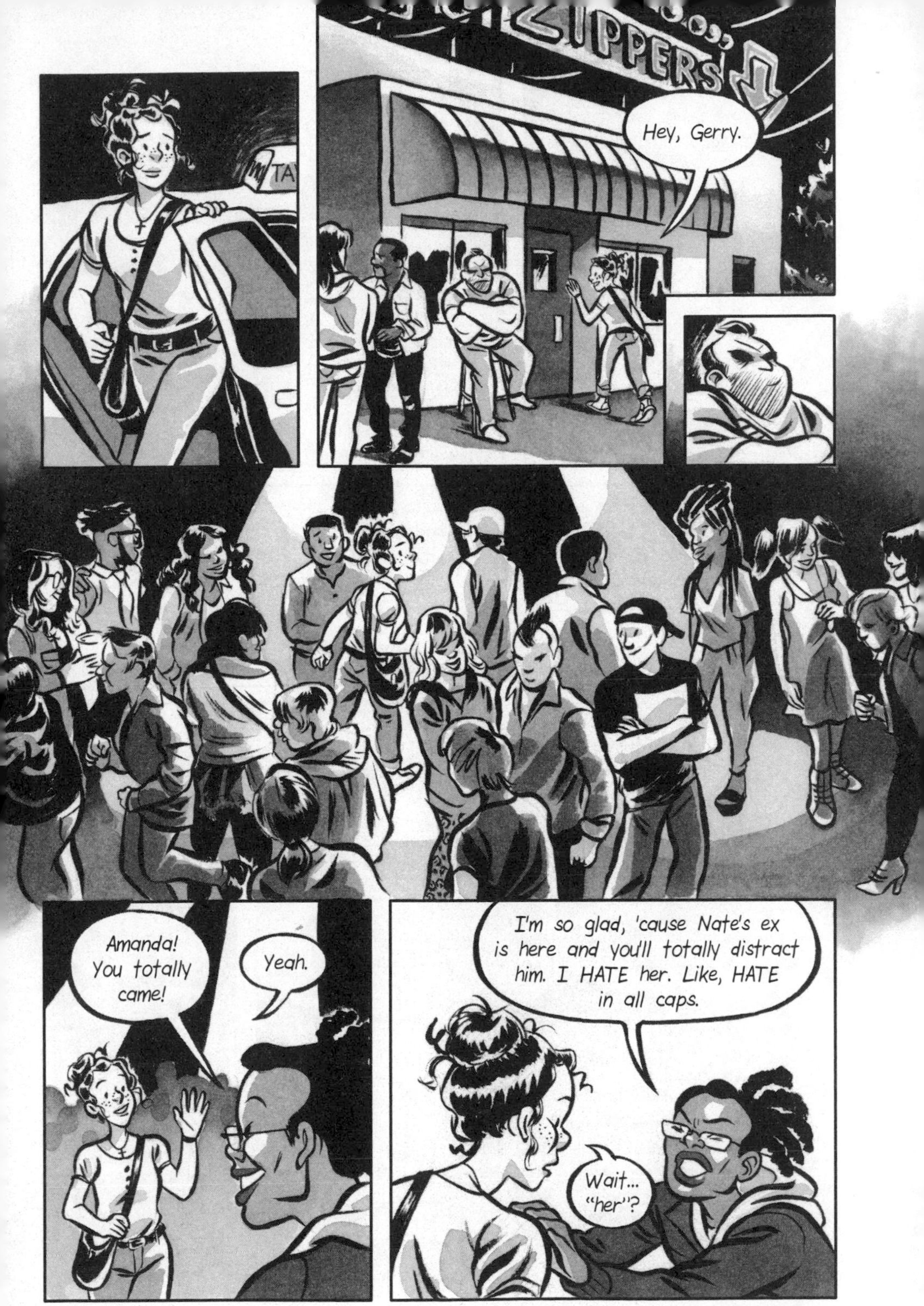

ZIPPERS
Hey, Gerry.
Amanda! You totally came!
Yeah.
I'm so glad, 'cause Nate's ex is here and you'll totally distract him. I HATE her. Like, HATE in all caps.
Wait... "her"?

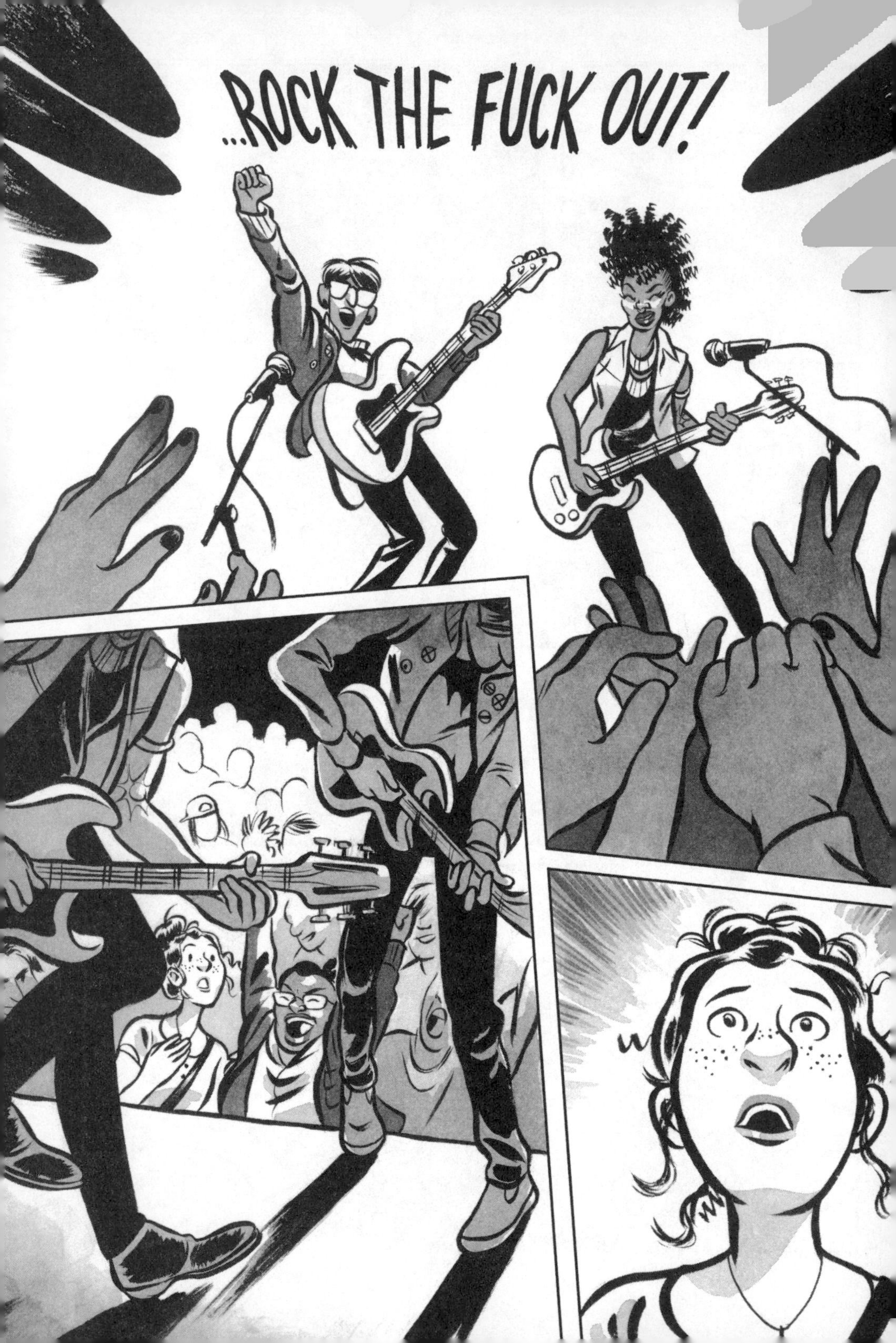
...ROCK THE FUCK OUT!

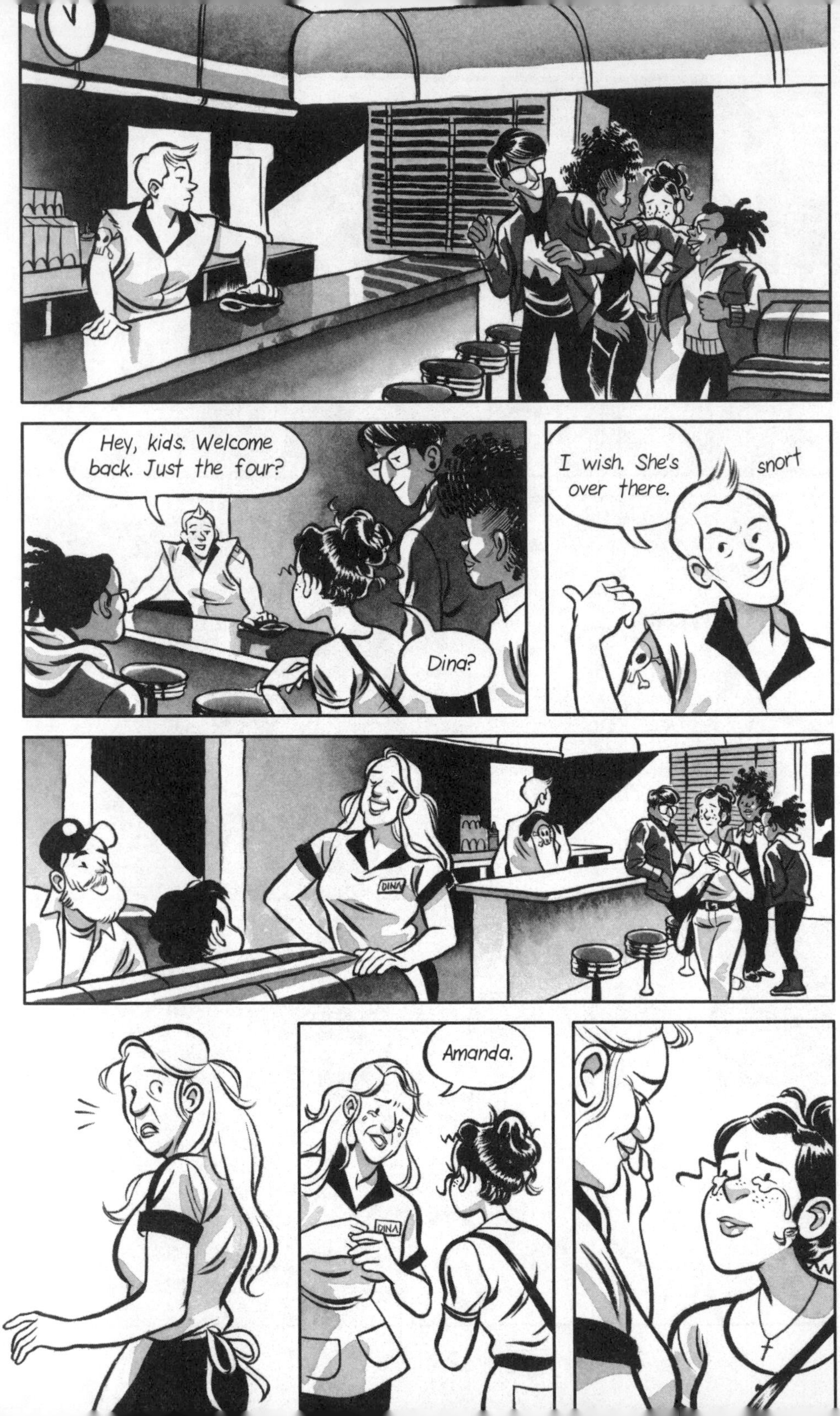
Hey, kids. Welcome back. Just the four?
Dina?
I wish. She's over there.
snort
DINA
Amanda.
DINA

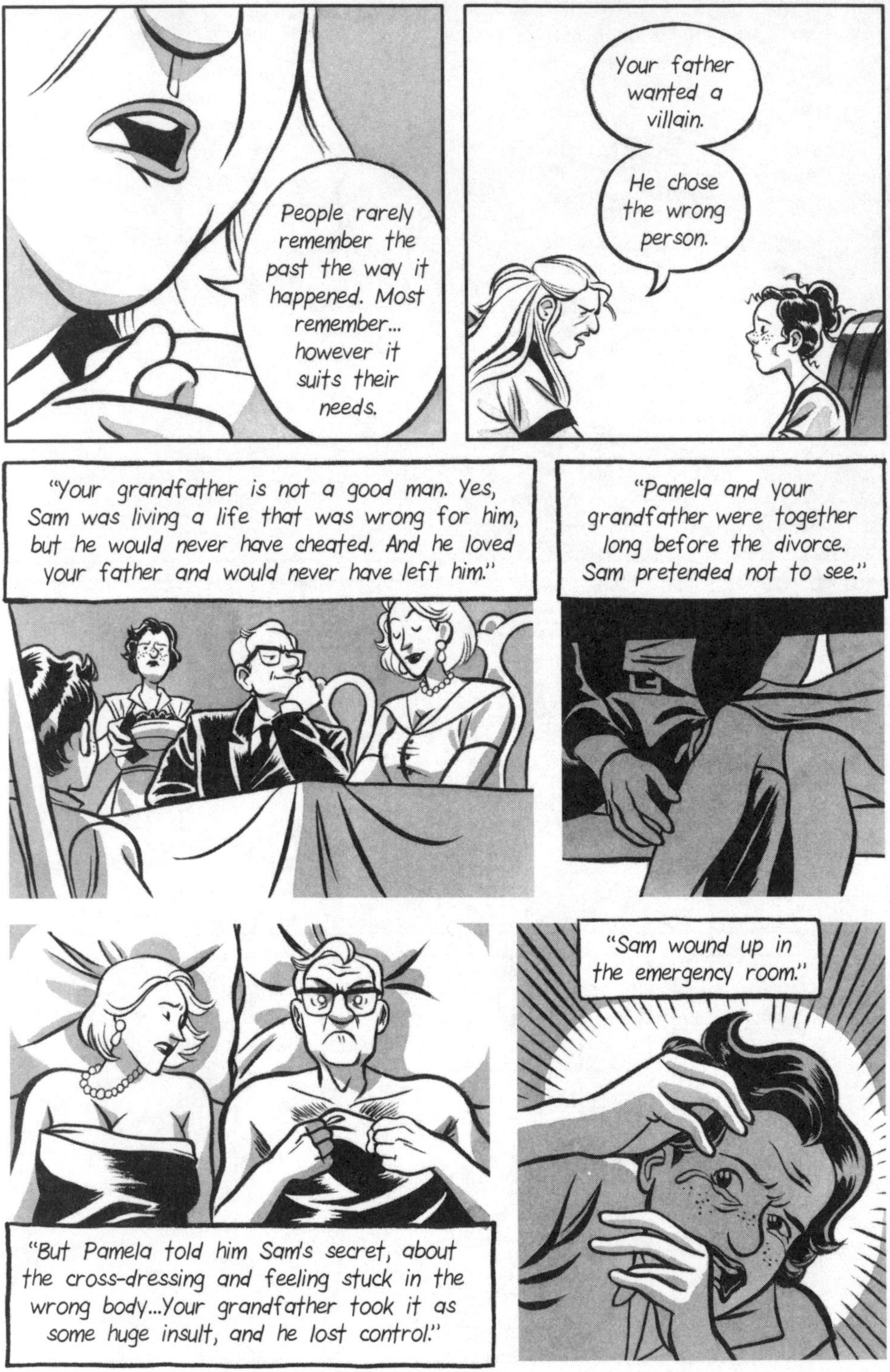
People rarely remember the past the way it happened. Most remember... however it suits their needs.
Your father wanted a villain.
He chose the wrong person.
"Your grandfather is not a good man. Yes, Sam was living a life that was wrong for him, but he would never have cheated. And he loved your father and would never have left him."
"Pamela and your grandfather were together long before the divorce. Sam pretended not to see."
"But Pamela told him Sam's secret, about the cross-dressing and feeling stuck in the wrong body...Your grandfather took it as some huge insult, and he lost control."
"Sam wound up in the emergency room."

279

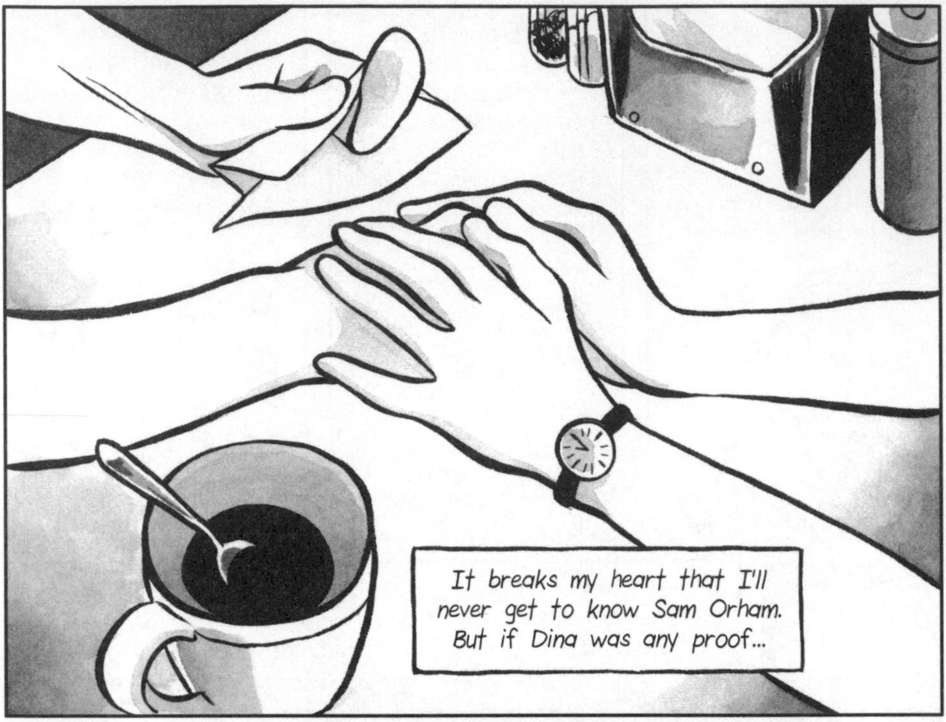
It breaks my heart that I'll never get to know Sam Orham. But if Dina was any proof...

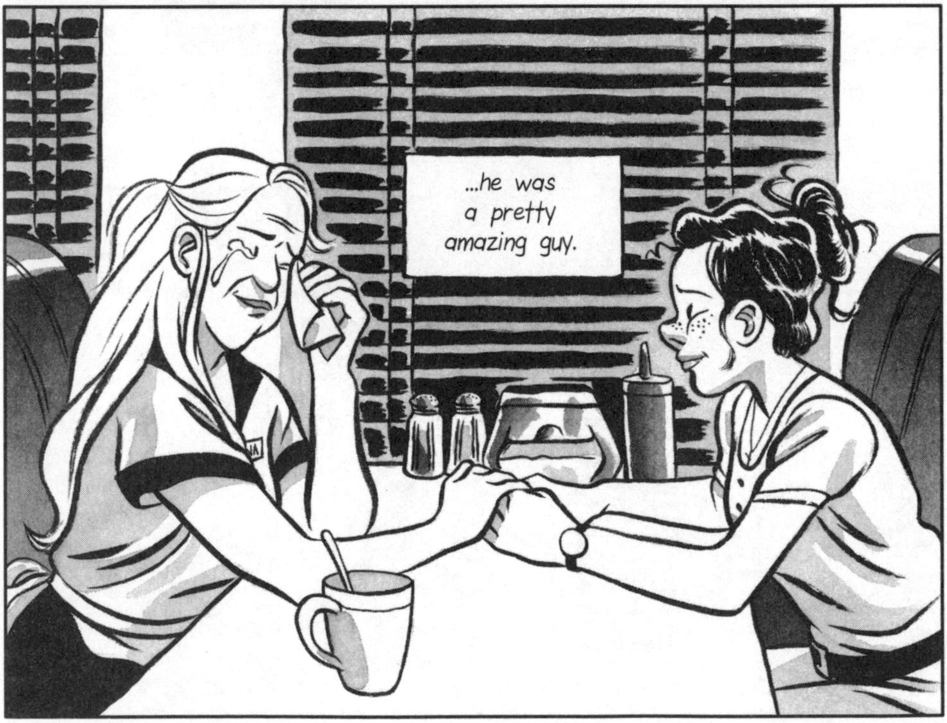
...he was a pretty amazing guy.

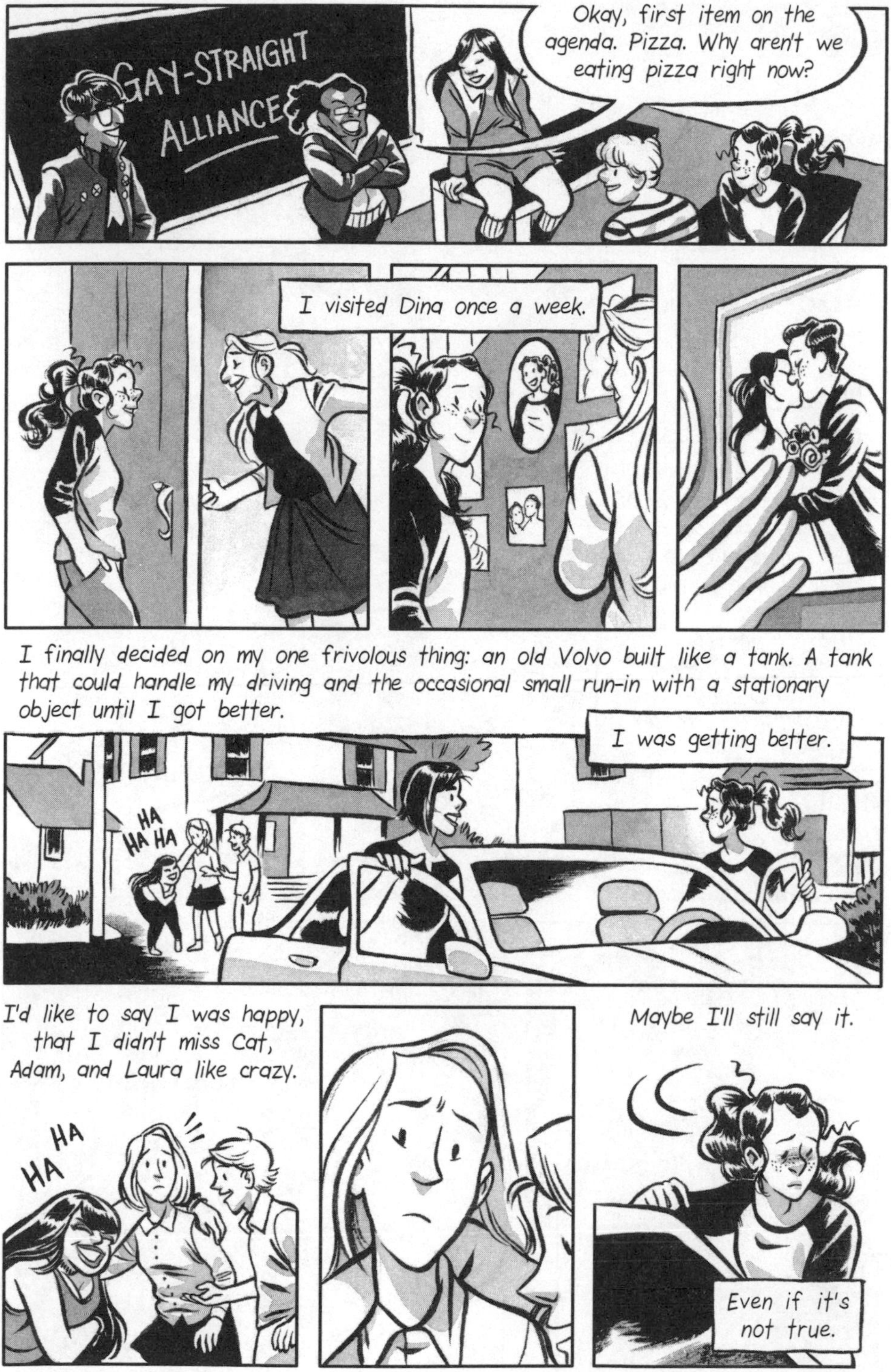
GAY-STRAIGHT ALLIANCE
Okay, first item on the agenda. Pizza. Why aren't we eating pizza right now?
I visited Dina once a week.
I finally decided on my one frivolous thing: an old Volvo built like a tank. A tank that could handle my driving and the occasional small run-in with a stationary object until I got better.
I was getting better.
HA HA HA
I'd like to say I was happy, that I didn't miss Cat, Adam, and Laura like crazy.
HA HA
Maybe I'll still say it.
Even if it's not true.

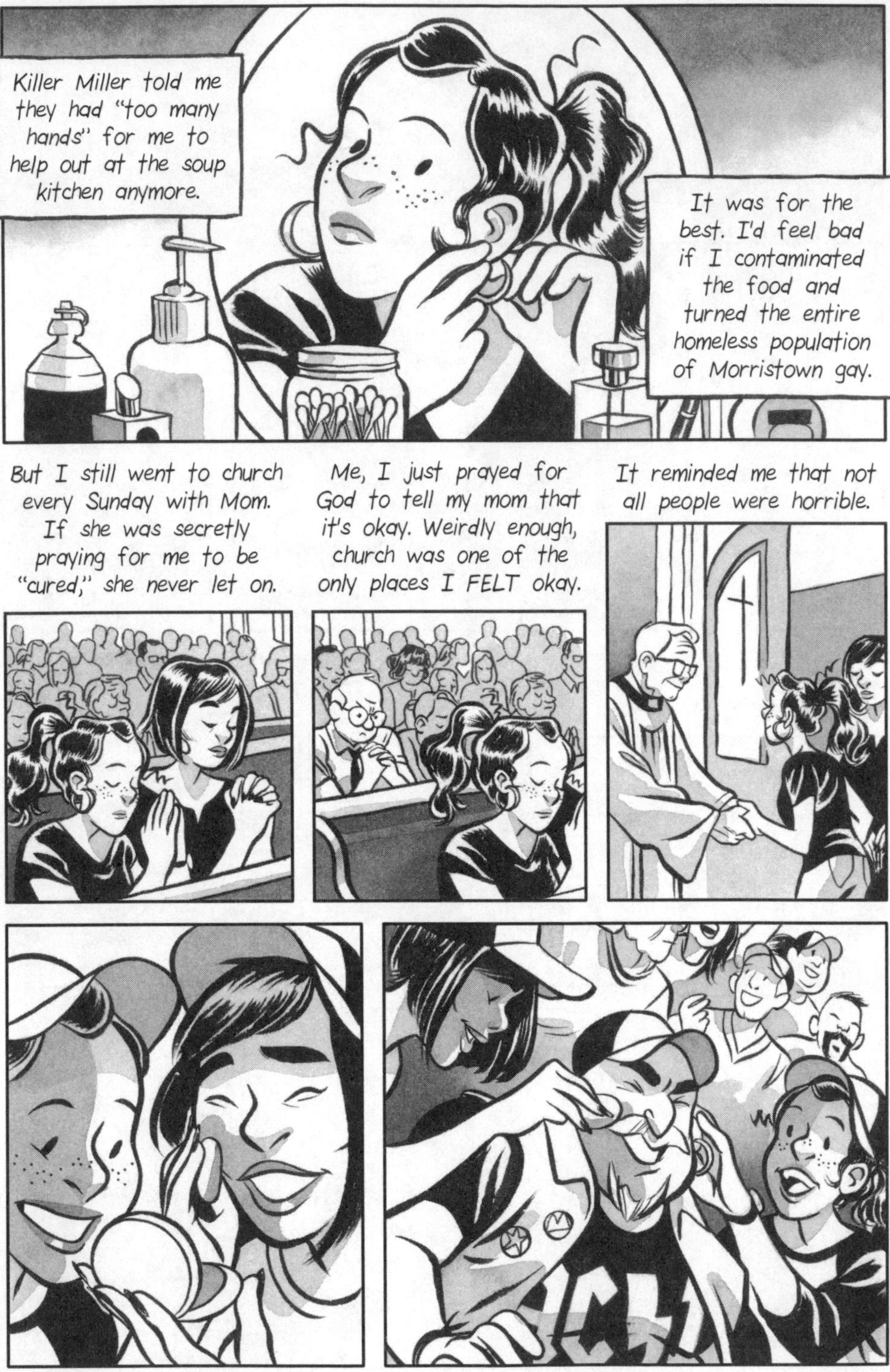
Killer Miller told me they had "too many hands" for me to help out at the soup kitchen anymore.
It was for the best. I'd feel bad if I contaminated the food and turned the entire homeless population of Morristown gay.
But I still went to church every Sunday with Mom. If she was secretly praying for me to be "cured," she never let on.
Me, I just prayed for God to tell my mom that it's okay. Weirdly enough, church was one of the only places I FELT okay.
It reminded me that not all people were horrible.

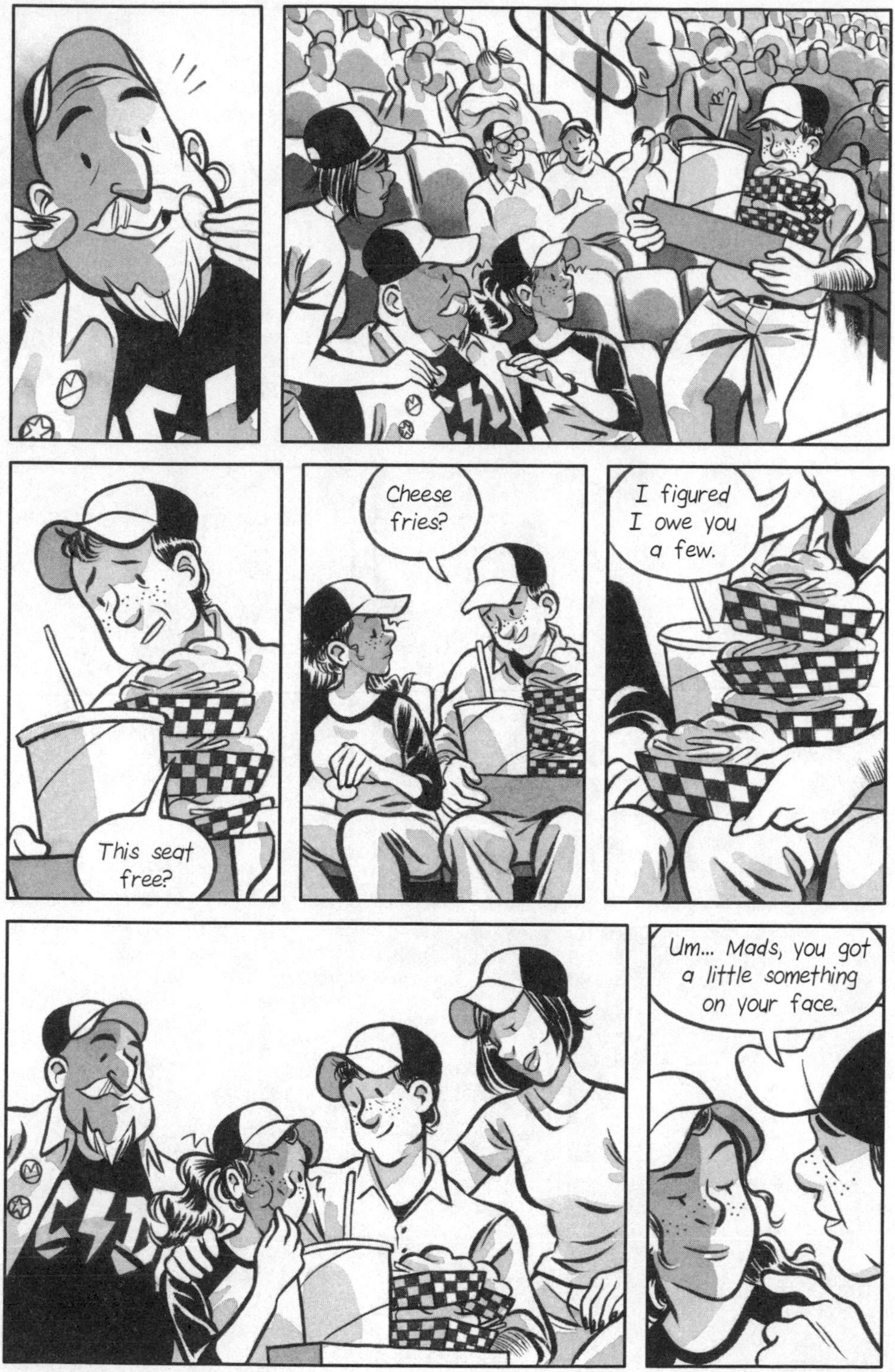
This seat free?
Cheese fries?
I figured I owe you a few.
Um... Mads, you got a little something on your face.

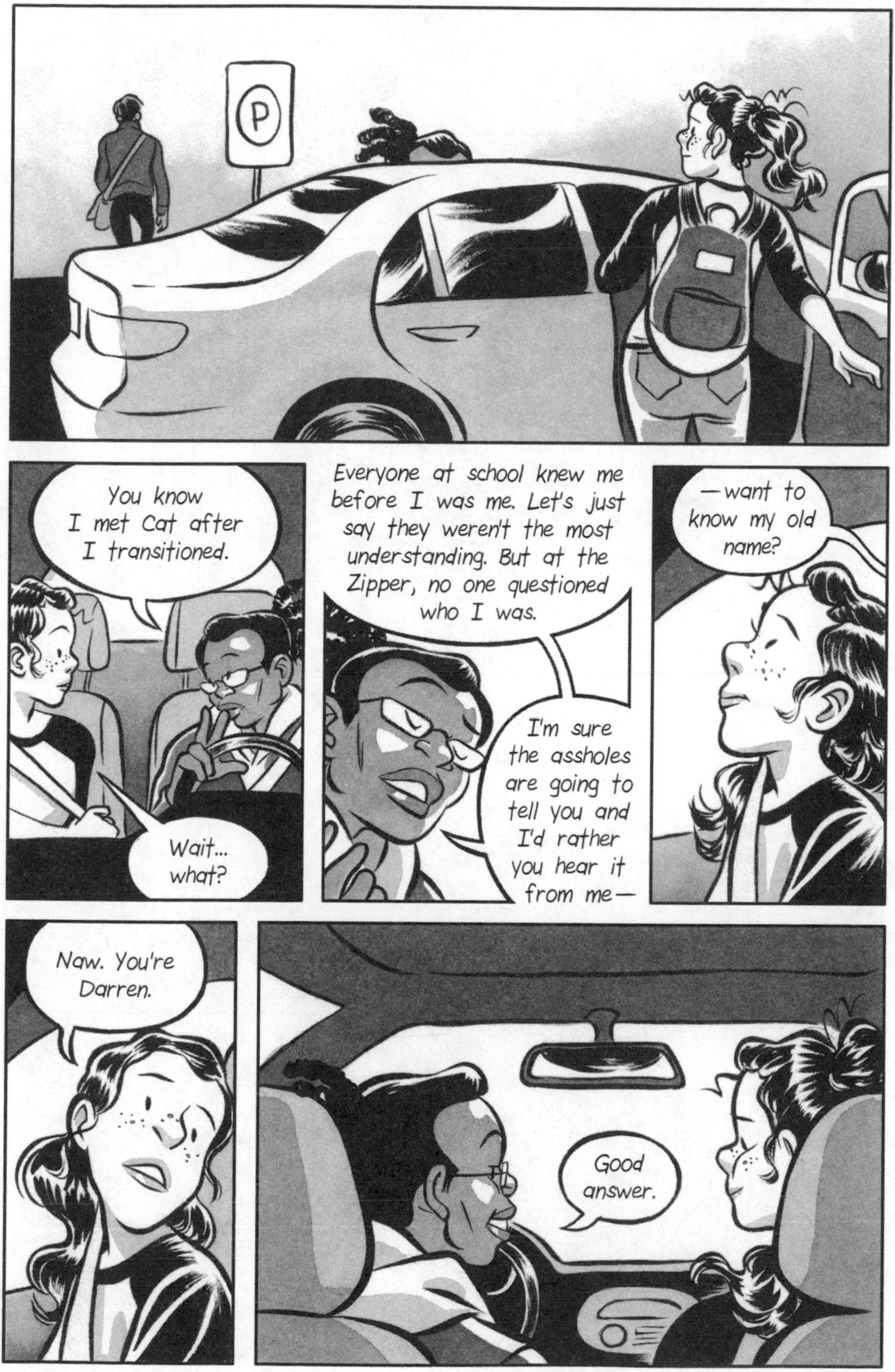
You know I met Cat after I transitioned.
Wait... what?
Everyone at school knew me before I was me. Let's just say they weren't the most understanding. But at the Zipper, no one questioned who I was.
I'm sure the assholes are going to tell you and I'd rather you hear it from me—
—want to know my old name?
Naw. You're Darren.
Good answer.

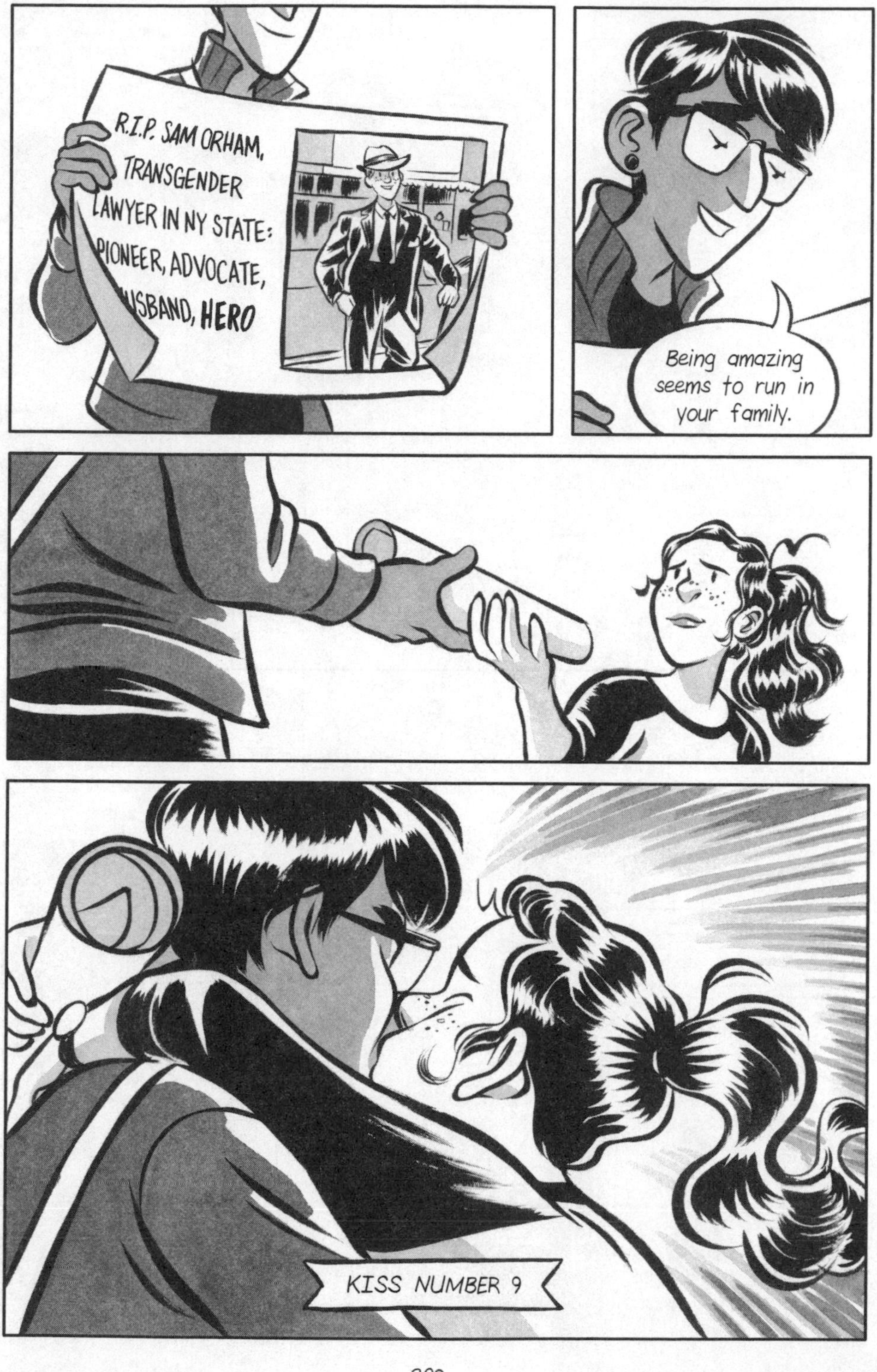
R.I.P. SAM ORHAM, TRANSGENDER LAWYER IN NY STATE: PIONEER, ADVOCATE, HUSBAND, HERO
Being amazing seems to run in your family.
KISS NUMBER 9

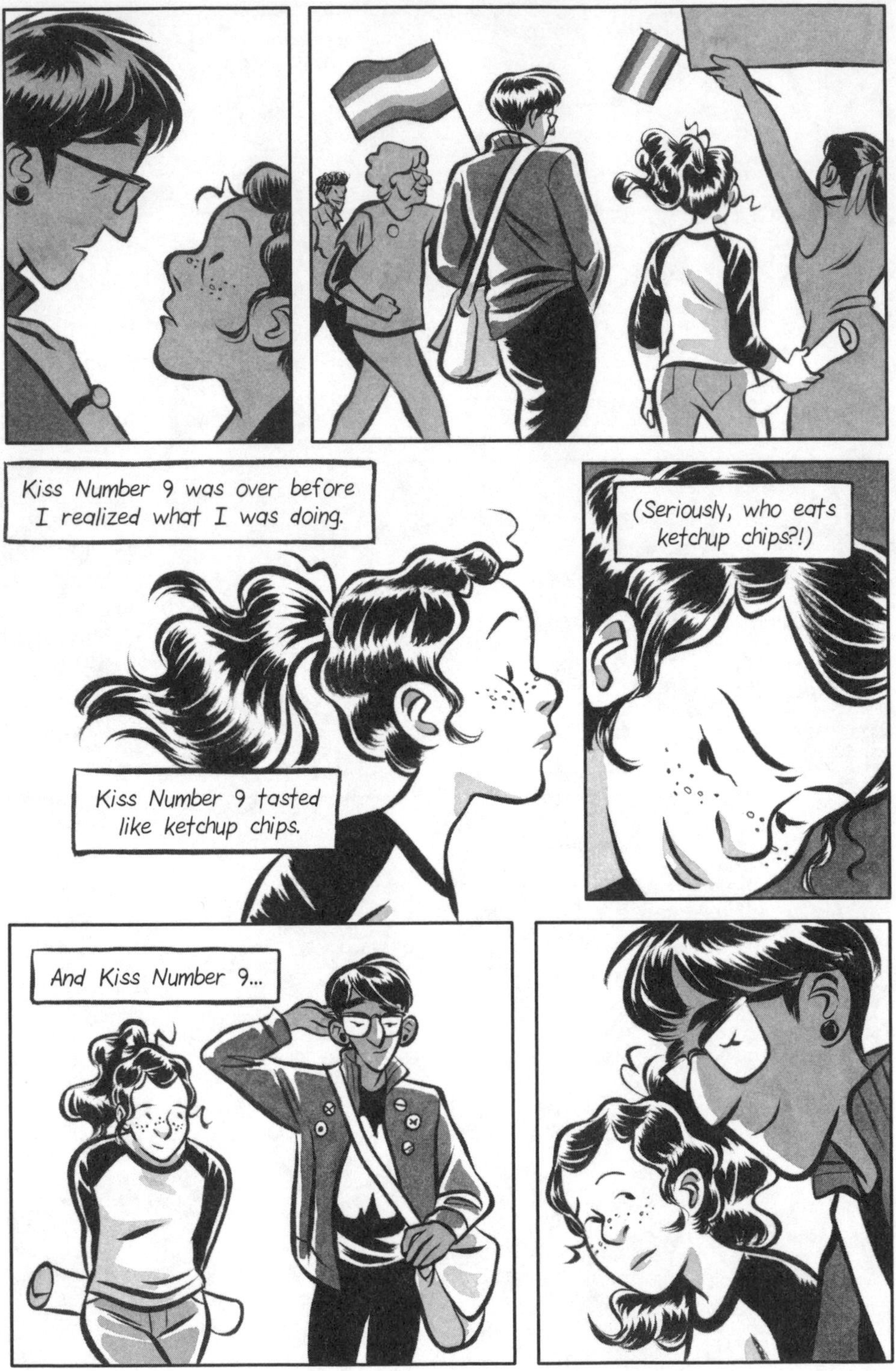
Kiss Number 9 was over before I realized what I was doing.
(Seriously, who eats ketchup chips?!)
Kiss Number 9 tasted like ketchup chips.
And Kiss Number 9...

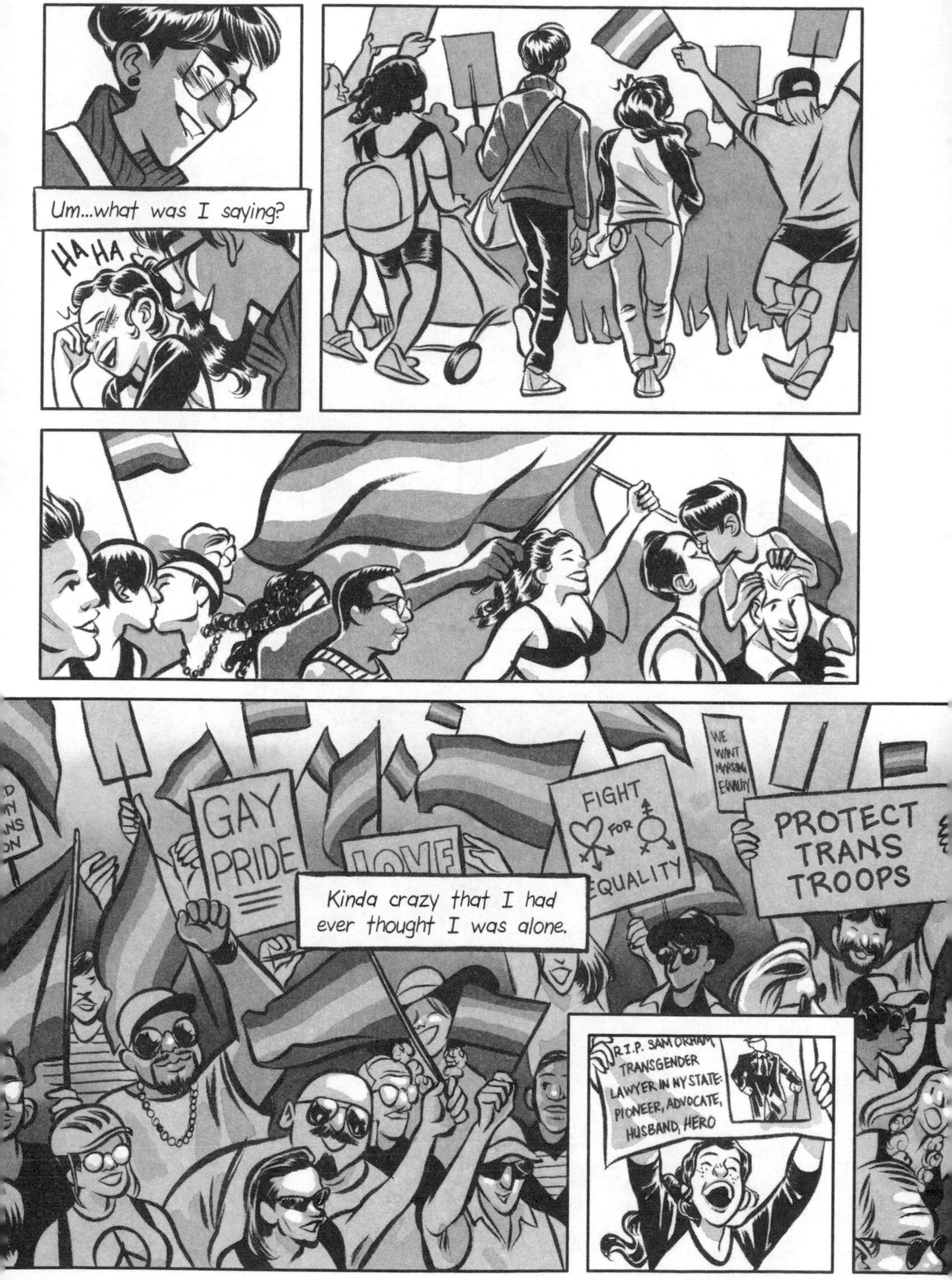
Um...what was I saying?
HA HA
GAY PRIDE
FIGHT FOR EQUALITY
PROTECT TRANS TROOPS
Kinda crazy that I had ever thought I was alone.
R.I.P. SAM ORHAM, TRANSGENDER LAWYER IN NY STATE: PIONEER, ADVOCATE, HUSBAND, HERO

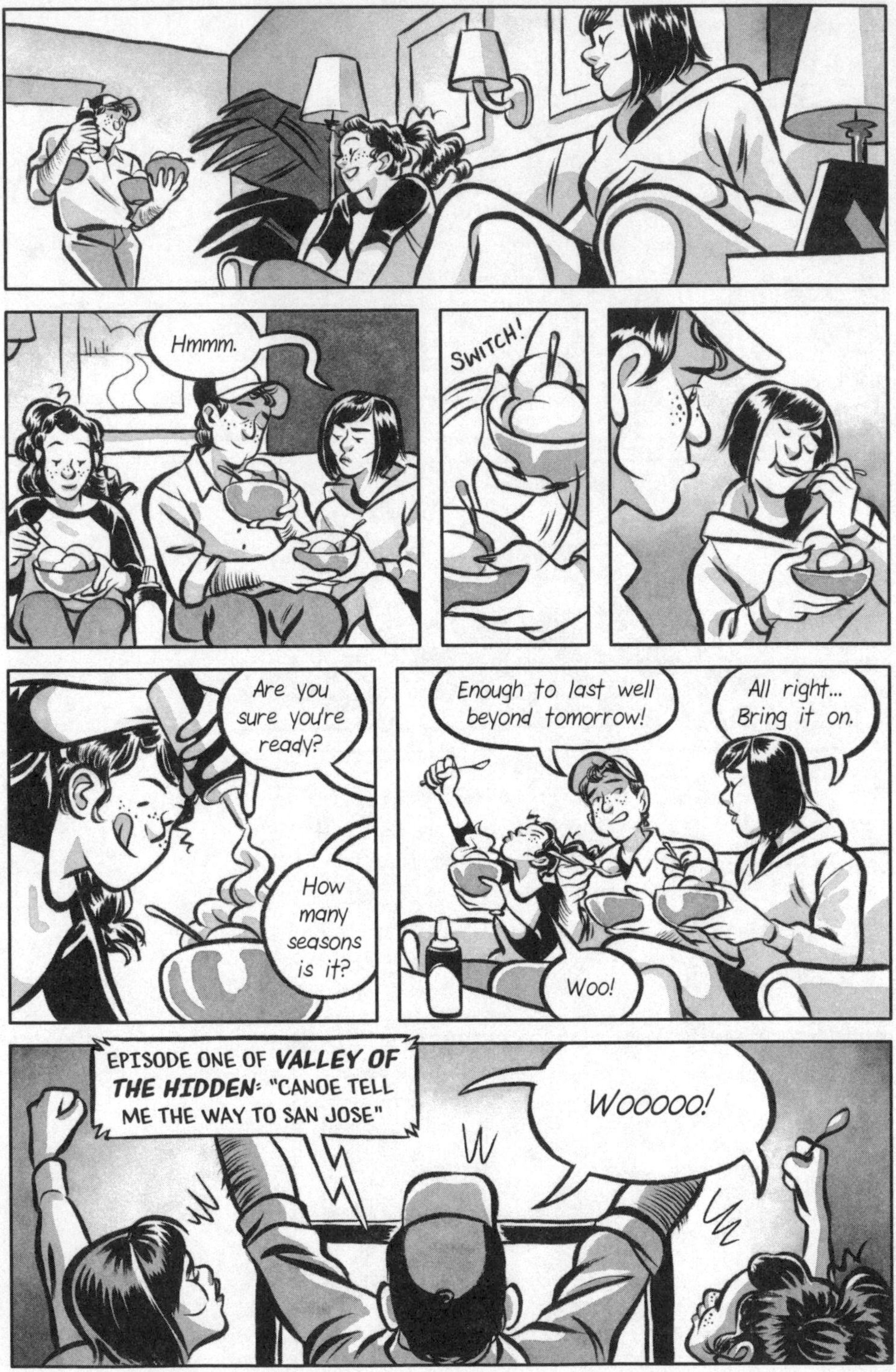
Hmmm.
SWITCH!
Are you sure you're ready?
How many seasons is it?
Enough to last well beyond tomorrow!
All right... Bring it on.
Woo!
EPISODE ONE OF VALLEY OF THE HIDDEN: "CANOE TELL ME THE WAY TO SAN JOSE"
Wooooo!
W
W
W

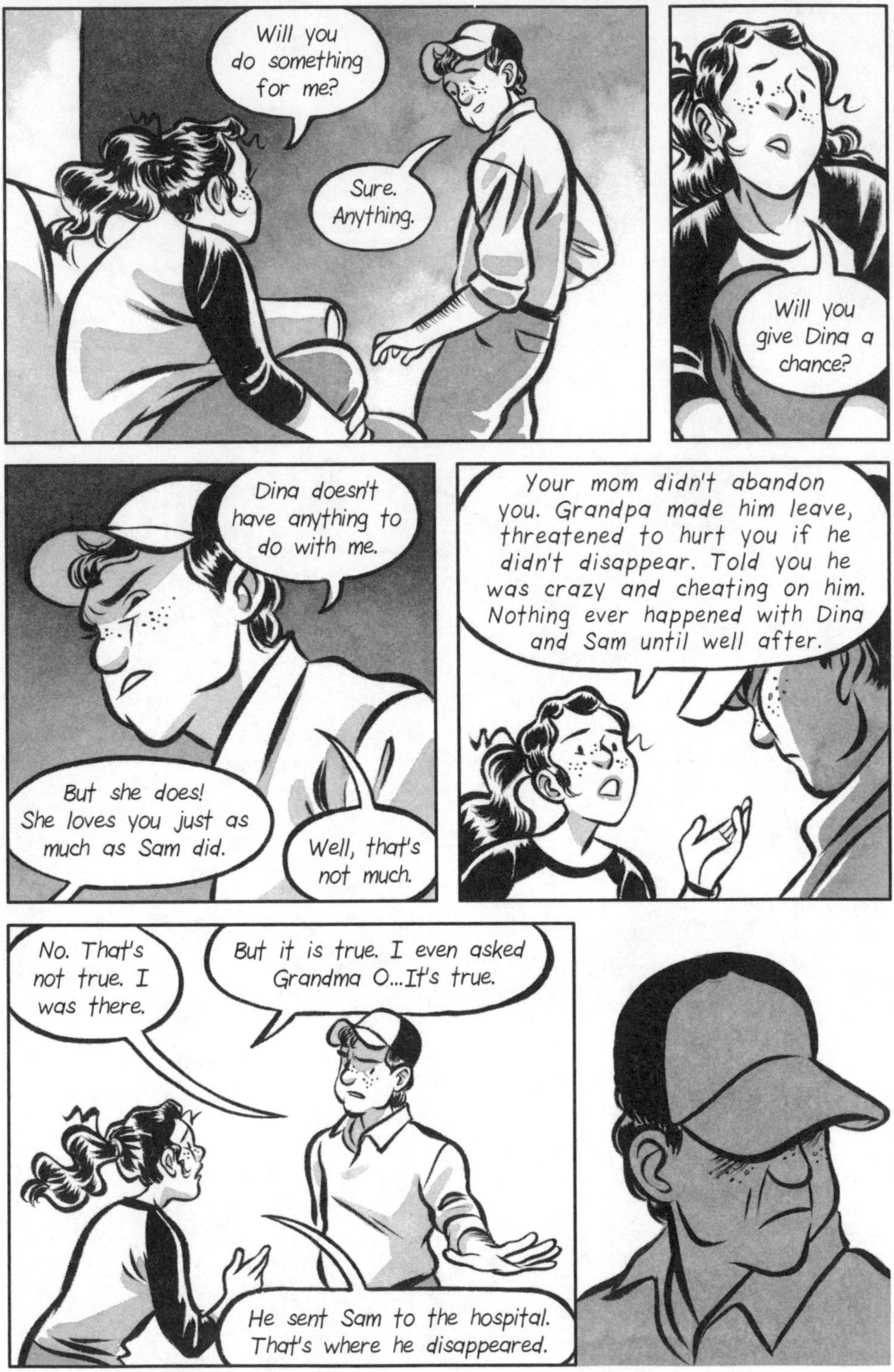

Will you do something for me?
Sure. Anything.
Will you give Dina a chance?
Dina doesn't have anything to do with me.
But she does! She loves you just as much as Sam did.
Well, that's not much.
Your mom didn't abandon you. Grandpa made him leave, threatened to hurt you if he didn't disappear. Told you he was crazy and cheating on him. Nothing ever happened with Dina and Sam until well after.
No. That's not true. I was there.
But it is true. I even asked Grandma O...It's true.
He sent Sam to the hospital. That's where he disappeared.

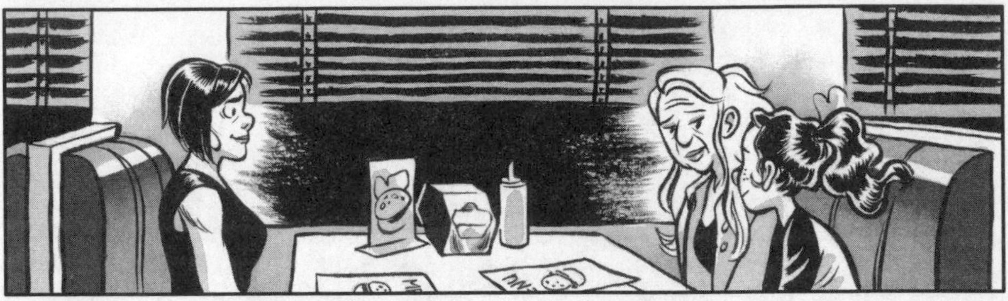

So Dad arrived. Dina and he got along amazingly. They're even talking about forming a bowling team.

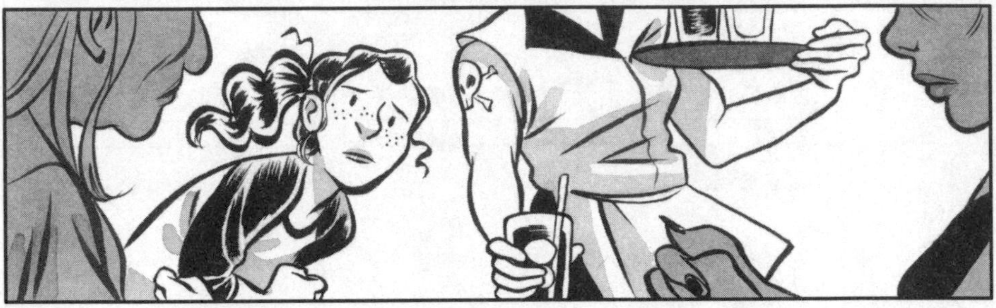

Oh, and Grandma and Grandpa Orham joined us as well. Grandpa must have apologized for three hours. It was really moving.

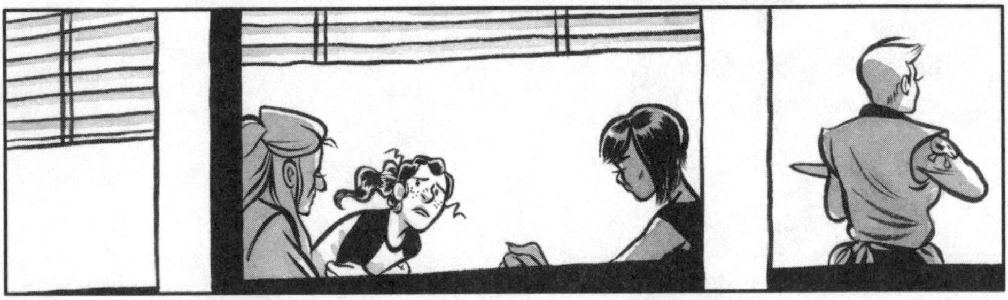

We ate with Laura and her new girlfriend, with Adam and Cat, and Father Tim and sweet Sara Miller. Jess and Nate's band played on the jukebox, since they had gotten pretty big by this point. Also, I finally got a superpower. Laser beams from my eyes. I would have done a demonstration, but I didn't want anyone to get jealous and ruin such a perfect evening.

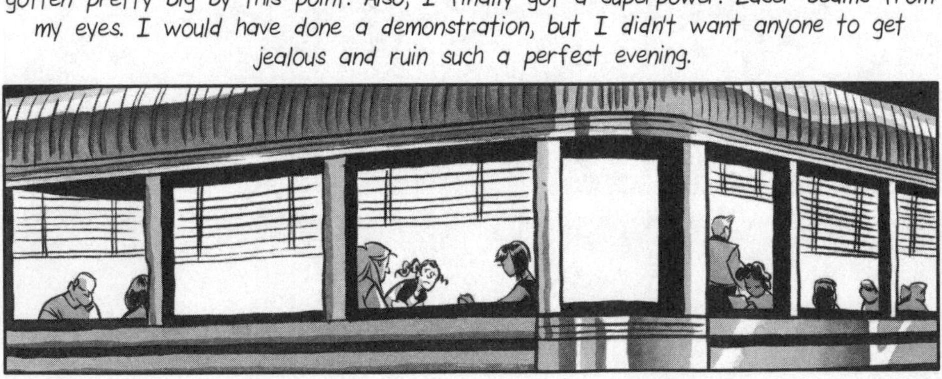

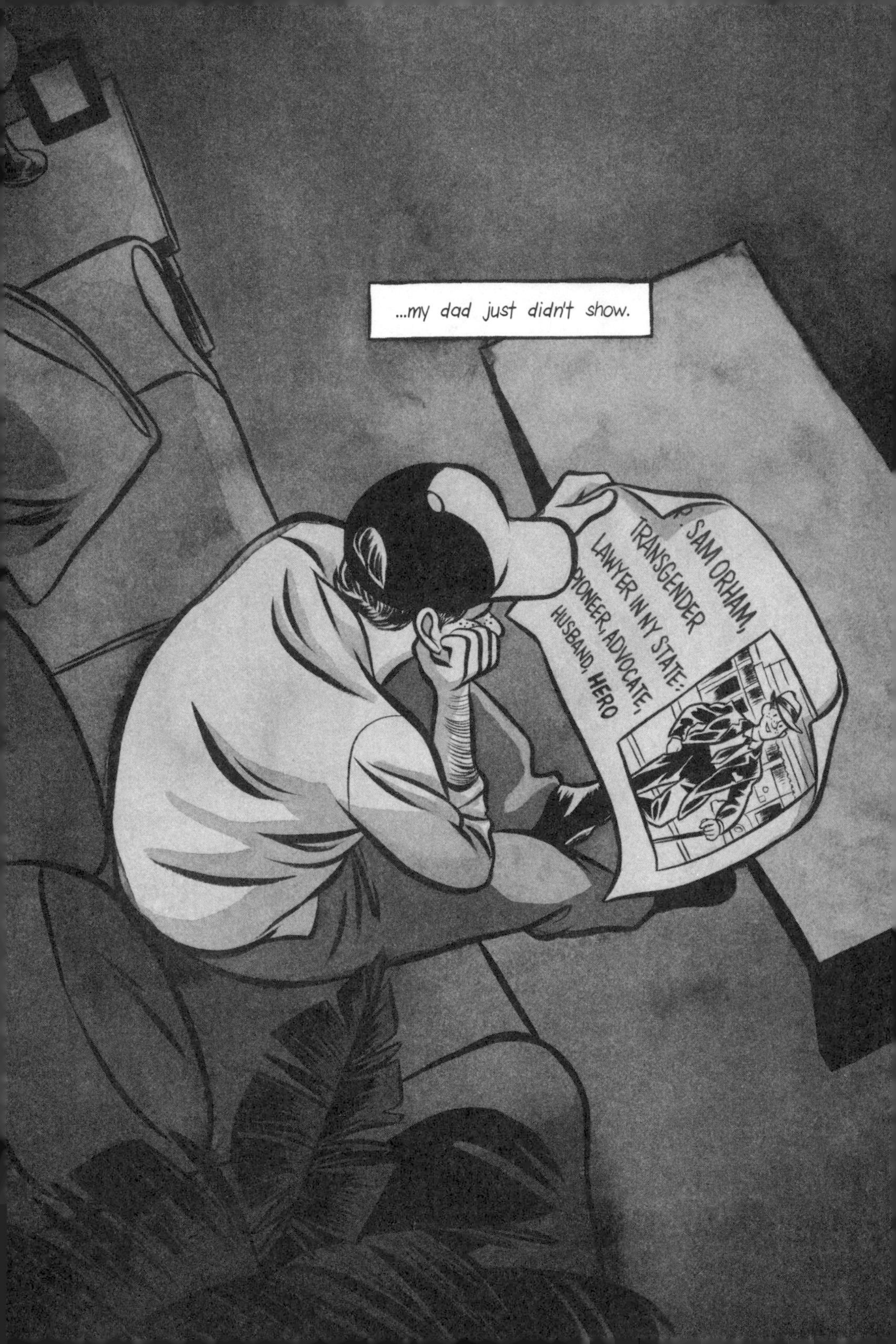
...my dad just didn't show.
SAM ORHAM,
TRANSGENDER
LAWYER IN NY STATE:
PIONEER, ADVOCATE,
HUSBAND, HERO

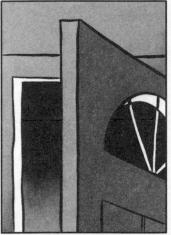

Mads, I just——

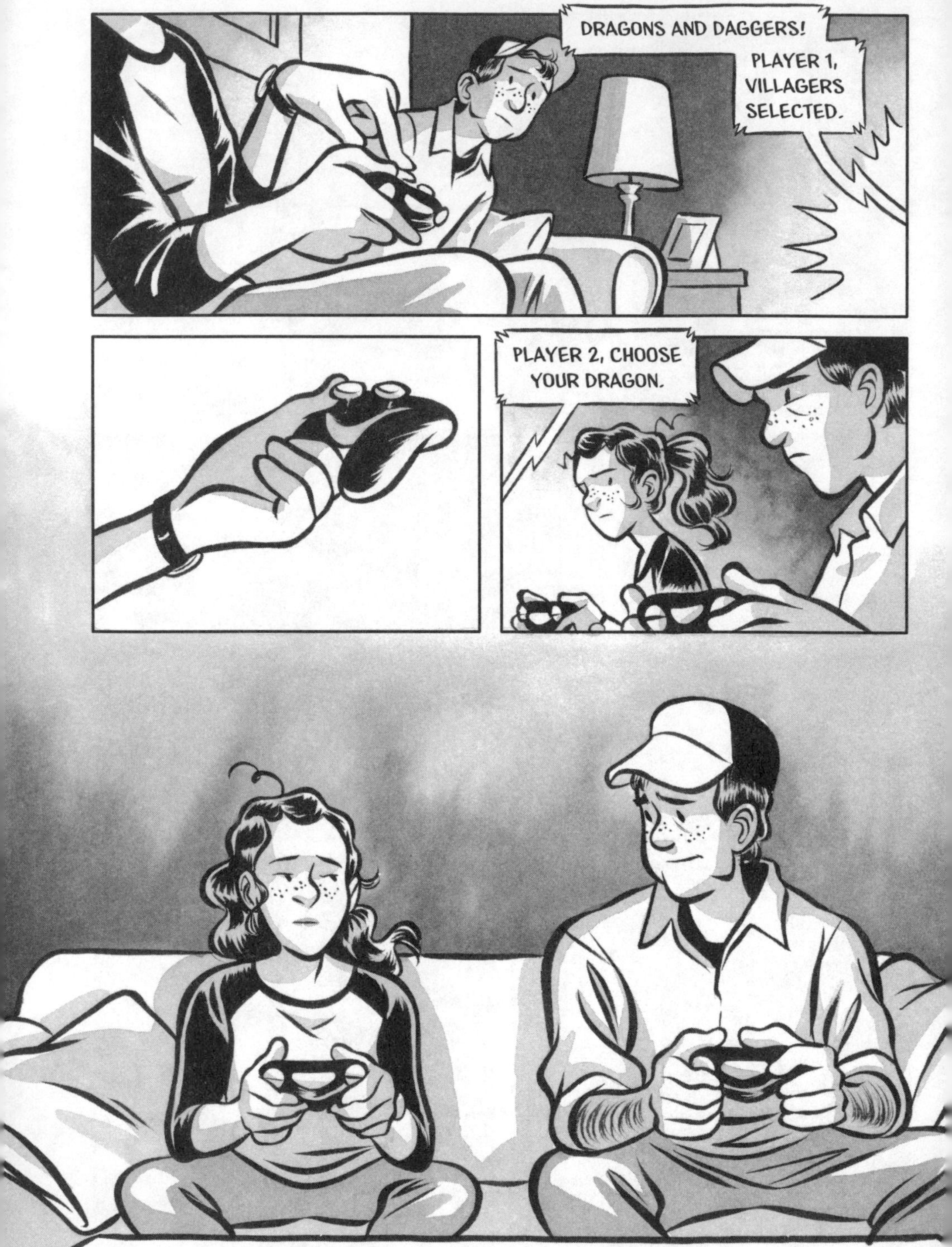
DRAGONS AND DAGGERS!
PLAYER 1, VILLAGERS SELECTED.
PLAYER 2, CHOOSE YOUR DRAGON.

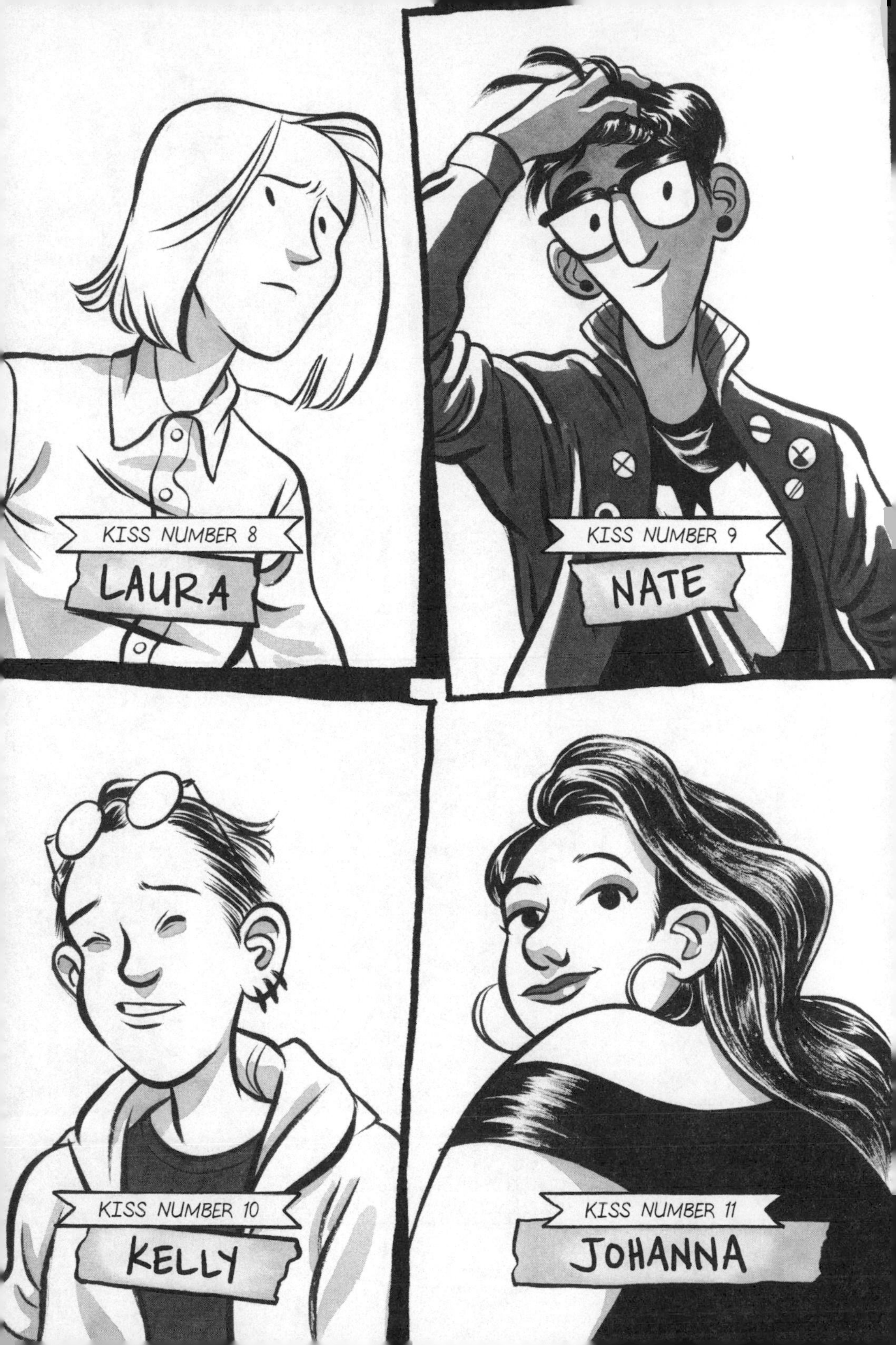
KISS NUMBER 8
LAURA
KISS NUMBER 9
NATE
KISS NUMBER 10
KELLY
KISS NUMBER 11
JOHANNA

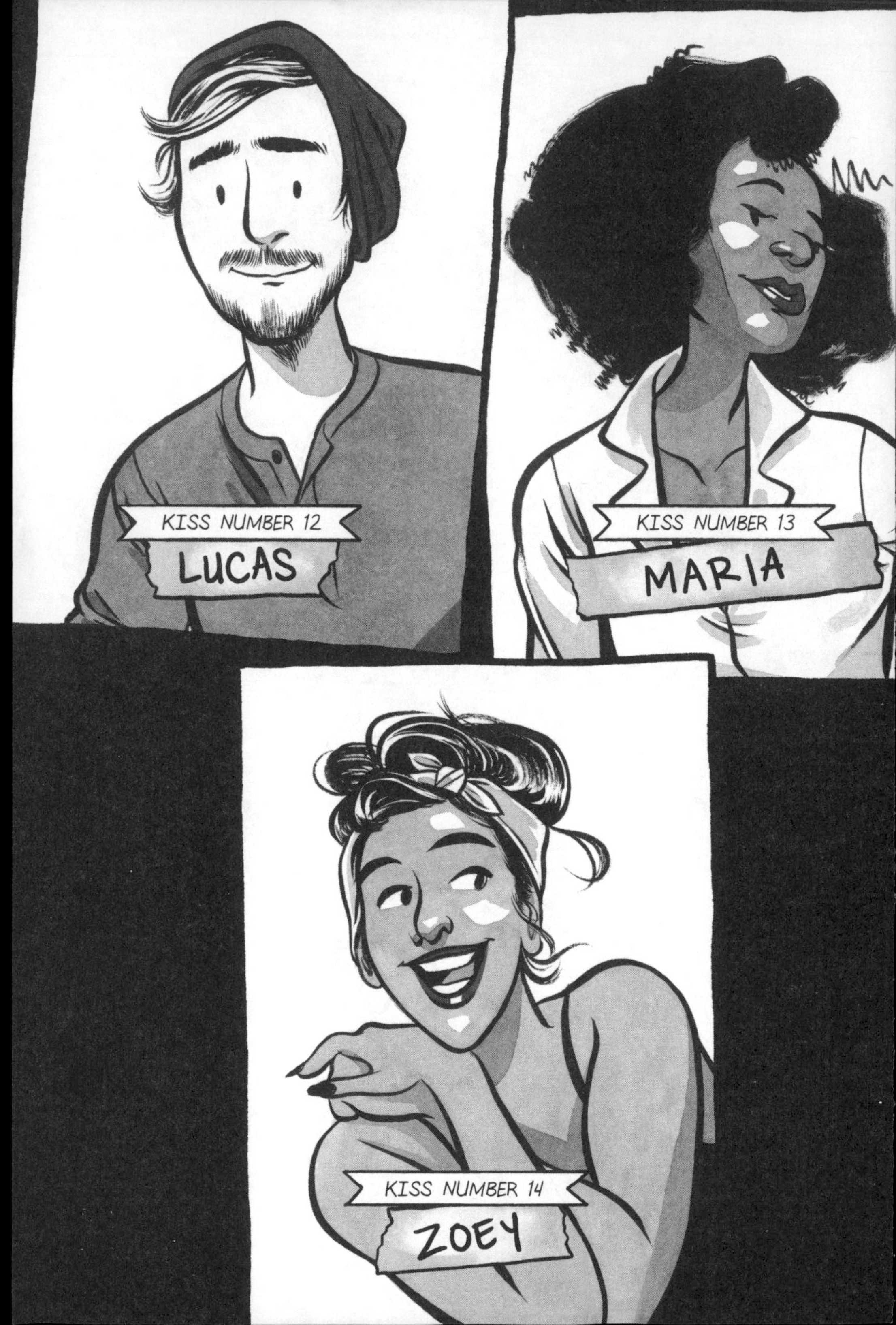
KISS NUMBER 12
LUCAS
KISS NUMBER 13
MARIA
KISS NUMBER 14
ZOEY

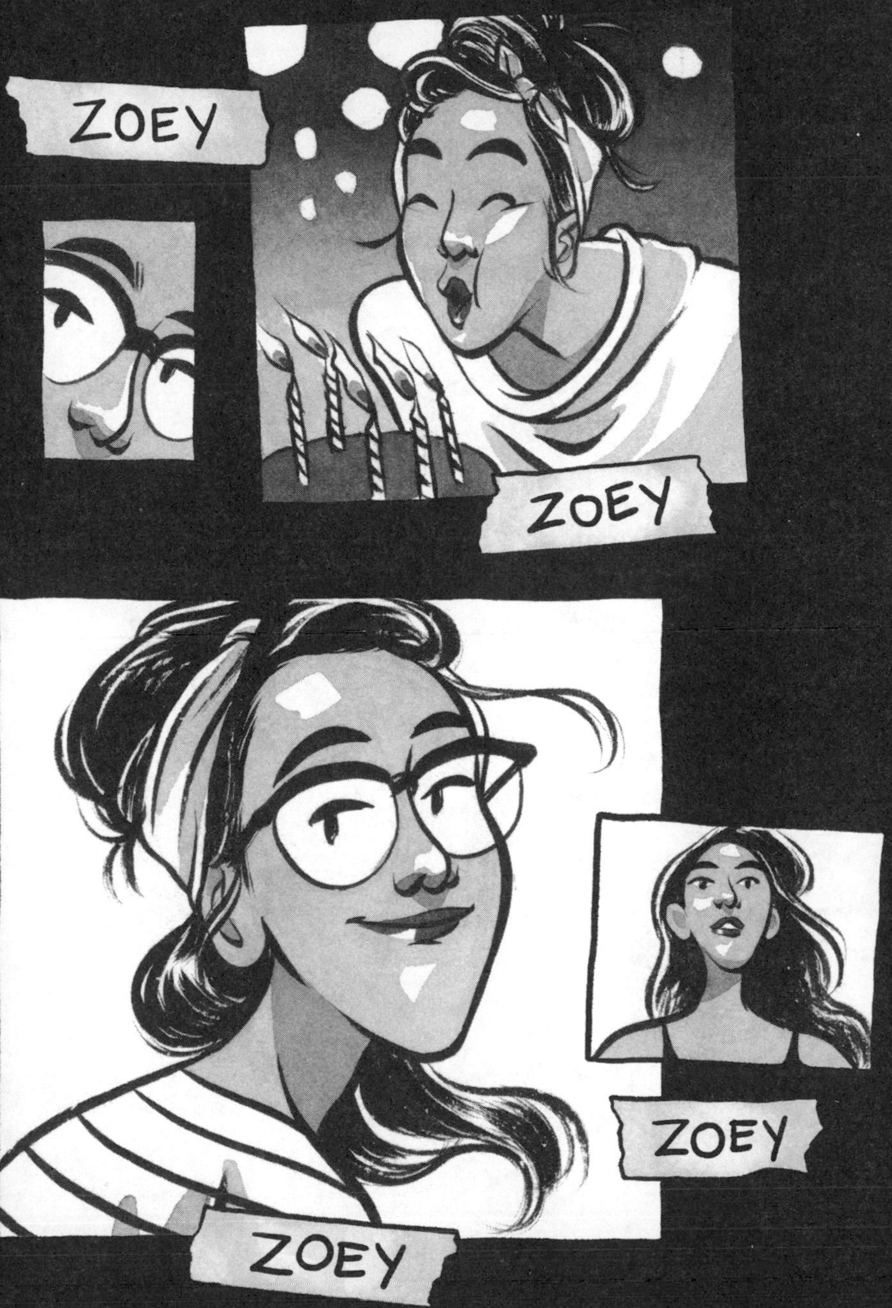
ZOEY
ZOEY
ZOEY
ZOEY

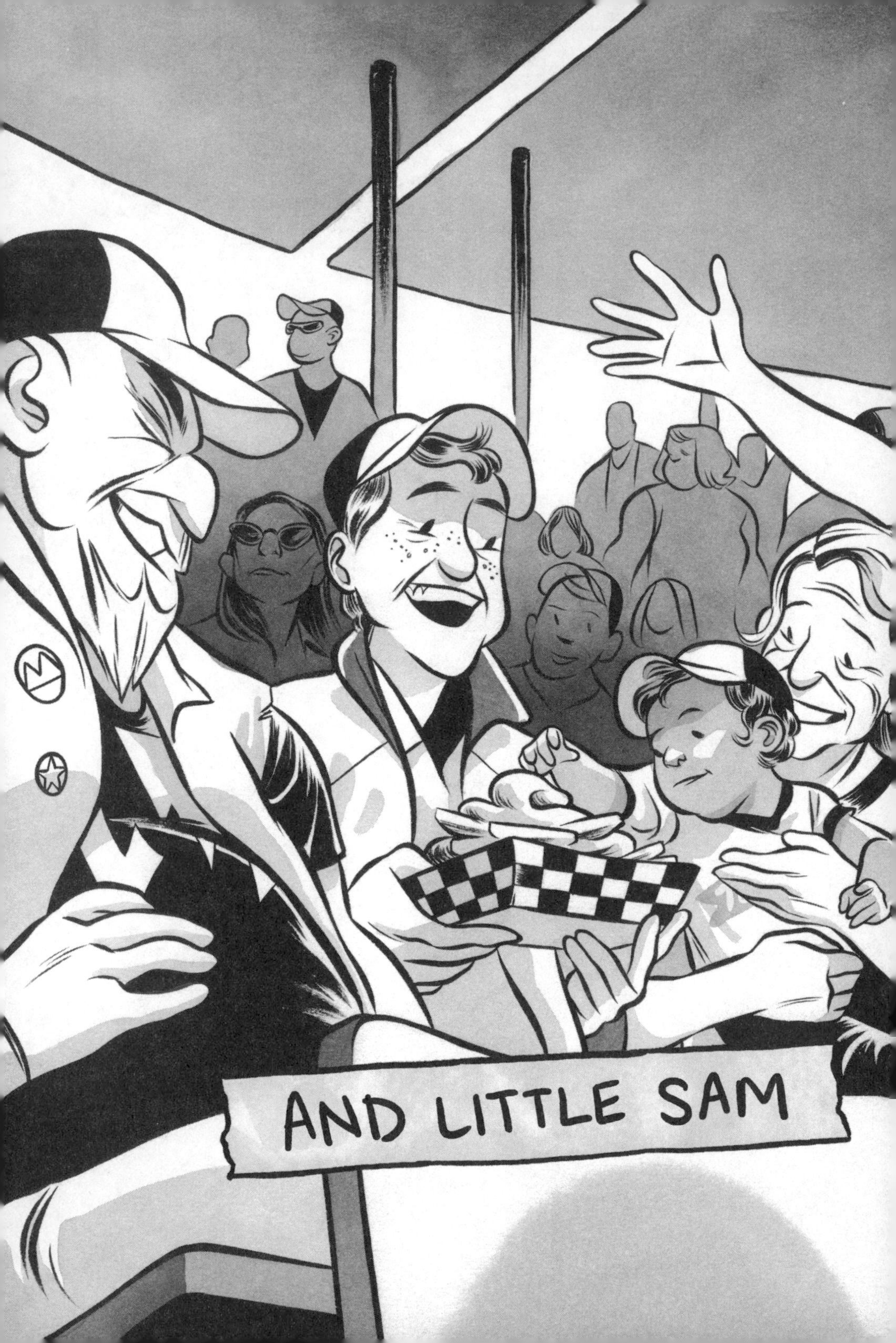
AND LITTLE SAM

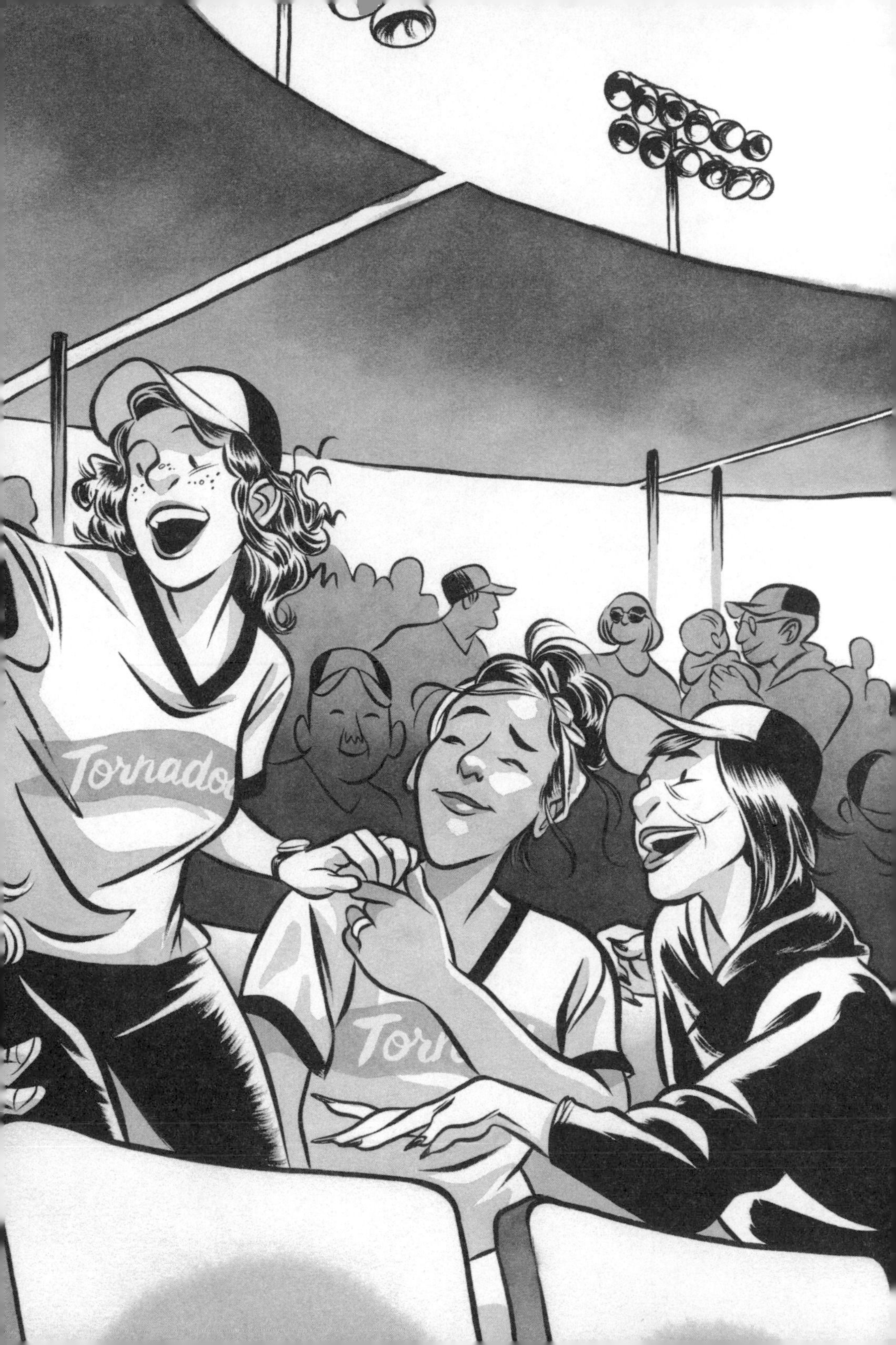

Q&A

with Author Colleen AF Venable and Artist Ellen T. Crenshaw

Colleen: What was your first kiss?

E: I was a freshman in college before I had my first kiss! He was an RA for my dorm network, so we were very secretive (or at least we thought we were—of course we weren't AT ALL stealthy). It was in his dorm room, he was a perfect gentleman, and it was a very good kiss!

C: Aw. My first was with my pillow, and if you ask me, that pillow needed a LOT of pointers. Luckily my first kiss with a HUMAN (now my kissing preference) was a lot better. I was fourteen and hanging upside down in the playground. My boyfriend of three months Spider-Manned me with a lovely sweet, short kiss.

E: He Spider-Manned you before Spider-Manning was even a thing??!? Dang, that's romantic!

Colleen: What was your worst kiss?

E: Okay, so maybe my first kiss was in high school, but I don't like to count it because I wasn't a willing participant. Senior year, a friend confessed his feelings for me in a note in my yearbook, and at our graduation he planted a big wet one on me and scampered away. I don't remember if we ever spoke again.

C: Nope. Definitely doesn't count. Let me guess, he's a "nice guy" who is always stuck in "the friend zone"? Excuse me while I scream into my old pillow boyfriend.

Colleen: If you could give any advice to your sixteen-year-old self, what would it be?

E: I think if I could give sixteen-year-old me advice, it would actually be to get in more trouble. And not to worry so much. I was a very uptight kid—much like Laura! Good to a fault. I don't regret being a goody-goody, but I could have spared myself some anguish by loosening up a little. (I could've had more kisses!)

C: What?! I don't believe this. You're too cool to have been a goody-goody. Are you just covering up your Buffy-style vampire-killing spree?

The advice I'd give myself is "Don't put your head in that half-solidified Jell-O vodka bowl. Yes, you'll win five dollars on the bet, BUT it will also dye your face red FOR A WEEK." Also "Don't starve yourself."

E: Colleen, you would've been the Buffy to my Willow. I would've taken you to TGIFriday's in the Grey Goblin (my car, an '88 Honda Accord—which, fun fact, is also Laura's car) and we would've shared a brownie sundae.

Ellen: Describe your high school best friend.

C: My middle school best friend, Brandy, moved back to Texas in eighth grade. She was super creative, wildly goofy, and brilliant. When high school started I became the sort of person who had lots of close friends but no real best friend. I jumped from social groups easily and didn't quite let anyone get to know me all that well (...or else they might notice I only ate two slices of fat-free bologna a day. Seriously, sixteen-year-old Colleen, stop that!). I focused on schoolwork, art, and making out with anything that moved. I dated a LOT in high school.

E: Aw, sweet Colleen! My high school BFF was Shanon (with one *n*). We went to elementary, middle, and high school together. She was a lot cooler and more popular at school than I was, but she never made me feel like I wasn't cool. Art connected us, and she introduced me to music that wasn't my mom's oldies cassettes or Disney musicals (which are still awesome, but that's all I knew!). We're still friends to this day, but she's not my BFF–she's my family.

C: Okay, that just made me tear up. If this was an episode of *Full House*, the music would totally be playing.

Ellen: What was your favorite band/musician in high school?

C: I was super into punk, but the nerdier side of it, like Atom & His Package, and Me First & The Gimme Gimmes. I listened to a TON of Beatles, and mystery mix tapes from friends who were too lazy to label them, and my love of witty lyrics made me fall for Barenaked Ladies, Blood-hound Gang, and Weird Al. I feel no shame! One of those three is still in my regular listening rotation.

E: I hope it's Weird Al.

C: "Another One Rides the Bus" 4 Eva!

Ellen: Tell me about your first high school rock show!!!

C: Went on a date to see Third Eye Blind at the Chance (woot-woot Hudson Valley, NY). They were okay, but the opening band was so weird and lovely it kinda blew my mind. They were called Thin Lizard Dawn because only three-word bands were allowed in the '90s, it seems. I accidentally crowd-surfed. It was an amazing night and made me realize there were a whole bunch of "pay $5 to see a buttload of weird bands you've never heard of" shows.

E: Third Eye Blind was your first show?! Get OUT of here. Mine was Jars of Clay at a local Christian community college. But I did get to see Third Eye Blind years later, headlining with Goo Goo Dolls, opened by Live. (To solidify this as the most '90s statement ever, I also feel it's important to mention that I got swept up in the short-lived swing music craze–no regrets!)

Ellen: With whom in *KN8* do you relate the most?

C: Personality-wise and in terms of making bad decisions, I'm very Amanda. In terms of sexuality, I'm totally a Dina–not into defining myself, with a preference for fellas or very masculine ladies (Hello, JD from Le Tigre). In my mind Dina didn't think twice about falling in love with Sam. If the right person comes along, no matter who they are, I'd like to think I wouldn't either. Also, I could live in diners.

Ellen: When I designed the look of the characters, I definitely drew on people from real life (no pun intended).

C: I drew on people, too, but it was just that one sleepover. I'm sorry, Kim's older brother!

Ellen: Did you base any characters on people in real life? Was anyone in particular a big influence?

C: The only character who came directly from real life was Franco. I actually love minor-league baseball, but mostly for the hot dog costume races and people like Franco: guys over their prime but still doing what they love. The real Franco played for the Pittsfield Mets from Massachusetts. I worked in Pittsfield one summer and eventually decided I didn't care who won as long as Franco got a home run. Most of the other characters were conglomerations of people I knew, but Mr. Orham was definitely influenced by Keith Mars. I was watching *Veronica Mars* mid-first draft and the quick back and forths of father-daughter goofiness made me so happy.

E: Oh my God, I based Mr. Orham's design on Mike O'Malley as Kurt's dad on *Glee*. Very similar physical type to Keith Mars.

Colleen: So funny! Who else did you model the characters after?

E: Some folks are based on actors—Grandma and Grandpa Orham are based on Helen Mirren and Spencer Tracy, respectively—

C: Helen Mirren! THAT would explain why I have a crush on Grandma Orham.

E: —but most of the character designs are based on people I know. This is not the first time I secretly raided friends' Facebook photos for reference. For instance, many of Cat's details—her black fingernails, bracelets, eye makeup, thumbhole sweater, and that sweet checkered belt—are based on the aforementioned BFF, Shanon.

C: Shanon just got even cooler in my mind. Um...can I be friends with her, too?!

Ellen: What inspired you to begin writing this story?

C: My older sister coming out in our very, very Catholic family. Suddenly I went from the bad kid (reminder: Jell-O vodka face) to the good kid just because I went on dates with guys. The other thing was that I started writing *Kiss* in 2004 and at that time the number of YA works that had any trans characters I could count on one hand. Hell, I probably only needed one finger! (*Luna* by Julie Anne Peters came out in 2004.) I wanted to write something for the teens trying to figure out who they were. And while I'm not religious anymore, I wanted to write a story of coming out where religion wasn't the bad guy. (I've got two amazing aunts who are nuns and they are the most caring, welcoming humans on Earth.) Also in 2004 there was a lot of backlash online for anyone who had come out as gay, but then realized they were bi. One web cartoonist in particular received such unkindness that I decided I wanted Amanda to not just come out of the closet, but I wanted her to keep exploring all sides of her sexuality once she was out.

C: How long did it take you to draw *Kiss*?

E: Just under two years. But I know the book had quite a history before I was attached to it. How long did it take you to write?

C: It took me three years of writing...then six months of submitting to publishers/peeing my pants with every email, then... Let's just say graphic novels take a LONG time to make.

E: Preach!

C: *Kiss* went from being a contemporary novel to a period piece, but I think it is more timeless that way. 2004 was a crazy rough time to come out as queer. Gay marriage wasn't even legal in 2004! It feels like a century ago... We've come a long way, baby! Wait, that's a cigarette slogan? Can we claim it back? "We've come a long way, don't-call-me-baby." There. Much better.

E: I actually love that this book has become a time capsule. There's internet, but smartphones were not common. AOL Instant Messager was the rage. It was equally likely that a person could have a portable cassette player, CD player, or MP3 player. It's like a major transition period: politically, socially, and technologically. There's a specificity to how the teens in *Kiss* communicate—Mads uses IMs and texts with Cat and Laura, but calls her grandparents on the landline and encounters their answering machine. Mr. Orham can take away Mads's computer and cell phone and not render her completely unable to do her homework.

C: I was even tempted to give Mads her own LiveJournal. R.I.P LiveJournal days.

E: I think the fact that she MOST DEFINITELY has a LiveJournal is implied.

Ellen: What is your writing process?

C: It's a three-step process: Hang out in loud places. Giggle at my own jokes. Eat pie. I'm a big believer in only writing a few days a week...though those other days I'm working out the story in my mind so when I finally sit at a computer, words just fall out of my fingers. If I sat staring at a blank screen every single day I think I would get discouraged. Also, maybe a human shouldn't eat that much pie every day. Maaaybe.

Ellen: What is it like, as a writer, to have your story interpreted and conveyed by another artist? Is there anything in particular that turned out differently than you imagined?

C: It is 100 percent the greatest thing! I get so so giddy about collaboration that it's hard for me to do anything other than squeal when I see your artwork. Little things, but mostly jokes that I wrote that were only half working until you made them work!

E: Aw, shucks!

C: And character designs: I'm not even sure how I imagined Nate, but as soon as I saw your drawing of him, I was like, *THAT'S NATE*. Those ears! I would have swooned super hard on him in high school.

Colleen: If you were sixteen again, which character in *KN8* would you have a crush on?

E: I mean, Nate, obviously! There's a reason he's designed like that! He's basically an amalgam of every boy I ever crushed on.

C: I'd love to think I would have chosen Nate, but sadly I think I would have been all about K. I liked the moody punks. Just ask my mom about the guy with the dog collar and foot-long green Mohawk. She loved him!

E: To be fair, I think the whole Zipper crowd is worth crushing on.

Ellen: Describe your typical weekend outfit when you were sixteen. (You wore uniforms to Catholic school, yes?)

C: Actually I lucked out, and despite being super Catholic, the only Catholic school by me was insanely tiny with a not-so-great rep. SO I went to Valley Central (not to be confused with Bayside's bulldog rivals) and covered myself in a LOT of neon and vintage, mostly stuff my mom wore in the '70s that I found and stole from our attic. My favorite outfit was a pair of red plaid pants with a pink mesh half shirt. Yes, HALF shirt. I am thankful there is no photographic evidence of this.

E: I, however, am extremely sad there are no photos! It sounds like you were the baddest babe on the block! I wore boys' camp shirts from Goodwill and cargo pants, plus these black Skechers that looked like they were from the Mickey Mouse oeuvre.

Ellen: Who was your favorite fictional character when you were sixteen? (Or who was your biggest crush?)

C: I had the major hots for Pavel Bure, the Russian Rocket, who played for the Vancouver Canucks. I wasn't into hockey until I saw him—such a graceful skater with blue eyes that could melt the rink—and my hormones were like, "YOU ARE SO INTO HOCKEY NOW." Because the internet was still a baby, the only way I got pics of him to drool on was to take photos of the TV during live games. Like real photos. With film. Because I am two thousand years old.
   You?

E: I don't mean to make so many *Buffy the Vampire Slayer* references, but Angel, hands down. Of course, nowadays I question the motives of a 241-year-old vampire in love with a sixteen-year-old girl, but at the time it was SO DREAMY.

C: You are so right! I remember friends crushing on Giles and me thinking, "Ew, he's an old man," but he was like two hundred years younger than Angel!

Colleen: What did your locker look like in high school?

E: I never had one of those tall lockers. At my school they were three rows high, and mine was at the bottom. I was too concerned with getting trampled to decorate it. You?

C: Someone once described my college dorm with my friend Jodie as looking like "an Applebee's threw-up all over our walls." My HS locker was the same way. Every single inch was covered in something, from Far Side comics, to cute stickers, to handwritten super-inspirational quotes like "Get high on milk because the cows are on grass!" and "Bad Spellers of the World Untie!"

E: I'm beginning to understand where Mr. Orham's excellent dad puns come from.

C: Those are in my DNA. Poppa V is the king of puns.

Colleen: I can't get over how amazingly you draw angsty teen body language. How did you get such great poses?

E: I take a ton of self-reference photos. Body language is my favorite, and I always try to say as much as I can with a pose. I'll even act it out sometimes if I need a little help figuring out the emotions in a scene.

Colleen: What's the hardest thing about interpreting a script?

E: My main goal in interpreting a script is achieving the right pacing and emotional beats, staying true to the author's vision while not sacrificing my own. If the script is well written, like *Kiss*, it's easy to translate it to the page. At worst I struggled making dialogue-heavy scenes fit, but page design is a fun problem to solve. The hard part is maintaining stamina when you've got over three hundred pages to draw! I've been making comics for decades, but this was my first graphic novel. It was like learning how to run a marathon while in the middle of a race.

C: I still can't believe this is your first book. The whole collaboration process was amazing! I'm totally going to get a T-shirt made that says "I got to work with Ellen Crenshaw first." Please remember me when you are working with...um...the most famous person I can think of is the Pope? Haha, damn you, Catholic roots!

E: It was a truly unique and wonderful collaboration experience with you. And it's not our first collab! We did a one-shot comic together about turning the tables on a subway creeper. It's how I knew we'd work well together on a big project.

Colleen: What advice would you give to aspiring graphic novel artists?

E: Estimate how long something is going to take you, and then triple it. Take lots of breaks! The suffering-artist trope is for the birds. Prioritize your health and well-being.

C: So true. We should do another book for teens that's just that last line four thousand times in a row.

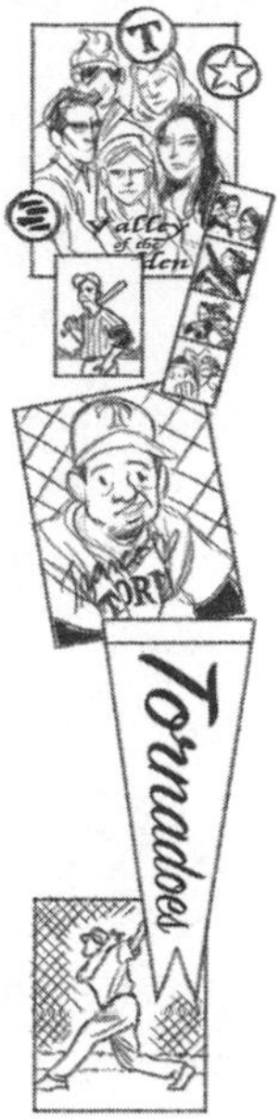
Tornadoes

Colleen: Art nerd time! What tools did you use to draw *KN8*?

E: I penciled the book in Photoshop using my trusty old Wacom Intuos4. Then I printed the pages in blue line onto Arches hot press watercolor paper. (My printer is an Epson R1900. You may note that my equipment is a few generations old, because I hate updating when something works.) I inked the pages with Dr. Ph. Martin's Black Star HiCarb ink and Winsor & Newton Series 7 brushes. (Many brushes died in the making of this book.) The tones were done with the same ink and a variety of synthetic watercolor brushes. Then I scanned each page with my Epson V500 scanner. Whew!

Colleen: The Tornadoes were inspired by my fave minor-league team, the Coney Island Cyclones. I like to pretend Coney Island is my backyard since it's only fifteen minutes from where I live, and I looooove the part where they dress people up in giant hot dog costumes with varying condiments and make them race across the field. Super-important question: Who wins: ketchup, relish, or mustard?

E: Mustard, Colleen. Mustard.

C: Buuuut if you cheer for ketchup and it's not winning, you get to yell "CATCH-UP, KETCHUP!" Eh? Eh? Get it? Okay...I'll see myself out.

E: Yeah, but when ketchup loses, you can say they didn't cut the mustard.

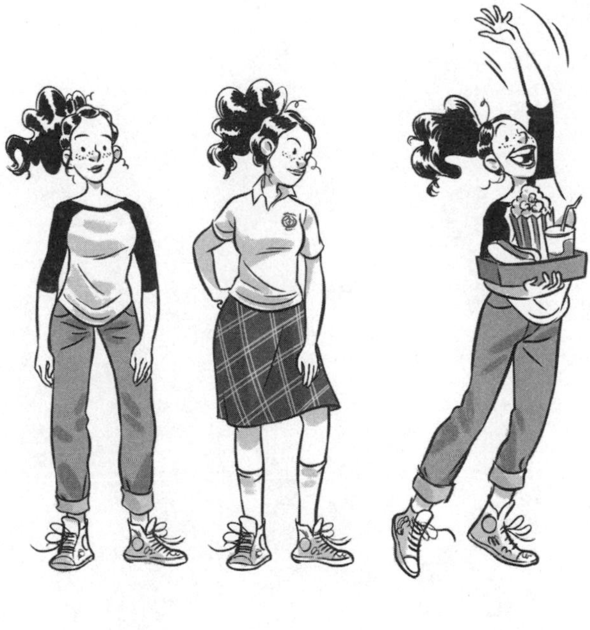

For Kath, the strongest person I've ever known.
—COLLEEN

For my family, without whom I
could not do what I do, or be what I am.
—ELLEN

Firs† Secͦond

Text copyright © 2019 by Colleen AF Venable
Illustrations copyright © 2019 by Ellen T. Crenshaw

Published by First Second
First Second is an imprint of Roaring Brook Press, a division of
Holtzbrinck Publishing Holdings Limited Partnership
175 Fifth Avenue, New York, NY 10010

Don't miss your next favorite book from First Second!
For the latest updates go to firstsecondnewsletter.com
and sign up for our enewsletter.

Library of Congress Control Number: 2018938071

Paperback ISBN: 978-1-59643-709-8
Hardcover ISBN: 978-1-250-19693-4

Our books may be purchased in bulk for promotional, educational, or business use.
Please contact your local bookseller or the Macmillan Corporate and Premium Sales Department
at (800) 221-7945 ext. 5442 or by email at MacmillanSpecialMarkets@macmillan.com.

First edition, 2019

Edited by Calista Brill and Aimee Fleck
Book design by Dezi Sienty and Molly Johanson

Penciled in Photoshop with Frenden's blue pencil. Inked and toned on Arches 140 lb. hot press
watercolor paper, with Dr. Ph. Martin's Black Star HiCarb ink and Winsor & Newton Series 7 brushes.

Printed in the United States of America
Paperback: 10 9 8 7 6 5 4 3 2 1
Hardcover: 10 9 8 7 6 5 4 3 2 1